THIS GAY UTOPIA

An Erotic Novel
by
John Butler

*A STARbooks Press
Publication*

Published in the United States
STARbooks Press
PO Box 711612
Herndon, VA 20170

Printed in the United States

Cover Painting, "In the Woods," by Andrew Potter
Provided by Adonis Art, www.adonis-art.com

Many thanks to graphic artist John Nail for *This Gay Utopia's* wonderful cover design. Please feel free to contact Mr. Nail at: *tojonail@bellsouth.net*.

Text formatting by Michael Huxley.

First Edition Published in the U.S. in Summer 2004
Library of Congress Card Catalogue No. Pending
ISBN No. 1-891855-56-5

DEDICATION

For DEREK,
with admiration and gratitude,
and — yes — love.
Who would have thought…?

Other STARbooks Publications by John Butler

"model/escort" (novel)
WanderLUST: Ships that Pass in the Night (novel)
Boys Hard at Work — and Playing with Fire (novel)
This Gay Utopia (novel)
The Boy Next Door (novel, in the anthology *Any Boy Can*)
The Year the Pigs were Aloft (novel, in the anthology *Seduced 2*)

John Butler editions

Seduced 2 (Co-editor)
Wild and Willing (Co-editor)
Living Vicariously — The Best of John Patrick (Editor)

Short stories included in the following anthologies:

Seduced 2
Fever!
Taboo!
Fantasies Made Flesh
Wild and Willing
Virgins No More

CONTENTS

THIS GAY UTOPIA

PREFACE

A riddle:

W hat is the malady that most commonly afflicts men of most ages, from puberty to late middle-age and even well beyond? At one end of the scale, it might be acne—at the other, perhaps prostate trouble; but between those two extremes it is neither of those, nor influenza, nor even the common cold. It is a complaint for which there is no medication that will relieve its symptoms, nor will vaccination prevent it—although a very special kind of injection can relieve it for a short period.

The only visible symptom of the malady is a considerable swelling—much more evident than the edema that accompanies certain other ailments.

Left untreated it can cause mental distress, anxiety, depression, despair, feelings of inferiority, and even physical pain. Strangely, it is not described in any medical books. It is called:

Involuntary Celibacy.

The following tale tells the story a number of men who, while potentially no more immune to it than the average male, escaped the clutches of the dread Involuntary Celibacy through a combination of timing, exceptional physical attributes, and pure good fortune. But equally important were the same three factors that

Realtors recognize as the most important to success: location, location, and location.

Most of the story takes place in a location so conducive to a gay man or boy's avoidance of Involuntary Celibacy that it might indeed be regarded as:

This Gay Utopia.

Imagine a small town where an all-male university and a Naval station are the only major components of activity in the isolated community. A university where the school's longtime-honored attitude toward homosexual activity is so tolerant it almost constitutes an endorsement of it, and where taking a shower in its vast dormitory is often as much a sexual adventure as it is a cleansing. Where even the vast majority of straight students are driven by their urges and the ready availability of sex to share the wealth of gay experiences their gay and straight schoolmates offer—and most of them find so much satisfaction as a result that they continue them long after they have graduated, moved on, and raised families.

All sailors are horny, and those at the Naval Station are no exception. In the absence of a significant number of females in town—and almost none on base—they eagerly pursue sex with each other and with the equally horny college boys. They find the pursuit is mercifully easy and quickly rewarded, and the results universally gratifying, since so many of the college boys in town are pursuing them.

Many of the men in town (if not most) are looking for sex with sailors and college boys, and achieve great success in finding it, depending on either their attractiveness or their willingness to pay for it. Hunky Marines visit from the Marine Depot a few miles down the coast, coming to town on weekends to gratify their sexual needs as well.

The town is so conducive to providing pleasure to men and boys who are either gay, or who enjoy 'playing with the other team,' that it is properly considered a Utopia.

Welcome to Hus Bay!

1.

STUDENTS AND SWABBIES AND JARHEADS, OH MY!

Between the Navy base and the University, there were as many attractive, horny young men and boys around town as a gay, cock-hungry, oversexed guy like Jason Boone could have asked for. And Jason asked for a lot of them — and usually got what he requested.

Not all of the sailors and college boys who liked sucking and fucking with other guys were gay — not by a long shot — but a slim majority of them probably were, although many might not have admitted it. A fairly significant percentage of them were just extremely horny, and needed whatever outlet might be available to them. Paulik University was all-male, and there were very few female sailors at the Hus Bay Naval Station — only a handful, really — and it seemed that of those, the half who weren't dykes weren't attractive. Jason was happy to provide a handy and extremely satisfactory outlet for horny sailors and college boys, whatever their motivation to seek his companionship.

Virtually all college boys and sailors need to bury their dicks inside hot holes to deliver that white load that drives them so crazy when it remains unexpended, and if their need to do so leads them to accept a guy's mouth or his ass as a viable substitute for the girl's mouth or pussy they might prefer, it's just the nature of the game. A surprisingly large number of those who cheerfully accept the substitute become sufficiently curious about why the men and boys who suck their cocks or take their dicks up the ass seem so deliriously happy to do so, that they try it for themselves. There are also some who practice cock-sucking and passive buttfucking purely as a way of returning the favor to friends or friendly strangers who suck them off or welcome loads of their cum up the butt.

But whether it is curiosity or compensation that is the motive for a TSG, a Theoretically Straight Guy, to offer full reciprocity in homosexual lovemaking, he is liable—and quite probably likely—to find he enjoys it, and to seek repetition of the experience. This does not really alter the status of his TSG-hood

The first time a TSG kneels in front of, lies below, or hovers over a guy with a hard cock that needs servicing, the sexual tension the throbbing prick represents is com-municable; he understands all too well the need it represents. The situation makes his own prick began to stiffen and grow, and he can even *smell* sex in the air. He can clearly *see* the need jutting out before his face, quivering at his mouth. He reaches out to encircle the shaft with his hand, and he can *feel* the pulse of unfulfilled lust coursing beneath the surface, and his own erection continues to swell and begins to throb. When his lips first open to admit the head of the needy hard-on, the *taste* of sex makes his blood run faster. The wider his lips have to stretch to accommodate the cock-head, and the farther his lips are able to travel along the shaft, the more excited he becomes; in short, the bigger the prick, the greater the thrill. *Hearing* the moans of joy that the man or boy who now begins to drive a prick into his hungry mouth maximizes the TSG's sexual intoxication, and he probably needs to stroke his own demanding cock as all his five senses come into focus and he begins to feel his *willingness* to service his fuckbuddy turn into a *hunger* to do so—even though that appetite may have begun as obligation.

The feeling of his buddy's asscheeks quivering and writhing as he drives that hard cock into his throat is very exciting, knowing from experience how exciting it is to be ramming his own cock into the hot suction of a hungry mouth while it is gripped by tightly compressed lips. He may gag at first, but as excitement grows, his ability to take more and more of his fuckbuddy's prick matches that growth, and somehow, there's even a sense of *pride* about managing to take it all—or most of it, in the happy event that the cock is so huge it's impossible to deep-throat it. Remembering only too well the ecstasy he always feels when he finally shoots his own load into a guy's throat, he resolves to take all the cum his partner can give him, without gagging or spitting it out.

Then his fuckbuddy's hands seize his head and pull his mouth as far down on the shaft as it will go, often burying the TSG's lips in a tangle of pubic hair at the base, and the cum spews deep inside his throat—and even though he may wonder if he *really* wants to eat the hot, viscous discharge, his buddy is so thrilled to offer it to him, gasping his relief and encouraging him to eat it all, that he swallows and licks the remainder from his buddy's still-hard prick. Like everyone else, whether they will admit it or not, he has often tasted his own cum, so he has a good idea what the load just blown in his mouth is going to taste like; he finds it doesn't taste bad at all—in fact, as his own orgasm arrives, which his continuous masturbation during cocksucking has brought about, he finds he loves the excitement-enhanced taste and is looking forward to sucking out another load very soon, hopefully in sixty-nine, with his fuckbuddy eating his own cum at the same time.

And that's only the beginning of the gratification the Theoretically Straight Guy finds in returning the favors a fuckbuddy has earned, and if he is perhaps just a bit less straight than he was before—perhaps he is now a PBG, a Potentially Bisexual Guy—he is that much more likely to enjoy what comes next.

Remembering how a casual sexual companion or a fuckbuddy registered pain while he entered him the first

3

time he fucked him, and how that pain turned to joyous thrill in short order, the TSG or PBG is prepared to accept the pain as a necessary prologue to that joy. If the amount of pain he feels when his fuckbuddy begins to fill his ass with hard dick is more than he expected, the blandishments his fucker coos into his ear, and the anticipation of the bliss he has observed *every* boy or man evidence while he fucked him, help to get him past the initial pain. Once the thrill takes over, the gentle encouragements his fuckmate has been whispering into his ear turn to fevered exhortations to enjoy the fuck. As the gentle encouragements were perhaps needed to prepare him, no exhortations to enjoy it are actually required once the fuck begins in earnest. In fact it is likely that the TSG himself will do the exhorting—urging and begging his fucker to hammer his ass harder, faster, and deeper, and to fill it with a hot load.

By the time the first spurt of cum has exploded in his ass, he will most likely have discovered that getting fucked can be much more exciting and gratifying than fucking, although to that point he had thought there *was* nothing more gratifying than fucking. The feel of a big prick slamming in and out of him is so stimulating that he often needs only a few strokes on his own cock to reach orgasm. After considerable experience, he will most likely decide that when it comes to taking a dick up the ass, and considerations of fucking technique being equal, the old axiom "the bigger the better" is applicable—within reason, of course.

If the Theoretically Straight Guy who has just enjoyed sucking his first cock is a little less straight than he was before, once he has learned not just the joy of cocksucking, but the thrill of getting fucked as well, he is exponentially less so—almost surely a PBG, and perhaps even a committed switch-hitter. Much to his astonishment, he might even find he is not straight at all! In any event, he will probably understand the position of the famous movie heartthrob James Dean, who — when asked if he had sex with men as well as women — said he didn't see any reason to go around with one hand tied behind his back!

Jason Boone had gone to bed with far more than his share of gay men and boys, and he had convinced more than his share of Theoretically Straight Guys to enjoy sucking dick and getting fucked — far, *far* more than his share, in fact. Almost a majority of his TSG conquests converted to PBG-hood, and quite a number confessed later that they had adopted a fully bisexual lifestyle; a few had been so pleased with the results of their sexual encounters with Jason that they now thought of themselves as principally gay — if not completely so. Those who were admittedly gay when they first climbed into bed with Jason just enjoyed the ride and hoped for many more.

On the surface, it was surprising that Jason was so successful, since his was not a face or body that *grabbed* the attention of another man or boy who was either gay or simply appreciative of masculine beauty. He was handsome, but he wasn't *gorgeous*. He had nondescript brown hair, dark brown eyes, and a rather bland face — but with a magnificent square jaw, a dazzling smile, and a dimple in his chin that at least put him in contention for gorgeousness. He had a good body, lightly muscled, and he worked out in the gym, but he wasn't the kind of gym-built hunk that causes gay heads to whip around when they see it. He was far better endowed than the average man, sporting just over eight inches of beautifully circumcised cock when it was erect. Add to that his uncommon sexual stamina, an unusual ability to produce multiple orgasms of considerable volume and velocity, and the fact that he was possessed of highly sophisticated and accomplished powers of both seduction and lovemaking, and it is understandable that he had been enjoying an extremely active sex life since he hit puberty.

Technically, he had begun even before that, in 1967, when he was a thirteen-year-old eighth-grader in Amarillo, Texas; on that occasion he had produced his first orgasm in his Scoutmaster's mouth, in the basement of his church one night after a Scout meeting—something the Scoutmaster had been working at producing for several months by that time. That same Scoutmaster nursed on Jason's dick for another year or two, helped out by the boy's Minister, who got wind of what the Scoutmaster was enjoying, and who was the first to get fucked by Jason's already formidable endowment. Jason enjoyed returning the oral favors his adult playmates bestowed on him, but he did not have fully reciprocal sex with a boy near his own age until the age of fifteen, when a high school Senior crammed a big dick up his ass and introduced him to receiving a kind of joy he had only been giving until then. He found that sex with his chronological peers was so much more enjoyable than what he had been sharing with his Scoutmaster and Minister that he cut both of the older men off, and proceeded to suck and fuck his way through a broad, appreciative swath of the student body at Bowie High School before his 1972 graduation.

During his high-school career, Jason spent too little time using the head on his shoulders, and much more time than he should have in using the head on the shaft of his large and widely admired prick. His grades were only fair, even though he was extremely bright; indeed, if he hadn't been unusually intelligent, he would probably have flunked out of high school.

When it came time to think about continuing his education past high school, Jason realized his choices would be limited as a result of his mediocre academic record. His parents had both attended West Texas State College in Canyon, seventeen miles down the road, and they earnestly desired to see Jason follow in their footsteps. He checked and found he could get admitted to West Texas State University, as it was by then known, but several of his high-school fuck partners who were now enrolled there reported that finding guys willing to fuck and suck wasn't very easy in Canyon. Perhaps there were too many girls there, they reasoned, and Jason considered how much more attractive an all-male college would be. It dawned on him that if he was considering those factors seriously, he was probably still thinking with the wrong head!

Although he knew he could succeed in college if he budgeted his time better between sexual and academic pursuits, he just didn't feel he was ready to do that yet. Knowing that since he had an extremely low draft-lottery number he would be drafted into the Army very quickly, and would probably wind up as a soldier in Viet Nam within a few months if he didn't go on with his schooling. So, he enlisted in the Navy before the Army could get him.

Whether justified or not, many gay men thought of the Navy as a place where sex between men is relatively common, and that appealed to Jason, of course. In addition, he simply thought sailors were by far the sexiest servicemen: Their tight uniforms certainly left less to the imagination than those of any other servicemen, and they seemed to have a swagger that suggested they were always ready to fuck. God knew Jason was always ready to fuck, so he regarded sailors in general as something like potential soul mates—and a specific experience with a sailor in his senior year did much to suggest he was correct in that assumption.

A handsome, well-built sailor with an extraordinary bulge swelling the crotch of his astonishingly tight sailor pants cruised Jason in downtown Amarillo one night, and took him to a motel, where he provided the boy with what was probably the hottest sexual experience he had enjoyed until that time—and which would remain a high-water mark for several years after. The young sailor not only had the biggest cock Jason had seen until then, but his sexual endurance and voracity were even greater than his own.

While Jason was blowing him after they had fucked each other the first time, the sailor told tales of sex with his shipmates that had the boy's cock-stuffed and (soon) cum-filled mouth watering, and his recently cock-stuffed and (still) cum-filled ass quivering in anticipation; the repeated cock and cum injections that ensued that night and the next morning only strengthened his belief in the sexual power of the United States Navy. Certainly the two Air Force men and the one soldier he went to bed with while he was in high school did not measure up to the sailor — who never gave Jason his name, but who gave him instead so much cock, so much cum, and so much to remember and treasure.

Since he wanted to experience both quality as well as frequency in his military sexual experiences, Jason chose the Navy. It turned out that he chose wisely.

As it happened, the Viet Nam War wound down, and Jason never went overseas. After a dangerously fuck-filled Boot Camp, he spent almost two years aboard the carrier *Kennedy* as a Yeoman — something like a Naval secretary. The cramped quarters and close living made sex fairly difficult to arrange aboard the ship, but he managed better than one might have expected. Like many of his shipmates, he wore carefully tailored pants, tight enough that they outlined the cock that hung down his left leg, and made it clear to any who might be interested that he had plenty to offer. Like so many of his horny shipmates, he courted those other sailors whose pants showed they were hiding enormously fat or long pricks; he shifted his wooing into overdrive if those same huge-hung swabbies were among those who frequently had a hard-on, not only showing they were ready for some action, but displaying a weapon of sufficient dimension to make Jason's heart catch in his throat — just one of the places he wanted to offer as a haven for such a monster erection. Fortunately, he was himself sufficiently well-hung that he drew his own share of pursuers, and he could frequently choose

8

from among the best-hung sailors who were as eager to receive really big dick as they were to give it. He never went on liberty without a fellow sailor to have sex with — and on quite a number of occasions, two or three accompanied him with that goal in mind!

By the time he was transferred to the Personnel Office at the Hus Bay Naval Station in South Carolina, in 1974, Jason's hormones had begun to calm down enough that he didn't spend almost all his free time trying to line up dick. Ironically, this came about at a time when he was plunked down in the middle of an environment incredibly rich in cute young boys who had an extremely limited number of heterosexual outlets.

The Naval Station was the site of a variety of Navy schools, and there were hundreds of young sailors being transferred in there for temporary duty every week — all in a transient status, and practically all starved for sex. The town of Hus Bay offered little in the way of available pussy for those horny sailors whose tastes tended toward the heterosexual, but with both the Naval Station and the all-male Paulik University located there, there was a near embarrassment of riches of attractive young men who might act as substitutes. The gay sailors and university students gloried in the imbalance, and the straight ones, the TSGs and the PBGs, settled for what they could get! Furthermore the word was out at the Parris Island Marine Depot a few miles down the road, where the Marines were just as horny as their Navy counterparts, and the opportunities to 'dip their wicks' or to get their Marine asses stuffed with dick were more limited — and the latter ambition seemed to be overwhelmingly more urgent to the tough, butch jarheads. On weekends it was common to see Marines strolling around Hus Bay with sailors and college boys, and smiles of either anticipation or satisfaction wreathing the faces of swabbies, students and jarheads alike.

John Butler
THIS GAY UTOPIA

Jason once spent the night with a Marine who said he had been stationed at Parris Island for over three years; he had come to Hus Bay every weekend, and he had never been fucked less than twice on every visit—usually three or four times—and once, in a special birthday orgy his buddies had arranged for him, he had taken eleven loads up his butt in one night!

Between his somewhat-lessened drive to have sex, and the unbelievable ease in lining it up when he wanted, Jason found he finally had the time to think seriously about getting around to a college education. Although he still had a year to go on his enlistment, he began to consider Paulik University, which offered a sufficient number of evening classes that he could begin work toward a degree in anticipation of becoming a full-time student there when he was separated from the Navy.

Paulik University was attractive to Jason on four levels: First, he could get a leg up on his degree work before he became a civilian; second, it was an all-male school, with little competition from women for the dick he wanted to get from hot guys who might be straight or TSGs or PBGs; it was located in a small town where a thousand or so horny young sailors and visiting fuck-hungry jarheads also walked the same female-devoid streets; and finally, it was reputed to be an excellent school. That he had put academic excellence at the bottom of the list for choosing Paulik indicated that while Jason had matured, he was still the same horny guy from Amarillo.

Paulik University was named after Janos Paulik, a Bohemian with a Hungarian first name, who came to America with the Hessian mercenaries to fight against the Americans in their War of Independence. After viewing the conflict at first hand, Paulik's allegiance shifted, and he gave up his pay from the British to assist the rebel forces as an unpaid volunteer. Being a talented, although instinctive, military tactician, he was of great help to Morgan in defeating the British at the Battle of Cowpens in South Carolina, and after the war a grateful American government settled a large land grant on him, which fronted on a deep-water bay on the South Carolina coast, part of Port Royal Sound, near the town of Beaufort.

Paulik named the bay for another Bohemian, the fifteenth-century religious leader Jan Hus. His plantation ultimately provided him with great wealth in producing rice, and at the time of his death in the 1840's (the exact date is not clear) he was almost ninety years old. He had been a bachelor all his life, and for his last thirty-two years he lived with a male companion forty years his junior, Edward "Ned" Farrar. Little is known about Farrar's years at Hus Bay, except that he was an exceptionally handsome man who was a faithful helpmate to Paulik, always at his side — rumored to be the old man's lover during their time together, and assumed to be in later years.

At Paulik's death, Farrar inherited half of his extraordinarily large liquid assets. The rest of Paulik's assets were devoted to the establishment on his lands of "An Academy of Classical Learning for Young Gentlemen," which was first known as Paulik Academy, and by the end of the Civil War had been re-named Paulik University.

The University remained steadfastly all-male when other institutions became coeducational, and since it accepted no state or federal funding for its operation, it was never required to admit female students. Indeed, even today the all-male atmosphere virtually extends to the faculty, administration, and staff, although a few women work in appropriate areas.

Admission to the fledgling university was highly selective at first, and has regularly remained so. As it was relatively expensive in the 1840's, it is even more so over a hundred and fifty years later. This academic and financial selectivity resulted in a very wealthy and influential body of alumni who over the years contributed to the University's endowment so liberally that it is one of the best-endowed institutions of higher learning in the country.

Certain students at Paulik love to refer to their University as tremendously well-endowed, implying that they, themselves, are personally thus gifted — and those who are able to prove it are unusually popular with certain of their classmates.

The town that drew its name from the Bay gradually grew up around the University, and during the Second World War the only other major activity was established there when the Navy built a base on the harbor, as they had established the Marine Base at nearby Parris island fifty years earlier.

When his presumptive lover died in the 1840's, Ned Farrar moved to the part of South Carolina almost diametrically opposite Hus Bay, to the village of Pendleton, where he lived until the Reconstruction Era, following the Civil War. He had invested his inheritance from Paulik in a large tract of land he found near the village of Oconee, on the upper reaches of the Seneca River, about twenty miles north of John C. Calhoun's plantation. By the 1870's he had moved to Oconee, and started work on his own academic gift to the State, another all-male academy of learning, which he himself named Farrar University when it opened in 1882, a few years short of his death; like his former partner and mentor, he lived an astonishingly long life for the time.

It was thought that Farrar's example — obviously inspired by Paulik's — motivated Thomas Green Clemson, in turn, to deed Calhoun's plantation to the State of South Carolina, to establish an institution for higher learning in the agricultural and mechanical sciences. Clemson had bought the estate from Calhoun's widow after he married the old man's daughter. The present-day Clemson University is, of course, the result. Both Farrar and Clemson began to admit female students in the 1950's.

*

Tuition and fees at Paulik University were so high that Jason Boone knew he would have to find ways to supplement his G.I. Bill assistance and the relatively small amount of money his parents could provide. He knew that while he was stationed at the Naval Station, quite a few of the sailors were selling their bodies to older men who either lived in Hus Bay, or who came to visit in order to avail themselves of the ready supply of horny young men. He had gone to bed with quite a few Paulik students who admitted to the same source of income. Sailors and students with truly impressive dicks commanded quite generous recompense for the services they provided for their clients.

Jason definitely did not disapprove of prostitution, but for a variety of reasons it did not appeal to him— chiefly because he was not interested in going to bed with a man whom he didn't find attractive, and doubted he would be able to *perform* satisfactorily with one. Further-more, it would almost always involve sex with an older man, and he only wanted sex with someone near his own age, or younger—preferably the latter. He had not had sex with a man much older than he since he stopped getting blown by his Scoutmaster and fucking his Minister. At the other end of the spectrum, he had been propositioned, when he was still on duty at the Naval Station, by a breathtakingly beautiful blond boy, the son of a Paulik University administrator who claimed he was sixteen, but whom Jason was reasonably sure was no older than fifteen. The kid gave Jason one of the most satisfying and artfully administered blowjobs he had ever received, both before *and* after he filled Jason's mouth with one of the largest and most forcefully delivered loads of cum the horny sailor had ever sucked out of a boy or man of any age. If the boy had been equally talented at fucking butt or taking it up the ass, Jason would probably have sought a

13

much longer-lasting union with the adorable blond past the three or four multiple-blowjob sessions they shared.

Probably because he was so interested in making new conquests, Jason allowed no real relationships to develop between him and his various sex partners, although many of them campaigned for such. He usually had repeat sex with the more attractive and satisfying boys he went to bed with, and a few of the best-looking or the most generously hung — who clearly understood they were *not* in a real 'relationship' with Jason — were welcomed into his bed quite frequently.

Since prostitution was not a viable option for Jason, he decided to find work in town when he was mustered out of the Navy and enrolled at Paulik as a full-time student.

2.

"I DON'T THINK I'M IN TEXAS ANYMORE"

In addition to his physical attributes, which drew an unusual number of gay boys to him, Jason Boone was extremely friendly and likable, and evidenced a genuine interest in people he met. Those traits drew many people to him, males of all sexual persuasions, and females as well. But the girls and women never learned of his more intimate physical qualities, since he had never once desired, or made love with one, although many had tried to seduce him. He was totally, unshakably, a fully homosexual man. The fact that he was also completely masculine, and could talk intelligently about sports and cars drew many straight boys into his orbit, and Jason's instincts—his 'gaydar' if you will—were sufficiently keen that he rarely mistook a non-seducible straight guy for a TSG, a PBG, or a self-confessed bisexual or homosexual. His instincts were not entirely instinctual: they had been clarified through experiences with all levels of gayness in his partners, including many straight boys who offered no sexual reciprocity at all.

If he never tried to put the make on a boy whom he pegged as straight and non-seducible, he could somehow tell which straight boys would probably be amenable to some one-sided sex play. On dozens of occasions he had lured boys into bed whom he felt sure agreed to go purely to get their rocks off, and who would not dream of responding in kind to Jason's lovemaking; even with the limited expectations those occasions aroused, he had usually enjoyed himself enormously with those boys—occasionally even on a spectacular level—and repeated the experience with them with surprising frequency.

One night in San Diego he picked up a sailor, Rex, a Bosun's Mate stationed aboard a cruiser visiting the harbor city, the *Albuquerque*. The sailor insisted he was strictly straight, and he gave off those vibes, as far as Jason could tell. But the sailor also said he was so horny he was more than willing to get a blow job and fuck some boy-butt. Jason watched in awe when they went to a cheap hotel room where Rex stripped, revealing a cock that grew until it actually attained the legendary dimension that seems to be every gay man's dream: a full twelve-inches! Jason sucked him off, taking a wondrously large load, which relieved the urgency of Rex's lust and allowed him then to deliver an extremely lengthy but very impassioned fuck—exhausting, but marvelously satisfying. His was the only prick Jason had encountered he was not at first able to take up his ass in its entirety. Still, the sailor was complimentary, noting that Jason had come closer to taking it all than most other guys or girls he had fucked.

After a solid forty minutes of hammering Jason's ass with his twelve-inch battering ram, in several different positions, Rex finally managed to drive his prick all the way inside with one brutal, inconsiderate-but-thrilling thrust just as he screamed in ecstasy and his load erupted deep within Jason, triggering a matching scream and the huge load of cum that shot involuntarily from Jason's prick, to cover Rex's chest and his own belly. Rex had been fucking Jason in missionary position when they came, and while the last spurts of his orgasm were still filling Jason's hungry ass with hot cum, he suddenly kissed him, astonishing Jason—and it was not a peck on the lips, but an all-out, extremely passionate soul kiss. Jason responded with as much tongue as Rex was giving him, and the two continued to kiss voraciously while their chests slid together in Jason's cum and the sailor's huge prick very gradually wilted and slipped out of Jason's ass.

Before they separated, Rex observed that it was the only time in his life he had ever kissed a guy, and told Jason that while he could never take a dick up his ass, he was willing to try sucking Jason off the next time — something else he had never done. He not only *tried* to suck Jason off a few nights later, but he did an excellent job of doing so. He didn't swallow Jason's load, though, instead squirting it into Jason's mouth, and their tongues danced around together in the slippery mouthful for a long time until Jason swallowed his own cum.

Their third and last time together — the cruiser was leaving San Diego the next morning — they sucked each other off in sixty-nine, each swallowing the other's load. Rex followed that up with another endless fuck — and this time, he did not hesitate to regularly drive his prick all the way inside Jason, who had apparently developed the ability to accommodate it all without too much pain the second time Rex had fucked him, a few nights earlier.

While they were embracing and kissing after Rex's fuck, the stud whispered that he wanted to try and take Jason's dick up his butt. "Who knows," he grinned, "I may wind up liking it as much as I like kissing you and sucking your cock." Jason was very slow and considerate in fulfilling Rex's request, and once Rex had Jason's eight-plus inches buried inside his ass, he began first to gasp and wriggle, but in a few moments was almost shouting with joy as Jason fucked him in earnest. A cock the size of Jason's is major meat for even a seasoned bottom, but the virgin Rex rode it like a champ until Jason filled his ass with cum for the first time.

Judging by the way Rex took a second load in his ass early the next morning, allowing very little time for him to get back to his ship before it sailed, getting his ass filled with dick was going to be a major part of his lovemaking in the future. Certainly the insanely erotic kissing he and

Jason had shared on their second and third meetings was something Rex was never again going to deny a sex partner just because he happened to be a guy—and he seemed to enjoy even the romantic kissing they had shared the night before and during their last moments together.

His parting words, breathed into Jason's mouth just before he left him that morning were, "You've got the sweetest ass I've ever fucked, and I guess you're probably the hottest piece of ass I've ever had—guy or girl. And nobody—I mean nobody—is a better kisser. Kissing you when you're on your back, with your legs in the air and my dick up your butt, is something I'll never forget." He laughed as he asked, "You tryin' to turn me queer or somethin'?" Then more seriously, he delivered his exit line, "If I wasn't shippin' out, you might just do it!"

Jason never saw Rex again, but six months after their time together, he got an envelope from him, postmarked in Guam, and addressed simply to "Jason Boone, Yeoman, U.S.S. Kennedy, San Diego," but with no return address. The envelope contained only a photograph of a shirtless Rex, with his sailor hat perched on the back of his head, and his apparently hard twelve-inch cock clearly outlined by his tight white uniform trousers. His arm was draped over the shoulder of another shirtless sailor—a young, gorgeous blond with a dazzling smile and a bulge in his tight pants almost as formidable as Rex's, and obviously just as hard. They were standing on what was apparently a wild and deserted tropical beach. On an enclosed sheet of paper, Rex had written, "I wanted to show you my new buddy, Kenny. I've been practicing what you taught me, and I want to let you know what a great teacher you are. Kenny says you're a great teacher too, and he sends his thanks. I think the guy taking this picture is drooling! It's a pity you're not here to teach him—you'd like to, I'll bet, almost as much as he'd like you to! He's not wearing as much as Kenny and I are, and if you could see where his white hat is hanging you'd know he's ready for a session

18

with the teacher! My thanks too, pal, and with *the 'L' word,*
Rex."

When he had first met Rex, and even during the first
hour or two of their initial lovemaking, Jason had the
monster-hung stud pegged as strictly straight, but willing
to accept an alternative hot male hole if necessary. He was
completely surprised that Rex kissed him after their fuck,
and astonished that he kissed him so passionately. It was
the first hint that Rex was a TSG or possibly even a PBG
(although judging by the picture and letter Rex sent, it was
possible he may have even become a convert since then).

Over the years, Jason had developed a kind of infor-
mal "Kissing Barometer," to gauge the sexual orientation
of a sex partner on the continuum between straight and
gay. While he didn't write it down, so he could consult it
at critical moments, it was something like the following:

1. He allows me to kiss him lightly on the cheek
or somewhere on his body, but only when he is
nearing orgasm, blowing his load, or within up
to fifteen seconds after he comes: He is straight.
(Note: If he allows no kissing whatever, of any
kind, he is not only straight, but unless he is
spectacularly hung or well-built or beautiful, I
probably don't want to get him in bed again
anyway. Note further that it does not count if,
while I am kissing him, my tongue is inside his
ass, or the shaft of his cock is between my lips.)

2. During those periods of sexual intensity
noted above under number 1, but only at those
times, he allows me to kiss his lips: He's
straight, but just the tiniest bit liberal about it.

3. He allows me to kiss his lips lightly at times
other than those sexually intense ones, but

there is no reciprocity: He's straight, but he may realize I have needs, too.

4. He kisses back and opens his mouth to admit my tongue during conditions noted under number 1-3: He's leaning toward our camp!

5. (a) While we're French-kissing during those conditions, his tongue is in my mouth as much as mine is in his, or **(b)** He allows me to kiss his lips, and occasionally enter his mouth with my tongue from the time we start actual love-making until he loses his hard-on: There's hope for him.

6. We kiss passionately as a prelude to actual foreplay: He's at least bisexual.

7. We kiss romantically before or after making love: If just 'before,' he's decidedly bisexual and probably leaning toward his gay side; If 'before' *and* 'after,' he's gay, whether he admits it or not.

8. He likes to kiss romantically, whether we're having sex or not: He probably admits he's gay.

9. He's got his tongue so far down my throat I'm almost gagging on it before I've even given him my name: Hang on to your hat, this boy is definitely one of ours!

Job openings in the small town of Hus Bay were relatively rare, but fortunately, Jason never really had to look for work to help with his college expenses — it fell into his lap.

During his two years living there while he was at the Naval Station, Jason had frequently browsed in the town's only bookstore. He was not a great reader, but he did like to keep up with the new works by favorite popular authors like James Michener and Alan Drury, or exciting new ones like Stephen King. The town library was almost non-existent, the library at the Naval Base seldom had anything he wanted to read that wasn't already checked out, and the University library was only for staff and students.

The bookstore, called "The Book Cellar," was housed — appropriately enough — in the cellar of a large two-story residence near the center of town. It was an old southern house, and the wrap-around front porch and entranceway were twelve steps above the street, so the cellar was basically at ground level.

The store was owned and operated by Max Koch, who also owned the house, where he had lived almost his entire life, the elderly last-remaining member of a wealthy family who had emigrated to America from Austria, and settled in Hus Bay for some reason. Max was born in Hus Bay, and attended the local public schools there, then graduated with a Master's degree in English Literature from Paulik University.

He spoke perfect English, but never quite lost a subtle German inflection in his speech and a very slightly Germanic manner of sentence construction, inculcated in him by the accent and speech patterns his parents used when they spoke English.

He went to Columbia, the state capital, to teach Language to high school students in the mid-1920s, but returned to Hus Bay ten years later to see to the needs of his ailing father, who had been widowed only two years before. The duty fell on Max because he was the last remaining member of the family.

At his father's death in 1938, the thirty-five-year-old Max indulged his passion for books by opening a book store in the cellar of the family home, where his lawyer father had formerly housed his law offices. The store prospered reasonably well during the last few years of the Great Depression, principally thanks to the patronage of University faculty and students, and when the government developed the Naval Station there shortly after the United States entered World War II, business seemed to boom.

The Naval Station was also a great boon for Max to indulge his primary passion—books had always been a secondary interest in life. The love of pretty boys had been his main interest since he had fallen in love with his first roommate at Paulik University, who had been a very pretty boy, indeed. His sex life had been active during his years at Paulik, and he readily found the same kind of willing playmates among the student body at the University of South Carolina during the years he taught in Columbia.

By the time he returned to Hus Bay, finding young bedmates was not so easy any longer, but he managed to find a few over the next several years—usually having to pay them to share their youth and their bodies with him, since there was so much attractive young cock available to them free on campus.

When the Naval Station opened, there were always a variety of sailors, usually in transient status, who keenly sought hot holes to play host to their hard cocks, and who were willing to settle for a boy or a man if female companionship was not available. They were afraid to do much on the base, so they cruised the campus, and many found their way to The Book Cellar, where Max very subtly let them know he was interested in finding hot young fuckmates, and was even willing to slip them a few dollars for a good time.

Until well into the 1950s, Max got all the dick he wanted, and found that by then the University students tended to be just as willing to put out for a few dollars as the sailors were. If he had to pay for it more often than he had before…well, that was the price of getting older.

By 1960, he found his sex drive was diminishing, and a bout with prostate cancer made him impotent, effectively spelling the end of his active sex life by 1965, when he was sixty-two years old.

The so-called 'Physique' magazines and eight-millimeter movies of young men wrestling (badly—but who cared?) or posing, and clad in as little as the law allowed, became the source of Max's gratification. He occasionally made it up to New York, or other major cities, and managed to find movies and magazines that were much more explicit. He began to stock duplicate copies of the more exciting magazines and movies he found, and secretly offered them for sale to a carefully selected clientele.

In 1972 he went to New York City to scout for some of the ever-more explicit films and photos he and his special customers enjoyed, and attended a screening of the movie he had been dying to see—Wakefield Poole's *Boys in the Sand*—and he found it was not only the hottest, sexiest movie he had ever seen, he virtually fell in love with the star, the blond Adonis, Casey Donovan, the most outrageously *sexual* man he had ever seen on the screen. Casey was adorable, he was reasonably well-hung, he had an ass to die for, he obviously adored sucking and getting fucked—and most miraculous of all, he was in the city just then, and could be *had* for a fairly reasonable fee.

Max arranged a meeting with Casey Donovan, and even though he was an old man, and impotent to boot, the blond sex god was gracious and considerate, and acted as though the licking and kissing and sucking Max applied to every inch of his fine body were the tributes of an admiring partner in lovemaking. The afternoon he spent with Casey was by all odds the most wonderful thing that ever happened to Max.

Back in Hus Bay Max began to stock the porn movies that were being released in ever-growing numbers — including *Boys in the Sand*, and the even sexier *Bijou*, which featured Bill Harrison and the biggest prick Max had ever seen, in person or in a picture.

All the gay pornographic material Max had for sale was upstairs, over The Book Cellar, and access was limited to those Max knew he could trust. And it was exclusively gay; there were no pictures of pussy to be seen in his upstairs sales area. He really didn't worry about the law, since the long-time Chief of Police had been one of his best customers since he first introduced his line of smut. When the Chief-to-be was seventeen years old, Max had picked him on Main Street one night when he was cruising for dick, and took him to the City Park, on the bluff, where he sucked him off. After Max had eaten the boy's load, the future Chief had surprised Max by producing a tube of Vaseline and bidding Max to fuck him while he bent over a picnic table. They exchanged occasional fucks and blowjobs for a few years, until the future Chief got married and Max became too old to be attractive to him any longer. Since then Max had often let the Chief use his Guest Room to have sex with the boys he liked to fuck; Mrs. Chief would never have understood if he brought them home.

Downstairs, in the book store proper, Max also added a complete line of mainstream magazines and certain newspapers. Even though he cut the number of hours the store stayed open, the job was becoming too much for him to handle alone, especially with the upstairs pornography section, so he decided he needed to find someone to help him run the business. Obviously, given the nature of the upstairs material, it needed to be a gay man, and if he was young and handsome and sexy as well, so much the better — Max could enjoy looking at him, even if looking was all he would be able to do. He could also provide some pleasant scenery for his gay pornography customers to appreciate.

Fortuitously, just about that time, a handsome, extremely sexy University student asked Max if he knew of any job openings around town. He knew Max casually, since he had been shopping in the store for a few years, and often enjoyed pleasant conversations with the owner. He was well-built and very well-hung—which was obvious when, as a sailor, he wore unbelievably revealing uniform pants. Max had often fantasized about paying the young sailor—now, later, a University student—the same kind of oral worship he had accorded the fabulous Casey Donovan, but he knew that Casey was a professional, a stranger he would never see again, while this was a local boy—at least for the moment. He would never even suggest a meeting to the young man like the one he had shared with Casey, even though he knew the young man was gay, a conclusion based partially on what magazines the boy studied, but more so on Max's near-infallible "gaydar," a power of intuition that had stood him in good stead all his adult life—developed long before the word 'gay' meant anything beside 'happy,' and decades before radar was invented.

The young man was Jason Boone, of course.

When it came time for Jason to get his degree in 1979, he had been employed by Max for almost two years, and the old man asked him to continue his work at The Book Cellar—indeed, to take over its operation. At the same time he invited Jason to move into the apartment on the second floor of the house, rent-free. During the depression, when Max's father needed an extra source of income, two of the three bedrooms over the first floor where the family lived had been converted into a kitchen and a full bathroom, respectively, providing a complete apartment; a set of stairs for outside access was added. The apartment had been vacant for years.

Jason loved living the free-wheeling sexual life Hus Bay offered, he even loved the business, and he had also come to love Max as a close friend, something of a surrogate father—or a grandfather, really, since Max was seventy-six at the time, and Jason only twenty-five. Besides, he had no specific career plans, so he readily accepted Max's offer.

There was no thought of Jason occupying the guest room on the first floor of the house, and actually sharing quarters with Max. Both realized that would be too much closeness; moreover, the guest room was also still used occasionally as a safe place where friends or important people could enjoy a sexual tryst if they needed one. The Chief of Police was a regular user, as were a few of Max's friends—mostly younger, and virtually all married. Jason had used it often, when the opportunity arose, to take an especially attractive trick to bed for an hour or so when he was working. Max was always willing to take over for Jason on those occasions, and the sly wink he tendered Jason as he left to go have sex with his trick suggested how glad the old man was that his attractive young assistant was able to get what he could no longer enjoy himself. Max often laughed that, to the best of his knowledge, no female had been in that room for fifty years, except for purposes of cleaning it, but that he had seen hundreds upon hundreds of different boys and men headed for it with lust in their eyes, and emerging with satisfied grins on their faces.

The Police Chief was by all odds the most regular user of Max's guest room, visiting it with some young man—often one of questionable legal age—more regularly than even Jason. The Chief always left by himself, slipping away quickly, telling the trick he had just had sex with to wait a few minutes before leaving. It was not at all unusual for Jason to chat with the Chief's trick for a few minutes after the Chief had left. There was obviously something about the Chief's tastes that resonated with Jason's own, and he was quite often sufficiently impressed with the appearance and the apparent horniness of the Chief's tricks that he made dates to do with them what the Chief had just finished doing, often immediately taking them back upstairs to get into the rumpled bed they had just vacated. Many of them were blond, slight of build, often underage, and just passing through town—usually as runaways. Those were the kind of boys the Chief stopped and talked with when he was patrolling the streets, often intimating that they were probably guilty of something, or doing something wrong, and offering his protection from any kind of trouble in exchange for an hour or two of servicing his cock, which he always fondled when he talked with them. Jason was careful to avoid the underage boys, however.

The second-floor apartment suited Jason's needs perfectly, and it was clear by then that someone should be living on the premises with Max; the old man's health was obviously failing, and he had absolutely no living relatives who might more logically be the ones to see to his possible needs. Max even paid for having the apartment spruced up and made ready for occupancy again, so that Jason moved directly into it from his dormitory room.

Living in the enormous main dormitory at Paulik University had been a great treat for Jason. He moved there directly from his barracks at the Naval Station, and it not only offered the privacy he had missed while living in the barracks, it offered a great deal of it.

All dormitory rooms at Paulik were singles, even though the residents of the halls where they were located shared the large bathrooms. The rooms themselves were lockable, and if the door was closed there was a long-standing, scrupulously observed tradition that one did not enter a room without knocking and waiting for permission to enter, and even then only doing so under necessary conditions. Part of that same tradition dictated that each room door was regularly left ajar or open if the occupant didn't mind company, and if it was closed, he didn't want to be disturbed. There was a sign on each door that could be shuttled into view, reading: "Studying, Do Not Disturb." If that sign was visible, everyone knew the door was locked, and they were expected to honor its injunction under any conditions except dire emergency. Everyone also knew that the likelihood the occupant was actually studying was slightly less than the chance that he had another boy in his room and was either working at seducing him, or that one of the two had his cock down the other's throat or up his butt. The standard joke was that at those times they were studying anatomy.

Jason had his "Do Not Disturb" sign showing with amazing frequency. Those who had been on the other side of that sign with Jason understood, since they had, through experience, learned how long the Texan former sailor was able to fuck—and how well he did it, either as fucker or fuck-ee—and how often he could provide encores that would stretch the time out wonderfully... gloriously.

The main dormitory was vast, with eight separate wings of three stories each. It had grown to that size gradually over the years, through the additions to it that were planned when the first units were built Most of the students lived in it. On each of the twenty-four halls there was a huge bathroom, with sufficient lavatories, urinals and partitioned private commode stalls to meet the needs of the eighty men who lived there. The single shower room had a dozen showerheads, spaced along two sides, without the privacy the commode stalls offered.

The boys at Paulik were apparently blessed with an extraordinary level of testosterone, although that blessing might have been a curse at a school less tolerant and accepting of its being applied. Given the prodigious amount of sexual activity that resulted, and the unparalleled acceptance of homosexual lovemaking, *relatively* little actual sucking and fucking went on in the dormitory bathrooms — although there was still a surprising amount of it.

Occasionally one might hear sounds emanating from one of the stalls that made it clear that although only one pair of feet was visible below the door, another pair was perched on the toilet seat while their owner was getting sucked or was squatting over a dick and riding it. If two pair of feet were visible in a commode stall, everyone could tell something was going on behind the door, and the direction in which the respective pairs of feet were pointing made it fairly clear exactly *what* was going on.

In the showers, everyone could see everyone naked, and it was not uncommon to see someone sucking a dick, and only slightly rarer to see one guy fucking another or burying his face in a hot ass. In any case, it was usually ignored. Seeing a boy showering with a full, throbbing hard-on was routine, but, oddly enough, drew more attention than observing a pair of boys actually having sex in the shower room; the paired-up boys sucking or fucking were obviously already engaged in doing what they wanted to do, and not only deserved some privacy to pursue it, but were probably not amenable to having someone join them. But a solitary boy with a raging erection might want some help with it. If he was stroking his hard-on with his eyes closed, apparently lost in his masturbation fantasy, he might be left alone to finish himself off — although another boy might step in to lend him a hand, or, just as he indicated he was ready to blow his load, even kneel and take the load in his mouth or on his face or body.

If the boy working on his erection was looking at other boys while he stroked it, he almost surely was ready to welcome a partner, or partners — whether just in masturbation or, more likely, something more advanced and gratifying. Usually those boys went off together to a room.

The most remarkable facet of the dynamic between boys in the dormitory shower rooms was they felt free to fondle and kiss each other when they touched, almost always leading to one or both of them developing a hard-on if they groped each other's cocks, sucked each other's tits, or caressed each other's asses, even if they hadn't been erect when they first embraced. Their kisses and gropes and fondling often became extremely passionate, surely the most intimate kind of interaction for the other boys in the shower to witness, but it was politely ignored with the same courtesy afforded those boys who were actually sucking or fucking there.

The showers also provided a ready showcase for all the residents of a given hall to see who was well-hung, who had a cute ass, who had great tits or was well-built, who studied other cocks or asses or bodies or tits, and — most importantly — who got a hard-on while he was checking out cocks and asses and bodies and tits. More episodes of first-time lovemaking between dorm residents began in the showers than anywhere else.

If the word got out that one of the boys was especially well-built or well-hung, or particularly attractive in some other way, boys from all over the dormitory might drift into the bathroom on that boy's hall from time to time, hoping to catch him in the shower and check out the accuracy of the report.

Jason had heard reports of dorm residents with monstrous endowment, fabulously cute asses, particularly muscular bodies, or — something that appealed to him almost as much as huge cocks — especially succulent tits, and checked them out by visiting their own shower rooms. He also went to those various shower rooms to check out the attributes of boys whose facial beauty he had observed elsewhere, and which appealed to him in particular, but whose other physical characteristics were yet to be assayed.

When the really beautiful boys, the most muscular, and—most notably—the ones with enormous cocks took showers, they were usually surrounded by other boys who were there to check them out, all hoping to be led by the exceptional stud—the Adonis or Hercules or satyr, the beau ideal—off to his room for glorious sex.

Jason was proud to think that he often scored in his sojourns to various shower rooms around the dormitory, seeking to confirm reports of the most impressive studs the student body had to offer. He had once been happily surprised to discover that not only did one of the cutest boys he had observed around campus prove to have an extremely impressive endowment—well over nine inches—but a trim, muscular body as well, and his surprise turned to thrill when the cute Sophomore agreed to come to his room for a night of sharing those splendid physical endowments with his admirer. If Jason had ever impaled a cuter, better-rounded or more wonderfully tight ass with his voracious prick, he could not remember it, and his lips had been bruised and his ass sore for three days from the boy's frantic kissing and the savage, relentless pounding of his nine-inch cock over the course of the two fucks he had given Jason, bookending Jason's second fuck, but before his final, third.

On another occasion Jason tracked down reports of a fabulous chest in a shower room that belonged to Brady Stone, a Senior bodybuilder, whose generous ass and massive arms and legs were reported to be in perfect proportion to his Herculean chest. To his delight, Jason discovered the reports were true. While Brady stood in the shower, flexing his body for the edification of at least a dozen naked and erect admirers, Jason boldly stepped up to him, bent down, and began sucking the most enormous, luscious tits he had ever seen outside of a porn movie or magazine—almost like one of the chests in the exaggerated, and heart-stoppingly sexy drawings of Tom of Finland come to life.

31

Brady's areolae were the size of half-dollars, and the nipples protruded a good half-inch above the swelling of his vast, hard breasts. Other boys were eyeing Brady's splendid ass and his hard cock; one moved in and started to eat his ass when he saw Jason begin to suck his tits, but the muscular boy clearly appreciated Jason's worship enough that he led him out of the shower and back to his room.

Although they spent most of the three hours they shared there with Brady lying on his back while Jason licked and sucked his tits, they also feasted on each other's cocks, each swallowing the other's load, and the body-builder fucked Jason in missionary style while Jason continued to worship his chest. Jason lay on his back and Brady rode his cock and took a load up his ass while Jason reached up and manually showed his admiration, caressing, fondling, tweaking, and running his hands adoringly over the swelling velvet firmness of those heavenly tits, so thrilled that his cock barely lost its rigidity when he shot his load inside Brady, who continued to ride while Jason returned to full erection and exploded inside him again.

Ken Harrison, the boy who was rumored to have the biggest prick on campus, was always besieged by offers in the shower room, and Jason managed to catch him there on one occasion. When Jason walked in on the scene, Ken was already stroking his awe-inspiring hard-on, and everyone else in the room was watching, almost all of them masturbating along with him. If Ken's prick wasn't quite the equal of the twelve-inch weapon Jason had been given by Rex, the Bosun's Mate from the *Albuquerque*, it didn't miss it by more than a half-inch, and since the boy was only a Sophomore, he might still have some growth left in him! Unfortunately, Jason lost out to another student who was bolder than he, who fell to his knees and took more of the monster cock in his mouth than Jason would have thought possible, eventually managing to actually deep-throat it. The other student released the cock filling his throat and looked up at Ken, saying, coolly, "I promise I can take every inch of it up my ass, as many times as you want to give it me, and for as long as you want to."

The super-hung stud smiled, leaned over and kissed the daring boy, not even attempting to lower his voice as he said, "I'm too close to coming to let you stop now. Suck me off first, then I'll take you to my room and fuck your brains out—all night if you want me to." The kneeling boy frantically took the gargantuan prick in his mouth again, and fondled the writhing ass that was brutally driving it in and out, until Ken seized his cocksucker's head and held it tight against his belly as he slammed his prick all the way inside, gasping while he obviously blew his load. After a few moments, he withdrew his cock, and the boy looked up at him again, grinning, with cum leaking from the corners of his mouth. Ken again leaned over, and lapped his cum off the boy's chin, then kissed him before he whispered, "Let's go to your room," and they left the shower—leaving a dozen or more boys so horny by then that most of them who hadn't already started to do so, began sucking and fucking each other then and there.

A cute boy who had deep-throated Jason's cock about the time Ken and his worshipper began to leave, pulled Jason down on top of him as he laid his back on the tiles. Jason reversed his body and knelt over the boy in sixty-nine, so they could suck each other off—which they did, most eagerly. By the time Jason had swallowed the other boy's load, but had yet to come himself, someone else had knelt behind him and was fucking his ass. Jason shot his own load in the other boy's mouth, but the cock up his ass felt so fine, he insisted the boy keep sucking him while the third boy—whom he never saw, much less recognized—kept fucking. At almost exactly the same time the third's boy's cum unloaded explosively inside him, Jason fed the other boy another load and had him turn his

33

body around so they could kiss and fondle, passing Jason's second load back and forth between their mouths, sharing it when they swallowed. While they were doing that, someone — presumably the third boy — ate out Jason's ass, apparently sucking out his own cum and swallowing it.

Later, Jason regretted not having identified that third boy, since he was clearly an extremely talented buttfucker, and liked eating ass as much as Jason liked having his eaten. Jason would have liked to enjoy his talents again and again. He didn't realize that the boy he picked up in the bathroom one night later that semester was the same one who had remained hidden behind him while he fucked him and ate his ass in the shower after they had been watching Ken Harrison. The fine fucking he gave Jason and his excellence in eating Jason's ass that night might have provided a clue, but it was not until after Jason had fucked him, had eaten his ass also, and shared an opening sixty-nine session when each sucked the other off, that the boy admitted, between what were to have been farewell kisses, that it had been he who fucked and ate out Jason that memorable time in the shower. A grinning Jason interrupted their farewell to fuck him again, and suck his own cum out of the boy's ass so they would be even.

Jason came close to scoring with monster-cocked Ken Harrison another time, but lost out to a very young-looking Freshman who was so cute that even Jason couldn't fault Ken's choice. He did finally get to *share* a fuck by Ken's fabled cock, at least. He and only two other boys happened to be in a shower room late one morning — so far only soaping up and eyeing each other's hard-ons when, miracle of miracles, Ken got in the shower with them. He washed thoroughly, well aware of the appreciative stares of his three admirers, who were by then just standing there and gaping, stroking themselves. Then Ken turned off the shower and turned to grin at the three while he began to stroke his already fairly hard cock until it grew to its full, stupendous size. "Who wants it?" he said. Then, before any of the three boys could voice his enthusiastic wish to have it, Ken laughed and said, "Shit, you all want it, I know. Get on your knees and I'll give it to all of you."

Ken let each of the three delighted boys suck his cock for a while before he had them kneel on all fours, side-by-side, while he knelt behind them. Then he knee-walked from one hungry ass to the next, fucking each for a few minutes before moving on, repeating the cycle several times. Jason had been the only one to come close to deep-throating Ken's prick, and he was the only one who was able to take all of it up his ass without groaning in pain — but the groans didn't cause Ken to lessen the force and depth of his fucking. When Ken's orgasm arrived, he happened to be fucking the boy in the middle, whose howl of joy at the thrilling eruption inside him all but drowned out Ken's own cry of triumph and domination, "Take my whole fuckin' load up that hot pussy!"

While Ken's glorious cock wilted inside the lucky boy who had taken his load, Jason shared long, passionate kisses with him while the other boy sucked his ass. Between kisses, Ken commented to Jason, "Shit, you can really take a dick, can'tcha? I've gotta get outa here now, but I'm gonna get you alone some time soon, and have you suck me off. Then I wanna fuck the hell out of that hot ass of yours, and when I do, I'm gonna fill you so fulla cum it'll be squirtin' outa your ears!"

To Jason's disappointment, the private session Ken said he wanted never came to pass, and not a single drop of Ken's cum ever entered his body. But he did manage to score with Bill Riker, the boy rumored to have the second-biggest cock on campus — and even got to do so privately. While Bill fucked him passionately, endlessly, and very, very deeply — probably at least eleven inches deep inside Jason's ravenous ass — he did not himself take it up the ass, and was only a mediocre cocksucker. Still, he was considerably cuter than the champ, Ken Harrison, and was a fantastic kisser — and, unlike the peerless Ken, deposited *lots* of cum inside Jason's mouth and his ass!

Jason's success in the shower-room derbies seeking the cutest, the best and the biggest was probably attributable in part to the size of his own prick — or perhaps, more accurately, to its *appearance*.

He did not have the biggest dick in the dormitory, by any means — he had been to bed with at least five or six bigger than his own, including Ken and Bill, the champ and the runner-up — but he was decidedly a *show*-er, not a *grow*-er, meaning that his flaccid cock was almost as big as his erection. Jason's eight-inch-plus erection developed from a prick that measured a *full seven inches* when it was completely limp, and was almost as big around when limp as it was when it was hard — and its girth was as admirable as its length!

Amazingly enough, there had come a moment during the sessions he shared with twelve-inch Rex out in San Diego when neither of them had an erection. Rex laughed when he observed, "Shit, Jason, your dick is the same size as mine!" And it was true, they each had about seven inches of meat hanging down out of their pubic nests — but while Jason's only grew about an inch-and-a-half when it erected, Rex's added an astonishing *five*. If, in the shower rooms at Paulik, Jason did not have a hard-on — which was seldom the case when he was taking his shower with one or more attractive boys — those who checked his equipment out were extremely impressed, and he was occasionally rumored to have a Ken-Harrison-class prick, one of the biggest in school. As a result he drew a good many fans to the shower room on his hall, and if they found his cock grew less than they hoped it might, it was still a very impressive tool, wielded by an extremely handsome, wonderfully talented, and fully versatile cock-sucker and buttfucker. None of them complained if Jason went to bed with them!

On his own turf, in the shower on his own hall, Jason almost never went back to his room without leading an eager boy along with him, unless he was in a hurry (seldom) or not in the mood for sex (almost never). Jason liked to amuse himself by holding his conquest's prick as he pulled on it, using it to lead the eager boy down the hall, back to his room

Naked boys in the halls were *de rigueur* in the dormitory at Paulik; no one went to the shower wearing anything but shower shoes, carrying his towel and toilet articles. If a boy did wrap a towel around his waist in the halls, it was sure to be yanked from him and draped on his shoulder, or if he wore underwear, it would literally be torn off—unless he was fat, unattractive, or unpopular. Attractive, and—especially—well-built or well-hung boys were expected to display their assets as they went to and from the shower. Swinging and bobbing hard-ons jutting out from those naked bodies walking the halls were so common that they drew little notice, unless they were especially large or beautiful—or, perhaps, unusually *un*attractive. Two boys walking together in varying degrees of intimacy, with (usually) or without (rarely) erections drew more attention, but the sight was extremely common. Jason leading another by the cock into his room provoked nothing but good-natured amusement or mild jealousy.

Boys stopping in the hall to kiss and fondle one another was a fairly rare sight, even though such behavior was both commonplace and fully accepted in the showers. In fact, the sight of boys openly kissing each other was thought of as somehow mildly distasteful, unless they were making love or doing so in a place of sexual expectation—like the showers, or the Hus Bay City Park. This attitude was partially reflected in the "Kissing Barometer" Jason developed, of course.

*

In spite of the wild, widespread sexual activity of the variety described in these pages, the boys of Paulik University were not predominately gay, although the percentage of homosexuals in the student body seemed to be—and more than likely was—much, much higher than in society generally. That can perhaps be at least partially explained by the fact that since homosexual acts were so widely accepted at Paulik—there was virtually no stigma attached—gay boys were less likely to stay in the closet, as they probably would have in communities where homosexuality is stigmatized.

Like the sailors stationed at the remote, virtually all-male Naval Station at Hus Bay—and like so many men concentrated in other similar situations, like those in prisons—many of the Paulik students became homosexuals of convenience, homosexual by default, if they wanted an active sex life. Most of them would revert to heterosexual lifestyles after they left, although many of them would become what most men really are, judging by surveys: avowed heterosexuals who occasionally enjoy sex with other males—bisexuals, really, balanced toward their masculine side. The heterosexual Paulik alumni no doubt went to bed with others of their own sex far more frequently than those heterosexuals in the general population, since it was not only an enjoyable sexual diversion, it was also a way to revisit the joy and the excitement they had experienced during the halcyon time of their college days.

Many sailors wanted to be stationed at Hus Bay, or at least to be able to spend some liberty time there when their ships put in. They knew they would get all the pussy they wanted there, but that the pussy would be college-boy pussy or sailor-pussy (but not the same old familiar sailor-pussies they regularly fucked aboard their own ships). Even straight sailors reasoned that pussy is pussy, and if a hole is really tight, and if the guy or gal taking your dick can really work it and show you how much he or she appreciates it, it's probably a tossup.

Actually, most boys or men who have been sucked off by quite a few members of both sexes will admit that a guy usually gives a better blowjob than a girl. And while kissing is kissing—a guy's mouth is as pleasant to share as a girl's—men and boys are usually much more ravenous and passionate when the kissing is hot; few girls will drive their tongues down into your throat while you suck theirs. Romantic kissing? Also a tossup, probably.

But the thing that might lead a basically straight sailor to *prefer* fucking with a guy is that if getting a blowjob or fucking a pussy puts him in the mood to suck a dick himself, or take one up his own 'pussy,' the girl can't offer him what he wants. After all, having seen how much a guy enjoys and appreciates sucking your cock or taking it in his ass—and guys are infinitely more likely to let you know exactly how much they enjoy it than girls are—it's only natural to want to experience some of that enjoyment for yourself from time to time, and if the mood strikes while you're having sex, you want your partner to be ready to provide you with the equipment needed to satisfy you.

Today, girls often bring dildos to the sexual table to satisfy part of that longing in their men, but there is still no substitute for a hot, throbbing, driving, real-flesh cock to suck on and drain; for that matter, dildos don't ever provide the warmth, the pliability, and the throbbing feel of the real thing, and while it's easier to pretend a hot guy is fucking you if your female partner straps it on while she slams it into your ass, feeling the cold, hard texture requires so much imagination that it greatly lessens the enjoyment.

As a result, many a modern woman who has discovered or cultivated in her man a longing for something up the ass, has discovered she occasionally needs to seek another man to join them for a threesome; if she doesn't, her own man might bring one in, or look for a twosome with one on his own. For a straight man with a wife or girlfriend, the traditional 'night out with the boys' is often a night *out of the closet* with the boys.

Best of all, for the sailors who especially wanted to be in Hus Bay, was the easy availability of Marine pussy on weekends. Nobody appreciated getting fucked like the jarheads who went in for it, and once you got one primed and ready, he'd take it as long and as often as you could give it to him.

It was, curiously enough, only the Marines who usually referred to their asses as 'pussies' when they were making love with a man. The sailors and college boys at Hus Bay seldom used the term when they talked about themselves, but usually did with the jarheads. The lucky man with his cock driving in and out of a sailor or University student at Hus Bay often heard, "Yeah, fuck my ass!" But if a jarhead's muscular ass was working your cock, you would likely hear, "Yeah, fuck my Marine pussy" (Or the Marine might preface 'pussy' with 'hot,' 'tight,' 'jarhead,' 'fucking,' 'hungry' instead, or even without an adjective when he could tell the cock up his ass was getting ready to unload, or his own cock was due to explode; at those times, his mind was too seized by fuck-frenzy to seek appropriate adjectives to spur his partner on to greater effort.)

The adjective 'tight' was very often the one used by Marines to describe their asses while they were getting plowed, and deservedly so. Marines are rightly proud of their muscle control, which apparently extends even to their sphincters, and most jarheads who have taken an inordinate number of really huge pricks up their butts an inordinate number of times will feel, to the fucker, like a boy giving up his anal virginity, The virgin boy, however, would very unlikely offer the Marine's wild shouts of appreciation, his furious cries of encouragement, the

40

writhing and humping of his ass, the pulsating grip of his chute as it works the invading prick, or the howls of joy that mark the explosion of his own or his fucker's orgasm—those display the experience of the seasoned bottom, who may, nevertheless, feel to the man filling his ass with dick that he is cherry.

It was fairly unusual to see two Marines cruise each other when they were out to score some dick in Hus Bay. They got all of that they wanted back at Parris Island, although they had to be *very* careful about doing so. The Marine Base was infinitely less tolerant of jarheads having sex with jarheads or other men—hence the exodus to Hus Bay on weekends when there was enough time to really enjoy getting their Marine-pussies stuffed. Weekdays and weeknights were for discreetly and carefully sharing Marine-pussies with other jarheads on base; weekends were for joyously and exuberantly sharing Marine-pussy with sailors, college boys, and affluent older men at Hus Bay.

Along with the dazzling array of advantages Hus Bay offered boys and men who enjoyed sex with other men and boys, a drawback—a limitation, really—was that there was a hell of a lot of competition for the Marine-pussy; the college boys liked it as much as the sailors did, after all, and too often the Marines favored a college boy over a sailor when they were in the mood to take some dick up the butt, since they could easily find a swabbie ready to give it to them wherever they were—even back at Parris Island, where there was a large contingent of sailors assigned. The Hospital Corpsmen there—the most likely sailor candidates for on-base Marines to have sex with—were usually as eager to bottom as the jarheads were, but many of them had to perform as tops with a Marine if they were to get him to top them.

The Hus Bay group that probably favored Marine-pussy more than any other was the gay contingent of University faculty and staff. The students were off-limits to them, and there was so much college-boy-pussy readily available to the sailors—to say nothing of the wealth of sailor-pussy that other sailors traditionally hungered for— that the Marines were particularly favored targets for the adults. Sailors could often be bribed for sex, but there was so much young cock available, they expected more money than the Marines, who tended to enjoy sex with adult men more so than with kids. A good-looking older man who whipped out a reasonably big cock to offer a cruising jarhead was almost sure to score, and if his cock was big enough, he could almost certainly keep his wallet closed.

There was one completely, openly gay bar in Hus Bay, *Janos and Ned's*, even though the several other drinking establishments tolerated a level of gay interplay almost as prevalent, if not as intense as that found at the real gay bar. Only *Janos and Ned's*, for instance, would tolerate boys or men actually making love with each other in dark, private corners—provided they were discreet about it, of course. There was even a full acceptance there of customers giving and getting blowjobs at the bar if they occupied the far side, basically against the wall, so the cocksuckers crouching down to suck a dick were not visible from the street or the rest of the bar, and only the upper parts of the recipients' bodies could be seen.

Like the other bars in town, *J and N's*, as the gay bar was popularly known, was a place where gay Paulik University staff and faculty tended to go when they were looking to score dick. There was a strict understanding at the University that faculty and staff did *not* fraternize sexually with the students. Discovery that one of them was doing so was usually grounds for dismissal. But the sailors and visiting jarheads were fair game, and bars were the places where they went to pick them up, or they cruised them on the streets. They tended to stay away from City Park since so many students went there to cruise or have sex.

Janos and Ned's had been officially 'off limits' to Naval personnel since a few weeks after the Naval Station had opened, even though it had been only partially gay then, and the gay activity was relatively restrained. Sailors and Marines—both of which were actually Naval personnel—had always ignored the restriction, but in deference to its spirit they never appeared there in uniform. It was easy to tell who the sailors and Marines were, however; that could easily be inferred from their shoes and haircuts. The shinier the black shoes, and the shorter the haircut, the more likely the serviceman was to be a Marine rather than a sailor. And the more likely that he was a Marine, the more likely it was that the guy who picked him up was going to get to fuck butt!

A pair of jarheads would rarely go off to have sex with a sailor. Marines tended to look down on sailors as inferior beings, and they didn't want another Marine to watch while they were getting fucked by a swabbie—even the most cock-hungry Marines were aware that bottoming connoted subservience to the man topping him.

If it was clear that a man had an unusually big prick—whether that was learned through groping the outsized prick when the man was dressed, if the man's reputation advertised his endowment, or if the guy simply pulled it out and *displayed* it hard—a pair of Marines was as likely to go with him to fuck as one Marine by himself would be. Perhaps even more likely, since jarheads loved to have other jarheads watch them while they took a really huge, potentially painful dick up the ass or down the throat. It was a display of real manhood such as appealed to machismo-conscious Marines. If one sees *three* Marines going off together to have sex, he can be sure at least one of them has a stupendous cock!

In general, any guy who picks up a Marine for sex had better be prepared to top him; he will expect it, and if you don't come through he will probably be pissed off. And even though he may crave getting fucked up the ass, giving up his Marine-pussy, he's a *Marine*—and a wise man does not want to get a Marine pissed off at him! However, if he discovers the Marine he expects to (and probably does) top has a sensationally big prick, he had better be prepared to bottom, too. Marines love to show how dominant they can be, as well as tolerant of pain.

In general, a good rule when trying to pick up a Marine who is clearly ready for sex with you is this: grope him and get his cock hard, and if it is enormous and you can't, or don't want to take that monster dick up your ass, move on to another prospect.

Marines are not exclusively bottoms in gay sex, of course, although even many of the dedicated heterosexual ones enjoy getting fucked by a really hard-fucking, huge-hung stud as a test of endurance and tolerance of pain. And some enjoy topping a really macho man as a display of their strength and dominance. Marines with huge cocks, and ones who are even manlier than most jarheads are extremely popular on Marine bases.

Finding two or more Marines willing to have sex with you is like striking gold, but you should probably be ready for a lengthy session, and be able to produce more than single load. Each Marine will want you to fuck him, but each will also want every other Marine present to fuck him as well, so everyone can see how well he takes it. By the time you're through, every Marine will have fucked every other Marine at least once—and each will have fucked you too, if you're lucky.

Every jarhead will want you to suck his dick, often insisting you swallow his load—often as many loads as he can give you—perhaps as a gesture of good faith. But don't be surprised if he doesn't suck you back, Marines are not noted as cocksuckers. However, if you have a really challenging prick, he will probably work hard to take it all, to deep-throat it if possible, and to swallow every drop he can suck out of it, in a display of the same kind of endurance and tolerance he shows when you fuck him.

Another good rule, if you are unusually well-built or extremely masculine: only contemplate going off for sex with two or more Marines if you know you can take all of them up the ass, while they fuck you hard and long, until they blow their loads—maybe inside you, but more likely splashed ostentatiously on your back or stomach for the edification of the watching Marine(s), whom they have hopefully impressed with their domination of a really butch stud.

3.

ONE ENCHANTED EVENING

Whether the participants in the wild gay sex that went on at Hus Bay were actually gay or not, between the all-male University, the nearly all-male sailor population, and the more limited crop of hot, horny Marine bottoms, there was opportunity and acceptance — and, therefore, prevalence — of man-to-man sex there that was unparalleled. Stories of especially gratifying experiences were as commonly relayed as were guesses about the weather, and the names of particularly studly boys or servicemen were widely bandied about. But the names and the stories were circulated orally — even though the subject matter was probably as much anal as it was oral — so there is almost no archival material a person interested in the history of the gay sex life of Hus Bay can consult or quote. Certainly, nothing was hinted at in the various newspapers or newsletters.

No doubt private diaries and letters recorded countless sexual activities in the town, but a vivid first-hand account of one especially wild occasion was eventually detailed in a published book. The name and location of the town was not specified in the account, so unless one is familiar with the background of the author, or is familiar with Hus Bay, it is impossible to tell where it happened.

The famous gay porn movie director, Spike Jefferson, was born in Hus Bay in 1929, and lived there until His high-school graduation. That was not his actual name — in fact, he adopted it in the 1960's, in homage to a contemporary physique model at the Athletic Model Guild, whom he had often been told he resembled so closely they could have been twins. His alter ego was called Spike Adams, and since Jefferson followed Adams in United States presidential succession, it seemed to him a good choice as an alias for his own 'physique' work—and besides, his real first name was actually Jeff. The co-incidence of his uncanny resemblance to Spike Adams was compounded: he had actually been nicknamed "Spike" when he was in high school. In spite of the implied egotism in his doing so, given their resemblance to one another, Spike Jefferson thought Spike Adams was un-believably cute and sexy.

He enlisted for a hitch in the Navy to avoid being drafted into the Army. He chose that branch of the service over others because he had so many fond memories of the Navy—all of nights and days and even mornings spent having sex with sailors in his home town. He scored his share of college-boy dick with the Paulik students, of course, but he had a special fondness for those sexy sailors and the way their tight pants advertised what they had to offer a cock-hungry boy.

He considered the Marine Corps briefly, because he also had some wonderful memories of sex with jarheads. He realized, however, that ninety percent of his sex with Marines had involved him sucking them off and then fucking them. Spike had loved that, of course, and wanted to repeat it as often as possible during his military service, but he loved taking a big dick up his ass above all things. If he became a Marine he figured that living among all those rabid bottoms, he would have only a ten percent chance of getting fucked when he had sex during his enlistment. He planned to have a *lot* of sex while he was serving his country, and if he was living among horny sailors, he knew only too well, from growing up in Hus Bay, that he would not only suck a lot of sailor cock and fuck a lot of sailor butt, he would have his dick in a lot of sailor throats and have a lot of sailor dick up his ass. Marines or Navy?

To use an expression that came into being much later, it was a no-brainer!

During his time in the Navy, Spike's sexual accomplishments actually exceeded his aspirations. He was adorably cute, he was boyish and very likeable—yet completely masculine; he had a mighty body and a huge cock, and the gay and bisexual sailors fell all over themselves trying to get him in bed—and unless they were unappetizing or unpleasant in some way, they succeeded. Even when there was pussy around for the straight sailors to fuck, an amazing number of them joined Spike in bed—and once there they acted pretty much like their gay counterparts in enjoying the same intense lovemaking he had to offer. The romantic kissing, the fondling and cuddling, the sweet, slow *foreplay* Spike almost always enjoyed with his gay or bisexual tricks when they began making love, was something he was able to enjoy less frequently with the straight sailors he fucked with, but every now and then he got a pleasant surprise when a raging heterosexual stud began their lovemaking by enfolding him in his arms and sharing sweet kisses. He was completely manly, but even straight boys could see his beauty was, in its own right, as winning as that of a beautiful girl.

But the romantic kissing and snuggling that Spike loved to enjoy in the *afterglow* of really good sex was something he very rarely needed to ask for, even with the straight boys. Sex with the young Spike Jefferson was so satisfying that almost all wanted to stay attached to him for at least a time, to savor for a little longer the extremely satisfying love they had just shared.

Spike was stationed in the Pacific or on the West Coast during his entire hitch in the Navy, and he stayed in California when he was mustered out of the Naval service in 1951. He achieved considerable initial success as a model, since he resembled the popular image of "The All-American Boy": tall, gym-built muscular body with

49

massive arms and acres of rounded, toothsome chest; light-golden, naturally blond hair, with blue-green eyes; brilliant white teeth and deep, adorable dimples that appeared when he flashed his ready, winning smile. He *looked* like a sweet guy, but still appeared to be extremely masculine. He *was* sweet natured, and his masculinity was equally genuine, even though his sexual appetites were limited exclusively to members of his own sex. He had fucked a girl or two in high school, strictly on an experimental basis, but abandoned the experiment for all time before he graduated. There was no question in his mind that he was exclusively gay—nor did any of his satisfied sex partners think he was in any way straight. The word 'gay' is used here in its modern sense, of course, although it was not used that way at the time. Rather, Spike and others like him thought of themselves as 'queer.'

By 1960 his taste in sexual companions and his modeling took him to "The Studio," in Los Angeles. He was thirty-one, but looked like a golden, phenomenally built twenty-year-old. The Studio was a photography studio-cum-movie-lot where a plethora of models—all male—hung out and posed for 'physique' pictures and movies. The camera loved Spike—as did many of the models! Still pictures and one-reel, eight millimeter, black-and-white movies followed, and soon he was extremely popular. He even distributed his own line of still photographs personally, through the mail, to his many fans

Unfortunately, Spike's modeling career spanned a time when pictures or movies that showed complete nudity or obvious sexual activity—even if the latter was only suggested—were not allowed, especially through the mails. He took a chance with the photos he distributed privately, posing completely nude for some of them, and hand drawing a small pouch over his cock with washable ink. His customers could easily wash away the ink to expose the beautiful big prick it had been masking, which made his private photos very widely subscribed to.

50

In spite of his wholesome, open, pleasant good looks, it was all but impossible to look at Spike and not be convinced he was a creature who relished wild, uninhibited and ecstatic sex. The image of a smiling, friendly, beautiful satyr helped make Spike especially popular, and since he never posed with anyone but other good-looking and sexy men, whose adoration almost glowed from their eyes as they looked at him in the pictures, or who fondled him adoringly in the movies under the transparent guise of wrestling, gay men assumed he was not only gay but was an especially hot piece of ass. The looks and the fondling Spike exchanged with his partners provided further clues that those assumptions were valid. In fact, they were valid.

Spike was able to choose the models he worked with, and he always chose ones whom he found particularly sexy, ones he most wanted to screw with. And he had sex with every single one of them, at least once—and often more frequently—at The Studio or in private trysts. It was quite common for a still- or movie-shoot to be interrupted when Spike and his partner got so horny that their unhideable hard-ons needed to be satisfied before filming could continue. When that happened, they would usually strip off their posing straps and fuck or suck in full view of the photographers, the director, and a group of hot young men—mostly other models—who were always hanging around The Studio, sunning by the pool, cruising each other, and scoring casual sex. Not surprisingly, a shoot involving Spike always drew a relatively large audience. Although he was not especially vain—in spite of how justified he might have been to feel that way—Spike was proud of his looks, his body and his big dick, and he loved to show them off, especially when he was making love. One of the things that made his work at The Studio gratifying for Spike was imagining the thousands of men all over the country jacking off while they looked at his pictures and movies. He really wanted to make movies while he was actually having sex, so he could feel those anonymous fans watching and participating by proxy.

The costumes worn in almost every minute of every movie, and in virtually every frontal still photograph, consisted solely of a tiny cloth pouch, a 'posing strap' that just barely contained the genitals of the wearer, suspended by an almost invisible string around the waist—basically leaving the buttocks completely exposed. The material from which the pouches were made was flimsy and elastic, and a great deal of cock growth could be contained inside—and the thin material actually did more to emphasize and outline every detail of what it was supposed to be hiding, rather than obscuring it. In fact, it is probably true that seeing a big cock bulging inside such a posing strap, rounding out or lengthening it so much that it protrudes from the body—threatening to break free—is more sexy and erection-producing than seeing a bare hard-on. Filming around the studio was constantly being momentarily suspended when one or more of the models got an erection. The company tried to leave in as much movie footage as they could where it was clear a cock was straining for release from one of the minuscule pouches, cutting or suspending filming only when it actually burst forth.

Several models he worked with made Spike's pouch regularly swell to the bursting point: the dark, smiling Latino Zaro Rossi, with a body and ass to die for and a cock almost down to his knees when he was inspired—as he often was—by Spike and some of Spike's other favorites; blond, sexy, hung Jim Stryker; the rather effeminate, but nicely built and almost supernaturally beautiful Bob Page; and the sexiest man Spike had ever laid eyes on, the dark, devilishly handsome, mischievous Monte Hansen, who loved nothing better than to display his perfect ass and huge erection in the most tantalizing poses imaginable, for the enjoyment of all with whom he worked. Lamentably, Monte had to stuff his luscious prick into a posing strap when the cameras rolled for commercial films.

Occasionally Monte allowed his sexual antics to be photographed, but only for private distribution, and underground photos of him fucking a boy in the ass, or getting sucked, and even ones where he has his lips wrapped around a big cock while it is fucking his mouth were commonly circulated. Spike longed to have Monte do all those things with him, but his greatest ambition was to bury his own big prick inside the dark Adonis's trim little ass, and fuck it forever. He also *ached* to feast on Monte's extremely fat prick and ride it until it discharged the kind of enormous load he had actually seen the stud blast onto a partner's back or ass—but Spike desperately wanted Monte to shoot it deep in his throat, or way up inside his ass.

Spike had seen photographic evidence of Monte engaged in everything but eating a partner's ass or taking a cock up his own ass, and he had actually watched the filming of Monte fucking and sucking with another man while some of those pictures had been taken.

In later interviews, Spike talked about his days at The Studio, and although he waxed rhapsodic about Monte Hansen, he never revealed if he had gone to bed with the sexy beauty, or even so much as sucked his dick, or realized any of his ambitions where Monte was concerned, until he published his memoirs at the closing of the century—and even then his comments were guarded and cagey. It seems extremely probable that Spike's popularity and importance on the scene at that time, and his manic desire to have sex with Monte, brought about at least a partial realization of his goals. After all, Spike was usually around, if he could arrange it, when Monte was posing or filming, and Monte almost always teased the gathered fans watching him work before the cameras by kissing them, momentarily giving them his ass or cock to suck and worship, even sucking a few cocks himself, and now and then shoving his cock up an attractive bystander's ass for an all-out post-filming fuck. It would have been unthinkable that the sexy stud didn't zero in on the magnificent blond stud to bestow those favors on him, at least a few times. There is photographic proof in Spike's book of memoirs that he did so to some extent, at least once.

So, while it is almost a certainty that Spike got fucked and sucked by Monte, and sucked him off in return, history will never know if the young Spike Jefferson ever buried his luscious cock in the immortal sex god Monte Hansen's equally luscious ass. Spike's tell-all autobiography skirts the issue, even though he devotes a great deal of space in the book to Monte's beauty and sexiness, and his own eagerness to share it. Fortunately, the book was published at a time when nudity, and even erection could be shown—and one of the crowning glories of the volume for many is a full-page photo of Spike and Monte standing, facing each other and grinning lewdly, completely naked. In the photo, each is standing with his 'upstage' arm draped over the other's shoulder and his 'downstage' fist propped against his waist; their enormous hard cocks are almost equally matched, jutting out straight in front of their bellies, with the tips *almost* touching. Another photo of Monte alone shows clearly that he is circumcised, but many photos demonstrated that Spike is not. In the dual picture with Monte, as well as in several others, Spike's prick is so hard that it is impossible to tell that he has a foreskin. A matched two-picture set of Monte and Spike in much more explicit poses also graces the book—but it will be described later

During Spike's days at The Studio, bare asses were allowed in all kinds of photographs, fortunately, and his fans got to see a great deal of the young Spike's completely naked and breathtakingly glorious ass. Except for his privately circulated photos, his extremely large, uncircumcised, and equally beautiful cock was hidden from the

54

cameras until very late in his modeling career, about the time he moved behind them to begin his work as a director. While images of his magnificent body, sublime facial features, and his infectious smile began to become relegated to the history of physique photography, Spike began producing and directing men of almost equal beauty and sex appeal in some of the hottest pornography of its day.

When Spike retired from the world of pornography in 1999, at the age of seventy, he published his memoirs in a book entitled *Shooting Stars — While They Were Shooting Loads*. Since he did not specify Hus Bay as his hometown, or specifically provide the actual name of Paulik University or the Hus Bay Naval Station, he referred to them simply as the town, the University, and the Naval Station. He gave a sufficiently detailed account of his days there that anyone familiar with the town knew where he was talking about, and often even *who* he was talking about.

The many, many photos of Spike at all ages made it clear to anyone who had known him at Hus Bay that 'Spike Jefferson' was really hometown boy Jeff Sikes, the incipient *fuckmaster* who had shared his beauty and his budding sexual mastery with so many local folks before moving on to fame and — in the eyes of some, perhaps — notoriety. A few former sex partners, high school classmates, had provided Spike with his nickname, "Spike Sikes," because of the huge, hard 'spike' he hammered into them, or let them suck — and quite a few appreciative sailors had enthusiastically agreed, through experience, that it was an appropriate moniker for the blond junior stud.

One of the most vivid occasions Spike remembered in *Shooting Stars* took place on August 14, 1945, when he was still several months short of his seventeenth birthday — but already a seasoned veteran of gay sex. It was a hot day, and not much was happening around town, when it was announced that President Truman would make a special radio address at 7:00 that evening. World War II was clearly running down, and everyone had heard about the unbelievably destructive 'atomic' bombs that had been dropped on Hiroshima and Nagasaki about a week earlier, so hopes for the announcement of an end to the war ran high. Consequently, almost everyone tuned in to hear the President's special broadcast.

Within a few minutes the town ran wild with ecstatic citizens and University students, and the even-more-delighted sailors who poured out of ships at the Naval Station, to celebrate the fact that the President had just said that Japan was ready to surrender. Although the official "V-J Day" — the "Day of Victory over Japan" — would not be observed formally for another two or three weeks, when the Japanese would sign the formal surrender, by eight o'clock that night the party was in full swing around Hus Bay.

For 'Spike' Sikes and a huge number of sailors, University students, and male townsmen, the best way to blow off steam on such a happy occasion was to blow off some cock! Like others who knew it was an excellent place to celebrate, Spike headed for City Park.

The South Carolina coast is almost universally flat, except for a large outcropping of bedrock that surfaces at the northwest end of Hus Bay, and rises sharply for about a mile, ending in a bluff that lines the north edge of the bay and overlooks it from a height of some sixty to eighty feet. The sea-level City of Hus Bay, at the west end of the Bay, and the adjacent Paulik University, are clearly visible from the park that was developed on the bluff, as are the ship moorings and the buildings of the Naval Station that crowd the south edge of the Bay.

There is ample soil covering the rocky bluff to support all manner of native plant life, including some rather heavily forested sections. The sea breezes, the seemingly cleaner air, the peacefulness, the lush plant life, the scenery, and—above all, perhaps—the *privacy* of the vast City Park, which had actually been planned by Janos Paulik in his late years, made it a very popular spot. One large clearing overlooking the Bay, on a precipice near the eastern end of the park, was sufficiently remote that most visitors did not penetrate that far when they wanted to enjoy the natural amenities so easily available to them closer to town.

The remote clearing inevitably became 'Lover's Lane' for the town, and an overwhelmingly large percentage of the sexual acts that went on there were male-to-male. Male-female couples making out there were more likely to be looked at askance than were the boys and men fucking and sucking. But the sexual orientation of the couples or the groups of all sizes that gathered there to make love really made no difference—sex went on in the open, freely, since those who were uncomfortable if anyone saw them screwing went elsewhere to play. While nighttime activity was more prevalent than daytime, that was probably a function of scheduling, rather than modesty. Every possible sexual act was celebrated in the clearing during full daylight as well as by moonlight.

The police never interrupted sexual activity at the clearing. It couldn't offend anyone who didn't see it, they reasoned, and since it lies at such a remote reach of the park, the only ones who went to the clearing knew why they were going there. Furthermore the *laissez-faire* attitude of the authorities toward sexual activity, even between boys and men, and the fact that many of the police had probably grown up sucking and fucking there, made them lenient toward sex-play in the clearing. When the policemen visited the clearing—and they often did, especially their Chief—it was usually done individually and on their own time; then, it was not to break up sex-play or catch anyone in the act, but to find a boy to fuck with. Unescorted girls never went to the clearing, but there were almost always a few lone boys or men there who were eager to make connection with a sex partner.

Spike Jefferson explained those things about the park in his autobiography, followed by his account of his visit there on the evening the imminent Japanese surrender was announced, but without specifying which town supported it:

I was at home when I heard the news [Spike began]. I grabbed a huge tube of Vaseline and headed right for the clearing in City Park when I decided to celebrate. I wanted to fuck some butt, suck some cock, and get at lest a few guys to stick their cocks into me any place they wanted. What better way to celebrate than by getting laid?

It was obvious a lot of other guys had the same idea, but not all of them waited until they got to the park. I saw all sorts of wild sex going on practically in public. In an alley, about fifteen feet back from Main Street, I saw two sailors standing side-by-side, with their backs against the building while they turned their heads toward each other so they could kiss; their white pants were pulled down below their balls, and two boys were kneeling on front of them, giving them blowjobs and finger-fucking their asses. I recognized the two boys sucking the sailors off; they were University students, but I didn't know their names, even though one of them had sucked me off and fucked me one night a few months earlier.

When I passed the campus, I saw something that was almost a preview of what I was going to find when I got to the clearing in the park: two naked guys were standing next to the statue of the founder of the university, bent over and hanging onto it while another naked guy and a sailor in uniform—with his pants down around his ankles—were fucking the daylights out of their asses. The two guys fucking were playing with each other while they slammed away into those hot asses, and the two getting fucked were practically yelling about how great it felt.

There was a fifth guy standing there, a classmate of mine at the local high school, completely naked and jacking off while he watched—waiting his turn, I figured. I only watched for a minute, but my classmate shot a big load while I was watching. I didn't think that anyone's getting off was going to slow down the action for very long, though—not that night.

I saw a lot of other guys having sex, often practically right out in the open like the five at the statue. Everybody was horny and looked like they were ready to go all night. Couples were walking around and standing around, holding hands and kissing—and the majority of the couples were made up of two guys, often a mix of sailor and civilian, but just as often two sailors or two civilians. None of them made any move to hide their affection from anybody else, and it was obvious that nobody cared that night, even though gay couples holding hands and kissing in public was very rare most times—except at City Park. For that one night, at least, it was anything goes—really, *anything* goes—and nobody gave a shit who was doing what, or with which, or to whom, to quote the old limerick.

I even saw a police squad car parked on a street corner, with the back door open, and the light from a streetlight was enough that I could see a sailor kneeling in the back seat, with his pants down to his knees and a cop eating his ass. There were almost no girls out, but I did see one lying on her back on the front lawn of a house while one guy was fucking her, and a second guy was fucking the first one's ass.

Going up to the park I ran into other guys headed there, obviously for the same purpose as mine, and we chatted and joked about getting laid to celebrate. A lot of us were shedding clothes as we walked, and beginning to grope each other. A few had brought flashlights, although there was a lot of daylight left. Several had also brought blankets, like I had; I planned to keep mine hot that night, and share it with as many guys as I could.

There were already quite a few guys in the clearing when I got there, most of them already sucking and fucking, and more were arriving regularly. All of them were completely naked, and there were piles of clothes all over the place, mostly spread out on blankets or draped over bushes. I spotted Dave, a really cute guy from my Trigonometry class standing there taking it all in, with his dick in his hand while he stroked it. I hadn't even known he was gay, and I didn't know if he knew about me, but as soon as I stripped, I went over to him, put my arms around him and shoved my tongue down his throat, tickling his tonsils with it while he responded just as eagerly. I figured by then he knew I was queer — or was at least open to sex with a guy!

While we watched the orgy developing, before we joined in, Dave stood behind me, with his arms around my chest, playing with my tits, and his prick sticking in between my legs while he kissed and sucked my neck. I reached behind to stroke the smooth skin of Dave's ass and pull his body even closer to mine. He occasionally reached down to stroke my hard cock while we watched the action for a while before we lay down on my blanket and necked and double-sucked for a while.

He was kneeling over me while we sixty-nined, and I was getting near to blowing my load, so I told him to stop for a while, that I wanted to pace myself, making the sucking and fucking last as long as possible. I knew I was good for three loads on even an average night, but with the special excitement in the air, I thought I might match my previous record — five loads — or maybe even exceed it. I figured we'd all be there for a long time, maybe even all night — who was going to be keeping track of anybody on this night-of-all-nights? Certainly not my parents. They never checked up on me, and besides, my dad would know what I was doing, if not where I was doing it — God knows he had caught me in bed with another guy often enough. He might even have had a pretty good idea where I was, since after he found out I was gay, he confided in me that he had spent a lot of time in City Park, sucking and fucking with the sailors and college boys before he met my mother and 'cleaned up his act,' as he put it.

For some reason, Dad thought my cocksucking and buttfucking were part of a 'phase' I was going through, just like the one he had. I assured him I knew I was doing what I wanted, and was planning to continue doing it for the rest of my life, until I was too old to get a hard-on. Later, I often wondered just how much that 'phase' was completely behind Dad: his once-a-week 'poker nights' with his asshole buddies were probably a front. I knew for a fact that at least one of his poker buddies was queer as pink peanut butter—God knows he sucked me off enough, and he was the second guy I ever fucked.

My parents died quite a few years ago, by the way, or I would never include those stories here!

When Dave and I took a break from sucking each other, we stood up to survey the scene before us, and what I saw has always been etched in my mind—even more so than that night at The Studio when all the models got together for a New Year' Eve party. That was the biggest orgy I've ever seen, by the way, with virtually all my favorites giving up their butts for me to fuck, and almost all of them giving me at least one load up my own in return—and those were just my special favorites. I took a total of something like twelve or fourteen loads of cum up my ass that night.

I don't remember how many guys fucked me, or how many blew their loads in my ass or my mouth the night the upcoming Japanese surrender was announced, but there were a lot of them. I remember that on the way back into town the next morning, Dave was walking on air, but his ass was sore as hell. He confessed he had taken at least ten loads of cum in his butt, maybe more, because of the ten different guys who had fucked him, three of them—one of our schoolmates and two sailors—had fucked him for a really long time, and he thought at least two of those had each shot two loads in him before they moved on to someone else.

Actually, I was the last one to fuck Dave that time. We had been so busy screwing and sucking with other guys that we didn't get around to fucking until it was daylight again, and we both wanted to be sure we did it before going back into town. He was the first guy I had sex with when I got there that night, and the last one the next morning. I stood behind him, holding his waist while he stood, leaning over and sticking out his ass for me to fuck while he held onto the trunk of a tree. The sun rising over the ocean was quite bright, and Dave's body was bathed in gold; he looked good enough to eat, but I had eaten him earlier, now it was time to fuck him. His ass was nothing short of gorgeous, by the way—small, but really well rounded, with velvet skin and an extremely deep cleft guarding his treasure, a cleft so narrow that his asscheeks would barely allow my prick to penetrate between them; it made it very hard to get my tongue as far inside him as it would go when I ate him out—which I *adored* doing!

Dave had been fucked so often by the time we began our sunrise fuck, and so much cum had been shot inside his ass, that when I shoved my cock inside him, it was like I had opened a floodgate. The first six or eight times I drove my prick inside him, it displaced a spurt of cum each time, and after that, cum trickled out of his asshole steadily while I fucked, flowing down the shaft of my dick and dripping from my balls. Dave reported something akin to that a little later when we exchanged places, and he finally fucked me—but only after he had sucked my balls clean.

Dave and I dated pretty regularly after that, but not exclusively—neither of us wanted to limit ourselves to just one guy.

Besides Dave and myself, I counted nineteen boys having sex in the clearing while we began to watch, following our first break on the night we first got together. It was a scene so exciting and—to me at least—unthinkably beautiful and inspiring, it seemed almost *holy* in its scope and its implications. All the nineteen boys were completely naked, except for quite a few sailor hats, so that I had no idea how many were sailors and how many were high school or college boys. I assumed the sailor hats were being worn by sailors, but I saw that one of my schoolmates was wearing one, and one of the University boys I had gone to bed with a few times also had one plastered jauntily on the back of his head—the sexy way the sailors wore them when they were on liberty. There was a sailor I had once had fantastic sex with standing there without his cap, and it eventually became clear that, for some reason, the hats were being worn by high school and college boys. I counted nine sailors caps, so I assumed that many sailors were mixed in the group of nineteen. Dave and I didn't wait very long before we made it a group of twenty-one!

There was still enough daylight left to see clearly what was happening—and even though it got dark soon, we were blessed with a near-full moon of unbelievable brightness, so we could continue to enjoy things visually before we were forced to mainly enjoy them tactilely, with the only light coming from a few flashlights placed strategically in tree crotches

In spite of the intensely bright moonlight, I frequently could not even tell who was fucking me, or whose cock I was sucking, or whose ass or lips were taking the record-breaking number of loads I was producing. The moon eventually moved so that the clearing was in shadows, but then we all went on kissing and fucking and sucking in the near dark, relieved only by the feeble glow from the flashlights many had thought to bring. By the time all the batteries had burned out, the flashlights weren't needed, since by the time the party broke up, dawn had also broken.

The wild scene that Dave and I watched for a while before we joined the fun ourselves impressed me so vividly that I can re-create it in accurate detail, although later on, more boys showed up, and developments became so wild and kaleidoscopic that it's all a jumble in my memory—but still, a fondly remembered jumble of *fucklust,* the likes of which I had never suspected could exist.

In the middle of the clearing, where a variety of blankets pretty well obscured the grass, three boys were kneeling in a row, on all fours, shoulder to shoulder—two wearing sailor hats on the backs of their heads. On their knees behind them were three other boys, fucking their asses quite enthusiastically; only one of those wore a sailor hat, and as he fucked the boy impaled on his cock with extremely deep thrusts, his ass cheeks opened and closed, alternately displaying and concealing his asshole. I couldn't see the asses of the two boys who were fucking without sailor hats, since two other boys were on all fours behind them, with faces completely buried between their undulating buttocks, feasting on hot ass!

Standing in front of the three boys who were getting fucked were three other boys—one facing away from them and bending over while his ass was being eaten, the other two facing them and getting their cocks sucked.

Another boy wearing a cap was fucking the ass of one of the ass-eaters at the back, making a row of five who were getting sucked, sucking while getting fucked, fucking butt, eating ass, and fucking butt again, respectively. The boy fucking the ass-eater, the back one in the row, was bent over the back of the boy he was fucking, and his upper body was perfectly still while his ass writhed and humped deeply, driving what was clearly a major piece of meat into the boy he was impaling. I recognized him—he was a University student whose dormitory room I had visited a few times.

Two couples lay on blankets, slightly apart from the cluster of twelve, each pair sucking each other off in sixty-nine. Another pair stood next to them, kissing hungrily while their hands feverishly fondled each other's bodies. Behind one of the standing pair, another boy, wearing a sailor cap was holding his ass tightly while he fucked him. I had seen the one getting fucked around town—he was a sailor, and so cute and well-built he was extremely memorable, and I had thought to proposition him, but so far had not worked up the nerve (I later did—with extremely gratifying results). The boy the cute sailor was necking with was another classmate of Dave's and mine, whose presence there surprised me, but not Dave—who had gone to bed with him recently.

As daylight broke, and we were beginning to wind up the night of unbridled sex, I realized that forty or fifty people had been involved at some point, and I had probably kissed or sucked or fucked most of them if only for a few minutes—and I had been kissed or sucked or fucked by at least an equal number. My jaws were stretched and sore from sucking dick, and my ass was just as sore as Dave's when we walked back down into town. It was full, bright daylight by then, and we encountered any number of townspeople who waved and grinned at us, obviously aware of what we had been doing, but so elated over the imminent end to the war that even the least understanding of them were happy, and, I thought, even happy for us.

Does the nineteen-man fucking-and-sucking tableau sound familiar to you? Yeah, it should; I recreated the whole scene in my video *Victory Orgy*, back in 1995—just the way I remembered it. The orgy it memorializes took place on a bluff overlooking a bay on the Atlantic ocean, but the video was shot on a bluff overlooking the Pacific Ocean, near Camp Pendleton in Southern California, and we shot it all in full daylight. It took about five days to film the orgy, and we actually began shooting it on the fiftieth anniversary of the day the real one began!

The video shows only my arrival and encounter with Dave, and the nineteen-man orgy that becomes a twenty-one-man orgy when we join it. There are many close-ups and cuts between fucking couples as well as a good many panoramic shots; the orgy part alone ran almost ninety minutes on video, while the part of the original orgy that I was re-creating probably didn't take more than forty.

My part in the orgy, as well as Dave's—to a somewhat lesser extent—were especially emphasized in the video. Hell, why not? It was my story, and I was the director—besides, I hired Steve Fox to play me, and naturally I wanted that fantastic body and gorgeous face of his to be seen at great length in the final product.

When I contracted with Steve to play the lead, I told him he was going to be playing the real me, fifty years earlier. He was a real sweetie, and said, "Do I look like you did back then? You're still a damned sexy man." Christ, I was sixty-five years old! I showed him pictures taken during my days at The Studio, and he was kind again, saying except for some facial features, we could have passed for twins. But I know that while our blond hair was almost the same, his body was even more muscular than mine had been—and that's saying something, because even if I say so myself, I was built like a brick shithouse back then. And I'm proud to say I had a lot more dick than Steve did—and that's saying even more, because there was nothing remotely small about Steve's.

I guess I should have been insulted that Steve wasn't familiar with my work back in those days of The Studio, but hell, why should he have been? It had all been done around thirty years before—about the time he was born! Plus, you have to remember that anything he *might* have seen with me in it would have been soft porn at the most, and he'd grown up looking at the really good stuff: hot fucking and sucking with cuties like Mike Henson and

66

Erik Houston, gorgeous hunks like Matt Ramsey and Ryan Idol and Tom Steele, muscle studs like Cody Foster or Brad Stone or Adam Hart, and those super-hung fuckers like Rick Donovan or Jeff Stryker or Tom Chase. Jesus, it's hard to limit the list of examples to so few. With guys like that fucking and sucking for the cameras, who would want to watch soft porn? And don't forget Steve saw the most beautiful and studly one of all every time he looked in the mirror. I guess you have to be into blonds who look like Adonis and are built like Hercules to appreciate Steve's looks as much as I did, but I thought he was the most beautiful man in porn.

Steve did great work on the movie, and we got to know each other really well, if you know what I mean. Up until the time he did my movie, he had almost entirely been a bottom on film; he was a spectacularly good bottom, and his physical, literal bottom was about as luscious as any I ever saw — or 'got to know,' to continue the euphemism from the previous sentence. In *Victory Orgy* he topped as much as he bottomed, treating six of his fellow performers to his persuasive topping.

I was amazed to find how many of those other studs involved in *Victory Orgy* Steve had been to bed with, and I won't reveal any names, but six of those eleven exceptional porn stars I mentioned a couple of paragraphs above were among the other lucky ones who had made love with Steve — including two who were strictly tops on film, but who gave up their butts to Steve in person. Only one of them, Brad Stone — he of the world's finest tits — was ever in the same video as Steve, but they didn't actually do a scene together — at least not in front of the cameras! (What a shame! Jesus, can you imagine how hot seeing Brad Stone's and Steve Fox's chests pressed together would be?)

If I can't tell you the names of the other famous porn stars who made love with Steve Fox off-camera, I will admit that one guy who sucked and fucked with him quite a few times, and kissed and snuggled, too — Jesus, he was a great kisser—was none other than yours truly! I must have spent more time eating Steve Fox's ass than I did eating lunch and supper that week we spent shooting *Victory Orgy*.

Speaking of Brad Stone, I am reminded of something that happened about twenty years ago, and I have to digress to relate it here.

I went back to my hometown for a visit with my parents. I was forty-five or fifty, and even though, by tradition, guys in my age bracket didn't normally go up to City Park to cruise for dick, I figured, what the hell? What could they do if I did go up there to cruise kids half my age, sue me? I hadn't had any dick or fucked any butt in about a week, and I was horny as hell—and unless things had changed a lot, there would be a lot of cute cock and ass on display up there. If I had trouble scoring, I could probably wave some money in front of a hot sailor or college kid and get what I wanted. So, I took a stroll to the site where the inspiration for my *Victory Orgy* had taken place.

It was early afternoon, and there weren't too many boys around. Things obviously hadn't changed, though; pairs of boys walking around and holding hands could be seen, a few pairs lying on the grass or standing around were eating each other's faces and groping each other's asses, and I spotted a guy standing at the edge of the bushes, with a sailor kneeling in front of him, sucking his dick, not far from another pair who were naked and locked together in sixty-nine, sucking each other off. I didn't actually see anyone getting his ass plowed, surprisingly. *Not* surprisingly, there were quite a few unaccompanied guys wandering around, cruising each other.

One of the solo cruisers was dressed in extremely worn and faded Levi's, ripped (or perhaps worn through) in 'key' places—sexy! Even sexier was the fact that his Levi's were unbelievably tight, and he was apparently not wearing any underwear, because the outline of his prick could clearly be seen down his left leg—*very* big, and obviously hard as flint. Between the cute boys all around me and the sight of this beauty, my own dick was straining for release. Sexiest of all, the stud was bare-chested, with his shirt tucked into the back of his Levi's, and the bare chest he showed literally took my breath away: It was *vast*—that's the only word for it—and if I'd ever seen rounder, broader, more muscular or more thrilling tits before that, I couldn't remember it just then. His tits were sumptuous—delectable, mouth-watering—and his arms were equally muscular, in perfect proportion to his awe-inspiring chest.

Naturally I started circling around, cruising the muscular tit-stud, and he didn't seem to be paying much attention to me, until suddenly he walked directly up to me and said, 'You're Spike Jefferson, aren't you?'

My heart thumped and my dick twitched as I confessed I was, indeed Spike. I asked him how he could know that. I wouldn't have been too surprised if he had recognized Casey Donovan, maybe—after all, Casey was still something of a poster boy for gay sex then, not one like me, whose place in the sun had faded long before then. The kid explained that he had recently visited with an old guy who had some pictures of me in his bedroom, and who told him all about me because the kid had been so struck by the pictures. "I told him I thought you were the cutest guy I ever saw," the kid told me—and I was really flattered, of course, but I was really pleased, too, since I knew then I was going to get in this sexy kid's pants for sure!

The old man—and he was *really* old, about eighty, the kid thought—was gay of course, and he ran a book store, where he had sold physique magazines back in the sixties and seventies, before the hard-core mags he later sold had come into circulation. He had spotted my pictures in *Physique Pictorial*, and thought I looked familiar. A local boy perhaps? He showed pictures of me to some of his gay pals, and finally identified me as a hometown kid. Whether it was that I was from his home town, or whether I was just the type of guy he really got hot over, he developed a kind of fascination with me—but really with Spike Jefferson, who is not really me, at least not all of the time.

The old guy collected every magazine he could find that had my picture in it, and he ordered my eight-millimeter movies. He even ordered the photo sets that I personally offered through the mail, and I remembered him, because I had been struck by the fact that someone from my home town was buying them—*collecting* them, really, because he bought every one I had for sale. I always included a little note with pictures I sent to customers, something like "I'm heading for the beach. Wish you were here to go with me. We could have a great day! Love, Spike." The man always included a note when he ordered pictures, but only said complimentary things about me, never saying anything about his age or the fact that he knew I came from his hometown.

The kid with the luscious tits, who was a student at the local university, said the old man had approached him on the street one day when he was walking around in tiny shorts and an underwear top—the kind of white, ribbed, tank-top underwear we call 'wife beaters' these days—showing his magnificent chest and emphasizing his heavenly tits. The old man apologized, and said he was too impressed with the kid *not* to offer him a business proposition that he hoped would not offend him. He promised to give him a hundred dollars to go with him to his house and strip naked. He assured the boy he would not do anything but fondle his body below the waist or above the shoulders. But he wanted to suck his tits—but would also be glad to suck anything else the boy would allow, if he wanted him to. He had actually laughed when he told the kid he couldn't get a hard-on anymore, anyway. I guess at eighty, you don't get embarrassed about something like that.

Young Mr. Tits went with the old man, of course, and posed for him. He let him lick and kiss and suck every inch of his chest for a long time, and the old man was so nice, and so respectful, that the boy let him suck him off and eat his ass, too—which made the old guy so grateful and happy that the kid actually collected *two* hundred dollars when he left.

When the kid had asked about the pictures of me, the old man told him I was Spike Jefferson, and made him promise not to tell anyone that I was really a local boy. He said he had some old black-and-white Spike Jefferson movies, if he wanted to see them. The kid said he wound up watching every movie, and by the time he left the old man's house, he was a complete Spike Jefferson fan.

The kid said, "When I left the old guy's house, two loads lighter and two hundred bucks richer, he gave me copies of a pair of pictures of you, naked, with another naked guy, ones that he had hanging over the dresser in his bedroom. In the first you've got a great big hard-on and you're kneeling in front of this dark-haired guy whose dick looks like it's about as big as yours, and it's almost touching your face. In the second picture, the other guy is holding your head, and his dick is all the way down your throat. The other guy is gorgeous, by the way—about as fuckable-looking as you'll find. I got my copies framed together as one big picture, and I keep it hidden in my room. And even though I get about as much live cock and ass as I can handle," he giggled when he said that, and added, looking down at my bulging basket, " —and I really love to handle cock—I get those pictures out and jack off to them quite a bit." He laughed and said, "I don't hide them because I'm afraid somebody would figure out I'm gay— shit, most of them know that anyway, especially the ones I've blown or got fucked by—but because they'd probably get stolen."

I told the kid, "Today's your lucky day. You can jack off with the real thing, but I hope you're gonna do a lot more than just jack off." He promised to do a *lot* more than just jack off We went to his dorm room and fucked and sucked each other all afternoon, with the pictures of me about to give a blowjob, and actually doing it propped up on the desk next to his bed. The odd thing about the photographs—and they were really good ones, obviously taken just a few minutes apart—was that I had never seen them before, although I certainly remembered the occasion; I hadn't known at the time that it was being photographed!

But the amazing thing about this story is that while I can't say the tit boy's name here, it was only *one letter* different from Brad Stone's name. I hadn't yet seen Brad Stone then, of course, but when I did, and was completely bowled over by his huge, beautiful chest and tits, I decided that the only chest and tits I had ever seen in person, much less gone to bed with, that were as fabulous as his, were on the student I had fucked that afternoon, whose name was almost identical to Brad's. Talk about coincidences!

I didn't see a picture of Brad's thrilling chest and realize the coincidence until about ten years after I fucked with Tit Boy in the dorm, but I remembered the kid's name well, since he came out to California to visit me a few times, and when he eventually started selling his body and cock—tits too, of course—I helped him get set up in the escort business there. Not long after that I also helped get him into porn, and he had a short-lived, but spec- tacular career as a porn star.

Once Mr. Luscious Tits was established as a famous porn star, he started bringing in the big bucks when he rented himself out to tricks, of course, and he kept on escorting for a long time after he quit doing porn. Last I heard he was still living with an incredibly wealthy businessman in the entertainment industry, who became his big-time sugar daddy, and got him to quit selling his ass and fantastic tits. He never sold himself to me, but he often gave it to me for free!

The first time he visited me in California, he brought an enlarged copy of the set of photographs of me about to give, and giving head, the ones that had watched over us while we made love that afternoon in his dorm room. There was a photography shop back in my hometown that would print almost any kind of pictures, no questions asked. Tit Boy had taken his copies there to be reproduced as a present for me. That same pair of pictures can be seen over on page 242 of this book, and you should be able to recognize the dark-haired sexpot I'm getting ready to blow, and whose cock is down my throat next—there are plenty of other pictures of him in this book. (Do the initials "M.H." suggest anything?)

Back to the subject of Steve Fox: I heard rumors that he was straight—was only gay-for-pay in his video work and in his personal life as a very successful and well-paid prostitute (you can call it 'escorting' if you want, but that doesn't change what it is). Given the intensity and the wonder of our lovemaking as both director and 'playmate' for a full week, I find it impossible to believe.

It was a real shock to learn about Steve's death a couple of years ago. Jesus, if Monte Hansen was the sexiest man I ever saw, Steve was the most beautiful one. I think Monte actually was 'gay-for-pay,' by the way—but god *damn,* he was the hottest stud a gay man could ask for if he was being paid! I was thrilled to find there were ways I could find to pay Monte when I was more-or-less broke, when I was hard-up with a hard-on. Unavoidably, my dick was always hard when Monte was around. I wasn't doing a lot of escorting back then (okay, prostitution), but any time I could get together with Monte, I'd sell myself to some guy and take the money I got paid for having sex with him and fork it over to Monte for the same purpose!

But anyway, Steve did look a lot like me back when I went up to that park to celebrate the Japanese surrender, but of course I was only around seventeen at the time, and Steve didn't look like a kid when we did the video re-creation. Oh no, if anyone looked like a *man*, it was Steve Fox—may he rest in peace.

Spike's book sold very well. Thousands upon thousands of gay men in the United State were fans of the videos he directed, and he had countless international admirers of his work as well. If they knew little or nothing of his earlier life as a model in 'physique' publications, they knew he employed the hottest studs for his movies, and he managed to inspire the best kind of dramatic and sexual performances in them.

Victory Orgy had an all-star cast in addition to Steve Fox, and it sold well, and when the word got out that it was Spike's best work, extraordinarily hot in addition to having a stellar cast, sales went through the roof. When *Shooting Stars Who Were Shooting Loads* was published, word of mouth was equally laudatory, and even gay men who did little reading bought it for the wealth of explicitly sexual pictures it contained—of the kind one normally does not find in anything but hard-core magazines. Those who had enjoyed the video, and learned that its genesis was detailed in Spike's new autobiography bought a copy as soon as they could lay their hands on it.

Gay residents of Hus Bay—townspeople, students, sailors, and even regular Marine visitors—soon learned that 'Spike Jefferson' was a local boy—although many of the older ones already knew that. They heard that the book had a very explicit section detailing a gay orgy that took place at City Park a long time ago, although no individuals were identified, nor was the name of the town ever specified. Old-timers, and the ones who were either gay or had practiced homosexuality back then, all had to read the book, hoping to learn if they, or anyone they knew, could be identified. Younger ones just wanted to get the dirt, and the current crop of students and servicemen wanted to share vicariously in the excitement of events that had taken place right where they were still practicing the sort of behavior described: in City Park.

Shooting Stars While They Were Shooting Loads was published by a relatively small house—major publishers would not touch a book as sexually specific as it was, especially considering that it contained many pictures that were outright pornography. It was available only from 'specialty' distributors, ones who handled erotica.

The Book Cellar was still the only bookstore in Hus Bay, and it sold hundreds and hundreds of copies of Spike's book. Probably two hundred were sold to townspeople, and at least five hundred to students at the University. Sailors and Marines had been more careful about buying it, in the wake of recent purges in the service and the absurd "Don't ask, don't tell" policy the government had adopted recently, which actually had the effect of bringing about the reverse of the liberalizing of the military services' attitude toward homosexuality among military personnel that it had been originally intended to alleviate—resulting in record numbers of discharges for homosexuality. Still, local sailors and Marines who visited regularly from Parris Island bought the book in fairly large numbers, and almost all of them who didn't want to buy it, or were afraid of possessing a copy, managed to read a borrowed one.

The Book Cellar had, by then, been owned by Jason Boone for almost twenty years.

4.

FILLING THE HEIR WITH
ROMANCE

L ess than six months after Jason moved into the
apartment over The Book Cellar, Max Koch died
peacefully in his sleep one night, at the age of
seventy-six. Jason was only twenty-five at the time.

Max's health had begun failing rapidly about the
time Jason took over the store for him; it was almost as if
Max waited to die until he was sure someone was on
board to stay the course of the business he had loved, one
who shared his own appetites, however many years
separated them.

From the time he first came to work for Max, when
he was still a student at Paulik, Jason was treated like a
beloved grandson by the old man. Even if Jason had been
straight, Max would probably have loved him — he was a
sweet, thoughtful, intelligent boy. But the fact that Jason
was extremely attractive, enormously *sexual,* and unapolo-
getically gay especially endeared him to Max, who saw his
own youth reflected in the young man's eyes and
behavior — a youth that Max had enjoyed enormously. The
old man especially enjoyed knowing how much Jason was
enjoying his own life. Only in the subtlest sense did the old
man re-live his own younger life vicariously with Jason.

Jason loved Max, too, and in spite of the great difference in their ages, he was never made uncomfortable by
the old man's frankness about his sexual past and the fact
that, although Max no longer really did anything about it,
he still enjoyed looking at pretty boys. Jason liked to watch

with him while they looked at the wonderful pictures and movies of other pretty boys, which had enriched Max's life so much over the years.

During the last two months of Max's life, when he was mostly confined to his bedroom, Jason spent a great deal of time listening to the old man reminisce about his fondly remembered sex life. Before then, Jason had never even entered Max's bedroom, although he was frequently welcomed into all other parts of the house. Jason had never heard of some of the astonishingly beautiful, sexy boys and men whose pictures filled Max's bedroom, standing in frames on most surfaces, and hanging on the walls in profusion.

Max had Jason dig out copies of old physique magazines to see more pictures of men like Spike Adams, Spike Jefferson, or Monte Hansen. His collection of Spike Jefferson pictures and films was vast, and he confided in Jason that Spike was a Hus Bay native. Jason set up the old eight-millimeter movie projector, and together they watched old physique films, old hard-core gay pornography and recent, more polished efforts. Max never owned a VCR or videotapes, which were becoming common only during the last year or two of his life, so he was never able to enjoy any of the flood of excellent pornography that was beginning to appear about the time he died.

Jason became enamored of the older stars Max doted on—in some cases, whom he almost obsessed over. In various parts of his house Max had large reproductions of paintings by George Quaintance, definitely gay, and decidedly erotic, but with no genitals or actual sexual activity depicted—not even kissing or embracing. Jason thought the subtle but very powerful eroticism of Quaintance's paintings, and the coy concealment of genitalia were actually more arousing than pictures of boys having sex. Bare chests and asses abounded, and Quaintance was a master of exaggerating those body parts to make them particularly erotic. The chests of his subjects were broader than in real life, the asses were more perfectly rounded. Tom of Finland would later do the same thing in his drawings, but in Tom's work, asses and chests and the gigantic muscles and pricks and cocks were exaggerated so much that they were totally unrealistic— but *very* sexy and erection-producing. A Quaintance painting made you feel warm and romantic, and anxious to make love with the beautiful subjects. Tom of Finland drawings made your prick spring to attention and throb while you fantasized about dominating or being totally dominated sexually, *wildly* fucking and sucking the most tantalizing ass and the biggest prick ever imagined, slurping cum or being showered with it.

There were enlarged photos of Glenn Bishop hanging throughout the house as well, but none showing his genitalia, or even a covered hard-on. He had the most astonishing ratio of broad, muscular chest to narrow waist Jason had ever seen, with muscular arms and legs that fell just short of being overly developed. He had dark, short, somewhat curly hair, and the face was that of an angel— truly one of the most classically *beautiful* men Jason had ever seen. Although he was occasionally posed with a supernaturally handsome blond named Richard Harrison, there was no sexual activity shown or even suggested. Apparently, Glenn Bishop actually *was* a physique model, not a hot stud who intentionally posed naked to titillate gay men and provide them with jack-off fodder.

The Quaintance drawings and the Glenn Bishop photographs were beautiful and sexually arousing, but not so sexually explicit that Max had felt they needed to be hidden in his bedroom.

Max obviously felt death was approaching near the end, since a few days before he died, he told Jason to contact his attorney immediately when he died; Jason noticed he had said *when,* not *if.*

Max's last words, whispered to Jason as he said goodnight to him the night he passed away, were inspired by the last movie they had watched together, playing on the late show on television: the quarter-century-old *Island of Desire*, starring a young, mouth-watering Tab Hunter. Max said, "My God he was beautiful, wasn't he? There were so many beautiful men Jason, and I made love with so many of them. I've had a wonderful life." He smiled and clasped Jason's hand gently, as he sighed, "I love you, my boy," before he patted it and added, "Good night."

Somehow, Jason sensed that it would be the last time he would see Max alive, but as he kissed him lightly on the forehead and turned out the light, he could not be sad about it. It was obviously time, and Max *had* enjoyed a good life.

The next morning, when it was clear that the end had actually come during the night, Jason called a doctor. As soon as the doctor had pronounced the old man dead, Jason called Max's attorney.

Jason had met the lawyer on several occasions, when he visited Max for some business or other. He told Jason over the phone that he was to inform the funeral home they should be prepared to cremate Max's body, and that he would stop by to see them within the hour, to give them properly certified permission to do so. He would then come to Max's house and tell Jason what should happen next.

Only a few hours later, the lawyer showed up at Max's house and informed Jason that it was now Jason's house. A year earlier, Max had prepared his will as a graduation present for the young man who had become such a trusted assistant—a present Jason was not to know about until the old man's death.

By the terms of the will, virtually everything Max owned became the unrestricted property of Jason Boone, to do with as he saw fit, except for twenty-five thousand dollars he left to Anthony L. ("Tony") Lowe, a young sailor said to be stationed at the Hus Bay Naval Station. Jason had absolutely no idea who Tony Lowe was.

Max's estate included the house and the city lots surrounding it, which Jason had always assumed were just part of one big lot on which the house sat. There was a five-year old Cadillac, which Max had stopped driving a few years earlier, but which Jason had regularly used since then. Naturally, the business, The Book Cellar, was included in the inheritance, especially so since it was in the house. There was also a considerable portfolio of stock holdings, and a surprisingly large amount of cash in addition to that earmarked for "Tony Lowe." Since Max had no living family whatever, it was virtually certain the will would not be contested, the attorney said. "There will be some tax to pay, of course — the entire estate is valued at around two million dollars — but I have already prepared a recommended list of stocks or properties you might want to sell in order to pay that.

"But why would he leave everything to me?" Jason asked.

"Well, obviously he wanted you to have it, and since he had no family, if he hadn't make a will, everything he owned would have reverted to the State of South Carolina. And he told me that he didn't know anyone else who would appreciate and preserve his 'treasures.' I guess you know what that means; Max didn't elucidate. I know he hoped you would continue to live here, and keep the bookstore open. That's not a condition of the will, by the way, just something he told me he would like to see happen. And he said he hoped you would move into his bedroom if you stayed on, and that you would preserve his 'shrine' there. I presume you know what that meant, too. It's all spelled out in the will, of course." The attorney presented Jason with a copy of the will, saying, "And you'll notice that he refers to you as his 'beloved' friend. I believe he meant that literally."

"Will you find this Tony Lowe?" Jason asked.

"I asked Max if I should do that, but he just smiled and said that eventually you would meet him, and you could be the one to let him know about his part of the inheritance."

Instead of a church funeral, Jason arranged a memorial service, as Max had requested in his will; Max was nominally Jewish, but he had never practiced his religion, and the closest synagogue was in Charleston, anyway. According to further specifications, the service was held at The Book Cellar, with Max's ashes on site for the service. Jason also arranged to later honor Max's wish to have the urn containing his ashes interred in the Koch family funeral plot in the Hus Bay Civic Cemetery, next to his parents' graves.

There was a fairly impressive turnout for the memorial service, but it principally comprised old men, mostly of Max's generation, many of equal years or more. There were a few younger men, mostly customers Jason knew casually from the store. There were only a few women in attendance—all wives of old friends. Jason chatted and shared reminiscences with as many of the attendees as he could, whatever their age or connection to Max.

One who showed up for the service was a dark young sailor who was strikingly handsome, wearing a uniform so tight that it not only revealed a fine body, a perfect ass, and a massive 'package' of cock and balls, it virtually *proclaimed* them! While Jason thoroughly enjoyed the sight, he actually felt the breathtaking sexiness of the uniform was not in good taste at what was essentially a funeral. He wanted to have a few words with the sailor, hopefully to find out what his connection to Max had been. He had to admit that he would want to spend some time with *any* young man as handsome and sexy as this one—hoping to do more than just talk, perhaps—but he put that out of his mind as inappropriate to the moment, like the sailor's uniform.

Jason was afraid the young stud might leave before he was able to speak to the several older men and customers who clustered around to tender their condolences. But the sailor lingered near the back of the shop, pretending to look at books; Jason guessed he might actually be stalling for time so they could speak privately.

Jason ushered the last old man from the shop, leaving only himself and the sailor. He turned to go to the back of the store and talk with the sexy stud, but when he turned to do so, he discovered the sailor standing only a few feet behind him.

"Jason?" The sailor extended his hand to shake, "I'm..."

"My God, you're Tony Lowe, aren't you?"

The sailor was clearly taken by surprise, but he smiled. In the somber mood the service had obviously engendered in him, he had been beautiful; with a smile lighting his face, he was *gorgeous!* "How did you know that?" he asked.

"I'll tell you in a minute. It's good to meet you, Tony Lowe," Jason said, shaking the boy's hand.

Tony appeared to be about nineteen, and was even cuter and sexier up-close than he was from a distance. Jason continued, "I haven't seen you in here before. How do you know my name?" He couldn't resist adding, knowing Max would probably approve: "I know I'd remember if I'd ever seen you." He had shifted into his seduction mode, if only for a second, so his quick glance down at the bulging crotch of Tony's white sailor pants was automatic — and highly gratifying.

And Tony noticed the glance.

"I think that's a compliment," Tony grinned.

"You can bet your..." Jason hesitated for a second before he continued, with a laugh, "I was going to say you can bet your sweet ass it's a compliment, but calling your ass 'sweet' might be a little inappropriate under the circumstances."

"Would it still be inappropriate some other time?" Tony asked quietly.

Jason waited a brief, *meaningful* moment before he replied, smiling crookedly: "Not at all. I'll bet your ass gets described with at least that much appreciation most of the time. You know, some kinds of Chinese food are sweet, but they're also spicy — they call them sweet and hot. That always sounded peculiar, but I can see that the term could easily apply if we're gonna talk about your ass." He laughed as he added, "and it looks like I'm determined to do that, doesn't it?"

"Yeah. Yeah it does," Tony laughed along with him.

"Christ, look at me. I'm almost trying to put the make on you, and Max's ashes are sitting right over there on that table. Talk about inappropriate! I apologize."

"First of all," Tony began, "thanks for the compliment. I've heard it before, but it's always nice to hear it again. So, if you think you might have shocked me, forget it. I can tell when a guy is coming on to me, and I knew you were, but it doesn't bother me, I promise you. If a guy who makes a pass at me looks like you, I really welcome it, in fact; some of the best times of my life started out that way. But to get to the point, your making a pass at me is not only welcome, it's actually appropriate that you do it while Max is listening in, even if it's only his ashes. He wanted you to."

"Whoa," Jason said. "*That* remark requires an explanation. So tell me who Tony Lowe is, and how you know my name, and how you knew Max — and how you knew that Max wanted us to..." He paused.

"To fuck?" Tony grinned.

Jason exhaled, with a laugh, "Well, I was going to say 'hit it off,' but yeah, also to fuck, I suppose. Come on, let's get a cup of coffee and sit down." He locked the door to the store, where the "closed" sign had been hanging since the morning Jason found Max's body, four days before. "We can talk over there," he concluded, nodding toward the sofa and a group of easy chairs in a secluded corner in the back of the store, where customers could relax to scan a book or magazine, or just chat over a light refreshment of the kind the store provided.

"Sounds good," Jason said.

Tony extended a hand, motioning toward the coffee urn over in the corner. "After you."

Jason smiled, "Age before beauty, huh?"

"Oh *sure*, right...age," Tony laughed. "You're really old. What, twenty-four?"

"Almost on the nose. Twenty-five," Jason replied. "And you are...?"

"Nineteen," Tony said.

"Well, I think you should go first—*definitely*. Beauty before age this time."

"Thank you, sir. You do say the nicest things," he said archly, as if quoting an outmoded expression—which he was. "But we're pretty close to the same age, and if you think I'm beautiful—which I'm beginning to think you do—we're pretty close there, too."

"My turn to thank you, because I decidedly think you're beautiful," Jason said, looking the sailor up and down, "if not a helluva lot more than that."

"Well, we're still matched in that department," Tony said seriously, looking Jason over. Then he laughed, "Hell, I think you want me to go first so you can look at my ass."

"Guilty," Jason replied, "but it might be nice if you walked backwards. The front is maybe even more impressive—and that means it is awfully goddamned impressive!"

"Let's just get some coffee and talk," Tony said. "We can do the mating dance later, if you want to."

Jason patted Tony's ass slowly and appreciatively— the material of his uniform pants was stretched so tightly, it felt like a second skin covering the firm swelling. "I believe I still have a place left on my dance card. Who gets to lead?"

"I like to lead, but I like following just as much." The sexy sailor grinned, "Following and swallowing too. How about you?"

"Call me Mister Versatile."

Sitting on the sofa in the corner of the store, over coffee, Tony explained that he had first wandered into The Book Cellar several months earlier, wanting to pick up a copy of the new Stephen King novel, *The Dead Zone*. Max had been working alone at the time, and even though he was discreet about it, Tony could tell he was cruising him.

"Were you wearing those same pants?" Jason asked. "If so, I can see how he wouldn't have been able to resist. They're pretty fucking impressive. Well, not the pants, but... well, you know what I mean."

"Yeah, I know," Tony chuckled. "That's why I have them tailored this way, after all—same reason most sailors do, who walk around in pants so tight you can count their pubic hairs. But it was still winter when I met Max, and I was wearing my dress blue uniform. By the way, if you call my uniform a 'sailor suit,' that's it—I'm outa here."

Jason laughed. "Believe me, I'd never do that. I spent a hitch in the Navy myself—just got out three years ago, in fact. And whenever I went back home on leave..."

"And home is where?" Tony interrupted.

"Texas. Amarillo. Whenever I went home, about half of my friends either commented on my *sailor suit*, or wanted to know why I wasn't wearing it, and it really pissed me off. And my Mom was the worst of all. I never could break her of the habit—or her friends, either. But go ahead—you were wearing blues when you first saw Max."

"Yeah—and blues don't...well you know, since you were a swabbie too, blues don't begin to advertise what you've got to offer nearly as well as whites do. But even in my blues, it's pretty clear that I've got a lot more dick than your average bear! From what Max told me, you're packing pretty near the same caliber weapon I am!"

"Jesus," Tony said. "What all *did* Max tell you about me? Let's get back to your story. You haven't really started. Max was cruising you, and...?"

"Right. I could tell Max was cruising me. But that didn't bother me, no matter how old he was. A lotta guys cruise me." He laughed, "Around here, I think it's most of them. I'm flattered when they cruise me, you know? I've got a huge dick, and I like for guys who appreciate big meat to know that. I'm not even gonna think about giving it to ninety-five percent of them, but it doesn't hurt me to let them admire it, whether they're old or ugly or in the closet, or even if they're straight. I like to think they might fantasize about sucking it, or taking it up the ass, and so I'm giving them pleasure.

"So anyway, I'm talking to Max—there's nobody else in the store—and I can tell he's checking out my dick, even though he never says anything to me that's out of line. He asks me my name, how old I am, what I do in the Navy, where I'm from..."

Jason broke in. "Which is where?"

"Florida, little town down near Jacksonville. Finally I ask Max why he's so interested in me—even though I've got a pretty good idea—and he says something like, 'Because you're a very impressive young man. You're so...' He stopped for a second before he said, 'Look, Tony, can I speak frankly with you? Looking the way you do, I know a lot of men approach you, probably proposition you....' I told him he didn't know the half of it. Then he went on. 'I'm an old man, sure, but if I was anywhere near your age, or even twenty-five years younger, I'd be one of those who propositioned you. As it is, I can only look, but I really like looking at you.'

"I can't recall Max's words exactly, of course, but I remember them pretty well, and I know *what* he said, if not exactly *how*."

Interestingly, Jason noticed that—whether consciously or unconsciously—Tony's speech took on a slight tinge of Max's very slight German accent when he reported the old man's words.

"I said, 'Look, sir, I'm flattered, but...' and Max broke in. 'Max. Please, call me Max. I feel old enough already without the *sir*.' So I said, 'Okay, Max it is.' I really liked him—he seemed like a sweet old guy, and I sure didn't hold it against him that he was gay. Shit, I sucked my first dick when I was thirteen years old, and sucked one this morning, and I've never even thought about wanting pussy in the six years between my first and my latest blowjobs. I'm not about to criticize a guy because he likes what I like, no matter how old he is. But that doesn't mean I wanna have sex with him, so I corrected the *sir* to *Max*, and went on.

"I said, 'Max, I'm flattered that you find me attractive, but I just couldn't...' 'No, no, no,' he said, 'I know there's not a chance of that. I'm interested in you because you're so—excuse me for saying this, I don't want to embarrass you—you're so beautiful, and almost as sexy as you are beautiful. I know most people don't use the word to describe men, but what else could you say about...about you, about Tony Lowe? Beautiful, that's the right word. And sexy? That goes without saying: look what's on display down there,' he said, waving his hand down at my dick. 'And with pants like that, you've got it on display, you have to admit that.'

"So I laughed, 'Guilty, Max, but you should see when I display it in my white uniform.' He laughed, too, and he said, 'Believe me, I know how much better things look in the white pants—and shirts too—and I wish you were wearing them. I hope you'll come around and give me a look when you switch to the whites. A big look—it'll take a big look to take it all in.' I promised him I would.

" 'But there's a special reason I find you attractive,' he said. I asked what that was, and he told me I looked like this guy from ten or fifteen years ago—in fact, he said I looked like his twin brother. The guy was somebody who posed naked for pictures in magazines, and was in some movies, too—not real movies, but those short ones that guys used to like watching while they jacked off."

Jason interrupted. "Who was the guy he was talking about? Did he give you a name?"

"Sure," Tony said. "I ended up seeing a lot of pictures of him that afternoon, and I guess I do sorta look like him, but not a dead ringer, like Max seemed to think I am. But I wish I did look just like him; the guy was fucking gorgeous, with a really cute ass and a pretty dick, even if he's not hung quite as well as I am."

"And his name was Monte Hansen, right"

"Right! So you think I look like him, too?"

"I didn't spot it at first, but I can see the resemblance. Come to think of it, it's a pretty strong resemblance—dark, same hair, same cheekbones and mouth. Looking at those pants, I can tell your cute little ass is every bit as fine as Monte's was, and you've probably got even more dick than ol' Monte had—and he had a big ass-reamer. Jesus, he was one of the best of those guys back then. I looked at a lot of his pictures, and watched a lot of his movies with Max. Monte Hansen. Yeah, he was, like you said, fucking gorgeous, and maybe the sexiest guy in any pictures from those days. And whether he looks like Monte Hansen or not, Tony Lowe is mighty goddamned gorgeous and sexy too."

"I might use those same words to describe Jason Boone, you know," Tony said with a grin.

"Thanks, Tony. Look, what do you think about...no, never mind that right now. Go on telling me about your meeting with Max."

"I'm pretty sure I know what you were about to ask me," Tony said, "and if I'm right, the answer is a great big, enthusiastic *affirmative!* But it can wait for a few minutes." He looked down at the bulge in Jason's crotch, and patted it firmly. "I guess it can wait, anyway."

Jason reached over and fondled the enormous tube of flesh outlined along Tony's left leg by the tightly stretched fabric. "But I don't think it can wait too long."

"Okay," Tony grinned, "I'll get on with my story." He leaned over and kissed Jason's ear as he groped his hard-on. "I promise it won't take too long." He leaned back, and continued.

"So, Max asked me if I wanted to see pictures of this guy, Monte Hansen, and I said sure. He said, 'I've got them upstairs, if you want to come up and look at them. I promise you, I'm going to keep my hands to myself.' So he wrote out a sign saying BACK IN AN HOUR, and hung it on the front door when he locked it. He grinned, and said, 'That ought to confuse Jason if he comes back before we do.'

"I asked who Jason was, and he said you were his helper, but then he smiled and said, 'No, he's more than that, he's like a son—more like a grandson, I guess—but we appreciate the same things. You get my meaning? Even so, I'd never lay a finger on Jason, but he enjoys looking at pictures of beautiful men and watching dirty movies with me. Monte Hansen is one of his favorites, too. Wait until I tell him about you—if you don't mind, of course.' I said I didn't. 'He was a student at the University when he started working here a few years ago—he's graduated now—but I've seen pictures of him when he was in the Navy, wearing those white uniform pants. Believe me, he fills them out just like you do! He's also a really handsome boy. I think the two of you could really enjoy spending some time together, if you know what I mean.' I assured him I did.

"We went upstairs, into his bedroom, which made me a little nervous, but he never did anything but act like a perfect gentleman, like he promised.

"He showed me pictures of Monte Hansen, and I had to agree he was really cute, and unbelievably *hot*. One picture showed him doing push-ups over a guy lying on his stomach, with his prick halfway up the guy's ass—and looking at the camera with a big, very sexy grin, almost looking like he might be saying. *'You're next.'* I was already half hard from looking at all the other pictures of him, but that one drove me over the edge. I really wanted to be next! I sprang a huge boner, and Max noticed it, but he never said anything except, 'I see you like Monte, too.' If I hadn't blown a load just a few hours earlier, I would have had to excuse myself to jack off right then.

"Max said he had to get back to the book store, but he asked me to come visit him again, if I would, even before time to switch over to whites—but that he was going to hold me to my promise to let him see me in whites some day.

"So, I left—you still hadn't come in—and I told Max I'd be back to visit him soon. I came back several times when I was walking around town, and we'd talk for a while, and he would close the shop and take me upstairs to look at more pictures. Not just Monte Hansen, either—a lot of other really sexy guys, too. And he showed me movies, but not ones with Monte Hansen. When I asked him why no Monte Hansen movies, he smiled and said he had a plan for the first time I got to see them. I didn't understand, but he enjoyed acting mysterious about it, until later, when he finally told me why."

"Why was it?"

"I'm coming to that."

"God," Jason grinned, I love to hear you say those words, *I'm coming.*"

"Believe me, you're gonna hear them again, soon—at least once. And I'm gonna be looking forward to hearing them from you, too."

"Oh you'll hear them all right, and I promise you you'll hear them at least *twice*. But getting back to Max, I don't understand why I didn't see you when you came in all those times," Jason said. "Believe me, I would have noticed you."

"Well, I'd always look, and if anyone was in the shop I'd just walk on, and plan to come back another time. I saw you several times, but I didn't get a good look at you." He snickered, "Shit, if I had, I probably would have fluffed up my dick to make it look bigger, and walked in so you could cruise me. But anyway, I figured if you knew how friendly Max and I were being, you might think I was taking advantage of him somehow.

"So, anyway, the first time I came in to visit Max after we switched to whites, he almost had a stroke checking out my box especially after I got a huge hard-on while we watched at a movie with...uh, Spike Adams playing around with this other young guy, both of 'em looking like they were about to have sex, and with those little pouches bulging so much it didn't look like they could wait much longer. Spike was fucking gorgeous—a total stud—and the other guy had the prettiest ass I think I ever saw."

"*Spike Adams vs. Bob Page*, I know the movie, and it gets me hard every time I see it."

"Well anyway, when Max spotted how hard my cock was—it woulda been pretty hard to miss, inside those tight whites—he asked me if I wanted to go into the bathroom for a few minutes before we went on watching movies. He laughed and said, 'I can see it probably wouldn't take very long.' I never cared when he talked about my looks, or my ass or my cock, he was always so complimentary; but still he never made a move, just like he'd promised he wouldn't. When I told him about some of the times I *used* my ass or my cock with another guy, it was like he knew he couldn't have me, but liked to imagine him being in on it. I learned a new word when he told me how he enjoyed sex with me that way, without going back on his promise to keep his hands off: *vicarious*.

"When Max asked me that day if I wanted to go away for a few minutes and jack off, I decided, what the fuck, it wouldn't hurt if I gave him a little thrill while I got myself off. But I didn't let him know what I had in mind. I went into the bathroom, and stripped, shoes and all. I left my uniform in there, and walked back into Max's bedroom completely naked, with all ten inches of my prick hard as a fuckin' rock, and standing straight out; I stood there for a few minutes, wiggling my butt so that my hard-on flopped all over the place.

"Max looked like he was gonna have a stroke, and I thought for a second that maybe I shouldn't be doing this—he was mighty damned old, what if he *did* have a stroke? But after he got over the shock, he whispered 'My God, Tony. You are so beautiful, and it is so big. So magnificent.'

"Max was layin' on the bed, fully dressed, with his legs stretched out and his shoes kicked off, and his back was propped up against the headboard. I stood at the end of the bed and stroked my cock, slow and sexy, but every now and then holding my fist still, and fucking into it really hard, so Max could see the shaft going in and out. I turned around several times, playing with my ass while I kept jacking off, sometimes bending over and shoving a finger up my asshole and keeping it there while I wiggled my ass around it, then sticking two or three fingers inside and fucking myself with them.

"All the while, Max kept breathing real hard, and gasping, telling me how hot and beautiful he thought I was. Finally, I was about ready to come, and I don't know what came over me—I sure hadn't planned it—but just as I knew I was going to blow my load, I stepped up to Max and aimed my cock at his face. He opened his mouth real wide, and I blew about half my load inside, and the rest all over his face and neck. While my prick was shooting, Max kept going, 'Oh! Oh! Oh my God!' When I shook the last drops of cum off the end of my prick, Max looked into my eyes while he licked his lips and cleaned the cum off his face and neck with his fingers. Then he licked his fingers clean and smiled like he was in heaven.

"He reached up and almost put his hand on my prick, but I guess he remembered he had said he wouldn't, because he snatched it back and kept smiling while he said, 'That was so exciting, Tony. It is the nicest thing you could have done for me. I thank you very, very much.' I leaned over, kissed his forehead and said, 'You're welcome, Max. I'm really glad it pleased you. You're a nice man. I wish I really was Monte Hansen, just for you, at last.' Max smiled and said, 'You look just like him, but you're even better, Tony.'

"That was the only time anything like that happened with Max, but you know, it didn't feel like it was dirty at all. I know, there I was, a young guy blowing cum in an old man's mouth, but it seemed…I don't know, just kinda *right* somehow, like I was just doing something nice for a really nice man."

"It was sweet of you, Tony," Jason said. "I'm really glad you could please him so much. I could never have done that for him. It seems funny to say it, but we were too close to do something that…intimate."

"The next time I visited Max," Tony continued, "he told me, when I was getting ready to leave, 'One of these days you will come to the store, Tony, and I won't be here any more. I feel it coming, and soon. But it's all right, I've lived a long time, and I've had a wonderful life—and one of the many fine things has been the way you've visited with me these last couple of months. In case I don't see you again….' I started to protest, but he waved his hand, like he was telling me not to interrupt. 'I hope you will promise to do something for me, something I know you will enjoy, and something that someone else very dear to me will enjoy just as much.' I told him, 'Sure Max, anything you want.'

" 'When I go, I want to be cremated, I don't want to be buried, and I don't want a funeral. I just want a simple memorial service, right here in the book store, where friends can gather and tell nice lies about me, and part of

94

the thing I ask that you do for me is to attend that service.' I promised him I would. 'And I want you to be sure to wear your white uniform, the tightest, sexiest one you've got—but then, every one I've ever seen you wear was about as tight and sexy as possible! I want you to intro-duce yourself to Jason, my young friend who runs the book store. You know who he is?'

"I told him I'd never really got a good look at you, but Max smiled and said, 'When you do, you're going to be impressed. He's beautiful like you, and he's hung like you, too. And I know how impressed Jason will be when he sees a Monte Hansen look-alike with a cock like yours bulging down inside those tight white pants. Tell him I asked that he show you the Monte Hansen movies up in my bedroom. That's why I've never showed them to you; I want you to watch them, but with Jason, because I know he's going to get excited by seeing Monte Hansen on the screen while he's got Monte's double lying there next to him. And I know how excited you're gonna get when you see your double in live action. I'm counting on you and Jason getting so excited that by the time the movies are over, you'll make love to each other. I want to think that will happen.' Then he smiled again, and said, 'In fact, I'd be willing to bet it does. But if I lost the bet, I wouldn't be around to pay off; on the other hand, if I won the bet, I wouldn't be around to collect. Anyway, if things work out, I want you both to make love here in my bed, with my ashes sitting right over there on the dresser, so I can be here with you both.' He laughed, 'Then they can take my happy ashes off to the bone yard.'

"I tell you, Jason, he really gave me the 'hard sell' about you. It's obvious he really thought you were the greatest. He told me that if he had been anywhere near your age, he would have done anything in his power to become your lover, but that it was good he wasn't, because if you hadn't been interested in loving him back, he would have been heartbroken."

"He never told me that," Jason said.

"He wouldn't have, would he?" said Tony softly, looking into Jason's eyes with great sincerity and sympathy, pressing one of his hands against Jason's cheek, and the other over his hand.

And then, finally, the tears came. Except for some minor choking-up, Jason had not yet cried over Max's death. Dying so peacefully, after having lived such a long, and, by Max's own admission, happy and satisfying life, had not stuck Jason as tragic in any way—nor was it. The revelation of the will's contents had been such a surprise that Max's magnanimity and love had yet to fully register with Jason, and the myriad details involved in bringing affairs to this point had occupied Jason's mind so much that he hadn't really had time to reflect, or to comprehend the fact that his beloved older friend was really *gone*. Max would not be appearing in the bookstore, nor would they ever again share a lunch or dinner, where they might discuss what was happening to Jason, or reminisce about his former sexual experiences and the sexual events in Jason's past. Never again would Max show how young he still was at heart—even though the youthfulness of his favorite organ, the one somewhat south of that one, was definitely a thing of the past.

The wonderful pictures and movies of the celebrated young men Max admired—and an amazingly large number of pictures of those less famous, but equally beautiful and virile, whose charms he had personally shared—were still there, but Jason knew he could never enjoy them as fully as he had when Max was there to enjoy them with him, to express his devotion to his beautiful idols.

But now it was really over, in the past. Max was gone, what had passed for his funeral had been observed, and here he sat with an unbelievably cute and sexy young sailor whom the sweet old man wanted him to enjoy, since age and circumstances had never permitted Max to share the boy's obvious charms.

96

When the tears began, they came fast. Jason began to sob, and Tony put his arms around his shoulders, pulling him close to his own chest, offering comforting words and embraces — and a much-needed handkerchief — for a quarter of an hour, until Jason calmed down and began to pull himself together.

It was then that Jason realized Tony had been crying too, but his tears had been more of sympathy for Jason, rather then grief over Max's death — or had they? Tony was mentioned in Max's will; obviously there had been a bond between them.

They refreshed their coffee cups, and Jason told Tony about the twenty-five thousand dollars Max wanted him to have. Tony was amazed. "Max shouldn't have done that. I can't take the money," he said.

"You have to take it, Tony. Obviously Max wanted you to have it, and I can see why. You were a good friend to him at the end — you gave him a lot of pleasure."

"But I still don't...oh what the hell, why not, if he really wanted me to have it? It won't hurt to have some on hand when it comes time for college. But talking about giving Max pleasure, do you think you're ready for me to give *you* some pleasure about now? Max apparently wanted me to have the money, but he also wanted me to have you — and I can't think of anything at the moment that I want more."

"Shall we take Max's ashes and go upstairs?" Jason asked.

"I don't know. I think when we do that, we should *plan* it, make a ritual out of it. I think that's what Max wanted — a formal ceremony," Tony said. "But I want you now. And besides, Max's ashes are still here, even if we do wait to do it exactly the way he wanted until later on." He took Jason's hand and guided it up and down his left pants leg, where Jason could feel the fat shaft growing and hardening alarmingly under his touch until it was straining the material from within. "I guess you can tell how much I want you," he said as Jason's hand worked is way up and down, finally cupping the big bulge of balls at his crotch.

By then, Jason's own prick was throbbing, and as Tony's hand found it and began to stroke it, Jason released Tony's prick and embraced him, whispering into his ear, "I guess you can tell I want you, too. I want that big fuckin' prick down my throat, and up my ass, and filling me with hot cum." He took Tony's head in his hands and held it as he studied his face. "Jesus, Tony," he whispered, "you are a beautiful, beautiful man."

Tony returned Jason's embrace, and their lips met. Their sweet kiss gradually grew more intense, and soon their tongues were dancing together in each other's mouths and they stretched out on the sofa together, with Tony on top of Jason, between his legs, which Jason stretched out to accommodate the young sailor. Tony frantically clasped Jason's chest to his while Jason's hands explored the firm young ass that ground and writhed beneath his appreciative touch.

"Max told me you had more than eight inches," Tony said as their lips disengaged and Jason began to tongue and blow in his ear "and I can tell he was telling the truth — and it's obviously a fat one, too."

"Every inch of it is yours — do anything you want with it," Jason whispered. "And I can tell yours is a lot bigger."

"Actually," Tony said, "it is — ten inches on the nose."

"Fuck 'on the nose,' I want it up my butt," Jason panted.

"Can you take it? Some guys can't."

"I once got fucked by a Bosun's Mate with twelve inches, but I never once got fucked by anyone as beautiful as you, whatever size his cock was."

"I've never even seen twelve inches, but I ran into a guy in Boot Camp who had almost a full eleven inches —

and I finally got where I could take most of it down my throat, and I could ride every inch of it when he had it up my ass, even the first time we had sex. He told me he'd never met anyone who could do him better. Fortunately, he loved to suck dick and take it up the ass, too, because we fucked three and four times a week all through Boot Camp. I was afraid we were gonna get caught some of the time, but it turned out he was feeding his cock to the Chief who was in charge of our company, too, and the Chief looked out for him."

Jason kissed Tony again and said, as he stood, "Enough talking. Let's get naked; we can't be seen from the street back here." He began to strip as Tony stood and followed suit. "Leave your pants on, though," Jason said, "I want to take them off of you myself. Jesus, do you realize how sexy your ass and your dick look in those pants?"

Tony snickered, "Of course I do. Why do you think I wear them this tight, and why I don't wear any underwear when I'm out hoping to pick up a guy? It sure as hell isn't because it's comfortable."

By that time, Jason was wearing only his knit briefs, and Tony was down to just his uniform pants. The sailor's throbbing cock was trapped inside his skin-tight uniform pants, and Jason's filled the entire left side of his shorts.

Tony quickly knelt and began to fondle Jason's bulging shorts. "Jesus, what a dick!" he exclaimed, as he hooked his fingers in the waistband and pulled them down, causing Jason's cock to spring out forcefully; Tony barely had time to gasp before he opened his mouth, and took most of it inside. While he sucked and licked it, he gradually took more and more, until his lips were locked around the base of Jason's monster, and the pubic hair was tickling his nose. Jason held the dark young stud by the head, and fucked his mouth fiercely, but Tony never gagged, just moaned his appreciation.

"My god, Tony, you are a helluva good cocksucker! Not many guys can take every bit of it like that."

Tony put a finger — then two — inside Jason's ass, and fucked it while he sucked. Jason groaned in happiness, but he was so eager to get what he was giving, that he pulled his cock from Tony's mouth and knelt before him. "Stand up and let me take your pants off."

Tony stood and unzipped his fly while Jason fondled his chest and stomach, with the sailor's navel directly in front of his face. Jason kissed and licked Tony's stomach while he pulled the pants flaps apart, exposing the boy's lush black pubic hair and the base of his prick. Reaching up again to play with Tony's tits, Jason told him, "Turn around. I want to see your ass first."

Tony smiled down and slowly turned his body under Jason's hands, which ended up caressing the mounds of his perfect, round ass-cheeks, still masked by the white cloth. Jason slowly, and with considerable difficulty, managed to peel the very tight pants down until Tony's cheeks were exposed. He whispered, reverently, "My god, what a beautiful ass!"

While Jason kissed and licked Tony's ass, he continued to work the pants down to the boy's ankles, and Tony stepped out of them. Then Jason spread Tony's cheeks with his hands, and planted his face between them. Tony gasped with pleasure, and bent forward as Jason's tongue penetrated him and danced inside for several minutes. Tony raised himself and turned around abruptly, causing his hard-on to slap against the side of Jason's head. "Eat my dick now!" he commanded.

Jason needed no encouragement. Tony's cock was absolutely enormous, but was not an insurmountable challenge for a talented veteran cocksucker like Jason. As Tony had done for him only a few minutes earlier, Jason took the boy's cock in his mouth, all the way to the root, and began to suck hungrily — masterfully.

Tony dragged Jason's body down to the carpet, at the same time keeping his cock buried in the hot, moist vacuum that engulfed it. Once on the floor, he rotated his body so that he could begin to suck Jason's cock again, and they lay in sixty-nine, each feasting on the other's mind-boggling, *throat*-boggling prick.

Max's ashes looked on, so to speak, but it was a pity that he was not able to witness in person the union he had brought about: two magnificent young men, naked, locked together in passion, each driving a gargantuan prick down the other's throat while moaning his appreciation for the monster cock he was being fed and for the virtuoso expertise of the man eating his own.

Jason had not had sex since the morning he discovered Max's body, and had only once yielded to an irresistible urge to have an orgasm, which he had accomplished in the shower the previous morning, and then only once — even though he was accustomed to blowing at least three or four loads a day. As a result, he was in dire need of relief. Still, it was Tony who first cried out that he was going to come.

Jason cupped Tony's frantically driving buttocks as the boy's cum began to flood his mouth. He sucked and swallowed the prodigious mouthful as it shot from Tony's cock, while the sailor gasped his excitement and appreciation long after Jason had drained out the last delicious spurt.

When he buried his cheek in Tony's pubic hair and expressed his thanks for what Tony had given him, Jason commented, "I can't believe I haven't come yet — I *really* need to get off. I may drown you when I do."

"God, what a way to go!" Tony commented, then added, "Kneel over my head and fuck my mouth until you're ready to come. Then pull out and blow your load in it so I can watch you shoot."

Tony lay on his back and Jason knelt over him, with his knees in the young stud's armpits, his balls dangling directly over Tony's chin, his cock stretching out for its full length over Tony's face. Tony whispered an awestruck "My God!" as he looked up in hunger and admiration. He reached up and cupped Jason's ass-cheeks as he smiled and said an obscene 'grace': "For what I am about to receive, may the good Lord make me truly thankful!"

Jason's body fell forward, and he planted his hands on the floor a foot above Tony's head, propping himself up. Tony opened his mouth wide, then closed his lips tightly over the magnificent shaft that began to drive in and out of them. At the same time, Tony forced his head up in sync with Jason's mouth-fuck, his lips countering each profound thrust of the shaft down into his mouth.

In less that five minutes, Jason cried out, loudly, "I'm going to come!" He rose up to his knees over Tony's head, pulling his cock rudely from the welcome heat and suction. He seized his prick and aimed the head at Tony's mouth just before it began to erupt. "Take it, Tony!" he cried, and the boy opened his lips as far as he could just as the first in an impossible number of huge gobs of thick white cum began to spurt forcefully. Jason tried to direct all his cum into Tony's mouth, and most of it went in, but inevitably some flew past Tony's head, or was deposited on the sailor's face and chest. When Jason was apparently finished, Tony took the fat shaft in his hand and brought it back into his mouth so he could suck out the last precious drops of the biggest orgasm he had ever seen—and the biggest Jason had ever produced.

They lay together on the carpet, embracing, their chests sliding together in Jason's cum while Jason licked more of it from Tony's face and neck, pausing now and then for Tony to suck it off his tongue. They kissed and caressed each other for a long time, smiling and exchanging thanks and compliments.

Jason's hands were fondling Tony's ass, and by the time he had put a finger inside it his cock had returned to full erection. Tony whispered, "I want your beautiful prick in my ass. Fuck me."

"I want to...I'm going to," Jason said. "I want to fill you with cum almost as much as I want an assful of yours inside me, but I think we should wait until we do the ceremony Max wanted—in his bed, with the movies playing."

"I can't wait," Tony said. "I'm anxious to see those Monte Hansen movies, too. I'll bet they get us ready for an extra-good fuck."

Jason laughed, " Shit, the second I see you naked in that bed, I'm gonna get as hard as I ever was. I really wish I could have fucked with Monte Hansen back when those movies were made, though."

"You were probably about ten or twelve years old then," Tony said.

"If I was ten, I might not have been able to fuck him yet, but I sure as hell would have made sure he fucked me," Jason said. "And if I was twelve, he'da had my dick as far up his ass as I coulda shoved it."

"And he would have loved it," Tony said, kissing Jason, and closing his legs over the huge hard-on pressing against his belly. "I can't wait to feel how far you're gonna shove it up my ass."

"You'll be happy to hear I can shove it a lot farther than I would have been able to when I was twelve. And you won't have to wait long, I promise you. Shit, I can't wait very long. Tomorrow. How's that?"

They decided to perform the ritual in Max's bedroom the next evening at 8:00. Jason still needed to blow another load right then, so Tony sucked him until he was near orgasm, then rolled onto his belly so that Jason could blow a load over his asshole. Jason tongue-fucked Tony through the pool of his own hot cum before he sucked it all out and swallowed it—which made Tony so horny that Jason gave him another blowjob before he left for the Naval Station, where he had to stand watch that night.

The next night Tony and Jason lay together in Max's bed, with the urn containing Max's ashes on the dresser next to them. They held each other and snuggled as the eight-millimeter movie projector ground away, showing Monte Hansen films on the plain wall opposite the foot of the bed—which Max had keep painted white, with nothing hanging on it, so it could serve as a movie screen.

Jason knew the films well, and always enjoyed them. He showed them to Tony in order of increasing sexiness. There was one only one that could be called actual pornography—where Monte got blown by a nondescript guy in a nondescript bedroom before he turned the tables and blew the guy who had just sucked him off. Then Monte fucked his partner in every way imaginable before shooting cum all over his face. But that was not the last one Jason showed; rather, it was next-to-last. The final film was a one-reeler in which Monte was unaccompanied, wearing a striped posing strap that was larger than he wore in the other films. The young Adonis romped around, grinning and posing for the camera, his teeth so white against his dark skin that they seemed to glow. The pouch of the posing strap grew alarmingly when he humped his ass and made it jump up and down, and in spite of its relatively large size, it was soon hiding a dick large enough and hard enough that it seemed to be bulging to the point of bursting. Except for the almost invisible string holding the pouch in place, Monte's ass was bare—looking perfect, and so enticing that even though there was apparently no photographic evidence to substantiate the contention, Jason felt sure that somehow Monte must surely have given it up to some unthinkably fortunate men's cocks. "Every guy who saw an ass that beautiful must have pleaded with Monte to let him fuck it," Jason told Tony. "There had to be a few who were persuasive enough, or had enough money they could offer—or could maybe even offer Monte something as sexy as his own ass to fuck in return — that Monte let them have it."

Tony agreed with Jason that the solo posing film was even sexier, more erotic, than the one where Monte fucked butt and sucked cock.

The two had agreed to keep their hands and mouths off each other until they had fulfilled Max's wish that they watch the films together. But as soon as the film ran out on the last movie, they began embracing feverishly, groping, kissing, sucking and rimming each other in turn or in sixty-nine. The projector kept grinding away, the tail end of the last film flopping as the reel continued to turn; it provided the only light in the room, but it gave ample illumination for them to enjoy the sight of each other while they made love.

They followed the example that Monte Hansen had set for them in his pornographic film, each fucked the other in every way imaginable, each gasped and shouted with the joy of taking so much fat dick up the ass. Tony was the first to come — erupting while he and Jason were embracing and kissing, with Jason lying on his back, his legs wrapped around Tony's waist while he got fucked missionary style.

Jason looked up in wonder at Tony's face while the cum filled his ass, and then when Tony finished and grinned down at him, Jason remarked, "Jesus, you really *do* look like Monte Hansen."

Tony said, "You look like the hottest piece of ass I've ever fucked!" Then he kissed him and smiled, "No wonder — you *are* the hottest piece of ass I've ever fucked." A courteous distortion, no doubt; Tony had fucked too many extremely hot asses to make such a judgment with any certainty.

Tony knelt on fours while Jason fucked him from behind, to blow his own load shortly thereafter. But instead of withdrawing once he had finished his orgasm, Jason pushed Tony's body down so that he lay on his belly while he, himself, continued to fuck—and fucked for another solid fifteen minutes before he blew a second load, with Tony by then on all fours again, virtually *howling* his joy. Jason pulled out of Tony's dripping ass and shared the kisses his splendid double-header fuck had earned him.

They both agreed that Max, wherever he was, had to be pleased with what he had brought about!

They had a bite to eat, and snuggled on the sofa in the living room for a while—still both naked. At Tony's request, Jason told him about his earlier life, and the story of how he went from being a horny kid in Amarillo, Texas, to being a cum-filled, happy man sitting on a couch in Hus Bay, South Carolina, with a gorgeous, cum-filled young sailor's head resting in his lap, kissing his prick.

Jason wanted to know Tony's story, of course, and the boy stopped kissing his cock and looked up into his eyes as he began to relate it.

5.

BLOW HIGH, BLOW LOWE

Tony Lowe was born and raised in Mar Vista, a rather new city on the east coast of Florida, below Jacksonville, near the oldest city in the country, Saint Augustine. He was not an unusually pretty child, but by the time he reached puberty, he was a complete knockout. He had a dark, coppery complexion—the heritage of his Greek mother and his half-Irish, half-Cherokee father. His black hair was straight and glossy, and Tony wore it slicked back from his forehead. He had unusually high, prominent cheekbones, brilliantly white teeth that dazzled the viewer when his infectious grin lit up his face, a trim, lightly muscled body with a broad chest and narrow waist, and long, *long* legs. The length of Tony's legs was not particularly apparent until he appeared in one of the minuscule bathing suits he favored; then they caused almost as many heads to turn as did the tantalizing bulges that filled the crotch and the back of his swim suit, just above them. By the time he reached his full maturity, about the time he enrolled at Atlantic High School, he had ten full inches of circumcised cock—as smooth and fat and beautiful as it was long.

He was not a novice at putting that stunning cock to work when he started at Atlantic High, however. He sucked dick seriously for the first time while he was in the first semester of eighth grade. He and his best friend and next-door neighbor, Jimmy, had played with each other sexually for well over two years by that time, and they had been casually sucking each other's cocks for a long time, until the night that Jimmy had his first orgasm, with his prick buried deep inside Tony's throat.

One of their classmates had proudly demonstrated his ability to produce cum to a group of boys in the school bathroom a month or two earlier, so Tony and Jimmy knew by that time what they were going for when they sucked each other's cocks. Jimmy's scream as his load erupted made it clear to Tony that his friend had reached the ecstasy their classmate had registered that day he blew a load to show them his cum, so Tony knew the hot liquid that filled his mouth was cum, not piss.

That earlier day in the bathroom, their classmate had blown his load in the palm of his hand, and offered it to anyone who wanted to eat it — as he assured them a high-school-boy friend of his regularly did. Neither Tony nor Jimmy took him up on the offer, but another classmate of theirs did, declaring he had eaten his own cum, as well as that of several other older boys. The cum-eating boy lapped up all that was offered, and declared it delicious, adding that he would be willing to suck the next load the boy could produce directly out of his prick, the way he had gotten it from the older boys — which he later did, but without an audience. Consequently, Tony never thought for a split second about whether he wanted to spit out his friend's load or not; he swished it around in his mouth and savored the taste before swallowing it, and smiling as he licked his lips. It was then that Tony's *serious* cock- sucking began.

Soon after that, Jimmy, who had learned by then to take almost all of his best friend's thrilling prick in his mouth, was licking Tony's balls one afternoon while Tony was jacking off. Suddenly Tony shouted, and blew his first load all over his stomach and belly. Jimmy lapped it up, and from that day he began sucking Tony off daily — often even more than once a day, and often sucking two loads out of his monster prick in quick succession.

The night Tony and Jimmy graduated from the eighth grade, they went down to the beach to celebrate, allegedly planning to suck each other off in the moonlight. Instead, they wound up doing what both had been aspiring to do for some time by then, something Tony had actually planned to bring about that night, instead of their usual mutual blowjobs: each fucked the other. Jimmy had great trouble taking all of Tony's monster cock up his young, untested ass, but he managed. Although he was also a virgin in anal sex, Tony had no trouble whatever in accepting Jimmy's prick; he took to bottoming as naturally and as enthusiastically as both he and Jimmy did to topping.

Jimmy moved away that summer when his father was transferred to Arizona, but Tony had no trouble in developing regular sexual liaisons with a number of new blowbuddies and fuckbuddies in his freshman year at Atlantic High — including a Senior football player who spotted the boy's gargantuan equipment in the shower room after a gym class he helped the coach teach. Tony's huge prick was so sumptuous and looked so appetizing, that the Senior kept him back in the shower after class that day, and sucked him off. When it became obvious that Tony adored returning the blow job, and stayed so hard after having been sucked off that he was ready for more, the Senior turned around and knelt on all fours in front of the huge-hung Freshman, where he took more dick up his ass than he had ever imagined he could.

In spite of his fine build, Tony was not naturally athletic, but his new, football-playing conquest suggested he come out for the team as a trainer. "We can see each other all the time, so we can arrange to get together a lot. Besides, you'll be around a lotta other guys — some really hot ones — who will be glad to give you what you want, and fall all over themselves to get what you've got hangin' between your legs." So, Tony became a trainer.

Tony sucked and fucked with the Senior for the rest of that academic year, but he never took a shower with the team members. Of course he wasn't on the team, he was only a trainer. *A trainer, shit — he was just a water boy who also passed out towels and laced up pads, and did crap work for the football players in the locker room.* He enjoyed the job, though, even if he didn't get to do the things he most wanted to do for a few of those players — beautiful young studs like Cary Dowd or Bill Rubich or the other gorgeous 'Bill,' Bill Counts. But Mark Epps was way past just beautiful. Mark looked like *God*, and his body looked like a young Steve Reeves; his dick hung halfway down to his knees — just like Tony's own, except Tony's dick hung even closer to his knees!

Tony knew he would get a hard-on if he got in that steamy atmosphere with guys like Mark or Cary or the two Bills walking around naked. That was why he never showered with the team, even though his cute little fellow-trainer, Randy Harris, always did. One of the Bills didn't have a lot of dick, but Cary and the other Bill both had impressive, *tempting* ones, whether they were soft or hard. Actually, he had seen all three of them hard at one time or the other — just like at some point he had seen almost all of the players with hard-ons. Bill Rubich's prick was big, and it was probably the fattest one Tony had ever seen.

Cary's prick was almost as impressive as Mark's, and he loved showing it off. One afternoon, after football practice, he walked out of the showers, with his towel slung over one shoulder and his big cock jutting out below his flat, washboard stomach, pointing slightly upwards, bobbing and swaying as he walked.

Tony was folding towels at a table halfway between the showers and Cary's locker, and happened to look up as the naked stud approached, hard-on flapping in the breeze. He couldn't tear his eyes away, and Cary could see that Tony was drinking in the sight — practically drooling, he thought. Cary stopped, and stood there as he put the towel over his head and began to rub his wet hair with it, which caused his hard-on to bob and sway wildly. He peeked out from under the folds of the towel a few seconds later, and observed that Tony was staring hungrily at his throbbing hard-on—exactly what Cary had hoped to find him doing. He had no reason to assume that Tony was cock-hungry—no one had ever said anything about it—but Tony was cute, and Tony was hung, and Cary was—as always—horny. His prick got so hard when he watched Tony watching it, that he decided the trainer was probably dying to suck on it, and he did his little 'trick' of using his muscles to make his hard-on jump up and down, without his touching it. No big trick, of course, a lot of guys could do that, but it seemed clear that Tony was really enjoying the show.

After a minute or so, Tony's eyes traveled up Cary's body until he discovered Cary was looking directly back into them, obviously having noted Tony's fascination with his prick. Tony was startled, and it clearly showed on his face. He blushed, knowing he'd been caught, and guessing (rightly) that Cary could tell what he wanted.

Tony was unable to shift his eyes from Cary's cool examination. He was terrified that the stud might take a swing at him, start to laugh, or maybe even yell something like "Tony Lowe wants to suck my cock!" Even though that statement would have been true, Tony didn't want everyone to know it. He wasn't even sure he wanted *Cary* to know, but his apprehension was tempered by the thought that if Cary knew how he felt, he might be willing to see how good a cocksucker the trainer was. That would be fine, because Tony knew he was a great cocksucker. Every guy he'd sucked off had told him so—but so far there hadn't been too many, certainly not enough of them! He wanted to add Cary's name to the slowly growing list of his conquests almost as ardently as he wanted to add Mark's!

After a long time staring nervously into Cary's eyes — probably only fifteen or twenty seconds, but it seemed like an eternity — Tony could see at the edge of his peripheral vision, that Cary had taken his bobbing monster in hand, and was beginning to stroke it slowly, while his solemn, *assessing* gaze turned gradually into a crooked smile, which he held for a long time before he looked down at the gargantuan bulge in Tony's sweatpants. He looked back into Tony's eyes, and his smile turned into a grin before he winked broadly at him and turned away. And the moment passed.

Tony watched the seductive up-and-down roll of Cary's tempting buttocks as he walked away, his heart actually pounding, and the racing of his blood roaring in his ears. Tony knew that Cary should have simply passed by him and headed to the end of the locker room, where his locker was. Instead, he had turned and walked all the way to the side wall before he turned again and went to his locker, giving Tony a chance to watch his departure for a longer time, made even longer by the slow pace of Cary's seductive walk. There didn't seem to be much question, given the sexy grin and wink that preceded Cary's exit, the circuitous route he took to his locker, and the exaggeratedly sexy walk, that he was well aware of how fine his ass looked when he walked, and how he wanted to provide Tony a good long time to study it and appreciate its beauty.

Tony quickly went into a toilet stall, closed the door, and continued to enjoy in his mind the vivid memory of what had just happened as he masturbated furiously, finally blowing a load, which he aimed at the toilet bowl, but most of which banked off the tile wall behind it. Aspirations to share Cary's huge prick with his own behemoth were born during those moments before his orgasm, although they seemed futile once he had shot his wad and calmed down while he waited for his hard-on to recede.

Futile or not, that grin and wink Cary had given him were sufficient to fuel Tony's ambitions, although he thought they might have meant only understanding and an acknowledgment of his admiration for Cary's quite admirable prick. It would not be long before Cary showed him that the wink and grin had been meant as a promise of great sex to come—to come in just a few days, as it happened, and if their encounter had not taken place on a Friday, that great sex might have come about the next day, but Tony did not regularly see Cary on weekends.

The presence of Randy's ass in the shower was another reason Tony avoided going in there; his dick began to swell every time he was privileged to see it. His fellow trainer was way past cute, the way Mark was way past beautiful. If Mark looked like God, Randy looked like Jesus. He had bland, even features, and when he smiled, he showed adorable dimples and blazingly white, even teeth—and he smiled a *lot*. He wore his hair medium length, and it was a glowing, golden-blond color. He looked like a movie star. He was only about 5'6", with a lean, trim body, and a decent-sized dick, which was hardly any longer when it got hard than when it was soft—but it got a lot fatter. Those qualities qualified Randy as someone for Tony to fantasize about while he jacked off, but there was also Randy's greatest asset: his splendid, sumptuous, glorious, *edible* ass! It was small, but its perfectly rounded, golden hemispheres of taut, young flesh protruded alluringly and defined a deep, narrow chasm hiding the secret place Tony longed to reach with his tongue or his cock.

Tony didn't eat ass very often, only with unusually sexy or cute guys—or ones he especially wanted to please, since he knew only too well, from extensive personal experience, how wonderful it felt. He had learned that the surest way to get his own ass eaten was to eat out the guy he hoped would do it. Of all the guys he knew, he wanted to eat Randy's pretty ass more than any one he'd ever

113

eaten or even thought about eating — and he wanted to do it because he desperately wanted to, not just it would be a pleasurable means to a possible end. He knew he could spend hours with his face pressed between Randy's adorable ass-cheeks, rimming him, kissing, licking, sucking, tongue-fucking, *feasting* on him!

Tony had playfully patted or slapped Randy's perfect little ass on any number of occasions — athletes always did that, and Tony was keen to emulate them; Randy's firm flesh was cool to the touch, and smooth as velvet. If Tony always let his pats on Randy's ass linger a little longer than might have been usual, the cute blond didn't seem to mind, or, perhaps, even notice. It was usually a vision of Randy's ass, and the phantom feeling of those adorable asscheeks clutching the driving shaft of his hard prick that dominated Tony's fantasies those times he blew his load while jacking off and pretending he was making love with the golden boy. But as far as he knew, tragically, Randy was straight. Still, even if he didn't want to suck cock or get fucked, he might be willing to get blown, or sink his pretty cock in a hot boy's ass; there was always hope, even if the possibility was likely to prove only one-sided.

From the talk he'd heard around the locker room, Tony knew that practically every football player loved to get his dick sucked — after all, what's not to love? From the reports he heard tossed back and forth, all the female cheerleaders sucked football-player dick, *at the least* — Tony knew from experience that the one male cheerleader not only sucked dick, but did so with unusual skill — and several other girls were mentioned prominently for their appetite and their ability. Quite ungentlemanly behavior on the part of the players, Tony thought. If those girls knew how they were being talked about, they would probably stop giving blowjobs to the football players, and turn their talents to others, if they weren't already doing so. Of course it was possible they only wanted to suck off or put out for football players because they were the big school heroes. Let the team have a few really bad seasons, and their dicks might get a little less attention!

Occasionally Tony had heard a player sneer that some guy or other had given him a blowjob, and everybody hooted, and acted like *he* would never be so horny that he would let a fuckin' *queer* have his cock!

Probably total bullshit. Several guys Tony fucked with claimed they also regularly blew some of the football players and got fucked by them, frequently even citing the names of the ones they serviced. Tony believed them—and he believed them when they told him most of the players liked to sixty-nine with them for a while before they started the fucking, frequently sucking them off while they did. Reportedly some would just get down and suck them off without needing to be inspired by a sixty-nine. He also believed their stories about the several football players who took it up the ass.

Tony once overheard an especially loutish fullback—who, in spite of his boorishness, was built like brick shithouse and had a stupendous cock—telling some teammates while they were changing, that he had let Danny Williams suck his dick when he was too horny to deny him the pleasure. "He didn't even do a good job," the lout laughed, "and he spit my load out when I blew it in his mouth. The least he coulda done woulda been to swallow it like a man, right?"

One of the other players said, "Hey, asshole, men don't swallow cum, remember?" All the players laughed and went about their business, saying no more about Danny.

Tony had to laugh, too, but not aloud. He was probably more aware than anyone how ludicrous the fullback's claims about Danny's poor performance were. Danny had sucked him off quite a few times, and Danny was an amazingly good cocksucker. Tony's cock was ten inches long—the longest one he himself had ever seen, up

115

to that point—certainly a lot bigger than even the huge-hung, scornful lout's. The very first time Tony gave it to Danny, Danny had managed to take all ten inches down to the root, burying his lips deep in pubic hair and actually managing to let his tongue lap the base of Tony's cock and the top of Tony's balls while he sucked. Later, just as Tony started to come, following a long, completely thrilling period of worship to his prick, Danny pulled his lips up to the middle of Tony's fat shaft, and while the six or eight spurts of a huge, explosively propelled orgasm filled Danny's mouth, he didn't gag when the cum splashed against the back of his throat, and continued to suck, moaning his pleasure.

Danny had pulled his head back and looked up at Tony, opening his mouth so that Tony could see his tongue immersed in a generous pool of thick white cum. Then he almost ceremoniously swallowed the delicious mouthful and smiled gratefully. Tony put his hands on the back of Danny's head and looked steadily down into his eyes for a long moment before he asked, "Want some more?"

Danny's smile turned into a grin as he nodded and whispered a simple, fervent "Yes." He opened his lips as Tony pressed his dick back inside and began to pull Danny's head in toward his belly, filling his mouth with a cock that seemed fully as hard as it had been the first time he admitted it.

"Take it," Tony whispered as he began to fuck the hungry boy's mouth again, until, after a deliriously long time, he again slaked the talented cocksucker's thirst.

Danny liked both sucking off the football players and taking them up the butt. There was only one thing, however, that Danny liked better than giving up his butt or his mouth to service the football players, and that was doing the same for Tony. Football players were exciting for Danny because they were *football players*, the school's macho-stud heroes, but Tony's dick was the biggest. And

116

for Danny, that meant it was the best. Also, damned few of the guys he sucked off, or who fucked him, were able to give him two loads in the brief span of time Tony managed it. If their lovemaking lasted as long as an hour, Tony would probably give him *three* loads—but the first two were all but consecutive.

Tony liked Danny pretty well, even though the boy was embarrassingly effeminate at times; he was a nice guy, he was always willing to help anybody out, and he was cute, too—with a sweet, if well-used ass. But claiming that Danny Williams was an inept cocksucker was almost heretical!

Some of Tony's less well-endowed fuckbuddies who screwed Danny (actually, *all* of Tony's fuckbuddies and regular friends were less well-endowed than he) complained Danny's ass wasn't very tight, even though his talent at using it more than compensated for that shortcoming. When Tony told one of them that he thought Danny's cute little butt was plenty tight enough, his friend laughed, and said, "Shit, Tony, anybody's ass would feel tight to that monster of yours!"

Following football practice on the Monday after Cary had put on his show for him, Tony was kneeling on the floor in the equipment room, tying some dirty laundry into a bundle, when Cary came in after his shower, this time with his towel wrapped around his waist. "Hey, Tony, I wonder if you'd be willing to help me with something."

"Well yeah, I guess. Sure, Cary." Tony sat down on the floor, and hugged his knees together, looking up at Cary. "Name it."

"Great. But first I wanna ask you about what happened when I saw you out there Friday afternoon." He nodded his head back toward the locker room. "You remember what we were talking about?"

"Cary, neither of us said a single word that I can remember."

He snickered, "Hell, we said a lot, we just didn't need words to say it. You know what I mean?"

Tony knew very well what Cary meant, but he said, "I... I don't know, Cary. What did you say? Maybe I'll figure it out if you put it in words this time."

Smiling that same crooked smile, Cary looked into Tony's eyes for a long moment before he began to untie the knot holding the towel around his waist. He untied it so slowly, it looked like a slow-motion picture to Tony, who nervously shifted his gaze between Cary's fingers untying the knot, and his unswerving stare. Not a sound was uttered, but Tony thought the beating of his heart must surely be audible to Cary.

The knot finally gave away, and Cary pulled the towel from his body, exposing his cock, which was only partially erect, but grew slowly as Tony gazed at it. Tony wet his lips nervously, and quickly looked up at Cary again, whose mouth was now fixed in the same broad grin he had flashed on Friday. Tony looked down again at Cary's swelling cock, and this time watched as Cary's fingers encircled his growing shaft and began to stroke it idly until it was again jutting out from his body in full erection.

Cary extended the towel toward Tony. "Here, Tony, you wanna put this in the laundry too?" Tony did not reply or take the towel from the naked boy, merely continued to stare hungrily at his fat hard-on. "Tony... stand up," Cary said, in a level voice. When Tony shifted his gaze to Cary's face, he found the boy was still grinning, and he favored Tony with the same sexy wink he had given him Friday.

Tony got slowly to his feet. His prick was tenting his sweatpants, but he made no movement to hide it. Cary knelt in front of him, seized the waistband of his shorts and sweatpants, and slowly began to pull them down. As the pants cleared the end of Tony's cock, it jumped out forcefully, like it was spring-loaded, and quivered in front of Cary's face.

Cary whistled appreciatively, staring in awe at the monster he had freed. "My God, Tony, I could tell you had a big one, but this is fuckin' incredible!" He grinned back up at Tony as he draped his towel over Tony's shaft, which easily supported it, even though it was wet and quite heavy. He reached up underneath the towel with one hand to run his palm over the underside of Tony's cock. "Don't want you to forget to put this in the laundry," he said sexily, then he took Tony's balls in his hand and gently squeezed them as he added, "I meant put the towel in the laundry, of course."

He stood, and pressed his body up against Tony's as he pulled the towel away. Tony's prick sprang up while Cary pushed his own cock down below Tony's balls, and his fingers encircled the throbbing shaft pressing up against his stomach ("*All the way to my tits*," Cary thought, in wonderment). "Maybe you can think of some place you want to put this," he said, squeezing Tony's prick. "I've got some good ideas." He leaned forward and whispered into Tony's ear, almost kissing it, "But I'll bet you've got some *great* ideas." He tickled the inside of Tony's ear with his tongue before kissing it slowly, and sweetly. "Now do you remember what we talked about on Friday?"

Spreading his legs slightly, Tony allowed Cary's prick to slip up, between his legs, where it nestled right under his balls. He reached around Cary's body and fondled his ass cheeks, which were already undulating as he instinctively began to fuck Tony's legs. "Now I remember what we said. I can think of a lotta ways to help you — and I really do want to. But where can we go? There are still some of the guys out there."

"I've got a place we can go," Cary said, "and even if you don't need it, I'd like to help you the same way, too." Cary put his hands around Tony to caress his butt cheeks, just as Tony continued to do the same to his.

Their lips were about an inch apart as Tony whispered, "I need it, believe me." He closed the gap between their mouths as he added, "I need it bad," and their lips touched, opening together to allow their tongues to explore.

Jesus, Tony thought, while he and Cary kissed feverishly and played with each other's asses, *Cary Dowd is going to suck my dick, and he's going to give me his! And even if he doesn't know it yet, he's gonna fuck me, too.* He now had a finger plunging in and out of Cary's ass, just as Cary's was fucking his. *He likes a finger up his ass – I hope he's ready for ten inches of dick!*

Cary wrapped himself in his towel again, and said, as he knotted it around his waist and Tony pulled his pants and shorts back up, "As soon as my dick goes down a little, I'm gonna get dressed, and I'll meet you out in the parking lot. You know where I park, don't you?"

"I know." Tony assured him, adding, "But why worry about hiding your hard-on? Hell, you walk around with it flapping in the breeze every day."

"Just when I'm trolling for cock," he chuckled, "like I was doing when I came up to you Friday afternoon. No... when I came *on* to you Friday afternoon. Jesus, why didn't you follow me? It doesn't usually take me two days to land a guy when I show 'em the bait."

"I...I wanted to follow you, but I wasn't sure you wanted me to...."

"Christ, Tony, I wanted you to, believe me. But now that I've seen your dick, I want you to even a lot more. Anyway, I'm gonna hide my dick and ass this afternoon, 'cause I don't want to get anyone else interested in following me – not today, anyway."

Tony laughed, "But you might get somebody interested for later, if you dangle the bait today. Hell, Cary, stores advertise in the Sunday papers, even if they're not open on Sundays, you know." He went over to the door and pulled it shut. He walked back to Cary and pulled the towel away

120

from his waist. Cary's prick was only semi-hard by then, but when Tony knelt and drove his lips down it, all the way to Cary's pubic nest, it returned to full erection in just a few seconds. Tony pulled his mouth away and grinned up at Cary, "That's better. Now go out there and show 'em what you're gonna give me today, 'cause they might wanna try for it tomorrow." He stood and kissed Cary again, then slapped him playfully on the bare ass and shoved him toward the door.

Cary opened the door, and turned around to wink at Tony. He said, simply, "At my car — ten minutes." Then, carrying his towel, with his prick bobbing from side to side, he walked out toward the locker room while Tony again watched the sexy roll of his ass.

Tony quickly tied up the bundle of laundry and dropped it next to the door. He reached Cary's car a few minutes before Cary showed up, and he got into it to wait; the car was a convertible, so it was not locked. Cary suddenly appeared, grinning broadly as he slipped into the driver's seat and started the engine.

As they pulled out onto the street, Cary put his hand on the inside of Tony's left thigh, and patted and affectionately squeezed the big tube of flesh snaking down from his crotch. "We can go to my house. Nobody'll be home for a couple of hours." Soon Tony's dick began to swell and grow stiff under Cary's hand. Cary whistled appreciatively, "Jesus, Tony, you've got some cock!"

Cary seemed as anxious to suck Tony's cock as Tony was to blow him. Neither had any great trouble in taking the other's dick down to the root when they fell on the bed in sixty-nine, nor did either show any qualms about swallowing the loads they sucked out only a few minutes apart. Cary was an accomplished and an appreciative cocksucker, and often complimented Tony's expertise in the same enjoyable field of endeavor, gasping his compliments around the enormous shaft filling his mouth.

If Cary seemed a little surprised, he didn't show it when, after a long period of snuggling and kissing, Tony got on all fours and looked back over his shoulder to say, "Fuck me!"

Cary reached for the tube of K-Y next to the lamp; he was not at all hesitant about complying with his partner's wishes. He fucked Tony for a long, ecstatic time, but finally stopped, saying, I've gotta rest for a few minutes before I finish. That was a big load I fed you."

Without asking permission, Tony rolled Cary to his back and raised his legs, placing them on his shoulders as he reached for the lubricant and prepared to enter his ass. He said, "I've gotta have some, too—and it won't take me too long." Cary offered no opposition. Rather, he cried, "Yeah!" as he bent his legs to lever his ass higher, closer to Tony's cock.

Tony greased them both up, and slowly, but relentlessly drove his entire ten inches inside Cary, who only muttered "Aaaaahhh!" the entire time it was going in. Once Tony's balls met Cary's, it was Cary's turn to say, "Fuck me." And Tony fucked him lustfully for about ten minutes before his cum exploded palpably, deep inside Cary, who screamed in joy as he felt it erupt.

After a short respite, Cary resumed his fuck, and this time managed to deliver the goods to Tony.

They snuggled and talked for a while, discussing what they had just shared, and how much they had enjoyed it. At one point, Cary said, "I wasn't sure you'd be interested in sex with me, but seeing what you were packing inside your jeans, I wanted it so much I finally got up the nerve to make a move. Sure glad I did."

"Me, too. I've been wanting you ever since I started with the team."

"Why don't you ever shower with the team?" Cary asked. "Believe me, there are quite a few guys who'd wanna go to bed with you if they knew what kinda dick you have."

"Aside from you and three other...no, four other guys, I don't think I'd be interested, and you and those four guys are so fuckin' hot, I know I'd just get a hard-on looking at you naked."

"So what, nobody pays any attention to a boner in the shower. Unless...well, unless it looks like yours."

"Well, I don't want to attract any of those other guys, really," Tony said, "and I don't think I even really want those four other guys to know they give me a hard-on, 'cause I don't think I'd give *them* a hard-on. So, what's the point?"

"I'm really one of the guys you were interested in?" Cary asked. Tony assured him that he was, and told him how excited he'd become when Cary began to put the make on him.

"I didn't have any idea you were gay," Tony said.

"Well, I don't know if I'm gay or not, I just..." Cary said, then laughed, "Aw shit, why bother to deny it to you? I guess you could tell when you rammed that big dick up my ass that I am."

"But you're going steady with Brenda."

Cary snickered, "My god, Brenda is no more interested in cock than I'm interested in pussy. We usually double date with...well, never mind, but when we go out and park, it's the girls in the front seat, and the guys in the back who are fogging up the windows.

"So, who are the four other guys on the team that turn you on?" Cary continued. "Maybe I can help set you up with 'em if they're interested in cock. At least I can probably tell you if any of them are."

"Okay, I'll tell you, but not a word of this to any of them. Right?" Cary nodded.

"The one I want most is Mark Epps. Jesus, he's beautiful, and he's built better'n anyone I know, and his dick is almost as big as mine. Then there's Bill Rubich and Bill Counts—both cute as shit, and Bill Rubich has a really nice dick and a *very* fuckable ass. Then the last one isn't really on the team, he's..."

"Randy Harris?" Cary broke in. "Has to be—talk about a fuckable ass. I'd be happy if he just sat on my face! And he has a good dick, too."

"Well, that's it," Tony said. "Do I stand a chance with any of them? Have you ever gone to bed with one of them?"

"Well, I'm pretty sure both of the Bills are straight, even though Bill Rubich's cock is hard in the shower once in a while. I don't have any reason to think that Randy is gay—he never pops a boner in the shower—but he's too goddamned pretty to be completely straight. It'd be a crying goddamned shame if that pretty little ass of his never gets fucked!"

"What about Mark, though," Tony asked.

Cary grinned. "I was saving the best news for last. Mark. Jesus, what a gorgeous stud! I think he'd be really happy to have you eat his cock, and he'd probably be just as glad to ram that monster of his up your tight ass. He's fucked me dozens of times, and I have no idea how many times I've sucked him off. His cock is damned near as big as yours, and it took me a long time to learn to take it all. " He grinned, "But I guess you could tell I'd been practicing with someone like that when I blew you and when you fucked me."

Tony grinned back. "Yeah, I suspected something like that. Most guys have trouble with my dick at first. But tell me more about Mark. Will he give head, or take it up the ass?" Tony asked.

"Well, that's the downside," Cary replied. "He *might* suck your cock some, if you get him excited enough; I've even got him excited enough a few times that he even sucked me off all the way, and ate my load. But he's never let me fuck him. He likes it when I tongue-fuck him, and he even likes a couplea fingers up his ass once in a while, but I think that would be as much as he'd let you put in there. Sorry."

"Does he kiss?" Tony asked. "That probably means more than anything."

"You think so? Hmmm. Well, anyway, if Mark's horny enough, he loves to suck face; he always eats my mouth alive when I'm on my back and he's got that monster cock up my ass. So, whaddya think?" Cary asked. "Want me to fix you up with Mark?"

"No," Tony replied. "I'm pretty encouraged by what you told me, but I wanna check it out in my own way."

"Sure," Cary replied, and while he himself was fucked out, Tony was still hard and huge, so Cary sucked him off again before taking him back to school.

Wednesday, just two days after Tony and Cary had made love, Mark Epps approached Tony in the locker room after football practice. Almost everyone had already left. "Tony, do you mind staying for a little while to help me out? I've got some new aches that really need massaging."

Tony knew instinctively that Cary had spilled the beans to Mark, even though he had promised not to tell him or the two Bills. Yet, he was grateful, since he might learn how far Mark would be interested in going with him. He sounded unusually friendly, Tony thought; perhaps his idol was going to allow him to conduct a worship service! His voice trembled with excitement as he said, "Sure, Mark. Glad to help you out."

"I usually get Randy to stay and help me out, but I'd rather have you do it today."

"Why, Mark?" Tony asked.

"I've heard that you're really good," he said simply, not sounding as though he were implying he had heard from Cary how 'good' Tony was in some other way, but the look he gave Tony after he said it was unnaturally long, and seemed to suggest there was a hidden meaning in his words. Tony hoped that were true, but as he covered a table for Mark to lie on while he massaged him, he resolved that Mark had to take the first step, that he would play along with whatever Mark had in mind just as long as he was reasonably sure what it was.

After the last student left the locker room — the coaches had departed some time earlier — Mark put a 1x6" board between the handles of the pair of outward-swinging doors, effectively locking them securely. He looked at Tony, who watched him. "Might as well have some privacy," he said, and winked. Except for the wink, neither his voice nor his look suggested anything untoward.

Tony told Mark to lie down on the table he had prepared for his massage. Mark walked over to stand next to the table as he removed the towel he had knotted around his waist, and dropped it to the floor. Tony checked out his cock, and was sorry to note that it was not at all hard — but my god, it hung a down a long way!

Stretching out facedown on the table, Mark purred with satisfaction as Tony oiled his hands and began to knead his huge muscular shoulders and upper back. "Yeah — that feels really good," he murmured as Tony worked his back and waist, then moved down to massage his massive legs. He wriggled his ass and said, "Do my ass, too. It's really tight."

With his heart pounding and his cock tenting his sweat pants, Tony began to work the hard globes of Mark's generous ass. "It really is tight," he said, and then let his hands begin to work down into the crevice between the buttocks. "Yeah, really tight," he said, in such a way that the double meaning could not be mistaken. He poured oil over the base of Mark's spine, and as it trickled down into the crevice, he rubbed it in, even following it down to the asshole. Mark responded by spreading his legs farther apart, and wordlessly murmuring his further satisfaction.

Meeting no objection as he rubbed his fingers over Mark's asshole, Tony was emboldened to insert the tip of a finger inside, and whisper breathlessly, "Really tight, Mark!"

"You should see what that's doing to me," Mark snickered. "Maybe you'd better start doing my chest now," he said, as be rolled over onto his back. His huge cock rested on his stomach, pointing toward his chin. He took it in his hand and raised it, then said, as he released it and it flopped back onto his stomach with an audible *whap!* "See what you did?"

Tony was still not sure how far Mark was willing to go, although he was reasonably sure he wanted to take this massage further. "It'd be pretty hard not see that," he said. "Jesus, Mark, what a cock!" As he replied to Mark's question, he busily began to massage Mark's broad chest and glorious tits, using all his self-control to ignore the thrilling monster cock that lay within easy reach.

Smiling as he reveled under Tony's busy hands, Mark said, "I hear your dick is even bigger."

Still massaging, but moving down to Mark's stomach and waist, where his hands inevitably pushed the fat, bobbing shaft aside as he worked, Tony said, "Yeah, I've got a big one. I don't know if it's bigger than this, though." That was true, although Tony suspected his cock was the bigger one.

"You wanna check it out, and see?" Mark asked, simply. He looked intensely into Tony's eyes for a long moment, before adding, "It would have to be really big." He turned his head to look at the enormous bulge in Tony's sweatpants, and smiled as he returned his gaze to Tony's eyes. "Looks to me like it really is!"

Tony's hand shook slightly as he encircled Mark's shaft with it while their eyes remained locked. Then he looked at the prodigious handful he was holding. It was enormous, and fiercely hard, throbbing under his touch. He added his other hand and squeezed the pulsing shaft gently—there was ample room for both of his hands. "I think I might have a slight edge over you, but this is still fucking amazing!" As he said that, one of his hands began to stroke up and down Mark's prick, and the other stroked the boy's inner leg.

"Maybe I should be massaging you," Mark said.

There was no question now where things were going, so Tony reached up to cup Mark's generous balls while his hand continued to slide up and down his big shaft. He said, "Maybe we should stop pretending this is a massage."

Mark smiled and reached up to pull Tony's head down, so that their lips almost met. "Maybe you're right. You made my dick too fuckin' hard to ignore." He kissed him lightly, running his tongue over Tony's parted lips, but not yet inserting it into his mouth. You wanna suck me off?"

"Yeah," Tony murmured, simply. He bent his head to begin his work, but with his lips poised at the tip of the beautiful, huge prick, he turned his head and asked, "You wanna suck me off, too?"

Mark only smiled at the question before he sat up on the side of the table and took Tony's head in his hands. Ignoring Tony's question, Mark pushed his head downward so that as Tony opened his mouth, his lips encircled the cock-head, and then sank all the way to the pubic hair.

For several minutes, Tony sucked profoundly as he drove his lips up and down the entire, considerable length of the fat shaft filling his mouth. Mark tousled Tony's hair and fucked upward, gasping in excitement.

Suddenly, Mark pulled Tony's head off his prick and continued to hold it as he slipped off the table and pressed his lips to Tony's. They both rose to stand, embracing as they kissed. Mark slipped a hand inside the waistband of Tony's pants and began to play with his ass. "Nice ass," he whispered into Tony's ear. "You ever take a dick in there?"

Tony began playing with Mark's ass, which writhed and undulated under his eager hands, as he answered. "Didn't Cary tell you I did?"

"Yeah he did," Mark laughed. "I figured you might guess why I needed for you to massage me today. And I guess you can tell I've got more cock to shove in here than even Cary's big one."

"I already knew that. The question is, will you?"

"Oh, yeah. I'm gonna fill your pretty little butt so fulla dick, you'll think you're in heaven."

Putting a fingertip against Mark's sphincter, and beginning to drive the first inch or two of the finger in and out of Mark's ass — still well lubricated from the so-called massage — Tony asked, "You ever go to heaven like that, Mark?"

Mark was silent for a few seconds — a meaningful pause, Tony thought, although he didn't know exactly what that meaning was. Then Mark said, "If what Cary tells me is true, I probably wouldn't be able to take it."

"Why don't you decide for yourself?" Tony asked, as he stepped back, out of Mark's embrace. He pulled the sweatshirt over his head, and threw it to the floor, then hooked his thumbs in the waistband of his sweatpants, and dropped them to his ankles, exposing the full glory of his astonishing erection.

Mark goggled. "Holy Mother of God — what a prick!" He dropped to his knees and reverently began to touch the monster shaft jutting out from Tony's body. He whistled in appreciation, "I thought Cary was exaggerating, but I can see he was telling the truth, the whole truth and every big, fat, fuckin' inch of the truth!"

One of Mark's hands began fondling Tony' balls, and the other caressed one of his ass-cheeks, so that when Tony's hand came to press against the nape of his neck, Mark merely opened his lips to accept the cock head resting on them. Tony exhaled his pleasure as Mark's lips sank farther down his shaft until the head pressed against

Mark's throat. Opening his throat further, and beginning to exert a strong suction as his lips traveled up and down Tony's shaft, Mark was soon taking all of the challenging cock inside his mouth as both hands frantically began to fondle Tony's ass, which was by then busily driving his cock in and out of Mark's hungry orifice.

Suddenly, Mark stood, and he gasped. "Eat my dick, too, Tony. I've gotta get off." He pulled the towels from the table, and spread them quickly on the floor. He lay on his back and held his hands up toward Tony. Tony began to kneel between his legs, but he said, "No. Sixty-nine. So I can suck you off at the same time." Tony reversed his body, and knelt over Mark. Soon each boy was hungrily sucking the other's gigantic dick.

Long before Tony approached orgasm, Mark thrust his hips upward, ramming his cock-head deep in Tony's throat, crying, "Take my load!" As his cum began to fill Tony's mouth, he gasped further, "Don't swallow it. Keep it in your mouth." A negligible amount escaped around Tony's lips, and flowed down Mark's cock, into his pubic hair, and, inevitably, he swallowed some of the massive flow, but he retained most of it according to Mark's injunction.

For some time after Mark's cock had ceased discharging its load, Tony continued to suck and lick it, still holding the cum in his mouth. Mark had gasped "Don't swallow it yet" several times while he groaned his satisfaction as Tony rolled his fat shaft and cock-head in his mouth, bathing it in hot cum. As Tony began to back off, letting Mark's prick slip from his tightly compressed lips, Mark again told him to refrain from swallowing.

Tony sat back on his haunches and looked down at the exciting stud he had just sucked off, he swished the mouthful of cum around in his mouth, savoring it, a look of utter bliss on his face. Suddenly, Mark turned over and rose to his knees, facing Tony; he seized Tony's head tightly with both hands, and drove his tongue deep into his mouth, wriggling it about in his own cum until he sucked it out of Tony's mouth, then let it trickle back in. They passed the load back and forth several times before Mark pulled away, leaving all the precious fluid in Tony's mouth.

Looking into Tony's eyes with intense passion, Mark gasped, "Drizzle it on my asshole, and fuck me!" He rolled quickly to his stomach, and spread his legs.

Tony was astonished. He had no idea Mark would even allow him to suck his prick, and he had counted himself impossibly lucky when it first became clear he might entertain that notion with any hope of success, but he had entered a state of ecstasy when Mark opened his mouth to provide the welcoming, moist suction for his own cock. Now, this unthinkable rapture: the prospect of putting his prick inside the beautiful ass writhing and humping hungrily in front of him.

Mark reached behind and used his hands to spread his ass-cheeks wide, exposing his winking pink hole, moaning, "Give me that huge dick!" As Tony drizzled the first drops of Mark's cum on the exposed sphincter, Mark gasped and began working his ass ring, opening and closing it as more and more of the viscous fluid flowed over and around it, and even into it.

Mark spread his legs wider, and Tony knelt between them, pressing the tip of his cock into the pool of cum guarding the precious target Tony had ached to reach in his wildest dreams. As he began to press forward into the cum-slicked entrance, Mark gasped, "I need it, Tony, shove every inch of it up my hole. I think I can take it. C'mon, Tony, *fill me up with dick* – your *dick!* I want it so fuckin' much! Give it to me, Tony, *I need it!*"

As the huge head of Tony's monster cock began to slip inside, Mark grunted and cried out in pain. "Shall I stop?" Tony asked.

"No. Oh Jesus, no! It feels great. But god *damn*, it's so fucking big!"

131

Tony continued to slip it to Mark slowly and gently, as his buttocks writhed; Mark had been holding them apart, pulling his asshole open to admit Tony, but as he released them, they snapped back together, gripping the fat shaft of Tony's prick in a vise, but one that was still sufficiently lubricated with Mark's own cum, that the cock continued to slide in imperceptibly. Mark's hands moved upward and gripped the cheeks of Tony's ass, quivering and undulating subtly to continue driving his cock ever deeper into the hot, unbelievably tight grip of his idol's chute. As he pulled down on Tony's ass-cheeks, urging his dick inside, Mark murmured, "Oh Jesus, Tony your ass! It feels almost as good as your prick. Come on and fuck me! Fill me up with that hot cum, Tony. But I want your ass after that, if you'll give it to me."

"It's yours, Mark, it's always been yours, like my dick — you just haven't known it."

"I wanna fuck your ass, Tony, I wanna eat it. Would you like that?"

"God, yes, Mark," Tony cried, as with a final lunge he buried his prick to the hilt; Mark screamed, but he immediately began humping back to welcome it, and grinding his ass around it. As Tony began a shallow, gentle fuck, Mark suddenly rose to kneel on all fours, shoving his ass fiercely back against Tony's cock, and riding it savagely as Tony picked up his tempo, and began fucking Mark's ass just as brutally, in perfect sync.

The load of cum Tony blasted inside Mark's ass was not long in arriving, and each boy shouted in ecstasy as it arrived. After a long period of post-coital kissing, they went into the shower room to clean up, but soon were lying on their sides on the heated, wet tiles as Mark positioned his body behind Tony, and after demonstrating his sincerity about wanting to eat Tony's ass out, he pulled his tongue out of it and rammed his huge prick inside with one long, violent thrust. Tony's cry was more of surprise and excitement than pain, although Mark's cock was one of the biggest—if not *the* biggest one he had ever taken. Eventually, Mark lay on his back while Tony rode his prick until it discharged, then fell forward and shoved his cock down Mark's throat and fucked it until he blew another load, which Mark swallowed eagerly.

In talking later about their first sexual encounter, Mark confirmed Tony's suspicion: Cary had told him all about fucking with Tony, and had also informed him of Tony's eagerness for sex with Mark. Mark also confirmed that "the two Bills" were straight, although he admitted he and Bill Rubich had sucked each other off once. "But Bill would never agree to do it with me again," he lamented, "even though I know one other guy who he fucked up the ass."

"What about Randy Harris? Tony asked.

"That's right. That's who it was. But how did you know?"

"I wasn't guessing who Bill fucked," Tony said, I was just asking you about Randy."

"Oh. Well, what can I say? Cutest little ass I've ever seen," Mark laughed.

"Yeah, that's for sure. So he let Bill fuck it, huh? Has he let you do anything to it besides look at it?" Tony wanted to know.

"Well... yeah, he has. But you can't tell anyone about it, okay?" Tony promised. "I know he's hot for my body and my dick," Mark continued, "but he said he'd only suck my dick if I sucked his, and he wouldn't let me in his ass unless I let him fuck mine, too." He grinned, "I agreed to do both, and it was *well* worth it, believe me! Anyway, Randy's a little guy, but he means what he says—and I want that ass of his bad enough, I'll do whatever he says. Jesus, Tony, it's so fuckin' tight, and he can work your cock with it like you can't imagine!"

"What's his dick like?" Tony asked. "I've never even seen him with a hard-on, even when he's around you or any of the other guys when your dicks are hard, so I just presumed he wouldn't be interested in sharing it with another guy. But Jesus, what a pretty ass!"

"He's got this thing he does," Mark said. "He doesn't want anybody to know he likes dick, unless it's a guy whose dick he wants, so when he's in the shower or the locker room, he thinks of things that turn him off, to keep from getting a hard-on." Mark laughed, "You wouldn't believe some of the crap he thinks of—stuff like his grandmother takin' a dump, or somebody throwing up on him, or running his finger along a piece of paper to get a paper cut, shit like that. It works, though. I've never seen him pop a boner unless he wanted to. And when he wants to, that boner is hard as a rock—and it's pretty big, but probably a couple inches shorter than yours or mine. And the little sonofabitch fucks like a demon. When he's through with you, you flat-out know you've been fucked!"

"Is he fucking with any other guys?" Tony asked.

"Jesus, I have no idea, except for that one time Bill Rubich fucked him," Mark said. "Knowing Randy, I'd be willing to bet Bill took it up the ass that time, too, but he probably wouldn't admit it. Hmm, I might have to check that out—maybe I can get Bill again, after all.

"Randy won't say a thing about other guys, but he took my dick all the way up his ass without batting an eyelash the first time, and he sucked it down to the root first time he blew me, so I figured he'd already been getting some big dick somewhere—bigger even than Bill Rubich's. Why? You want him too, Tony?"

"Christ, Mark, think about his ass. Do you really have to ask?" Mark laughed, and admitted the answer was obvious. Tony continued, "You suppose he'd give it to me if I let him fuck me or if I sucked him off?"

"I think he might, if he knew how you're hung," Mark said. "You want me to ask him for you? I could just sound him out, without mentioning your name."

Tony smiled, "Tell me how you'd describe me if you did."

Mark leered, "Cute guy, with a good build, loves to suck dick and get fucked, with maybe the biggest cock I've ever seen—bigger than mine, even—and he fucks with it like a goddamned professional."

"Shit, that oughta do it. Hell, with that description, I'd fuck me in a heartbeat!"

"But hasn't he seen you with a hard-on?" Mark asked.

"That's just it, I don't know. I almost never get in the shower with you guys, 'cause I get a boner every time I see you, or Randy, or Cary, or the two Bill's in there naked."

"I know at least five or six other guys on the team who'd love to get that dick of yours inside 'em," Mark said. "One of 'em even asked if I thought you'd want to play around with him. You wanna know who they are?" He leered, "Don'tcha even wanna know who got my cherry? You know him. He's the one who wanted to know if I thought you'd fuck with him." He laughed, "We got each other's cherries about two years ago. Then, just a couple weeks ago, he told me he'd seen your cock hard, and he really wanted it—and his dick is about as big as yours."

Tony was very curious, but he said, "Not right now. I'm getting about all the dick I can handle, 'specially after today. We *are* gonna do this more than just once, aren't we?"

"Well, maybe only once today," Mark smirked, "but you can plan on getting my dick as often as you can fit it in your schedule."

"As often as I can fit it up my ass, you mean."

"That, too," Mark snickered, and kissed him.

"And I *know* I could find time to fit Randy in my schedule."

"Jesus, he has a sweet ass, doesn't he?" Mark mooned.

"No shit, Dick Tracy," Tony laughed. "Anyway, I guess I'll have to start playing Randy's game if I want to enjoy the sights in the shower room. But a lot of the guys have seen me with a hard-on, anyway. But maybe Randy hasn't—he tends to keep to himself in the locker room."

Three days later, Mark told Tony to hide in the locker room after everyone had left except him and Randy. He said he had asked Randy if he might be interested in getting together with a hot guy with a dick even bigger than his own, who was interested in doing whatever Randy wanted for a crack at his ass. "Randy said he might be, but I didn't tell him who it was, or when I would tell him. We're gonna fuck after everyone leaves this afternoon. Be quiet so he doesn't know you're there until we're goin' at it hot and heavy, then pretend you fell asleep and just woke up and heard us making it. Be sure you're naked, and your dick is standing straight out. I'll bet once he gets a load of it, he'll be willing to ask you to join us." He laughed, "He'll probably want to get a load out of it!"

"All right!" Tony said. You gonna want a load out of it, too?"

"I'd like a load out of it right now, but there's no time. Guys are already starting to leave, so hide, okay?"

Tony stretched out on a bench behind a row of lockers, and waited, pretending he was asleep. He might have actually dozed had he not been thinking about Randy's ass, and how much he wanted it. Eventually it was quiet, and then he heard Mark slip the board into the door handles, and say "All clear."

He heard Randy say, "I hope you're ready for some serious fucking—I'm horny as hell today."

Mark said, "You know I'm always ready for serious fucking with you. I can't wait to get inside this beautiful ass." There was complete silence for a few minutes, during which Tony assumed—rightly—that the two boys were kissing. "Grab some towels, and let's go in the shower room," he heard Mark say.

Randy said, "Jesus, that looks good. It looks even bigger than usual," as their voices faded, and their footsteps padded away.

Tony remained on the locker room bench for ten or fifteen minutes, then stripped naked and edged toward the door into the shower room. He could clearly hear the gasps and moans of Randy and Mark making love. He had no need to fluff up his prick as he stepped into the shower room—it was as hard as it had ever been, anticipating what might lie ahead.

Mark was lying on his back on the tiles, a towel under him and his upper body propped up on his elbows, so he had a clear view of the door. Randy was bobbing up and down, riding Mark's enormous cock, with his back toward Tony. Randy's head was thrown back, his eyes apparently closed as he gloried in the fuck he was getting, so he could not see Mark smile as Tony came into view, nor did he see Mark motion with his head for Tony to come over and join them.

Tony approached the pair silently, and stood just behind, and to the right of Randy's body riding up and down on Mark's cock, with his own rigid cock flopping wildly. Randy was moaning in pleasure, occasionally muttering "So fuckin' big!" or "Give it to me!" Keeping Mark's cock in his ass, he leaned over to kiss him, and said, "You're the best fucker I ever met," which provided the opening for Mark to acknowledge Tony's presence.

Mark turned his head to look up at Tony, and smiled, "Hi, Tony."

Randy sat up, and whirled his head around, gasping in surprise, "Tony!"

"Randy, meet the guy I was telling you about," Mark said.

Tony was holding his prick out, extending it right at the level of Randy's face, so the first sight that met Randy's eyes was a monstrous hard cock, even bigger than the giant one inside his ass. "Wanna ride this one too, Randy?"

"Tony, I..." Tony could see the realization of how much dick he was being offered dawn in Randy's eyes. "Christ, Tony...my god, what a cock!"

Mark put his hands on Randy's waist and began to thrust upward into his ass again as he grinned, "What a pair of cocks, Randy. Today's your lucky day."

"Shit, Randy, we'll all be lucky," Tony said. "How about a hot three-way?" He knelt and reached down to fondle Randy's cock. Randy's surprise at discovering Tony there had caused it to wilt, but it returned to full erection as Tony said, while he stroked it, "And I want this slammed up my ass at least once for every time I shove mine in your ass. How about it, Randy?" Randy's cock was not huge, like his own or Mark's, but it was still quite generous, and Tony looked forward to sucking it and taking it up his ass.

"He's a mighty fine fucker, Randy, I promise you," Mark said. Rather than replying, Randy seized Tony's cock and turned his body so he could lick at it and kiss it, and finally to take it in his mouth. As he sucked it voraciously, Mark laughed, "Good answer, Randy."

Randy was clearly an expert cocksucker, apparently having practiced diligently on Mark's mouth-stretching prick, at least. He continued to suck profoundly, continuing to bob up and down on Mark's thrusting cock as Tony moved to stand astraddle Mark, providing better position for Randy's efforts.

As he sucked, Randy feverishly fondled Tony's ass, frequently gasping admiration for the two monster cocks invading him, doing so around the one in his mouth. After five minutes, Mark cried, "I'm coming," and levered his ass high off the floor.

Randy ceased his bobbing and screamed, "Give it to me!" when he felt Mark's cum begin to explode deep inside him. He let Tony's cock slip from his mouth as he cried out, although he held it tightly in one hand as both he and Mark panted and moaned while Mark finished blowing his load.

Mark's body collapsed to the floor, pulling his cock from Randy's ass. Immediately, Randy shifted to a kneeling position on the floor and looked up at Tony. "Stick your dick in my ass! I'm full of Mark's cum — put that big cock inside me and fuck me in it!"

Tony lost no time in complying with Randy's urgent request. He knelt behind him, took his waist in his hands, and plunged his entire prick deep inside the boy in one fierce thrust, eliciting a scream of pleasure from Randy. Mark had provided ample lubrication. Randy immediately began slamming his ass backwards to counter the deep hammering Tony was giving it.

Tony was ecstatic. This sweet little ass he had been wanting for so long was *his* at last, and his cock was slipping and sliding in hot cum from another boy he had wanted for a long time — one he had finally conquered only a few days earlier. He grunted as he fucked savagely, accompanied by Randy's appreciative moans, and Mark's cries of admiration. He gasped, "What a beautiful fuckin' ass! Jesus, Randy, I've wanted you for so long! You're so full of cum! Your cum is fuckin' *hot*, Mark!" His hammering prick was displacing squirts of the enormous load Mark had just put in Randy's ass.

Mark and Tony kissed passionately over Randy's body while Tony fucked, and soon Mark moved behind Tony to fondle his driving ass. In a moment, Tony gasped as he felt Mark's tongue entering his ass, dancing, plunging, exploring. It was Mark eating his ass so hungrily that pushed Tony over the edge. Far before he wanted it to, his cum began to erupt inside Randy's perfect ass; both he and Randy howled in thrill as it did so. Mark continued to tongue-fuck Tony for a moment before he moved his head downward and began to lick his own cum from Tony's balls, where it had collected after being displaced from Randy's ass.

As Randy and Tony collapsed together following Tony's orgasm, Mark returned to eating Tony's ass. "Jesus, your ass tastes so good, Tony," he remarked. Tony's ass-cheeks muffled Mark's remark somewhat, but it was nonetheless understood by the boy to whom the remark was directed as well as by the one who still had that same boy's monster prick buried deep inside his own ass.

"Eat my ass, Mark," Tony groaned.

Randy said, "Get it ready for my dick, Mark. I'm gonna fuck some ass now. Okay, Tony?"

"Jesus yes, Randy," Tony whispered, kissing and sucking Randy's neck. Randy turned his head so they could share kisses while Mark did his best to prepare Tony's ass.

Soon Tony pulled his cock out of Randy and knelt next to him, saying "I'm ready. Give it to me, Randy."

Mark kissed Randy as Tony got into position, saying "How about me? You gonna fuck me, too?"

Randy was not a large, muscular boy like the two who had just fucked him, and he seemed to be fairly shy and sensitive, but it was clear his physical appearance masked a commanding sex partner when he growled, "Get down there next to Tony. I'm gonna fuck the shit outa both of you!"

And if Randy didn't—fortunately—*literally* fuck the shit out of the two eager boys kneeling there for his pleasure, he fucked them both roundly and royally. And if his cock wasn't enormous, like those of the boys he was screwing, he used it so forcefully and so expertly, he gave the kind of satisfaction that would appease any but the most single-minded size queen.

When his orgasm arrived, after having fucked Mark's and Tony's asses in rotation for a good fifteen minutes—a *great* fifteen minutes, actually—Randy blew it inside Tony, which inspired Mark to kneel behind Tony and, as soon as Randy relinquished Tony's cum-filled ass, fuck Tony in Randy's cum, as Tony had fucked Randy in Mark's cum. It

140

took Mark quite a while to get another load, and by that time Tony was sufficiently inspired that he fucked Mark again, and Randy fucked Mark in Tony's cum, although it took a very long time before his load arrived.

It had been an extremely satisfactory three-way fuck, which was frequently repeated during the remainder of their time together at Atlantic High, and the three met in pairs even more frequently for the same kind of activity.

Tony was able to adopt Randy's method for avoiding a hard-on to some extent, and he began showering occasionally with Randy and the football players, although the system occasionally failed him, and he would duck out of the shower to take care of a throbbing hard-on.

Only once did Tony intentionally let Randy's system fail him. He and Bill Rubich happened to be the last two in the shower one afternoon, and Tony purposefully contemplated the other boy's body and face. His prick grew to full length almost immediately, and bobbed and swayed as it jutted out from his body. Bill pretended to ignore it for a while, until finally he asked, nervously, "That thing doesn't get any bigger, does it, Tony? How long is it, anyway?"

Tony began to stroke his cock as he said, simply, "Ten inches. It doesn't need to get any bigger, does it?"

Bill's own cock filled out and rose as he watched Tony stroking his.

"I've always been proud of my eight-incher, but jeez, I wish I had ten," Bill said, with obvious admiration.

"You've got a great dick," Tony said. And it was true. Eight inches is a *big prick*, and it was an unusually fat eight inches Bill held in his hand. But at that point, Bill might have been playing only a round of the *You show me yours, I'll show you mine* game, rather than opening negotiations for the sex Tony hoped might develop, so he added, "But if you mean you wish you had *this* ten inches…" as he pointed his throbbing prick at Bill.

"Oh God, no, Tony, I didn't mean…I meant I…"

Tony smiled seductively during the silence that followed Bill's faltering denial. Then he said, very quietly, "C'mon Bill, no one will ever know. And I'll tell you right up front, it won't be one-sided." He grinned lopsidedly, "Eight to ten is a pretty close score, after all."

"Still, I don't know," Bill whispered, but as his hand gradually reached out and timidly encircled Tony's cock, he whispered reverently, "Jesus Christ!"

Tony knew he had him. He reached out and firmly grasped Bill's cock—so fat that the tips of his thumb and forefinger did not meet when his hand closed over the shaft. He grinned, "I couldn'ta put it better—Jesus Christ!"

Sinking to his knees, Tony opened his mouth wide—extremely wide—to allow Bill's fat lip-stretcher to enter. Bill gasped with pleasure as Tony's lips sank down to the base of his shaft and sealed it off while he began to exert suction on it. "Oh God, Tony. Jesus, that feels so good!"

After he had enjoyed Tony's service for only a minute or two, Bill suddenly backed away, unceremoniously pulling his cock out of Tony's mouth with a distinct *plop!* "Wait, Tony, we've gotta see if anyone else is around. Stay here."

Bill strode out of the shower, and Tony murmured *"Cute ass!"* to himself as he watched the boy's ass-cheeks roll when he walked. In a moment, Bill returned. "Everybody's gone. I put a board in between the handles of the doors, so we're safe."

Tony laughed, "Mark's trick, huh?"

Bill blanched, and then smiled sheepishly. "Yeah—Mark's trick." He dropped his eyes and whispered, "But it was only once."

Tony walked up to Bill and put his arms around him. "Mark's quite a trick, though, isn't he?" He put his lips to Bill's, but Bill averted his head.

Finally Bill's arms went around Tony to return the embrace, and his hands began to stroke Tony's ass-cheeks as he put his lips only an inch away from Tony's, whispering, "Mark is a helluva trick" as his lips opened to admit Tony's tongue.

They kissed and fondled each other for several moments, humping their hard cocks together while their asses undulated excitedly under each other's hands. Tony released Bill, and was about to sink to his knees again, when Bill went down and began to suck Tony's monster prick. He was obviously no novice, Tony thought; he never gagged or even hesitated when he deep-throated the enormous organ.

After enjoying Bill's sucking for a few minutes, Tony lay on the floor, pulling Bill over him in sixty-nine. The tiles were wet, but still retained their heat for a long time as the boys feasted on each other. Their orgasms arrived at almost the same moment, and each swallowed eagerly, licking his lips in appreciation of the other's fine gift. Tony reversed his body and the two embraced and kissed for a long tine until Tony whispered, "I want to fuck you."

Bill hesitated for a moment before he said, quietly, "I don't think I can take a cock as big as yours up my ass. I've never tried…No, that's a lie, I have tried, and I have taken one almost as big."

"Only one?" Tony asked.

Bill blushed and admitted, "No. Quite a few, actually."

"But do you want mine, Bill?"

"Do you want mine" Bill asked, apparently not ready to commit.

"More than I can say," Tony grinned. "And yours is damned near as long as mine, and a helluva lot bigger around. I promise I'll be as easy with you as I want you to be rough with me."

"Can you fuck me so soon after…after I sucked you off?" Bill asked.

"Can't you feel that I'm ready," Tony whispered into Bill's ear as he kissed and tongued it.

Bill groaned and rolled to his stomach. Spreading his ass-cheeks with his hands, he said, "Fuck me, Tony. Go easy putting it in, but then just fuck me until you blow another load — all the way inside me this time."

Tony kissed his ear again, and said, "Keep that thought, and stay right there while I get some Vaseline. I've got some in my locker."

It took Tony less than a minute to return to the shower room. Bill lay there still, propped up on one elbow and smiling. His hesitancy seemed to have vanished in the short period of time Tony had been gone. He again rolled to his stomach, but Tony said, "Roll onto your side. That's the best way to take a really big one if you're not used to it."

Bill did as Tony had instructed. Tony lay on his side behind him, and took a generous gob of the lubricant in his hand and began to smear it over his cock and between Bill's cheeks, using a finger to pierce the boy's sphincter and prepare him. "Raise your leg," Tony instructed, and the head of his prick began pushing against Bill's asshole. Bill gasped and demurred as he slowly began to accept the throbbing monster cock inside him, but his objections only caused Tony to proceed slowly, not to cease his impalement of the boy.

As the last inch or two of Tony's prick entered him, Bill's protestations turned into encouragement and welcome, and once Tony's stomach pressed against his buttocks, he cried out feverishly, "Give me that big dick, Tony. Nothing has ever felt this good before. Fuck me!"

And fuck him, Tony did — thoroughly, expertly, and at great length. As he fucked, he rolled Bill to his stomach, and Bill gradually rose to his knees the longer he thrilled to Tony's wonderful fuck-lust. At long last — but still sooner than either boy really wanted — Tony leaned over and wrapped his arms tightly around Bill's chest, ramming his cock as far inside as it would go, and freezing in that position as he filled Bill's writhing, humping, ravenous ass with the load of cum he was by then loudly begging for. Bill quickly rose to his knees and threw his arms behind him to pull Tony's body as tightly against his back as he could. As he did so, and without his touching it, his cock began to shoot ropes of thick, white cum out onto the tiles in front of them. He actually screamed Tony's name with each jet that shot from his wildly bobbing prick, before he turned his head enough that he could share passionate kisses with the incredibly virile stud.

The floor had become fairly cold by then, and the two boys wrapped up in towels and went into the locker room, where they leaned against a bench while they kissed and embraced for a long time. Bill could not sufficiently praise Tony's power as a *fuckmaster*, and during the course of their conversation, he confessed to having fucked Randy and several others, and to having shared blowjobs with Mark and quite a few others. He admitted he had screwed up in limiting his sexual experiences with Mark to a single mutual blowjob, and said he planned to re-open negotiations with him at some convenient time in the future.

There were also several boys who had fucked him — only one of whom Tony knew, a football player.

The biggest surprise was that the cock that Bill had taken up the ass, the one that was almost as big as Tony's, had been wielded by the head football coach, a man with a wife and four children!

Bill had gone into the coach's office very late one afternoon to ask him something, and had caught the coach drinking from a bottle of Jack Daniels and stroking his huge prick, with a bodybuilding magazine spread out on the desk in front of him, opened to a photo-spread of extremely muscular men. Rather than acting startled or guilty, the coach had merely smiled at Bill and turned on so much seductive — if a bit boozy — charm that he had Bill

145

bent over his desk and taking it up the ass almost before the boy knew what was happening.

Bill had ample opportunity to study the magazine while the coach drilled his ass, and he found a handwritten note on the desk as well, which said "Coach: Your wife is beginning to ask me some very odd questions. I think she may know what we're doing, so I think it best that we quit. *Right away!* I'm going to miss your dick as much as I think you're going to miss my ass, but it's over!" The note was signed "Steve." There was no way to tell who 'Steve' was, but it seemed clear to Bill that the coach was probably thinking of what he was missing with him while he had been jacking off over the magazine, and when he blew his load up Bill's ass. If Steve looked anything like the muscular studs pictured in the magazine, Bill wished he could find out who he was, so he could replace the coach in Steve's bed — or wherever they had been fucking.

The coach turned Bill over and sucked him off after he finished fucking him, but he never alluded later to what happened with him that afternoon, or even hinted at it, so Bill wondered if he even remembered what he had done under the influence of the whiskey!

As Bill and Tony cuddled and exchanged such confidences, Bill told Tony he was really eager to fuck him, but doubted he could come a third time.

"You wanna try?" Tony grinned. "I'm not in any hurry."

Bill was in no hurry either, and while Tony lay on his back on a bench and they kissed hungrily, Bill fucked him at great length, until his third load of the afternoon finally filled Tony's greedy ass. He spent a long time running his hands up and down Tony's long legs as they rested against his shoulders, and whispering his admiration: "God damn, Tony, your legs are almost as beautiful as your dick!" Tony was so inspired that once Bill's load has exploded inside him, he put his feet on the floor and commanded Bill to mount his furiously hard cock and ride it again. Bill bounced up and down, licking his lips and playing with his own tits for only a few minutes before he had taken another load from Tony.

Bill eagerly promised Tony he would meet with him frequently to make love, but he insisted that it be their secret, that not even Randy or Mark should know about it. Tony promised, and while he continued to make love with Randy and with Mark, and frequently with both of them as a threesome, he kept his promise to Bill. Bill continued to date the girls he had always dated, but apparently saved his homosexual lovemaking to share only with Tony.

And so it remained until both Bill and Tony graduated from Atlantic High and went their separate ways. Randy graduated at the same time, but Mark had graduated a year earlier. Mark had gone off to the University of Florida, and Randy followed him there a year later; during Mark's senior year at Atlantic High they had become serious lovers, although each freely dated (i.e., fucked around) during the year they were separated. Bill went to Florida State, and married a girl he met there during his sophomore year.

Danny Williams continued to enjoy secretly all the cock his effeminate behavior attracted while he was a student, and even after he graduated and became a florist in Mar Vista, many of the boys who had sex with him while they were in high school continued to visit secretly with him, and many of the high school boys who succeeded them knew that the back room of Danny's Flowers was a place where you could always get a blowjob or a piece of very hot, very appreciative man-pussy. On a surprisingly large number of those occasions, gentle, submissive, effeminate Danny also *received* a lot of blow-jobs and fucked a lot of man-pussy himself.

Tony, of course, joined the Navy, and found such a wealth of sexual playmate material it was a near embarrassment of riches, especially when he was assigned to the Hus Bay Station.

6.

A DAY AT THE RACES

Neither Tony nor Jason was ready for a real love affair. Had either one been ready, they would probably have become a couple. They fit together nicely, they liked each other enormously, their sex was especially gratifying, each was cute, hung and horny. Moreover, Max's matchmaking from beyond the grave had the effect of bringing them together even more closely. Still, even though they often made love to each other, each continued to pursue sex with other men—many other men, actually. They consciously decided they would be better off as fuckbuddies instead of lovers.

At twenty-six, Jason was more ready to look for a long-term partner than the younger Tony, but the lure of new dicks was still too strong for him to contemplate settling down, even with a monster-hung, Monte-Hansen-look-alike Adonis like Tony. He felt no jealousy or pain on those occasions when Tony brought a horny student, a sailor or a Marine to the guest room above The Book Cellar for a casual fuck; frequently, in fact, he was invited to join Tony and his partner-of-the-moment for a threesome, and unless he had something of his own lined up, he usually accepted. Less frequently, but still fairly often, Tony accepted an invitation to bring his ten inches of hot prick to Jason's bed to supplement the eight inches Jason was offering a man or boy he had interested in sex.

When Tobey Barksdale walked into The Book Cellar one day, Jason's jaw dropped. The boy was dressed only in worn, faded Levi's, so tight they almost seemed painted on his massive legs, and an equally tight, sleeveless undershirt. The crotch of his pants bulged roundly, but did not reveal a cock snaking down the leg. Jason didn't get around to looking at his face for several minutes, because the enormous, broad chest that filled the undershirt—seemingly to bursting—and the large nipples straining against the fabric dazzled him, as did the huge, muscular arms. He didn't remember ever having seen a chest that came so near to the magnificence of Brady Stone's unforgettable tits, which he had worshipped in the dormitory when he was a student.

At length, Jason looked at the gloriously built boy's face. It almost seemed unfair that any guy as well-built as he was could be cute as well, but such was the case. He wore his light brown hair in a fairly short crew cut He had large, slightly prominent hazel eyes, a high, intelligent forehead, with heavy brows, a wide face, and very full, luscious lips. Perhaps most beautiful to Jason was his prominent square jaw—a feature Jason found especially attractive in a man, which was one reason he had found the blond 1950's movie actor Tab Hunter so irresistibly hot in his early films, and a reason why much later he would be similarly smitten with the stunning beauty of Casper van Dien. Tobey glanced at Jason and smiled briefly before he looked away, but Jason had time to enjoy the warmth of that smile, and the brilliant array of prominent teeth it revealed.

The boy turned to examine a table of new books, and his revealing Levi's displayed a small, but well-rounded ass. Jason lost no time in approaching to see if he could be of assistance. He was sure the boy had not been in the store before—at least not while he was there; there was no way he could have missed this body, even had it been dressed less provocatively.

"Could I help you?"

"Oh, hi. No, I'm just looking around." He smiled, and Jason's heart fluttered. "Killing time, actually."

"Well, this is a great place to do that," Jason said. "Make yourself at home." He extended his hand, "I'm Jason Boone, by the way. Let me know if there is any way I can be of help." Jason wanted to stress *'any* way' and leer suggestively at the boy as he said it, letting him know what he was really offering, but didn't want to scare him off. Anyone as gorgeous as this Jason wanted to *get* off, certainly, but if he *scared* him off, he would have no chance to make a play for him. That usually took time and careful planning.

The boy grinned and returned Jason's handshake. "I'm Tobey Barksdale."

"Student? Navy?" Jason asked. The haircut meant he could be a sailor, or even a Marine. The awesome body might indicate the kind of development Marines pursued.

"Student, actually. I'm a Sophomore at Paulik. My dad wants me to major in Business Administration, but I'm holding off before I decide—hoping I can find something more exciting to do with my life than that."

I can think of something very *exciting to do with your life,* Jason thought. *Something that would make* my *life a lot more exciting at the same time.* Visions of the hours he had spent that unforgettable afternoon, worshipping Brady Stone's tits, made his cock begin to grow in his pants. He stepped behind the table of books Tobey was examining, to conceal his erection.

Tobey looked around for a twenty minutes or so, and Jason had to focus his attention on another customer, but when he saw Tobey beginning to leave, he asked the other customer to excuse him for a moment, and he called out, "Tobey!" as he followed him (followed his *adorable* ass) toward the door.

At the door, Tobey turned and said, "Yeah?" as Jason caught up with him.

"I just wanted to tell you it was nice to meet you." He figured, what the hell, and added, "*Really* nice to meet you."

"Well, it was nice to meet you, too…uh…."

"Jason."

"Right. Jason."

"And please come back soon."

"I will, Jason," the boy said, and flashed his killer smile as he turned and left.

Tobey was accustomed to being wooed subtly by all sorts of men and women—mostly men, he realized—and he knew that was what Jason was doing. If he thought that Jason might be preparing the ground to make a pass at him—as he had discovered many of the men (and even boys) who were so friendly were actually doing—it would make no difference to Tobey; he would consider it a compliment, and would let it go at that. If Jason was gay— and Tobey sensed that he was—he was handsome and manly enough that he could probably get all the gay sexual action he wanted, without having to lure Tobey into bed, too. But he had to admit he had found Jason's attentions especially flattering, since he seemed very nice, and he didn't come on so strong that he seemed predatory, like so many did. Tobey was turned off when a complete stranger, whether male or female, tried hard to put the make on him immediately. He knew how attractive his body was—he'd spent years making it that way, after all— but he was also a *person*, and had a mind.

The idea of sex with a male was not repulsive to Tobey, but except for some fairly innocent sex play with a few friends when he was going through puberty, he had never tried it seriously, no matter what blandishments men or boys had offered—and he had been offered every-thing from embarrassingly lavish flattery to considerable amounts of cash, to the immense hard cocks several had produced to impress him. He was not a virgin, and he had a strong sex drive, but he was still relatively inexperienced when it came to making love. He had dated a couple of girls back in Lugoff, his home town, in the center of the state, but had only fucked one of them—and he had only done that three times. The girl had also sucked his dick each time, and, like the fucking, it had been fun, and fairly exciting, but not the great thrill his horny friends had led him to believe it would be.

Since coming to Paulik University, he had contented himself with 'five finger love,' even though he found it necessary to seek that kind of satisfaction at least once a day—and often twice or three times. He was constantly being propositioned in the dormitory, especially in the shower, where he frequently observed boys sharing blatant gay sex, and he always declined invitations to join them. He was polite, but firm in refusing sexual offers, and basically tried to take his showers when others were not around.

Tobey returned to The Book Cellar about a week after he had met Jason there, and Jason's unrestrained pleasure at seeing him again reinforced Tobey's feeling that the older man wanted to seduce him. Again, however, Jason was a gentleman, and made no overt moves or said anything specific to make the boy feel uncomfortable, or pressured in any way.

Jason desperately wanted to pressure Tobey, and make whatever moves might be necessary to get him in bed, with his awe-inspiring body naked and ready to accept Jason's worship. However, Jason got no 'gay vibes' when he talked with the muscular Adonis, nor did the boy say anything that might in any way suggest he was interested in sex. Instinctively, Jason put his hopes of seduction aside, without abandoning them; he knew you had to 'keep your eye on the prize'! Although Tobey Barksdale was straight—as far as he could tell—Jason *really* hoped the University Sophomore would someday prove to be one of those to whom he could offer the joys of a fuckbuddyship that would turn into a mutually satisfying, two-way relationship. Not since Brady Stone had he been given the opportunity to worship tits like Tobey's.

By his third or fourth visit, Tobey felt fully comfortable around Jason, even though he was still sure Jason was trying to get him in bed. Their visits were warm and friendly, and he looked forward to them. If the store was not crowded, Jason always took time to sit down and talk with Tobey in the reading area at the back of the store, and if Jason was fairly reticent about sharing details of his past and personal life—which would have been so strongly homosexual that he thought they might make Tobey uncomfortable—Tobey was completely forthcoming about his own life, even the meager details about his limited sexual experience.

Gradually Tobey began to step in and assist Jason when multiple customers needed attention. For some time Jason had been thinking he needed to hire someone else to help in the store. Considering how wonderful it would be to have Tobey's stunning body around to ogle on a regular basis, and thinking how fortuitous it would be if he were at hand should Tobey ever decide he wanted to try out gay sex, Jason naturally thought about asking the delectable boy to work at The Book Cellar.

There is a time-honored dictum in the business world that says, *You can't work 'em and fuck 'em.* While Jason was not yet a widely experienced businessman, he was still aware of that precept—his father had explained it after two of his business partners had run afoul of it. However, it didn't look like he was going to have a chance to fuck with Tobey, no matter how much he wanted to, so he offered him a job as a sales clerk.

Tobey jumped at the opportunity, and although he was unable to work more than twenty or so hours a week, because of his academic schedule, he was a great help around the shop, learning the ropes very quickly, and dazzling all customers—male and female—with his physical magnificence and his winning smile. Dozens of Jason's gay customers asked him about the possibility of Tobey being interested in sex with them, but they were all told — honestly — that the prospects probably ranged from zero to 'no chance.' The stupendous strength to which Tobey's body attested was not something any of them would willingly wish to provoke if they offended him, so Tobey remained relatively unpropositioned as he worked.

One of the first things Tobey expressed a desire to use his wages for, was the rental of an apartment in town. He didn't mind living in the dormitory, but the steady pressure from so many of the other dorm residents to have sex with them — both tacit and expressed — was so strong, he often felt uncomfortable there. He constantly had to watch for times to shower when the shower room would be relatively unoccupied. If he could have occupied a dorm room with a private bathroom and shower, he would have done so, but there were none.

Paulik University was an expensive school, and even though Tobey's father was affluent, he had also just sent his identical-twin daughters off to study at the Juilliard School in New York — an institution even more expensive to attend than Paulik — and Tobey did not feel right about asking for additional funds to rent an apartment. He wasn't comfortable with telling his father why he felt uneasy in the dorm, since his father had lived there for four years when he had been a Paulik student. His father had never hinted at the kind of rampant sexuality Tobey found in the dorm, so Tobey presumed the situation had been different a quarter of a century earlier. His father was an enormously handsome man, and pictures taken during his student years at Paulik showed him to be even more attractive and very well-built, if not as Herculean as his only son would become.

Tobey assumed his father had not been troubled with the same kind of sexual pressure he, himself experi- enced in the dormitory, but if he was, he had been better able than his son to resist it. *Wrong on both counts!* Walter Barksdale was one of the hottest residents in the dorm during his tenure at Paulik University. His great beauty and fine body assured him plenty of attention, but it was the mind-boggling cock that hung down between his legs — and, it seemed, almost as often jutted out below his belly — that drew the greatest interest from the other boys in the dorm. And Walter had not been hesitant about sharing his stunning assets with his eager schoolmates. Tobey often had occasion to see his father nude, but never when he had an erection; he would doubtless have been astonished at how well-hung his father actually was.

When he sent his son off to live in the dormitory at Paulik, the elder Barksdale assumed Tobey would share the same kind of harmless homosexual escapades he himself had enjoyed there — and he had enjoyed them enormously! It hadn't made a queer out of him, he reasoned, so why not let Tobey have his fun?

While it was true that his experiences at Paulik University hadn't made a queer of him, it should be noted that before leaving home to go there, Walt Barksdale had been fucked by, and had sucked off almost as many boys (and men) as he had fucked or been sucked off by. Furthermore, he did not lay aside his gay sexual appetites when he married, as he had assumed he would do. Like Jason's father, Walt knew that "you can't fuck 'em and work 'em," but he had apparently never heard that "you can't suck 'em off and work 'em"!

Tobey's father did not regard himself as 'a queer;' he held a more narrow definition of the term, and continued to enjoy a mutually gratifying sex life with his wife, so he regarded himself as bisexual. And he felt no remorse that he still loved cock. In church one Sunday a visiting hellfire-and-brimstone evangelist had railed, quoting Lev- iticus 20:13, *If a man also lie with mankind, as he lieth with a woman, both of them have committed an abomination,* etc. Walt smiled, and once again his narrow definition prevailed: both he and the hitchhiking University of South Carolina boy he had picked up the night before had not lain together at all — they had driven out into the country where they had stood, leaning up against a tree while they fucked each other, so no abomination was *technically* perpetrated. But Walt's view was: *Fuck Moses, and every book of the Bible he had allegedly written.* What he did with his dick was his own business, and, by another of his narrow definitions, not even his wife's.

Although he was well aware of how stupendously attractive his son was, Walt had absolutely no inclination to have sex with him—he might be a bisexual philanderer, but he was not inclined to pedophilia or incest—nor would he encourage those among his sex partners who expressed their desire to bed both father and son. He had, he hoped, trained Tobey to have an open mind when it came to sex, however, and he had been successful in that: whatever his sexual activities and attitudes, the boy was not a homophobe. Walt wanted his son to be happy in his love life, as in all things, and he wanted grandchildren, but if Tobey turned out to be gay—or only bisexual, like his father—he hoped the boy would enjoy himself as much with boys and men as he, himself always had. He knew that Tobey's astonishing masculinity did not rule out homosexual activity—he had, in his time (and even very recently), fucked too many hyper-masculine studs to think that.

By the time Tobey told Jason about his hope to move off-campus, he already knew that his employer was gay. In fact, Jason had indirectly made sure the boy knew he was gay; if he ever decided to proposition him—or perhaps *when* he decided to proposition him—he didn't want him to be led into something he wasn't aware might occur. If Tobey ever responded positively to a homosexual advance (please God, *when,* not *if!*), Jason wanted to be sure they would be having at least one-sided (but hope- fully, reciprocal) sex together.

Tobey had often visited with Jason upstairs in the house, after business hours. The many homoerotic, but not

157

explicitly erotic pictures hanging around the house would have made any but the densest clod aware the resident was gay. To be absolutely sure, Jason had the boy use the private bathroom that opened off his (formerly Max's) bedroom, so that he was inescapably confronted with the *extremely* explicit pictures there. The large diptych-style framed pictures of Spike Jefferson almost getting sucked off, and actually getting sucked off, alone would have made Jason's sexual orientation and appetites obvious to Tobey, if they were the only ones in the bedroom. But Tobey had never commented on the content of the pictures and photographs he saw anywhere, except to say on one occasion how much "the dark guy in the two pictures framed together" resembled Tony Lowe. He said nothing about the activity shown in the photos, and Jason merely agreed with his statement—somewhat surprised that the boy had spotted the resemblance. Tobey knew Tony, of course, from his regular visits to see Jason—and Tobey assumed that his boss and the handsome, monstrously hung sailor did more than just visit when they retired upstairs together.

With a heart pounding with hope, and reservations about the advisability of doing so floating around in his mind, Jason suggested that Tobey might wish to move into the second-floor apartment where he himself had lived before Max's death. "It's set up for separate gas and electric bills," he said, "and you could pay those along with your telephone and cable TV, but there wouldn't be any need for you to pay rent; I'm not going to rent it out to anyone else, that's for sure. You could consider it part of your pay for working here."

"That's really generous, Jason, but... Look, don't get pissed off, but I think I should ask, just so we're clear about things. I know you're gay, even if you've never done anything or said anything to me that was out of line. But you've gotta know I've never said anything to you that would make you think I was gay, or even...interested. I like you a lot, Jason, and I really enjoy working with you, and visiting with you in your house. And I've gotta admit all the pictures are sexy as hell, but...well, would I be kinda stepping out of the frying pan into the fire if I moved in here? Would you expect me to pay rent by... well, you know. No offense intended, but I just think we need to be perfectly clear where things would stand."

"No offense taken, Tobey. It's right of you to ask. I guess you've probably never met a gay man who wasn't interested in your body — and if so, that record remained unbroken when we met, if you know what I mean." Tobey smiled and blushed as he nodded his understanding. "To be honest with you," Jason continued, "I have to admit I would love to have sex with you, but it's strictly up to you. I won't make a pass at you unless you make it clear you want me to, okay? I've never pressured a guy for sex, or tricked him into a sexual situation. I've propositioned a lot of guys who said they weren't interested, and I've let them alone — and almost always managed to stay friendly with them. I lost a few friends who said they wanted to have sex with me, but after we did it, they decided we had done something wrong, and held me guilty. I was sorry, but there wasn't anything I could do about it after it had happened, except apologize, but they had made themselves feel guilty."

That was substantially true, but not entirely so. During the formative years of his sexual life, before he 'hit his stride' sexually, Jason had, on several occasions, done a few things to try and convince some boy or other to go to bed with him — or, more often, to do something the boy was not interested in doing after he had already gone to bed with Jason, presumably for sleep only.

"So, anyway," Jason continued, "having sex with me is not part of the deal if you move in here. I hope maybe it will happen some day, but it's strictly up to you."

"Jason, I don't know if it will..." Tobey began.

Jason put his hand over Tobey's mouth to interrupt him. "No, don't say anything. I'm gonna *hope* you come around in any case, so just let me hope, okay?"

Tobey extended his hand and smiled, "I guess it isn't going to do any harm if you hope. As Jason shook his hand in agreement, Tobey added, "But am I free to bring somebody else home to go to bed with me? Are you going to be jealous or upset?"

"Jealous? Hell yes, I'll be damned jealous, if I should happen to know about it; but I probably wouldn't know — I'm not going to be keeping tabs on you, after all. But if I am jealous, I won't show it, and I can deal with it; it'll be my problem, and I promise I won't make it yours. But upset? No — it wouldn't be any of my business; it's going to be your apartment after all. I won't even go up there unless you ask me to."

"I know there's an outside entrance to the apartment," Tobey said, "and I'll use that so I don't interrupt you." When Jason had lived in the apartment, he regularly passed through Max's quarters to go to the store in the cellar, using the same stairs Tobey had been using in going between the store and those same quarters, where Jason now lived.

"Don't be silly," Jason said. "If there's any reason I might not be wanting you to pass through, or to drop in for a visit some time, I'll let you know — or I'll lock the door coming down from your apartment if I don't have time to let you know in advance. Besides, if you catch me fucking with some hot guy, you might get inspired to branch out!"

Tobey laughed, "Who knows? We'll see. I guess it depends on how hot the guy is, huh?"

And so it was settled. Tobey moved out of the University dormitory, and took up residence in the apartment over Jason's house. The apartment was completely furnished, and Tobey's possessions from his dorm room provided everything else he needed.

Tobey proved to be a good worker and a valuable addition to The Book Cellar, working about twenty hours a week—mostly in the late afternoons, because of his class schedule at the University. Jason and many of his customers constantly stole surreptitious glances at Tobey's magnificent body. He frequently visited with Jason in the evenings, but also had his own life—going out with friends his own age, and having some of them over to visit him. Jason was by then convinced that sex with the muscular boy was, sad to say, something that was not going to happen.

Tony Lowe befriended Tobey, and as far as Jason could tell from talking with either one of the boys, nothing sexual was going on when they visited. Tony, in fact, frequently bemoaned the fact that Tobey was obviously not interested in sex with him—although he had made it crystal clear to Tobey that he *was* interested in sex with him. Tony always wore his gloriously tight uniforms when he visited with Tobey, and he confessed to Jason that he had made sure Tobey got to see his erect cock in its full, ten-inch glory! Jason figured that if his new roomer was not interested in a boy as beautiful and as superbly hung as Tony, he had to be straight—and he was able to relax in the presence of the beauty and sex appeal that he was *not* going to get to share.

When Tobey began agitating for Jason to install a hot tub in the back yard, Jason gave in easily. He knew it would be enjoyable in its own right, but would also be a great place to initiate—and perhaps even consummate— sexual encounters with tricks. Also, it would be a place where he could probably enjoy the sight of Tobey's sublime body on a regular basis, and probably the sight of Tobey's cock as well—strangely enough, something Jason had yet to see, although the big, rounded bulge of his crotch promised something very impressive.

The hot tub went in, located in such a way that it was completely screened by either the back of the house, or by shrubbery, allowing for it to be used at any time of the day or night without worrying about someone seeing nudity or sexual activity there. The tub was eight feet in diameter, and was made of cedar, lined with vinyl. It had a variety of underwater jets and lights, and built-in underwater seating all around it. They kept the water at about 100°, and Jason insisted it be no deeper than twenty-eight inches, although it could have been almost a foot deeper. When Tobey asked why he didn't keep it full, Jason explained that there was plenty of room to lie back against the sides, with legs stretched out, which allowed for immersion up to the neck, but one could also avoid getting overheated by sitting up. Tobey laughed, "Yeah, and if somebody stands up in it, his cock and his ass are gonna be out of the water for you to see, right?" Jason laughed, and admitted that was a major consideration.

The first evening the hot tub was usable, Tobey came down to join Jason, who was already seated in it. Tobey was wearing only a robe, which he slipped out of before he climbed into the hot water. He was not at all shy about showing Jason what he had apparently been hiding, but which he had, in fact, never revealed to him because no occasion had arisen to warrant his nudity. When he dropped the robe, he trumpeted "Ta-DA!" and laughed. "Here it is at last, the famous Barksdale dick! What you've been dying to see, right?"

"Yeah, but I guess it's just for show, not for blow, right?"

Tobey laughed, then said, seemingly with genuine regret, "Right. Sorry, Jason. Well, as you can see, it's nothin' special, anyway—but you may notice that the famous Barksdale balls are pretty impressive."

Tobey climbed into the tub, standing on the seat so that he towered over Jason, and lifted his cock to reveal his scrotum. His cock, though sizable, had obviously not been erect when he revealed it, but it had jutted out slightly as it drooped downward. When he lifted it up, it was clear why it had protruded: the testicles that buoyed it up were enormous—apparently fully the size of golf balls, and contained in a hairless sack that held them up tightly below the shaft of his penis. It was no wonder his crotch bulged so prodigiously, and so roundly when he was dressed. Then he turned around, saying, "And the renowned Barksdale ass, of course!" He looked back over his shoulder and grinned, "For viewing, not for doing!"

The perfection of Tobey's rounded ass almost overcame Jason's resolve. As he looked up at the two muscular hemispheres, and the profound chasm between them, it was all he could do to refrain from reaching up to caress and kiss them. Fortunately, Tobey stepped down into the tub and stood in the middle, facing him. He looked down at his cock and then peered up slyly at Jason. "Yep, when you get your next fuckbuddy in here, his cock is gonna be right there for you to see when he's standing up." Then he playfully seized Jason's body under the armpits, and dragged him to his feet as he said, "And he's gonna get a load of what you've got for him."

As Jason rose to his feet, his own cock was, of course revealed, and it was fully erect—standing straight out from his body, throbbing and bobbing, wet and glistening. Tobey whistled, "Jesus, Jason, no wonder you get so much dick—that's some bait you got there!" He pushed Jason back onto the seat, and went to sit opposite him. "Your cock is damned near as big as Tony's—and that's the biggest one I ever saw. Look, Jason, it's none of my business, but when you're with him, are you able...nah, never mind."

"Go ahead," Jason said, laughing. "I'm sure I know *what* you're gonna ask me, if I'm not completely sure about what part of my body your question is going to apply to."

"No, that's okay," Tobey grinned. "More information than I need. Talking about that isn't going to help you with that problem you've got going on down there, is it?"

Looking at Tobey's awe-inspiring tits as they visited, and all of him as they got out of the tub, the 'problem' Jason had going on *down there* did not evaporate until he had gone back to his bedroom and jacked off. He had been encouraged by Tobey's interest in showing off his cock and ass for Jason's pleasure, but no follow-up revelations occurred during the first month they used the hot tub—although during that time Jason and Tony had sucked each other off and fucked each other in it several times. There was something so sexy about the hot water and the steam rising from it, that Jason had also seduced two other University students in the tub during that month, with much greater ease than he might have expected—and each had come back for more.

Finally, inevitably, Tobey climbed into the hot tub with an erection, and while he didn't actually *display* it for Jason's admiration, he didn't hide it from him, either. It wasn't apparently fully hard, since it drooped downward as it projected outward over Tobey's gigantic balls. But even in partial erection, it was extremely impressive.

"Jesus Christ, Tobey," Jason whistled in awe, "talk about bait! That's a big one!"

"Not as big as Tony's," Tobey grinned as he stroked himself a few times, causing his prick to erect fully. "We compared them once, and he's got me beat by a couple of inches."

"That means you've probably got eight inches or so," Jason said, "and it's fuckin' beautiful!" He stood in the water, exposing his own very impressive cock. He guessed that Tobey's hard cock was actually about seven inches long, maybe a bit more.

Tobey took a step toward Jason, and put his hands on Jason's shoulders as he leaned in and pressed his lips to Jason's. "Thanks, Jason," he said as they kissed for long time, their tongues darting in and out of each other's mouths. Then he held his cock alongside Jason's. "Hell,

164

yours must be just a little bit shorter than Tony's," he said. "Major cock!"

Jason's hand cupped Tobey's enormous balls. "I sure don't have anything like this. In fact, I don't know anyone else who does."

Stepping back quickly, which caused his balls to slip from Jason's grasp, Tobey said, firmly, but kindly, "No, Jason."

Jason stepped forward and embraced Tobey, reasoning that since the boy had initiated their kiss, he wouldn't object to a hug. He clearly didn't object; he returned Jason's hug, and their cocks slid together, Tobey's poking into Jason's stomach, and Jason's poking against Tobey's balls. "I'm sorry, Jason. Maybe someday—I just don't know right now."

"I'm sorry, too, Tobey. I'm so fuckin' horny," Jason said.

"Why don't you jack off, then?" Tobey asked. "Do it here, I won't mind."

It took no second invitation for Jason to begin masturbating. He stood in the middle of the tub, his legs spread and his eyes closed as he stroked his cock, while Tobey sat down and leaned back to watch. By then, Tobey was as horny as Jason. He stood and began jacking off, his eyes riveted to Jason's cock. Jason opened his eyes, and was surprised to discover Tobey standing next to him, punishing his own prick so eagerly. "Godamighty," Jason gasped in admiration for Tobey's organ, "beautiful fuckin' dick, man!" In a few minutes he began to pant, "I'm gonna come!" He looked up into Tobey's eyes, his own eyes unfocused, delirious with the approach of orgasm. Jason pointed his cock at Tobey's busy hand, and the cum began to spurt from it to coat the boy's hand and the tip of his prick, which excited Tobey so that he stepped back and huge gobs of thick white cum shot out of his own prick to cover Jason's chest and stomach—and even his chin.

Still stroking his cock with his left hand, Jason's right hand scooped Tobey's cum from his body, and he lapped it up eagerly, sucking his fingers and licking his palm. Tobey watched, whispering, "God, that is so fuckin' hot!"

Jason smiled dreamily as he licked, "Your cum tastes great!"

Tobey impulsively took Jason in his arms and they kissed passionately for several minutes before he grinned and said, "It does taste good, doesn't it?"

"I want to suck it out of your dick next time," Jason whispered into Tobey's ear.

Pulling his head away from Jason's, Tobey looked deeply into his eyes and smiled, ruefully, "No, Jason. I can't do this. Not now, anyway."

"When?" Jason asked.

"I don't know," Tobey said. "Maybe never. I know you saw me in here with Tony and that's the same thing I told him. I shouldn't have even let this happen tonight. But I promise you that if I decide I want to go all the way with a guy, I'll do it with you first, okay?"

That seemed to be the best Jason could hope for, so he let it go at that—but he didn't give up hope.

In March, Tobey's parents came down to Hus Bay from their home in Lugoff, to check out the boy's new living arrangements, and to meet his roommate. Knowing Hus Bay, Walt fully expected to find his son had taken on a 'boyfriend,' and he rather hoped he had. He saw nothing in Tobey's apartment, or in the observable dynamic between Jason and his son that would suggest they were anything but friends. He had fairly reliable 'gaydar,' and although his son had never set it off, he was sure that Jason was gay. Still, his gaydar was not infallible, and just as he had halfway hoped to find that Tobey had taken a boyfriend, he fully hoped that if he had, it would be the pleasant and sexy Jason.

166

Both of Tobey's parents liked Jason, and both heartily approved of the boy's residence in his house. They took Tobey and Jason out to dinner on their last evening before returning to Lugoff, and, assuming Tobey would be coming home for the Carolina Cup, asked Jason to come along, and spend the weekend with them.

The Carolina Cup is a steeplechase race held each April in Camden, South Carolina, a larger city than Lugoff, only a few miles up the road from it. There are various annual events, like the football game between the Universities of Florida and Georgia, that style themselves as "The world's largest outdoor cocktail party." The Carolina Cup is another event often so described. As Jason was to discover, it certainly was more of a cocktail party than a race, and it was very large—probably accurately described as "The world's largest *elegant* outdoor cocktail party."

There is actually little attention paid to the races. 'Tailgating' parties are always in full swing, but many are held along the rows of Rolls-Royces, Bentleys, and other very expensive luxury automobiles—so elegant they could not be compared to the kind held along the rows of more mundane vehicles typically found at football games. Rather than spreading simple blankets on the ground, many in attendance spread expensive oriental rugs, weighted down with potted flowers, not the picnic coolers or stones that secure the less elegant blankets. There is plenty of fried chicken and potato salad, of course, but caviar, crudités, finger sandwiches and petits fours also accompany the champagne and fine wines that are served to the more prosperous (and snooty) attendees. Many people—perhaps the majority—pay no attention to the races at all, preferring instead to concentrate on socializing elegantly.

Jason had once attended another in-state event of even greater significance—the annual football game between Clemson and the University of South Carolina—

167

but he had never gone to the Carolina Cup, had never, in fact ever been to Camden. Walter Barksdale declared Jason owed it to himself to come to Camden for the Carolina Cup weekend.

"The girls will be home, and they're bringing some friends from school, so space is going to be at a premium, but if you don't mind sleeping in Tobey's room, you've got a place to stay at our house," Walt said.

Jason told Mr. and Mrs. Barksdale he would very much like to come for the weekend, but would need to check out a few possible conflicts, and would let them know in a few days. He had the strangest feeling that Tobey's father was coming on to him, but on behalf of his son. He shrugged the idea off as wishful thinking.

Tobey's parents had no more than left for Camden than Jason asked the boy what he wanted him to do on the Carolina Cup weekend.

"I want you to come with me, of course. Why wouldn't I? It's a lot of fun."

"Well, your Dad said I would be sleeping in your room, and I thought..."

Tobey grinned. "Don't you want to sleep with me?"

"You know goddamned well I want to."

"Well, before you get too excited," Tobey said, "you ought to know there are two beds in my room — and we'd be using both of them. Sorry." He kissed Jason very lightly, adding, "You still want to come?"

"Of course I do," Jason said, "even if that's not the way I *really* want to come when I visit with you."

So, the next day, Jason telephoned the Barksdales and accepted their invitation. Although he would be sleeping in Tobey's room, it did not mean he was going to bed the beautiful boy in the usual sense of the term, but he felt he might have a better chance of actually doing so than he ever had to date.

*

The weather for the race in Camden was perfect, and Tobey went out of his way to make Jason feel welcome at each social occasion—and there were quite a few in the space of only two days. He never wandered off to visit with his old friends from high school days, leaving Jason alone; rather, he took Jason along, and introduced him around as his friend, quite unself-consciously. Most of those old friends were male, and most had dates along with them; two of the girls Jason met had dated Tobey during high school. Tobey joked about 'dating' his boss— also his landlord—this year. Jason detected no irony or suspicion on the part of Tobey's friends, except for one of the girls Tobey had dated—who acted as though she suspected Tobey was not joking when he said he was 'dating' the older man. Most of Tobey's male friends were good-looking; one or two were gorgeous, and another one or two were extremely sexy. Jason would have loved to go to bed with almost any of them, but not one of them was as attractive or as sexy as Tobey.

The steeplechase races were enjoyable, what Jason actually saw of them, but it was clear they were secondary to the social aspects of the day—which Jason enjoyed enormously, especially with his gorgeous 'date' constantly in attendance.

The night before the race had been frustrating. Jason had provided endless openings for the boy to respond positively to his sexual innuendoes, but to no avail. They retired to their separate beds, and Jason dozed fitfully, always hoping that Tobey would either get into bed with him, or invite Jason to come into his own bed. He had done neither.

By the time to retire on the night following the race, Jason had given up hope of having sex with Tobey—at least in Lugoff. He could have had no inkling of the bizarre mixture of gratification and frustration that was about to ensue, or how much greater his frustration would become during the long night ahead, while he was at the same time in the process of realizing some of the sexual ambitions he had sought with the boy for so long a time.

Both stripped down to their undershorts. Tobey used the bathroom adjoining his bedroom, then Jason followed him. When Jason returned, he found that the lights had already been turned out, but there was ample illumination from a light-pole in the yard to see that Tobey was standing at the side of the bed Jason was to sleep in. As always, his body was magnificent, his tits beggared description. Jason noticed, with chagrin, that while the crotch of Tobey's shorts was huge, filled with his prodigious balls, it was clear his cock was not erect.

Jason walked up to Tobey and put a hand casually on his shoulder. "G'night, Tobey. Thanks for a wonderful day."

Tobey reached out and took Jason's shoulders in both hands. "I had a good time, too. Everybody likes you." There was a moment of silence, while they looked into each other's eyes, and Tobey's hands moved inward a bit; his thumbs began to stroke Jason's neck. "I like you, too, you know." His massive arms encircled Jason's body and he pulled it in to press it against his own. His head moved in toward Jason's, and with their lips no more than inch apart, he added, "I like you a lot, Jason."

Jason returned the boy's embrace — feeling like a boy himself, being held in such gigantic, muscular arms. Their lips met, and they kissed gently, romantically, murmuring their pleasure, but Tobey evinced none of the heat or passion Jason wanted to bring to their kiss. Jason opened his mouth slightly, and sought to probe Tobey's mouth with his tongue, but the boy refused to admit it. He only murmured gently, and continued to kiss tenderly.

One of Jason's hands crept to Tobey's chest, and cupped one of the boy's huge, swelling breasts as he whispered into Tobey's mouth, "You've got the most exciting tits I've ever seen." Not quite true, in light of Jason's experience with Brady Stone, but close enough.

Pulling Jason's hand from his chest, Tobey smiled at him. "Just kiss me, okay?" Then he leaned in, and they returned to their sweet kissing.

They kissed for a long time, each one's hands affectionately roaming the territory of the other's shoulders and upper back. Each time Jason tried to roam farther south of that territory, Tobey would reach around behind Jason's body and move his hands back north, whispering simply, "Kiss."

After more than a quarter-hour of this sweet, romantic kissing, Tobey took the initiative: he pressed his tongue forward to part Jason's lips. Jason opened his mouth to receive Tobey's tongue, just as Tobey opened his mouth to accept Jason's. Their lower bodies were pressed together, of course, but each time Jason began to hump Tobey's, the boy asked him not to. They continued to kiss, with slowly growing excitement; their embraces became equally passionate, but their fondling never got below the belt. Each held the other by the nape of the neck, to press their lips together even harder. They tousled and pulled each other's hair, their mouths occasionally separated so they could kiss each other on the face, the ears, the neck, the shoulders. Eventually Tobey failed to object when Jason fondled his tits, ever more appreciatively and worshipfully, and their kissing became even more lustful. But when Jason would stoop over and attempt to suck Tobey's huge nipples and breasts, the boy would again object.

Although Tobey would not allow their kissing and embracing to go further, Jason was in paradise, delirious with the miracle of the boy's lovemaking—however limited the extent he would allow. They lost track of time entirely, and Tobey finally whispered, "We have to quit this and go to bed."

"Oh god, yes—at last!"

"No, Jason. You go to your bed and I'll go to mine."

"But, Tobey, I want you so much, I..."

"I know. But I don't know when yet, or even *if*," Tobey said. Go in the bathroom and beat off," Tobey said, "then get some sleep. But Jason," he whispered as he took Jason's head in his fingertips and kissed him lightly, "Don't give up, okay?"

With his balls aching from the need for release, and his lips and jaw sore from their frantic, lengthy kissing, Jason went into the bathroom and blew a huge load into the commode. It was then he realized that daylight was beginning to break. Unbelievably, he had spent almost *five hours* in Tobey's embrace!

Nothing was said the next morning about their night-long lovemaking except for Tobey noting that they both needed to wear shirts with high collars for a few days, to hide the hickeys each had given the other on the neck and shoulders.

Life continued as before for Jason and Tobey, with no further sexual contact until one night, as Jason lay in bed watching television shortly before midnight. He looked up when he heard a rap on the doorjamb (the door was standing open) and looked up to see a smiling Tobey standing in the doorway, wearing only his briefs. "Can I come in? I hope you don't mind me just barging in without calling you first."

"Of course not, Tobey." Jason said, sitting up in bed and leaning against the headboard. "You know you're welcome to come in anytime, unless the door from upstairs is locked." He laughed as Tobey came in and sat on the edge of the bed, "But I never remember to lock it, so if I'm in the bedroom, listen first to see if I'm with some guy."

"Actually, I came down to visit last night, but you *were* in bed with some guy—with Tony, I think—so I tiptoed out, and went back upstairs." He grinned, "You sounded like you were both having a helluva good time."

"We were," Jason grinned back. "In fact, I was having a full ten inches of fun! So, what did you want?"

"I just needed a goodnight kiss," Tobey said, and leaned over Jason, placing their lips together. "Could I get one tonight, instead?"

"Jesus," breathed Tony, putting his arms around the boy, "you can get anything I can give you."

Tobey returned Jason's embrace as they kissed. Again their kiss was tender and sweet, but this time it turned passionate and lustful after only a few minutes, and while they embraced and kissed, Tobey stretched out on the bed while Jason slid his body downward to lie next to him. After several minutes of the same kind of feverish kissing they had shared for so long at Tobey's house, the boy stopped kissing and slid his body upward, so that his chest was over Jason's face. He whispered, "You still wanna suck my tits?"

Jason's reply came immediately, in the form of worshipful licking, sucking and kneading the miraculous breasts. Tobey gasped, "God, that feels good. I believe you like my tits even more than I thought you did."

Jason paused only long enough to say, "I love your tits, Tobey," before he returned to his sucking. His hands roved appreciatively over the boy's back, and slipped inside the waistband of his shorts. He fondled and caressed the muscular, rounded mounds of Tobey's by-then writhing ass as he said, "Christ, what a sweet little ass. I love everything about you, Tobey."

"It's a good thing," Tobey smiled, " 'cause if you didn't, I'd have to force you." He rolled them to their sides, and put a hand in the back of Jason's shorts, where he began to stroke his buttocks. "You've got a pretty sweet little ass, yourself."

"Like I said, you can have anything you want," Jason said, as he forewent worshipping Tobey's tits to resume their kissing.

They lay next to each other, kissing and playing with each other's asses for a long time, humping their bulging crotches together. Finally, Tobey asked, "You mean it? I can have anything I want?" Jason nodded, and Tobey whispered, "What I really want is a blowjob. While I stood outside your bedroom last night, listening to you and Tony, I got so fuckin' horny I had to jack off. I was smearing my cum all over my tits while Tony was fucking you."

Jason rolled Tobey to his back and leaned over him, kissing him again before he said, "I'm going down now — and one blowjob is coming up!" He pulled Tobey's shorts off, and as the waistband cleared his cock, it sprang back and slapped audibly against his belly. His gigantic balls were exposed, pulled up by his erection.

Jason began to kiss and lick Tobey's magnificent chest again, and gradually worked his way downward until his lips found the throbbing cock. He kissed the head, and licked down the shaft until he reached Tobey's balls. "This is the biggest set of balls I've ever seen," he breathed in awe before he began to lick and suck them, finally opening his mouth very wide to take one ball inside; there was no way he was going to be able to suck both of them at the same time.

"Jesus, that feels so good!" Tobey placed his hands on Jason's head and held it, squirming in delight at Jason's worship. "They're so full of cum for you. I wanna fuckin' drown you in hot cum."

"Do it!" Jason said urgently as he raised his head and drove his lips all the way down the shaft of the boy's prick. Tobey began to hump upward, fucking Jason's mouth zealously as his fingers wove through Jason's hair, pulling it and massaging his head at the same time he held it down to receive the fierce thrusts of his cock. "I've been wanting you to do this since I first put my tongue in your mouth."

"Why didn't you tell me sooner?" Jason managed to gasp around the fat seven inches of dick filling his throat.

"I don't know, now," he answered. "You give a fantastic blowjob—best I've ever had!"

It was true; Jason was giving a superlative blowjob, inspired by the length of time he had desired Tobey, the fierce fucking Tobey was giving his mouth, and the feel of the boy's succulent tits and his frantically humping, muscular ass. Furthermore, he had deep-throated Tony's ten inches only the night before, so Tobey's dick presented no great challenge, and Jason was able to lavish extra care on it; although it was almost three inches shorter than Tony's, it was still a delicious mouthful, wielded by a beautiful young Colossus.

Tobey said no more for ten minutes, except to moan his ecstasy. Then he gasped, "I'm gonna come in a minute. You want to eat my cum?"

"Shit yes, I wanna eat your cum. Do you want me to rest for a few minutes and make it last?"

"No, keep sucking," Tobey said. "I've gotta blow my load, but I can work up another one soon, if you want me to."

"I'll want you to!" Jason intensified his sucking and his fondling of Tobey's ass; Tobey increased the intensity of his fucking, until after a few minutes he forced Jason's head down savagely and held it there as his prick began to erupt.

The force and volume of Tobey's orgasm was such that Jason was unable to contain it all in his mouth; he had to swallow halfway through to make room for the cum that kept coming! In fact, a few drops of the first blasts of Tobey's discharge leaked from the corners of his mouth before he was able to get it under control, after which he greedily sucked and continued swallowing the largest load he could remember having eaten.

Having fed Jason all he could for the moment, Tobey relaxed, and his hands now held the expert cocksucker's head tenderly while he lay there in temporary exhaustion, and Jason continued to nurse his cock gently. "Jesus, Jason, you can suck cock better than anyone I've ever got blown by. Thank you. It was great!"

"Thank you. What a mouthful you gave me. What a couple of mouthfuls!" Jason whispered. "Your cum tastes like honey."

"I don't think anything has ever felt as good as that did," Tobey replied.

"No? How about this?" Jason asked as he raised Tobey's legs until the boy's knees were pressed against his shoulders, and he buried his face inside the chasm Tobey's ass presented, immediately driving his tongue deep inside the sphincter, where it danced around and plunged in and out.

Tobey cried out in complete joy, "Ooooh! Aaaaahh! Oh God! Oh God, Jason—*eat my ass!* " His cries turned into whimpers of ecstasy as Jason tongue-fucked him, and his hands fondled Jason's head feverishly while his ass gyrated around the hard muscle plunging in and out of it.

Jason stopped rimming Tobey long enough to look up at him from his position between his legs. "I thought you'd like that."

Tobey pulled Jason's head upward and kissed him passionately. While they were kissing, each was masturbating. Suddenly, Jason cried, urgently, "I'm gonna blow my load!" He rose to his knees, still jacking off, and was soon spraying his hot cum all over Tobey's chest and belly, while his other hand fondled Tobey's tits and began to rub his own cum into them.

While Jason had been covering him with cum, Tobey had cried out his appreciation and encouragement. When it was clear that Jason had finished, the boy scooped the cum from his belly and smeared it over his prick. "Suck your cum off my dick, and then keep going; I need to shoot another load."

176

Leaning down, Jason licked his own cum from Tobey's glorious breasts, then kissed the horny boy, who eagerly sucked his tongue, not commenting on the fact that he was tasting Jason's cum, in effect, eating part of Jason's load.

"What a fuckin' stud," Jason smiled as he went down on Tobey again, and resumed blowing him. While it took a long time for Tobey to shoot another load, it was time well spent, during which Tobey rolled Jason to his back while he continued to fuck his mouth, and blew his second load straight down his throat.

The two cuddled and kissed tenderly for some time before Tobey whispered, "I'd better get back upstairs."

"No, stay and sleep with me," Jason said. "Let me blow you again in the morning."

"Jason, I…I enjoyed this tonight as much as I've ever enjoyed anything, but…well, I don't know where this is going. Or where I want it to go. Give me time to think it out, okay?"

"Okay," Jason smiled. "When you're ready, let me know." Tobey kissed him again, put on his shorts, and went back upstairs to his own bedroom. Jason had to jack off and blow another load before he was able to sleep.

The next morning, his bed smelled of Tobey, and with images of the young stud's magnificent body in his mind, and the taste of the boy's cum still in his mouth, Jason started his day by jacking off.

Tobey visited Jason's bed several times after that, but he did not yet return Jason's blowjobs or ass-eating. He did, however, lessen the one-sided nature of their meetings beginning with the second one in Jason's bedroom, when he started freely stroking Jason's dick while they made love. Several times Tobey made Jason come while he was jacking him off.

Finally, as Jason was lying on his back one night, early on during their session that evening, Tobey straddled

Jason's body, facing his feet, and sat all the way down on his face. Jason had sucked Tobey off only a few minutes earlier, and told the boy to give him his ass to eat while he finished jacking off. Jason eagerly ate Tobey out, and the boy was gasping his usual thrill at Jason's tongue-fuck when he suddenly fell forward and took Jason's prick in his mouth, all the way to the root, and began sucking hungrily.

"God, Tobey, I've waited so long for this," Jason cried as he stopped eating Tobey's ass for a moment. Tobey walked a step backward on his knees, so that his cock hung down directly over Jason's mouth. Jason quickly opened his mouth so that Tobey could fuck his mouth as eagerly as he was fucking Tobey's.

They rolled to their sides and sucked each other in sixty-nine until Jason rolled them over so that he was lying on the bottom again. Tobey immediately abandoned Jason's prick to bury his tongue deep inside Jason's ass, which thrilled Jason almost as much as it surprised him. Jason alternated between continuing to suck Tobey's prick and crying his thrill at the boy's eager rimming until he began to gasp, "I'm gonna come," Tobey abandoned his asshole and began sucking his cock again, so that at the moment Jason's cum began to erupt, it all went into Tobey's throat, and Tobey hungrily sucked out and swallowed every drop of it.

Tobey disengaged himself from their sixty-nine and took Jason in his arms. "I've never done that before, but I think I've wanted to for a long time now. Sucking your dick and eating your ass was great, but the best was when you shot your load in my mouth."

"Let me taste it," Jason whispered, and they kissed long and lovingly.

They cuddled and necked much longer than usual that night. When Tobey said it was time for him to go back upstairs, as he always had done, eventually, Jason pleaded with him to stay and spend the night as he had always done in answer. Tobey changed his mind this time, saying. "If I do, can we suck each other off again?"

Jason agreed, of course, and they not only sucked each other off before going to sleep, they began the next day the same way.

A few days later, about four o'clock in the afternoon, Tobey finished classes and came to work. He and Jason were working in the store together when Tony came in a quarter-hour later, dressed in his tightest white uniform, and looking impossibly sexy. Jason did not miss the way Tobey examined the sexy bulges of Tony's uniform. Everybody studied Tony's bulges when they were as large and prominent as they were when he wore his tight white uniforms. There were some who might not be particularly interested in getting their hands or mouths on the toothsome parts of the anatomy that created those amazing bulges, but they were surely a sparse minority.

Naturally Tobey had contemplated the glory of Tony's body before, but today his examination was closer and — given the steps in gay lovemaking he had so recently taken — more focused.

Jason had told Tony that Tobey was probably straight, and since Tony got all the dick he wanted, from boys who were eager to give it to him, he never tried to put the make on the boy, although he was as taken by Tobey's beauty and his glorious body as any sane gay man would be.

Tony and Tobey greeted each other warmly that afternoon, before Tony drew Jason aside and asked if he wanted to go upstairs and make love.

"Sure. We're not busy. I'll have Tobey watch the store."

"You think he'd be interested in joining us after that? He seems...I dunno, more interested than I've seen him before. He always cruises me, but..."

Jason laughed, "Shit Tony, everybody cruises you when you're showing your dick like that. They may just be amazed instead of interested, you know!"

"Whatever," Tony said. "Today, he looks more like he's interested than he ever has before."

"He probably is," Jason said. He went on to explain to Tony the developments in his relations with Tobey. "So far we haven't fucked, but I don't think it's very far away. Why don't you wait until that happens? I'll let you know, and we'll see where it goes."

"Jesus, his body is incredible. Does he look as good naked as he does in clothes? He could do anything to me he wanted if I could just suck those tits and eat out that cute little ass!"

"Believe me, " Jason said, " he looks even cuter when he's naked — if that's possible. Just give me some time to get him ready; you know he's not gonna be able to take your dick up the ass without some groundwork. If I can get him, ready, I'll tell you."

Tony laughed, "That dick of yours isn't exactly training-size, you know."

"Maybe not," Jason said, "but eight inches is a lot easier to start with than ten."

"Speaking of that, let's go upstairs. It feels like I've got twelve inches to give you this afternoon."

Jason called Tobey over. "Tony and I are going upstairs for a while. Will you watch the store and lock up at six?" He asked. "Just leave everything, and I'll come down later to count up and get ready for tomorrow."

"Sure," Tobey said, "go ahead." He dropped his gaze to brazenly study Tony's white pants, where the sailor's cock was clearly outlined, and just as obviously well on its way to erection — if not quite at its full ten-inch glory yet, not far from it. Tobey looked back up and grinned lewdly, "You guys have a good time." He winked and turned his attention back to the store, where a customer had entered.

Tony could not stay very long; he had duty that evening, and had to get back for chow before beginning his watch at 7:45. Still, there was ample time for him and Jason to share all the fucking and sucking they wanted, although the kissing and cuddling interludes they normally interspersed their lovemaking with had to be truncated somewhat.

At 6:45, Tony left by the front door, and before Jason had time to get dressed, Tobey appeared at his bedroom door, taking Jason by surprise as he was smoothing out the bedclothes. He leaned against the jamb and asked, simply, "Did you guys suck each other off?"

Jason was completely naked, but made no move to hide it as he stepped toward Tobey. He smiled, "Yeah, we did."

"God, his cock is enormous! How much of it could you suck?"

"Every bit of it," Jason said, with justifiable pride. "And before you ask—it's ten inches."

Tobey whistled appreciatively, "God, I'd like to have ten inches for you to suck."

"You can have Tony's ten inches for the asking. He said he'd be really glad to give it to you any time you want it." Then he grinned as he added, "Any way you want it."

Ignoring that statement, Tobey asked, "Did you fuck him?"

Jason smiled, "Oh yeah." And held out his prick for Tobey's inspection. It was still glistening with lubricant and cum. "Can't you tell?"

"Jesus, Jason," Tobey said nervously, and began to grope the ever-growing bulge in his pants. "And I presume he…"

"Fucked me? Yes. And before you ask, all ten inches." Then he turned around and arched his back, using his hands to spread his ass-cheeks, looking back at Tobey over his shoulder as he said, "Can't you tell?"

Tobey put his hand in between Jason's buttocks, and began to slide it slowly, seductively back and forth in the slippery lubricant residue. "Sure feels like it."

"But does it feel good?"

"Oh god, Jason, can I fuck you, too?"

"I've been waiting to hear you say that for a long time, Tobey." He turned around and embraced the boy, who put his arms around Jason and fondled the cheeks of his ass hungrily. "You can put that big dick of yours all the way inside me, right where Tony's monster was. It's still greased up and ready for you, and my ass is still full of cum. You wanna fuck me in Tony's cum?"

Tobey was quickly pulling off his clothes as he panted, "I just wanna fuck you — and if Tony's cum is in there to make it even hotter, that's great!" He was by then naked, his prick standing out and throbbing. "How do you want it?"

"Where I can see your face and play with your tits while you fuck me the first time. After that, any way you want it." As he said that, Jason backed up to the bed and lay down, raising and spreading his legs to welcome Tobey, who knelt between them.

Jason was, indeed, full of Tony's cum, and while Tobey fucked him savagely, it made a squishing sound, and enough was forced out that it coated the base of Tobey's cock and dripped from his balls. The feeling of fucking Jason's ravenous ass — amazingly tight, consider-ing it had just been stretched by Tony's ten-inch monster — with his prick plunging in and out of the hot pool of Tony's cum, was so exquisite, and the moment so fraught with fuck-frenzy, that Tobey's orgasm was not long in arriving.

Long after his load had exploded inside Jason, Tobey continued to fuck frantically, gasping his satisfaction. His cock remained as hard as it had been when he first entered Jason, and while he fucked and gasped, he cried, "You wanna fuck me now?"

"Are you sure, Tobey?"

"Shit, yes," Tobey panted as he pulled out of Jason and positioned himself on all fours next to him on the bed. "You still have some cum left for me? Or did you give at all to Tony?"

Jason had seized the bottle of lube and was preparing Tobey's ass. "I'll always have cum for you, Tobey." He lay on his back next to the fuck-hungry boy, saying, "You'd better settle down on my dick and ride me the first time. It'll be easier on you."

Tobey quickly straddled Jason's body and positioned the tip of Jason's prick at his asshole. "I didn't think I'd ever do this, but I've gotta have your dick up my ass!" He closed his eyes and licked his lips as he very gradually wriggled and sank down, occasionally stopping and retreating the least bit as he cried out with pain, until his ass was resting on Jason's stomach. With a huge sigh, he exhaled, "Oh Jesus!"

"Are you okay?" Jason asked. Tobey nodded and smiled ecstatically. "How does it feel?"

"It feels like I've gone to heaven," Tobey said as he tentatively began to ride up and down, eyes still closed and still smiling.

Jason reached up and began to fondle Tobey's magnificent tits and pinch his generous nipples as he began to lever his hips up and down to fuck the boy in sync with his ride. Soon Tobey pushed Jason's hands aside as he began to tweak his own nipples while he rode Jason's prick ever more frantically. Jason held Tobey's waist and pulled his body down to slam it against his own groin as he fucked upward—over, and over, and over, endlessly, deliriously, while Tobey gasped and moaned in ecstasy, until Jason reached up and pulled down on Tobey's shoulders as he cried, "I'm coming!"

While Jason's cum spurted and filled Tobey's ass, the boy quickly seized his cock and began to stroke it, so that even before Jason had finished his climax, Tobey's load was shooting out onto Jason's face and chest. As soon as his cock had stopped discharging, but while he was still panting in excitement, Tobey leaned over and licked his own cum from Jason's face, then shared it with him in a long, passionate kiss.

The final steps toward sexual fulfillment between Jason and Tobey had finally been taken, and both were in rapture as they lay together in bed that evening, kissing and caressing for hours. Jason was fucked out; he had blown a load in Tony's mouth and another in Tony's ass that afternoon, and had filled Tobey's ass with yet another. Tobey was not as nearly satiated, however, and after he had fucked Jason again, in doggie position, he lay on his back while Jason nursed on his tits until they both fell asleep.

The next morning, they rose early. Tobey had to get to class, and Jason needed to finish up the previous day's business in the store. But as they showered together, Tobey fucked Jason again, and then sucked him off; the boy's ass was too sore to get fucked again that soon, but he was ready by the next day. And Jason was there to accommodate him!

7.

COME ONE, COME ALL

To a certain extent, almost every gay man falls in love with the first man who fucks him, as long as the fuck is welcomed. Whatever happens subsequently, however many other men fuck him or whom he fucks, that love stays forever in some part of his psyche. So it was to be with Tobey.

From the first awakenings of his sexuality, Tobey had known he was attracted to other boys—and it was only later he learned he was far less attracted to girls. He thought he was passing through some sort of phase in his development that he would outgrow. By the time he spent a whole night kissing Jason in his bedroom the weekend of the Carolina Cup, he was beginning to realize the minor sexual skirmishes he had experienced with girls had really meant nothing to him, and the minor sexual skirmishes he had experienced with boys were the ones he remembered and desired to repeat. Still, he didn't *want* to be gay; who would, after all? Making love with other boys would almost surely prove to be much more complicated than heterosexual, socially acceptable relationships. He was right, of course. He also assumed being gay would prove to be more frustrating than being straight, but he was probably wrong—the frustration of developing and maintaining personal relationships is difficult for every-one, whatever the sexual orientation of the parties may be.

Whether he wanted it or not, Tobey began, in the days following the night he spent kissing Jason, to try and accept the likelihood that he was gay. Still, he was filled with trepidation, and wanted to proceed slowly. In his previous sexual encounters with boys he had only groped and fondled and necked with them, and allowed them to suck his dick. As his lips closed around Jason's cock the night they first went to bed together, it was the first time he had *actively* done anything sexual with another guy past kissing and groping, and he admitted to himself he was probably a *queer*. Later that night, when he tongue-fucked Jason's ass and sucked him off, there was no longer any question in his mind, although he still proceeded slowly with acceptance of his nature.

When he finished fucking Jason for the first time, feeling the heat and viscosity of the incredibly sexy sailor Tony's cum bathing his hungry prick inside Jason's voracious ass, he gave in completely, and his cry of "Will you fuck me now?" as he knelt on the bed a minute or two later and invited Jason's cock up his ass, had been his complete capitulation to his homosexual nature. And by the time Jason sucked him off in the shower the next morning, he knew he was in love.

In a very real way, Tobey felt that Tony had also been there with him the night he fell in love with Jason — after all Tony's cum, as well as his own, had been dripping from his cock while Jason fucked him the first time. As he sought out repeat sexual encounters with Jason — now, thankfully, completely realized — he also wished to make love with the handsome, incredibly hung sailor. In truth he had wanted to have sex with Tony for a long time, but could only now accept that fact and act on it.

But he felt that he should consult Jason before having sex with someone else; he wanted to belong to Jason, just as he wanted Jason to belong to him, but he knew only too well what a variety of other boys Jason bedded — in addition to Tony. Tony was the only other one among Jason's sex partners he knew, although he had seen many of the others going up to Jason's room or leaving the house, and had even overheard Jason making love with a few of them, as he had with Tony.

Once he had fallen in love with Jason, Tobey's initial feeling when he thought about Jason's other sex partners was jealousy. Still, he realized that it would be foolish to expect his new lover to be monogamous with him — even he, himself, wanted to make love with Tony, after all. And he had to admit that although he would enjoy making love with Jason and Tony at the same time — as he already had in only a symbolic way — he wanted to make love with Tony *alone*, to have the fabulous stud all to himself.

Without being vain, he also knew his body attracted constant admiration from gay men — but he had no idea that his facial beauty was equally attractive. He knew full well there was a world of experience he was now free to taste; he was young, he was hung, he was full of cum, and he wanted to live out some of his thus-far sublimated fantasies. Jason had been one, Tony was another — and who knew what other exciting boys and men he might make love with? He knew he could still love Jason if he pursued other sexual partners, and he felt that Jason loved him, and would continue to do so while he also maintained the free-wheeling sex life he had been enjoying. As for Tony, Tobey hoped the stunning sailor would be interested in a continuing relationship like the one he shared with Jason.

Tobey had never had sex with more than one person at a time, and did not, in fact feel sure he would enjoy a threesome all that much, but he was eager to engineer one with himself and Tony and Jason. Jason could prepare him for the invasion of Tony's monster cock, and be there to hold him and see him through the much-to-be-desired ordeal.

For such a young, inexperienced man, he considered his situation in a very mature fashion. He did the wise thing: he talked with Jason about it.

Jason was quite frank in what he told the boy, knowing that complete honesty would be important, since — like Tobey, although the boy had not yet confessed

187

it to him—Jason wanted to actively continue their now fully reciprocal sexual relationship without being restrained by monogamy.

"The very first time I saw you," Jason told him, "I was hot for you—*really* hot. You're about as handsome and well-built as anyone I've ever known, but as I got to know you better, I resigned myself to the probability that I wasn't going to get you in bed. Even after that night in Lugoff, when we spent the whole night necking, I didn't think it was going to happen." He kissed him. "I sure am glad it finally did. I want to be honest with you, Tobey, I love you, and I want us to keep making love to each other, but…"

"I'm in love with you, too," Tobey interrupted. "I really am, Jason, but…"

Jason laughed, "Sounds like we each have to add 'but' when we're saying we love each other, doesn't it? What I mean to say is that I love you, but I still want to love other guys, too. That's why I said I loved you instead of saying I was *in love* with you. To me, being *in love* means you don't want to be with anyone else, so I'm careful about what I say. You said you were in love with me, but I get the feeling the 'but' you put on the end of your sentence means the same thing as mine."

"But I am in love with you," Tobey explained, "still, I want to have sex with other guys, too. Can't I do both?"

"Of course you can. We can be lovers who don't have to make love only with each other. It doesn't matter what you call it, as long as we understand where we stand. How's that?"

"That's perfect," Tobey said. "We're lovers, and I know now I'm gay, and that makes me happy." He explained the genesis of his acceptance of his sexual orientation, concluding by saying, "And it makes me want to ask you an important question. Does Tony want to make love with me? If he does, will he want to fuck me?"

Kissing Tobey, Jason smiled, "Baby, I think everyone wants to make love with you. Do you have any idea how awesomely attractive you are? As for Tony, yes, he definitely wants to go to bed with you. He's said so quite a few times, and since he once asked me right after he'd blown a load in my ass, 'You think Tobey could take my dick?', I'd say for sure he's interested in fucking you. I think Tony is damned near as cute and sexy as you are, so I figured you might want to fuck with him. Hell, you'd have to be crazy *not* to want Tony, I guess. Beautiful, sweet guy, fantastic in bed, and a dick to die for. What's not to want? He could have about anybody he wanted, so I feel really lucky he keeps wanting to have sex with me."

Tony grinned, "I know why he wants to keep having sex with you. You're the best."

"That's sweet," Jason grinned, "but I think you're prejudiced."

"Damned right I am" Tobey said, "but I still think you're the best."

"You might not think that if you start riding Tony's dick. You want me to set you up with him? Not that you couldn't set it up just by smiling at him and saying you wanna screw."

"What I really want is to have sex with you and Tony both the first time I get together with him. It's gonna be hard to take ten inches of cock, and I'd like for you to be there to help me out. I know that's not very romantic, but..."

"Maybe not, but it's pretty fuckin' hot," Jason said. "I'll be there to help you, but you're probably gonna get more than just Tony's dick up that sweet little ass of yours: I'm gonna want to give you something, too."

"Sounds great to me," Tobey grinned.

As it happened, Tobey needed little encouragement or help in taking Tony's ten inches.

*

Tony had been very pleased to hear that Tobey wanted him, and promised Jason he would be over on a Thursday night, for a hot-tub soak that was intended to move indoors to Jason's bedroom and become a threesome. Jason thought the relaxing effect of the hot water would be helpful in preparing Tobey for Tony's formidable invasion.

Tony appeared a few minutes before 9:00, the time The Book Cellar closed on Thursday nights, wearing his white, deliriously tight and revealing uniform. Tobey was working until 9:00 also, and when the hour arrived, Jason sent them off to the hot tub, saying "I'll close up here and join you in about ten minutes." It was actually almost twenty minutes before Jason approached the hot tub, bearing drinks.

It was obvious that Tony and Tobey had begun getting acquainted, since Tony was sitting in Tobey's lap, facing him. Tobey leaned back, with his head thrown back and his eyes shut; the sailor had his head bent down so he could suck Tony's tits. They were so engrossed in what they were doing, they did not hear Jason approach. As Jason reached the hot tub, he could see that Tony was actually riding Tobey's cock while he sucked the boy's tits.

Jason watched for a minute or so before he cleared his throat. The two in the hot tub turned to face him, smiling. "I see you got started," he said.

Tony dismounted and stood—his prick jutted out, in full bloom. "How could I resist? I've never seen juicier tits. Or bigger balls, for that matter," he added, kissing Tobey.

"And I've never seen a bigger cock," Tobey said as his hand emerged from the water to encircle the giant shaft. Jason put the drinks down on the wooden lip surrounding the hot tub, and quickly shed his clothes. He said, "Juiciest tits," as he kissed Tobey, "and biggest prick I've ever seen, too," as he kissed Tony. A minor fib. If

Brady Stone, at Paulik, had an even more sumptuous chest, and if the sailor Rex's cock was even two inches longer than Tony's colossal weapon, what of it? What he confronted just then was almost as spectacular, and they were both here together.

Tony waded up to the seated Tobey and rested his cock against the boy's chest, centering it between his breasts. The sailor pressed Tobey's breasts in toward each other, forming a sheath for his prick, and he began to hump up and down inside the passage he had created. The head of his prick pressed against Tobey's chin each time he thrust. Tobey reached behind Tony and played with his busy ass-cheeks while the sailor—in effect—fucked his chest.

Jason moved to stand behind Tony's ass, and he said, "Hold it open for me, Tobey." Tobey's hands pulled Tony's ass-cheeks apart, revealing the pink hole, winking at Jason. Jason put the tip of his cock at Tony's asshole, and began to press forward. Plenty of lubricant had obviously been used when Tobey had started to fuck Tony, since Jason's prick slipped in easily, accompanied by a great sigh of pleasure from the sailor.

While Jason fucked, Tony pushed Tobey's body away from him, so that the tip of his cock trembled only an inch or so from the boy's lips. "Eat my cock while Jason fucks me," he growled, and Tobey opened his mouth wide and complied.

Jason peered around Tony's body to watch Tobey suck the sailor's cock. The boy was moving his lips up and down Tony's shaft, working so hard to do a good job he often took too much dick inside his mouth, and gagged. When Jason began to watch, Tobey was only taking about two-thirds of the shaft of Tony's cock in his mouth, but within just a few minutes, he was taking almost all of it, sucking hard, and moaning in excitement.

When Tony's load began to shoot, it discharged so forcefully that Tobey spluttered and gagged for a second or two before he got it under control and ate everything else Tony could give him. Tony had no more than finished blowing his load before Jason cried, "I'm coming," and filled his ass with cum.

Tobey had sucked every drop of cum out of Tony's cock, but he waited a minute or so for Jason to finish his orgasm before he stood and pushed Tony rudely away, bending him over the side of the hot tub, and thrusting his prick inside the sailor's ass in one fierce plunge. "Jesus, Tony, you're full of cum!"

While Tobey fucked Tony mercilessly, Jason knelt behind him and tongue-fucked his busy ass. In short order, Tobey's load was supplementing the pool of cum inside Tony.

Eventually, when all had calmed down, Tony stood and faced Tobey, taking him in his arms and kissing him. "You're a great buttfucker!" He reached out to Jason, who stood and joined the embrace. "Two great buttfuckers," Tony added as he kissed Jason. "Okay, when do I get to fuck some butt?"

Tobey was anxious for Tony to fuck him, but he confessed that he wasn't sure he could take all of his prick.

"Sure you can," Tony promised. "I'll take it easy, and before you know it you'll have ten inches of hard cock inside that pretty ass."

They adjourned to Jason's bedroom, where Tobey was, indeed, able to take every inch of dick Tony could give him—while Tony cooed in his ear and slipped his monster prick in slowly, and while Jason held him and whispered encouragement. Once Tony had all ten inches inside, he began to fuck slowly at first, but as both boys grew more and more excited, it turned into an all-out, no-holds-barred serious fuck that had both fucker and fuck-ee screaming in thrill and triumph as Tony's load blasted palpably ten inches deep inside Tobey's voracious ass.

The three made love for several hours, each fucking, each getting fucked, each sucking off one of the others, each getting sucked off. Near dawn, they called it quits for the time being. It was getting light as Tony headed back for the base, leaving Jason and Tobey nestled in each other's arms, each as satisfied sexually as he could imagine.

While Tobey and Tony and Jason got together for threesomes, they also met in various twosome combinations—Tobey and Tony, Tobey and Jason, Tony and Jason—and they met for sex with others on their own,—without apparently being troubled by any jealousy.

From his usual post in the store, Jason could see the stairs leading up to Tobey's apartment, and he frequently saw him taking tricks up there. He also observed boys and men in the store hook up with Tobey—often ones he had earlier hooked up with himself. Tobey usually shared stories of his sexual escapades with Jason, and made frequent trips downstairs to Jason's bedroom at night to either have sex with him, to introduce him to a trick who was interested in a threesome, or to offer to join Jason and a trick he was having sex with at the time; no one *ever* objected to having the beautiful young Adonis with the build of Hercules join him and Jason in making love—and some of those were often seen later, ascending the stairs to Tobey's apartment for a private tryst.

One afternoon, Jason observed Tobey leading a child up the outside stairs leading to his apartment. The boy stayed upstairs for about two hours, and then left by himself, grinning dazedly, seeming to be walking on air, his shirt pulled out of his Levi's, where it had been tucked in when he went upstairs—in short, exhibiting all the signs of the happiness that follows a good fuck. It was impossible for Jason to get a close look at the boy, but he appeared to be about twelve years old—far, *far* too young to be having sex with a boy ready to begin his junior year in college!

Jason tried not to worry; what Tobey did was his own business, after all. But he did love the boy, and

193

couldn't help worry that he might be heading for trouble with a minor sex partner. He confronted his young lover with his concern that night.

Tobey laughed. "You're talking about Sean. Sean Gayle. Believe me, he's no kid."

"I saw him going up to your apartment yesterday. I wasn't spying, but I was curious when I saw how young he looked—like about twelve! You know, if you go to jail for sex with a minor, you're not going to be able to pick your sex partners—and I doubt any of the ones who pick you are going to look like Tony Lowe!"

"Jason—he's nineteen years old. He's a Freshman at Paulik, but he's just really small." Tobey grinned, "He's not small everywhere, though, believe me. You wouldn't believe the dick on him. You wanna see it? Prove to you he's not a kid?"

"You don't need to prove anything," Jason said. "You say he's eighteen, I believe you." Then he grinned, "But yeah, I'd like to see it anyway. Will he show it to me?"

"I'm sure he'd like to show it to you. He says he loves to show it off. Guys come on to him in the shower in the dorm, and he likes to tease 'em, and usually fucks one of 'em or lets one suck him off—especially if there are other guys hanging around to watch. He says if a guy is really cute he'll suck his dick or take him up the butt, even if there's no one around to watch—but he likes it better if he has an audience. He gets a lot of action out at City Park—that's where I first saw him.

"I went into the clearing, and there were a bunch of guys clustered around a picnic table. I went over to check it out, and there was this big, really muscular guy bent over the table, naked, while a naked kid was hammering his ass. The guy was really cute, too, and he was so much taller than the kid fucking him—Sean, of course—that he had his legs bent under the table to bring his asshole down to the level of Sean's dick. There were five or six other guys standing around, jacking off while they watched—a couple of them were naked, and the rest had their dicks pulled out. I still had my cock in my pants, but it was hard as hell.

"I began to realize the kid wasn't as young as I had thought. Watching his ass while he fucked, it was obvious he was shoving a *lot* of dick up the guy's ass. Once his cock slipped out, and he stroked it a few times before he rammed it back in; it was fuckin' *enormous!* He mighta looked like a midget fucking a giant, but the midget had a lot bigger dick than the giant. He pulled it out again at the last minute, and blew a huge load all over the big guy's back, while the guys standing around whistled and clapped. Then the little guy leaned over the big guy to kiss his neck, and when he stood up there was some of his own cum smeared on his chest—most of it was on the big guy's back, of course. One of the other naked guys stepped up next to Sean, and he stepped aside. The new guy shoved his cock in where Sean's had been, and started fucking while he licked Sean's cum off the big guy's back."

Jason asked, "The new guy wasn't you, by any chance, was he?

"No," Tobey grinned, "but I was hoping to be next in line—the big guy had a fabulous ass. Sean had stared at me a lot while he was fucking the big guy, and he came over to me after he finished—his dick was still pretty hard, and he had a lot of his own cum on his chest, and a string of it hanging down from his pee-hole. He started playing with my chest, and asked me, 'Did that turn you on?' I told him it had—in a big way—and he started to unbutton my pants. He said 'Show me how excited it made you.'

"I pulled my pants and shorts down below my dick—needless to say, it was hard as a rock—and he dropped to his knees and pulled 'em down to my ankles. Then he took my cock in his mouth, all the way to the base in one swoop, and started sucking like crazy, while one of his hands reached up under my shirt and played with my tits, and his other one scooped his cum off his chest before he brought it up between my legs and smeared it on my asshole, lubing it up for his finger. Then he started to finger-fuck me while I hung on to his head and fucked his mouth as hard as I could. I wanted it to go on forever, but it was too fuckin' exciting; I blew my load in his throat after only about five minutes.

"Sean stood up, with this little smile that looked kinda... I don't know... *cramped*, until I realized what he had done. He had kept my load in his mouth, and when he turned to face the guys who were standing around watching us, he let the cum drizzle out into the palm of his hand. He grinned back at me, showing the handful of white cum he had, then he turned back to the others and licked it out of his palm until it was all gone. He got another good round of applause for that.

"We kissed, and I could taste my cum on his tongue. There was still some of his cum on his chest, and I licked it of before we kissed again. He whispered, 'I want you to fuck me almost as much as I wanna fuck you. But just you 'n' me, someplace where we can take our time and do it right. How does that sound?' Well, I'd already decided I wanted to fuck with him, but when he told me he thought I was gorgeous, and I had the best body he'd seen in a long time, I knew it was gonna happen." He laughed, "I say that with all modesty, of course."

"He obviously has good taste," Jason chuckled.

"If you say so," Tobey said. "Anyway, we made a date to come over here, and that was when you spotted him. He left the clearing that afternoon—well, he went off into the bushes with another naked guy—and I hung around and watched while a couple of other guys fucked the big guy on the picnic table.

"You mean you didn't fuck him, too?"

"Yeah, I did; you know me too well, Jason! But after I shot my load up his ass he turned around and sat on the edge of the table. He wrapped his arms around me and pulled me in to kiss me. He said it was his turn, if I was willing. The guy was cute, and he was hung, and his body was fuckin' fantastic. So, I climbed up on the table and sat down on his dick, and I rode it while we necked with each other, until he came inside me. By that time, nobody was watching — they were all making out with each other. Hell, I made dates with a couple of other really hot ones before I left.

"The day after Sean came over here, I met with one of those guys in his room on campus, at the dormitory. We fucked and sucked for an hour or so, and then he asked if I would go to the shower with him — he wanted to show me off. You remember me telling you how I hated going to the showers in the dorm when I lived there? Well, it was fun this time. We walked down the hall to the showers with our hard-ons wagging, and it was like we were Pied Pipers — guys followed us down to the shower, and it turned into an orgy. Hotter'n hell! But anyway, to get back to your question…"

"Jesus, I've forgotten what it was, after that story," Jason laughed.

"You asked if I thought Sean would show you his dick. Obviously, you can tell he'd love to show it to you, and I'm pretty sure he'd wanna do more with it than just whip it out so you can see it and admire it."

"There are a lot of ways to show admiration for a big dick besides just looking at it, and if he's as hot as you say, I'd like to see how many ways I can admire his. When can you get him to come back? I'd love to try a threesome."

"Well, I ought to tell you, when you get in bed with Sean, and start holding him, or when you're hanging on to him while you fuck him, it's a little creepy," Tobey said.

"Creepy? How so?"

"Well, he's so small, that you get the feeling you're holding a kid in your arms, especially when you're hugging and kissing him, but almost as much so when you play with his body when you're fucking him. When he rides your dick, though, it's not a problem. Looking up at him and watching the look on his face and the sight of his dick flopping, there's no mistaking that he's a man. You'd never mistake him for a young boy while you're sucking his cock, or while he's fucking you with it; that prick could only belong to a man!"

Undeniably, Sean was childlike in stature—he was less than five feet tall, and weighed slightly under a hundred pounds—but while his body was diminutive, it was perfectly proportioned and lightly muscled. Seen next to a normal-size man, he looked like a child, but if seen alone, with nothing next to him that might be used for comparison, he looked perfectly normal. If he was naked, however—seen alone or next to another—his cock was not at all in perfect proportion to the rest of his body, nor could he be mistaken for a boy.

In actuality, Sean's prick was slightly over nine inches long when it was fully erect, and extremely fat in proportion to its length. On a man of average height—say, six feet—a fat, nine-inch cock looks tremendous...*is* tremendous, in fact. But when that same prick juts out from a body that is more than a foot shorter, it looks twenty percent longer in comparison. In effect, Sean's cock appeared to be about eleven inches long—something past tremendous, a prick that appeared breathtaking, even mind-boggling to anyone who is attracted by large cocks—and damned few gay men are *not* attracted by large cocks (there are few exceptions to the old adage that declares 'There are only two kinds of gay men, size queens and liars.').

By nature, Sean was friendly and sweet, but when it came to sex, he was a different person. He used his outsized cock with an intensity that demonstrated the consummate mastery—*artistry*, even—that he brought to the art of lovemaking. He wanted to dominate his sex partner, and—considerations of personal chemistry between him and the other man or boy being equal—the greater the disparity between his size and his partner's, the more he wanted to dominate him. Yet his lovemaking was basically affectionate, no matter how intense it might become; there was nothing sadistic or brutal in his domination—he just liked being *in charge.*

A psychiatrist might have said Sean's attitude toward lovemaking was symptomatic of a "Napoleonic complex," a way of compensating for diminutive stature, but Sean also liked to be dominated when he bottomed. Although he was more oriented toward topping his sex partners, he loved sucking dick and getting fucked almost as much—and he wanted his partners to fuck his mouth or his ass with the same ferocity he employed when he fucked them. Even in bottoming, however, he often demonstrated his propensity to take charge; if someone wasn't fucking him hard enough, Sean made sure he did! When he was snuggling and kissing with another boy, not actually having sex, he was a different person, submissive and seemingly dependent; he adored being held tightly in the arms of a big man—the more muscular the arms, and the bigger the man, the better—feeling protected, and *safe.*

Safety was something Sean had felt little of as a child, growing up. He was bullied because of his size, and it was not until his freshman year of high school that his life changed—and it was mostly because of sex. Oddly enough, he had matured much more quickly than his peers. He had his first orgasm when he was barely twelve, and had begun masturbating at least twice daily after that. When other boys of his age had proudly displayed a wispy growth of pubic hair over their cocks, Sean had a full pubic bush over his outsized member, and he had already begun shaving when he entered high school, although not yet daily.

When Sean was a Freshman in high school, a Junior—a member of the wrestling team, with an awesome body for his age—had one afternoon come across three boys roughing him up in the woods near their school. He sprang to Sean's defense, and the bullies quickly fled from the huge, muscular boy who stepped in to protect their would-be prey.

Left alone, the two sat down next to each other, with their backs against a tree, while Sean gave vent to his frustration, telling his protector how miserable his life was. As much as he did not want to, Sean broke down and began crying. The older boy—Danny—took Sean in his arms, cuddling and consoling him until he calmed down. Sean felt so protected with Danny's massive arms wrapped around him, that he made no move to leave that protection. They talked about inconsequential things, and Danny discovered that he was holding a fourteen-year-old in his arms, not the much younger boy he had assumed Sean to be.

Lying there in the comfort of his savior's arms, Sean began to get an erection. He had never had sex with another boy—although he had wanted to for a couple of years by that time, and was already positive that sex with a girl was not something he wanted at all. The size of his erection attracted Danny's attention; two years earlier, the older boy had decided that he liked boys better than girls, and that he liked boys with big dicks much better than he liked other boys. Soon the two were lying on the pine needles, making love to each other the way Sean had dreamed of doing. Sean's stepfather had a collection of gay male pornography, which the boy had often studied in secret, and he knew exactly what he wanted to do with another boy if he ever got the opportunity.

Although he had never had sex before, within two hours after being rescued from his tormentors that afternoon, Sean had realized virtually all his ambitions. He had adored being sucked off, and when he took Danny's dick up the ass, he realized why the actors in his stepfather's porn collection—Casey Donovan, for instance—had looked so happy and thrilled when they were getting fucked. Danny's prick had not been unusually large, so Sean easily deep-throated it when he sucked him off, and the pain was not too great when he took it up the ass — moreover, Sean had practiced with dildos of various size he had also found in his stepfather's dresser, so he was ready.

The older boy had a fairly active gay sex life, but he had never yet had a cock the size of Sean's. He eagerly commanded Sean to fuck him — ever deeper, harder, and faster — and was so thrilled by the boy's performance that his praise inspired Sean to a level of lovemaking that completely belied his inexperience, but which revealed a great natural aptitude. Had Sean told the boy to whom he was giving his virginity that it was his first time to make love — which he didn't — Danny would not have believed him.

They continued to have sex with each other until Danny graduated, although they did not confine their activities to one another. Each time they made love together — on well over a hundred occasions — Sean's confidence grew, until by the time Danny graduated, *no one* gave Sean any more trouble because he was small — his new attitude and his reputation insured that. And by then Danny was like sexual putty in the hands of the diminutive *fuckmaster* during their lovemaking, but whom he always enfolded and protected in his huge arms following their coupling.

Everyone in the school who cared about such things knew that little Sean Gayle had one of the biggest cocks in school, and fucked like a lion! The boy with the *biggest* cock in school, according to those same people who cared about such things, reported that Sean was one of the very few boys or men he had ever fucked who had taken every inch of cock he had to offer, and wanted — no, *commanded* — even more.

His newfound assurance opened all sorts of extracurricular avenues for Sean to pursue at school, but aside from having gay sex—his principal interest and avocation—the thing that came to occupy most of his time was drama.

Because of his size, Sean was always cast as a child, which did not bother him—after all, he was smaller than almost everyone he shared the stage with—and even though his speaking voice was deepening normally as he grew older, he was able to project it in an upper register, so that he could even sound like a child. He proved to be a very capable young actor, and was soon a mainstay in the high school drama group and the local community theatre as well. When his high school graduation drew near, he was offered a scholarship in drama at Paulik University. Sean was excited; after all, Paulik was a good school, and it was rumored to be Utopia for a gay student. He ac- cepted the scholarship, and discovered that its reputation in both academic and sexual areas was well deserved.

Tobey brought Sean into The Book Cellar one afternoon, and introduced him to Jason. It was clear that Sean was a child only in stature, and Jason felt no com- punction about accepting Tobey's offer to watch the store for him while Sean and he went upstairs to make love. As it happened, Jason found that Tobey's description of the feeling he had while he made love with the diminutive, but very studly boy, was on the mark—'a little creepy.' He had to admit that while he sometimes felt like he was having sex with a child, it excited him mightily, and it made him feel slightly guilty for being so turned on by the experience. Fortunately, the size of Sean's cock, and his persuasive lovemaking constantly reminded Jason that he was no child, which eventually dissipated Jason's uneasiness. When Sean was actually making use of the man-sized-*plus* instrument that hung between his legs, Jason was fully aware that he was in bed with a fully mature young man; all guilt vanished then.

When Tobey locked the store and came upstairs at 6:00 that evening, he immediately stripped and joined them in bed. Sean welcomed him so eagerly that he and Tobey were for a while oblivious to Jason's presence. The odd feeling of perceived pedophilia came back to Jason while he watched the tiny boy and the much larger, superbly muscled older boy making frenzied love to each other. Jason found he was far more turned on by watching the mismatched studs having sex than he expected he would be, just as he been surprised at his excessive enjoyment while he, himself, had made love with this boy who felt like a child in his embrace. Yet, he still felt, in some small corner of his mind, that he was acting like a pedophile, although he knew he was not.

Tobey and Sean did not at first shut Jason out of their lovemaking intentionally, but each was so wrapped up in what he was doing with the other that he frequently forgot Jason was there — and Jason didn't mind; he was enjoying the show they were putting on. After Tobey had taken the edge off his horniness by blowing his first load down the boy's throat, Jason joined them in an all-out, extremely satisfying threesome. During their threesome, they did something none of them had done before:

Tobey had gone into the bathroom, and when he returned, Jason and Sean were lying on the bed, hugging and kissing. Tobey turned a side chair so that it faced them, and he sat down to watch them make love. Jason became aware that Tobey was sitting there, instead of joining them. He said, "What are you waiting for?"

"I'm just enjoying the sight of you two guys making it," Tobey replied, stroking his hard cock, which stood straight up out of his groin. "Hot!"

Sean broke Jason's embrace and jumped out of bed. He walked over to Tobey and straddled his legs. He bent down slightly and kissed his mouth. "We missed you," he said, He then stood, and aimed his cock at Tobey's mouth, which opened wide to admit it. Sean fucked Tobey's mouth as Tobey's hands fondled his ass. After Tobey had sucked his cock for a few minutes, Sean reached down and behind himself to hold Tobey's cock in position at his asshole as he sank down on it until it was completely buried in his ass. Sean wrapped his arms around Tobey's neck, and they began to kiss as the boy bobbed up and down, fucking himself on Tobey's big shaft. Tobey rose to his feet and began to carry Sean to the bed, his enormous arms wrapped around the boy's trim little body and his cock still planted all the way in his little ass.

Tobey stopped after a couple of steps and said, grinning into Sean's face, "Wish I could ride your dick like you're riding mine."

"I love it," Sean said, and began bobbing up and down on Tobey's cock again.

Jason stood and stepped up behind Sean, positioning his cock at the boy's asshole, which was already filled with Tobey's own cock, of course. "Can you take two cocks at once?" he asked Sean.

"I don't know," Sean smiled, turning his head to look at Jason. "I've seen it done in a movie, but I never tried it. Let's see what happens."

Very gradually, but firmly, Jason pressed the head of his cock against Sean's sphincter, which was stretched tightly over the fat shaft buried inside his ass; Sean's ass and both cocks were already well lubricated, and Jason's prick gradually began to slip inside, alongside Tobey's. Sean grunted and puffed, cautioning Jason to go easy, but he never called a halt. Soon the boy had two pricks inside him, and he gasped, "Jesus Christ, that feels incredible. Fuck me, both of you!"

Very tentatively at first, until they established a rhythm, both Tobey and Jason began to fuck Sean, and the grip of his ass was amazingly tight—not surprising, considering the volume of cock inside it. They soon realized that if one drove his cock in while the other was pulling his back, the friction of them rubbing together added to the sensation. Sean screamed his excitement, and tried to bob up and down on the two dicks inside him, but once Jason and Tobey established their alternating thrusts, he was unable to do much more that just sit on them and enjoy it, held in the air by Tobey's strong arms and the two pricks impaling him — and he enjoyed it about as much as he had ever yet enjoyed anything in his life! It was uncommonly gratifying for Tobey and Jason as well, and the three were lost in fuck-lust, Sean kissing Tobey voraciously, and Jason sucking and biting Sean's shoulders and reaching between his two partners to play with Sean's dick and Tobey's tits.

The massive Tobey was extraordinarily strong, and Sean was extremely light, so fatigue did not become a problem as Tobey continued to stand there, holding the boy up the entire time he and Jason double-fucked him. The singular excitement of the dual penetration probably would have added greater endurance if it had been needed.

Presently, Tobey cried, "I'm coming," and both he and Jason stopped fucking, holding their cocks still — held together so tightly that Jason could actually feel, with the shaft of his cock, Tobey's cum coursing up through *his* shaft on its way to eruption within the confines of Sean's ass. A split second later, Jason could feel Tobey's hot jism spilling out forcefully over the top of his own cock, and flowing around his shaft. Tobey cried "Aaaaahhhh!" just as Jason heard Sean echo Tobey's scream, and felt Sean's cum begin to shoot out and flow downward to coat his hand. It was so doubly exciting, that Jason needed no further stimulus; his own orgasm exploded to add to the hot, viscous pool that his and Tobey's cocks were bathing in, and his voice made the chorus of excitement and satisfaction a trio.

After a few moments, they fell to the bed in exhaustion, breaking their union, leaving Sean on his back between them. All three laughed and gasped their happiness for a few moments until Sean leaned over and licked his own cum from Tobey's chest—that awe-inspiring chest—and Jason followed suit, licking Sean's cum from the boy's own chest. They embraced and fondled and kissed as a threesome for some time before they got in the shower together—where their sexual horseplay made for an unbelievably extended and inefficient cleansing, but a thoroughly enjoyable aftermath to their lovemaking.

All three of them had a rather surprising number of boys with whom they had continuing sexual liaisons, although none of those relationships were serious, or seemed likely to develop into real *affairs*. Jason could easily have fallen in love with Tony, Tobey could easily have fallen in love with Jason *or* Tony, and Sean might have already fallen in love with Tobey. But all resisted any inclination toward monogamy; they were having too much fun sowing their wild oats broadly.

Living on campus, and given his physical unique-ness, Sean was presented with far the greatest variety of opportunities for wild-oat sowing, and he took advantage of them. As a result, he visited with Tobey and Jason less frequently after their first threesome than he might have liked to, but he did visit regularly. Tobey, with his glorious body, appealed to the diminutive Sean more than anyone he was having sex with regularly, and they met in Sean's room at the dormitory more frequently than they did in Tobey's apartment at Jason's house; there, they usually got together as a threesome with Jason in his bedroom. Sean liked Jason very much, and if Tobey was not at home when he came to call, he happily went to bed with Jason alone, if it was convenient. Still, although it was Tobey he was really interested in, even when he and Tobey were both making love with Jason, the double-fuck that Tobey and Jason invariably gave him at some point every time they got together was something he particularly enjoyed. They had developed a few different ways to achieve their double penetration—more comfortable, although not any more exciting—than the standing one they had employed the first time they did it. Sean had done it with a few other couples after his initial foray, but it was the Tobey-Jason pairing that seemed *right* to him, and most enjoyable.

Sean never let two boys fuck him simultaneously when he was making love publicly, in the showers or in the clearing at City Park, or in the occasional orgy he participated in—like those that were relatively common in the shower rooms, or the tangle of fucking, sucking actors and male techies he had once been part of on the stage of the empty Community Theatre; he was afraid things could get out of hand, and to take two dicks in his ass at the same time required more trust and care than he could count on if they did.

8.

LIFE UPON THE WICKED STAGE
— ACT ONE

When Jason learned about Sean's work in the theatre, he realized he had seen him before, although the name had not 'rung a bell' when they first met.

Sean had played the part of Tommy, the youngest family member in a Paulik Players' production of *Ah, Wilderness!* earlier that year — normally a child's role, since 'Tommy' is supposed to be eleven years old. Jason had seen the show, and was especially attracted to the very cute boy playing the part of Richard, an older brother. That same boy was a sometime customer at The Book Cellar, and however sexy he was, Jason had never made a pass at the eighteen-year-old, although he could tell immediately the boy was gay: He and the other student who always accompanied him were obviously boyfriends. Jason had not read the cast bios in the program for *Ah, Wilderness!*, so he did not realize that the actor playing Tommy — Sean, of course — was not a child; had he done so, he might have felt less guilty about his distinctly sexual response to the presumably pre-teenaged boy.

While in the Navy, and as a Paulik student as well, Jason had himself been active in both the Paulik Players and the local Community Theatre. He had not appeared on stage since his graduation from Paulik, but he never missed seeing a show staged by either group. He often visited with the Artistic Director of the Community Theatre, Lake McCoy, a flamboyant gay man whose considerable professional ability had made him a much-loved and respected part of the community for decades, and whose caution and tact in his sex life had enabled him to practice it without endangering that community acceptance. Lake was also a frequent Guest Director for the University drama group.

There is an unusually high percentage of gay men in almost any theatrical group, especially among those involved in the 'artistic' aspect; the techies (those working in technical areas) are usually far less likely to be gay. In Hus Bay and at Paulik University, given the unique situation and the tradition, percentages in both areas were higher than might normally be expected. Jason had enjoyed many satisfactory sexual adventures that were born of his involvement in the local theatres. He had often been involved in plays where every male member of the cast was either openly gay, or simply enjoyed gay sex. Among those latter, Jason felt that many of them were not just bisexual, but were more likely closet cases.

The extreme preponderance of males in Hus Bay had bearing on the shows the theatre groups presented. Plays that required a majority of male actors were obvious candidates for selection, and all-male casts were not uncommon. Prison dramas like *Fortune and Men's Eyes*, and military dramas, like *Mister Roberts* or *Stalag 17* were a mainstay of the repertory in Hus Bay. As a student, Jason had enacted the title role in the Paulik Players' production of *Mister Roberts,* and fucked his way through almost the entire large cast before the run of the show ended.

Jason was four years older than most of his classmates, and he was apparently so effective in playing the part of characters who were supposed to be considerably older than his own actual age, that he was frequently called on to do so.

Nudity began to find its way into mainstream American theatre in the late 1960's. *Hair* opened in 1968; *Oh, Calcutta!* and *Fortune and Men's Eyes* were not far

210

behind. By the time the nude scene in the prestigious *Equus* came along, no one was much shocked by it any longer. Lake McCoy was excited by the liberation of theatre that nudity in live drama represented to him. While that attitude was genuine, he also loved to see naked boys on stage, and especially working with naked boys in the role of Director.

At about the same time that nudity was becoming accepted on the stage, gay-themed plays were also appearing and gaining acceptance. Lake's special interest in this area of theater was similarly motivated by both his pioneering spirit and his homosexuality.

Watching a gorgeous, young, naked Don Johnson, the future television star, seemingly being raped by another man in the 1969 New York production of *Fortune and Men's Eyes* was so exciting to Lake that he was fired with a determination to treat Hus Bay audiences to both nudity and gay drama as soon as he could.

Both City and University officials were progressive enough that they supported Lake's projects; considering the prevailing climate of permissiveness toward gay sex in the city and its environs, it was not a great stretch for them. With the Community Theatre he directed a production of the very mild 1953 play *Tea and Sympathy* — a show about a student in an all-male prep school who is perceived by fellow students as gay — although he is probably not — and which does not include any nudity. Later in the same season Lake pulled some strings and was able to receive special license to stage the con- troversial, uncompromising, all-male gay drama *Boys in the Band* with the Paulik Players — no nudity yet, but a huge step forward in preparing audiences and adminis- trators to accept the trend toward gay theatre. Both shows were wildly popular, and had extended runs.

Lake waited a season before he brought nudity to the stage in Hus Bay, when he directed *Fortune and Men's Eyes*, with the University group. The boy who played 'Smitty,' the gay rape victim, had been carefully selected from an amazingly large number of students auditioning specifically for the part, each of whom understood that if he won the part, he would be appearing naked on stage for several minutes, while another naked boy stood behind him and simulated fucking his ass. In addition to dramatic skill, Lake considered each auditioner's further qualifications regarding his facial beauty, his physique, the size of his cock, and his ability to keep from getting an erection while another boy's cock was pressing and humping his ass — in effect, dry-fucking him (Lake was sure audiences were not ready to see hard-ons on stage!).

Auditions for the role of Smitty, and an unusual number of 'call-backs,' were as pleasant and as stimulating for the actors trying out for the part as they were for Lake. Each boy had to strip at one point and lean over a chair, propping himself up with his arms, while another naked auditioner stood behind him and dry-fucked him. Quite often the one simulating the fuck popped a boner, even though the one pretending to be fucked did not; Lake was not worried about that — he could block the scene to conceal that actor's hard-on, if necessary.

Considering all factors involved in making his selection, Lake was left with two candidates who met all criteria except adequate control of their erections, Joey and Clay. Both finalists were extremely well-hung, and both were show-ers, rather than grow-ers, so that even when their cocks were dangling limply, they looked extremely large.

Joey was able to avoid getting a hard-on while Clay was pretending to fuck him, but when he got behind the other boy and humped his ass, his cock grew hard *and enormous* almost immediately, as it had done with most of the other boys he pretended to fuck during the whole series of call-backs. Clay had kept his erection under control with every auditioner except Joey. As soon as Joey so much as touched his ass with his prick, his own came to attention. Naturally Joey was cast as Smitty, and Clay won the role of the prisoner who fucks him.

After Lake told the two finalists of their respective assignments, Clay confessed that he was gay, and that he was basically a bottom. He looked at Joey as well as at Lake when he confessed he also thought that Joey was so unbelievably hot he couldn't avoid a hard-on when he felt his cock touch him. He added that even though he was a bottom, the other boy's ass was so perfect he couldn't avoid getting a hard-on when he stood behind him, pressing his prick against it.

Joey grinned and confessed he was also gay, but was mostly a top. "You got a pretty hot ass yourself," he said, and walked over to Clay as he added, while he played with the boy's tits, "and that's some dick, too. It feels really hard, and really good when you're back there pretending to fuck me. You won't try sticking that up my ass one night during the show, will you? I may be mostly a top, but I enjoy takin' a cock up my ass once in a while, and you may be mostly a bottom, but I'll bet you've fucked a lotta butt, too. I'm not saying I wouldn't enjoy you fuckin' my butt, but who knows what would happen if I suddenly felt you slipping it to me in front of an audience one night?"

"Okay, guys," Lake broke in. "Clay, you have to promise not to actually fuck Joey no matter how excited you get. Right?" The second boy agreed. "But just to be sure, let's find out. Fuck him."

"Really fuck him? Now?" Clay asked, as shocked at the suggestion as he was excited by it.

"Yes. That okay with you?" he asked Joey. "I mean, you both sound like you're ready to go to bed together as soon as you leave here, anyway."

Joey bent over the chair and grinned at Clay. "Give it to me," he said as he reached behind and spread his ass cheeks. Lake reached into his briefcase and produced a tube of lubricant, which he threw to Clay. He had

anticipated that this problem—or one something like it—
might arise.

As soon as he began to grease Joey's ass, Clay's prick
grew fully hard—throbbing and bobbing, and jutting out a
very impressive distance. He applied lube to it, and
pressed the head against Joey's asshole. "You ready?" Joey
nodded his assent, and Clay steadily pushed his hips
forward as his cock sank deep inside Joey. Joey gasped
and groaned as it entered him. Clay asked, "You want me
to go easier? Or stop?"

"God no!" Joey said. "It feels wonderful—give it all
to me." And Clay not only gave it to Joey, he hammered
the boy with it. He may have fancied himself as primarily
a bottom, but it was clear he was an extraordinarily
effective top. Both boys were panting and crying out in
abject lust, but even though Clay's huge prick was driving
in and out of him ferociously, in the kind of deep strokes
only possible if the top has a dick as long as Clay's, Joey's
cock retained its flaccid state. It was extremely long—a
length that would have done most men proud if it were
what they attained in erection—and in truth it had grown
somewhat, but it still dangled down and swung back and
forth while Clay fucked his ass so exuberantly.

Lake was so excited that he had opened his pants
and pulled out his own cock. He masturbated while he
watched, but the two boys were so involved in what they
were doing, they never noticed. When it became clear that
Clay was about to blow his load, Lake moved to stand in
front of Joey to watch his cock for signs of a hard-on. With
a huge cry, Clay threw his head back and squeezed his
eyes shut as he discharged his cum deep inside Joey's ass,
and he held on tight to the boy's waist and kept his prick
buried inside the tight chute as his lust began to subside.

Joey looked up at Lake, grinning. "Did I pass the
test?"

"Yeah," Lake said, panting with excitement and still
jacking off.

214

"That was because I wasn't doing what I normally would while someone was fuckin' me. But since the test is over... "Joey reached behind and pulled Clay's ass in tightly as he began to revolve his hips, and hump his ass back and forth on the still-hard prick inside it. Immediately, his own prick began to swell and lengthen, and as he stood up, causing Clay's prick to slip from inside him, it stood straight out, trembling, fat and glorious. "You want some of this, professor?" he asked Lake.

Lake had apparently been oblivious to the fact that he was masturbating, but Joey's question brought him back to reality. "Jesus, Joey, I... You're absolutely fuckin' gorgeous, but I don't fuck around with student actors when I'm directing a show. Do I *want* it? Hell yes, who wouldn't? But no, I can't, Joey."

"Well you sure as hell need some relief," Joey grinned as he knelt in front of Lake and looked up at him. "This is a special occasion, though, and since I did this to you..." He leaned forward to pull Lake's hand away from his cock, and to drive his lips all the way down to the base of it. He sucked profoundly, and Lake was unable to resist. While Joey sucked, Lake held his head tightly and fucked his mouth wildly. In only a few minutes Lake's body tensed, and he shot his load deep in Joey's throat. Joey swallowed the cum hungrily, then stood and smiled at Lake. "That better?"

Lake was so excited he was having trouble replying when Joey turned away from him and walked up to Clay. "I've gotta get off too. You said you were a bottom, didn't you? Give me the lube and get down there while I show you why I'm mostly a top."

Offering no objection, Clay kissed Joey and applied lube to Joey's cock. As he started to grease up his own ass, he asked, "How do you want me?"

"Get on your back and get your legs up in the air," Joey said, forcefully. As soon as Clay was in position, Joey knelt between his legs and thrust his prick deep inside the boy's ass in one fierce lunge. Clay screamed, more in surprise than in pain, and as Joey began to fuck him, he moaned and gasped his joy while Joey's cock slammed into him, ever more brutally.

While he was thrilling to Joey's fuck-frenzy, with his legs thrown over Joey's shoulders, Clay seized his prick and began masturbating; it was again fully hard. Joey noted this, and spoke to Lake, without looking at him. "He's hard again. Get down here and suck him off, professor."

"I can't, Joey; I told you...."

Joey turned his head and looked fiercely at Lake, continuing to fuck as he snarled, "I said, suck him off — give him what I gave you. I told you this was a special occasion, and you know you want to. Now, clean his dick with that T-shirt so I can watch you blow him while I fuck him."

Lake was still caught up in the delirium of the occasion, and quickly grabbed the T-shirt Joey had indicated and knelt to clean off Clay's cock. Clay grabbed his head, and forced it down over him. Had Lake not been such a widely experienced cocksucker, he would have gagged as Clay's enormous prick slammed against his throat.

Clay's body was immobilized by what Joey was doing to it, so he could not fuck upward into Lake's mouth, but he held the teacher's head tightly as he drove it up and down the length of his shaft. His tight grasp turned into loving caresses as Lake made it clear he needed no forcing to offer the kind of blowjob Clay wanted.

Being both fucked and sucked so expertly, Clay howled and gasped his appreciation for some ten minutes, until Joey seized his legs and raised them as high as they would go, thrust himself inside his ass as far as he could, and froze there while his load exploded inside his body. Joey's discharge was so forceful, that Clay could actually feel it spurting, which excited him so much that he again gripped Lake's head and blew his own load inside the director's mouth.

After they all calmed down, Joey apologized for being so dictatorial with Lake, commanding him to blow Clay. "I was so fuckin' worked up, I didn't know what I was doing."

Lake laughed, "You knew exactly what you were doing, Joey. I think you probably always do." Joey grinned, and admitted the truth in what Lake had said. "But look, you guys, this was — like you said, Joey — a special occasion. I just don't think it's right for me to have sex with my actors while I'm directing them — and the University definitely feels that way, too — so it's not gonna happen again."

"But it's still now, professor," Joey said, "and look: Clay got off twice, but you only got off once. That's not fair. Clay's got a perfect ass for fucking, believe me, and right now it's full of my cum. Why don't you fuck him in my hot load? That sound good to you, Clay?"

"Sounds great. C'mon and give it to me," Clay said, kneeling on all fours and wriggling his ass for Lake's admiration.

"Okay, Joey," Lake said as he rose and began to strip. "You're manipulating me again, but what the hell? I've already sucked him off tonight, might as well fuck him, too. He knelt behind Clay, between his legs, and applied lubricant to his cock. Lake's cock was not as big as either Joey's or Clay's, but it was nothing to be ashamed of.

"You're not gonna need to grease up Clay," Joey snickered. "I got him ready for you in a big way."

Clay looked back over his shoulder and said, "C'mon, give it to me."

Joey hissed in Lake's ear, "Fuck his ass, professor; give him another load." Lake seized Clay's waist and drove his cock deep inside with one fierce plunge. He began to fuck as Clay moaned and murmured encouragement. Joey asked, "How does my cum feel in there?"

217

"Christ, it's so fuckin' hot, Joey," Lake panted, " and you really filled him up." As he said that, he felt Joey's hand on his ass, smearing lubricant on his asshole.

"And I'm gonna fill you up, too," Joey whispered seductively in Lake's ear. "I've gotta get another load, too; it's only fair. Right, professor?" Lake was so drugged with passion that he didn't bother to reply, or to tell Joey to stop calling him 'professor,' since he as not a faculty member. He only removed his hands from Clay's waist and reached back to spread his ass-cheeks to welcome Joey's cock inside.

Fucking Clay while Joey was fucking him was somewhat awkward for Lake, and it took few minutes to arrive at a satisfactory rhythm, but once that was attained, all three enjoyed themselves enormously—and for a marvelously long time.

Lake was particularly happy: the handsome, well-built, endlessly sexy Joey was driving an enormous cock in and out of his ass while he panted his enjoyment and bit Lake's neck; Clay's ass was not only unexpectedly tight, it was writhing and humping ravenously, while he fucked himself on Lake's dick almost as much as Lake was fucking him. The sensation of Joey's hot cum inside Clay's ass, bathing his prick while he fucked into it, was thrilling to Lake. Clay was pinching his nipples and groaning in excitement while Lake fucked him, reaching around to stroke his cock—which, miraculously, was once again fully erect.

Amazingly, before either Lake or Joey blew their loads, Clay had a third orgasm, which flowed down Lake's hand while he continued to masturbate the boy. Lake and Joey's orgasms were not far behind, arriving only a few seconds apart. When Lake felt Joey's cum spurting fiercely inside him, it was all it took to put him over the edge, and he added his cum to Joey's inside Clay.

None of the three had ever experienced an audition that inspired the degree of enjoyment that one had—nor were they likely to ever do so again.

During the run of the show, Clay and Joey performed their parts well, and on two different occasions, Clay actually did fuck Joey during a performance, but Joey was able to keep his detachment by not working his ass around Clay's cock, but on both of those occasions he turned the tables and fucked Clay in the dressing room right after the final curtain—but there was actually nothing unusual about that, he did that after almost every performance!

Jason was a student at Paulik the year the Players presented *Equus*, and he played the part of young Alan Strang, a character whose age was supposed to be almost exactly that of Jason's at the time he portrayed him. Jason normally played characters older than his actual age, but, ironically, the student who played the other principal role, the older psychiatrist, Dysart, was younger than Jason. There is nudity in *Equus*, involving both the boy Alan and the girl Jill. As Alan, Jason had his first experience in appearing nude before a large audience; he had often appeared naked—and would still frequently appear that way—in front of relatively small audiences, when he took part in sexual threesomes, foursomes, and even orgies in the University dormitory, at the clearing in City Park, and a variety of locations.

The boy who played the psychiatrist was not especially attractive to Jason, so there was no real danger of his getting an erection in their long scene together when he was naked. Furthermore, the boys playing 'horses' were not evident when Alan was naked on stage with Dysart, which was fortunate, since the horses were quite another matter, and could easily have led Jason to get a hard-on had he been able to see them.

The boys who played the horses in the production were, to a man, extremely well-built and sexy; that was no coincidence, since Lake was guest-directing, and had cast them mostly because of their stunning bodies — with large chests and arms the principal criterion for selection. Almost no acting ability was required of them. The horses were bare-chested throughout, and wore low-slung tights that left little to the imagination about what was under them. Between the prominent codpieces they wore under the tights, and the way the stretched cloth outlined and emphasized every contour of their asses, their lower bodies were more arousing than if they had been completely naked. Seeing them frequently made Jason's cock hard, and following performances, all but one of them personally helped him get rid of an erection at least once during the run of the show.

By coincidence, the next play in which Jason would assume a role on stage with the Paulik Players after his graduation, a few years later, bore some surface resemblance to *Equus*. There was nudity, and a group of extremely well-built boys were involved, much like the *Equus* horses, but these would be even closer to naked than the horses had been.

The play was called *Absalom,* and it was Sean who indirectly involved first Tobey, then Jason in the production.

Although the local Community Theatre largely stayed with the tried-and-true repertory, the Paulik Players presented at least one new play each season, often fairly daring or even avant-garde — and usually directed by Lake McCoy. Lake always kept an eye out for new plays with all-male, or *almost* all-male casts. There were not many, and he constantly asked playwrights whose work he knew and admired, to write new scripts for Paulik that would be suitable for the all-male school, and his efforts were frequently rewarded. *Absalom* was such a play.

The man who wrote *Absalom* for Lake had known him since they were in school together at Yale, where they had often had sex together, and were even lovers at one point. Since then he had won a number of prestigious awards for new dramas; shortly before he wrote *Absalom*, he had been nominated for a Pulitzer Prize, and according to inside sources, had come close to winning it.

Normally, Lake would not have specified elements he wanted in a play being written for the Players; he often suggested some optimal elements he might like to find, but accepted what was written. With the new play that was eventually to be called *Absalom*, he felt free to specify a few things he wanted in the play, drawing on his long friendship and old relationship with the playwright, sealing the deal with an intense all-night threesome with the playwright and his current lover.

The features Lake wanted in the new play were: some nudity on the part of a character (or, better yet, characters) in the play who would be strong and virile — a warrior, or warriors, for example — and opportunity for plenty of mostly naked he-men to grace the stage. If the playwright could come up with artistic justification for plenty of fully undraped he-men, so much the better, but Lake wanted lots of eye-candy, in any case. Some element of homosexuality would also be most welcome.

The horses in *Equus* were cited as an example of the sort of eye candy Lake had provided for audiences a few years earlier, as was the nude scene with 'Alan Strang.' Ultimately, the playwright managed to adapt those elements from *Equus* into the tragedy he ultimately wrote for Paulik — a drama about King David and the death of his son, Absalom. It called for a Greek chorus of warriors — specifying in the script (at Lake's request) that they be clad only in sandals and a wide cloth sash around their waists. The title character, Absalom, is a very manly youth, who in the final section of the play is carried in from the battlefield, completely naked, where he dies in his father's arms in a lengthy scene that would provide the audience with a long, lingering view of the actor's naked body.

When the script arrived, it was perfect—embodying everything Lake wanted, in an outstanding, brilliantly written drama.

Lake asked Sean to play the part of Absalom as a child in the opening scenes of the play, and had asked him to be on the lookout for students with unusually impressive bodies whom he might contact as prospective cast members; the eight warriors who made up the Greek Chorus did not need to do much acting, but, ideally, they needed to be ultra-hunky and gorgeous. As he had with *Equus*, Lake especially wanted to cast hunks with broad chests, muscular arms and legs, and luscious tits.

Tobey Barksdale had the broadest chest, the most muscular arms and legs, and the most sumptuous tits of anyone Sean had ever had sex with, perhaps of anyone he had ever seen. Fortuitously, Sean and Tobey connected while Lake was formulating plans for *Absalom*, and his was the first name Sean suggested to Lake. After Sean had described Tobey's body, and Lake had checked out Tobey's picture in the University annual, he asked Sean to recruit the young stud while he continued scouting others.

Tobey had no theatrical experience, but he agreed to talk with Lake about it, and was assured that his duties would require minimal acting demands, a relatively small number of lines to be memorized, and the willingness to stand around almost naked while he watched the action on stage and occasionally commented on it in chorus with the other warriors of the Greek Chorus. In addition, he would have to strip completely naked in the final scene, but would show his genitals only briefly while he positioned himself facedown on the stage, displaying only his naked buttocks for the last few minutes of the show.

Tobey felt he was easily up to the demands of the role, and was definitely interested in being cast. He not only had no compunction about exposing himself on stage, but was eager to work with seven other extremely well-built boys who would be exposing themselves on stage – and hopefully working with some of those who might be willing to do more than just expose themselves when they were off-stage together.

The Director was flabbergasted at Tobey's body when he had the boy strip to see if he would fit the mold for the Greek Chorus he wanted to assemble. When Tobey was down to only his briefs, Lake whistled appreciatively, and said, "Wow, what a body! You've got the part if you want it."

He asked Lake, "You wanna see it all?"

"I'd love to see it all," Lake said, and then added, with regret, "but it's not really necessary."

"What the hell," Tobey said, as he pulled his shorts down and let them drop to his ankles. As he stepped out of his briefs, he could see that Lake was studying him like a starving man contemplating a seven-course dinner. He was excited to be showing himself off to someone who obviously appreciated his physical attributes. It didn't give him a full erection, but his cock was sufficiently engorged that it arced out alarmingly over the enormous bulge of his gigantic balls. He turned around slowly, so that Lake could study the perfection of his rounded buttocks. Lake was dumbfounded at the boy's body and his beauty.

"You'd better get dressed, Tobey, before I do something I shouldn't."

Tobey began stroking his prick, and it immediately began to stand out in front of him as he said, "Maybe I'd like to do something *we* shouldn't."

Lake explained about his avoiding sex with students he was working with in the theatre. "And besides, you don't have to do anything to get the part; believe me, you have it. I'm looking for guys with fantastic bodies – Jesus, there's no question you've got that!"

Tobey had continued stroking his dick while Lake spoke, and replied, "Even if you don't wanna have sex with me, is it okay if I..."

Lake laughed, "Tobey, I never said I didn't want to have sex with you, I just said I'm not going to."

"Well, is it okay if I beat off before I get dressed? I guess you can see I need to." He smiled, "I don't think it's gonna take long."

Lake gulped "Sure," and as Tobey began to jack off in earnest, he began to grope himself, and soon unzipped his trousers and pulled his own cock out. He began stroking it with ever-increasing excitement as Tobey wrapped the fingers of his right hand around his own prick and held them immobile while he fucked his fist, reaching behind with his left hand to finger-fuck his writhing, humping ass as he did so.

With the head of his cock poking in and out of his fist as he fucked it, and moaning with the thrill of the finger probing his ass, Tobey gradually walked up to approach Lake, who sat in his chair, savagely beating his own prick. As he came to stand only a step away, he used his fist to again stroke all the way up and down the shaft of his cock, and his left hand came around to grope his huge balls. He gasped, "I'm gonna come in a minute!"

"Oh *God*," Lake cried, "me too!"

Standing so close that the head of his prick was no more than six inches away from Lake's panting mouth, Tobey hissed, "You want it, don't you!" It had not been a question, nor did Lake bother to answer; he only opened his mouth wide.

The cum began spurting from Tobey's cock, as he screamed "Aaaaahhh!" and stopped masturbating to aim the hot white discharge into Lake's ravenous mouth. Most of the enormous load, which Tobey delivered in six or eight large spurts and innumerable smaller ones after that, went directly into Lake's mouth, but when Tobey had finished, there was cum all over Lake's lips, his chin, his cheeks, and his forehead.

Tobey grinned down at him as Lake swallowed and licked his lips before he released his cock and quickly swiped a hand over his forehead and chin, scooping up most of Tobey's cum. He smeared the handful of cum over his own prick, and resumed jacking off, using it as a lubricant. He slid forward on the chair, spreading his legs wide, and in a moment was shooting his own copious load out onto the floor in front of him. When he had completely finished, he slumped back on the chair, and seemed to collapse in exhaustion.

Tobey had watched carefully the whole while, and said, "That was really hot, Mr. McCoy." He walked forward and straddled Lake's legs, putting the tip of his cock to his lips; it was still dripping cum. "Kiss it goodbye," he whispered, and Lake opened his lips to suck the last few drops of cum from Tobey's cock before he bestowed the farewell kiss on the head.

"Tell me when we begin rehearsals," Tobey said, and winked before he turned around and began to put his clothes on. Lake watched his fabulous ass while he dressed, and asked Tobey to encourage any other extremely well-built students he might know, to audition for the Greek Chorus also. Tobey promised he would do so, and left.

Many of the most awesome bodies on campus were to be found among the members of the Weightlifting Club, but they were generally not interested in being associated with the drama group — *their* members were reputed to be gay — and although the weightlifters were not necessarily anti-gay (they were, after all, students at Paulik University!), they held themselves aloof as models of masculinity. Most of their sexual activity was intramural, confined to the membership of the club, involving mutual body worship, as well as the usual sucking and fucking and rimming that so many of their other fellow-students enjoyed; the only significant difference was that the weightlifters tended to kiss each other only while they were actually deep in the throes of heated sex.

Tobey had associated with the Weightlifting Club for a short time when he started school at Paulik, but the supposedly straight hunks were always hitting on him for sex, and he was always seeing them having sex with each other. At that time, he was still unaware how much he was interested in gay sex.

Although he had little success in recruiting members of the Weightlifting Club for *Absalom*, Tobey convinced one of them to audition, and a few other exceptionally well-built students as well. Sean also found several, and Lake had kept his eyes open for especially hunky boys on campus — as he always did, actually — and managed to find a sufficient number of others, so that the full complement of eight Greek Warriors was soon cast. While none of them auditioned as uniquely or excitingly as Tobey had — there were always two or three boys auditioning at the same time — Lake got to see every one of them completely naked, and one pair became so excited seeing each other naked they got hard-ons. Tobey had told one of that pair how his own audition had gone, so he was emboldened to begin to stroke the other's hard prick. Not surprisingly, Lake made no objection when that boy knelt in front of the other and sucked him off before he bent him over and fucked him.

Lake had one student in mind to play the title role in *Absalom* before the play had even been completely written: Thom Nelson.

Thom was a Junior at Paulik University, and had appeared in several productions of the Players and the Community Theatre. He was one of the most talented young actors Lake had worked with in years. He had short black curls wreathing his face. His large, light blue-gray eyes, were deep-set under an overhanging brow, with heavy eyebrows shaped like flattened "V"s, skewed dramatically to the outside. His prominent teeth were dazzlingly white, and his lips voluptuous. A broad face and prominent cheekbones combined with his heavy brow to suggest the facial structure of an Asian peasant. His muscular body also suggested that of a well-developed workingman — without the excessive development of a bodybuilder like Tobey. Thom was extremely handsome and physically striking, but he was not *beautiful*. Mostly he projected an earthy, almost palpable air of uncommon sexiness — ultra-masculine, but with no suggestion of brutishness. Both in face and in body, he resembled Rudolf Nureyev, in that great ballet dancer's younger days.

In auditioning for the role of Absalom — an audition that was mostly *pro forma*, since Lake was already all but sure he was going to cast him — Thom was required to strip. As many times as Lake had worked with Thom, he had never seen him without clothes, as much as he wanted to. Now he actually needed to see him that way. Absalom would be lying naked in front of an audience for almost ten minutes at the end of the play, and that could be a problem if the boy had an especially small cock, or even an enormously big one — either could be embarrassing, although Lake knew the latter would draw no complaints from audiences at Paulik or in Hus Bay, and would probably increase ticket sales considerably.

Thom was not hesitant about stripping in front of Lake, even though he was well aware the director was gay. He had spent a lot of time in showers and locker rooms over the years, and furthermore had been propo- sitioned by so many guys whom he liked and respected, that he had no special problem with homosexuals — although he was not interested in having sex with them.

There was a dearth of girls in Hus Bay who were within the proper range for Thom to date, but he managed to find enough pussy to keep his sexual needs under control by supplementing the available girls in the appropriate age range with mature women who were thrilled to fuck with a gorgeous young stud like him.

Thom had visited Paulik University when he was a Senior in high school, considering enrolling there. A friend who had graduated Thom's high school a year earlier played host to him the weekend he came to Hus Bay to look things over. Thom stayed with his friend in the dormitory, on condition the friend did not hit on him sexually, as he had done several times — unsuccessfully — when they were in school together. There was only one bed in the room, so they shared it, but although Thom's friend jacked off twice during the night when they were in bed together, he kept his hands to himself.

The shower was quite another matter, of course. Thom was amazed by the sexual activity in the shower room, which he visited when an exceptionally well-hung student was using it, one who always drew a good crowd of onlookers, and who inspired a fairly wild orgy when he let three boys suck his cock, and fucked two others. Thom was a little shocked, and a little amused, but he was also — inevitably — a little titillated. He got a hard-on, but he was not interested in doing anything about it. He fended off several boys who wanted to blow him or play with his ass, and watched while his friend got fucked. Thom's friend had warned him that he might have sex in the shower room, and Thom had assured him he wouldn't mind, even though he was not going to take part. Thom was horny enough that he did finally yield to his friend's pleading to beat off and blow a load in his face. It was the closest to all-out gay sex Thom had ever engaged in to that point, except for a couple of occasions during eighth grade when he had slept over with his best friend, and wakened some time during the night to find his best friend sucking him off.

Thom liked Paulik University, but, not surprisingly, did not want to live in the dormitory. He rented a room in a house near the campus.

When Thom stripped for Lake, the director was pleased that what he revealed was going to be good for the show. While the Greek Chorus members were called warriors, they looked like gods, Thom looked down-to-earth, extremely masculine, like a real warrior—albeit a remarkably handsome one. Perfect for the part. His ass was ample, without even a suggestion of fat; it was well-rounded, all but hairless, and the buttocks were very tight, completely concealing the asshole deep inside the chasm between them. His flaccid prick was about six inches long, and its circumference was extremely impressive in relation to its length. His balls were covered with a light fuzz, and were unduly large. Even without a hard-on, Thom's genitalia were imposing—powerful—and when he got excited, he had nine inches of hugely fat cock.

Lake wondered if there was any possibility of Thom getting an erection on stage, which—while most of the audience and cast members would almost surely enjoy seeing it—would no doubt seriously distract the audience from the emotional impact of his death scene. He told the boy he would like to see if there was any danger of his getting a hard-on when he was naked on stage. Thom said he doubted there would be any problem, that being naked in front of an audience would probably have the exact opposite effect. He admitted he was not certain, and Lake asked him if he would mind taking a few tests to be sure. If he could pass those tests, he would definitely be cast as Absalom. The first would involve Thom watching while a couple guys—probably two of the studly warriors from the Greek chorus—got naked and did what they could to give him a hard-on, without actually touching him.

"Okay, I guess, if I'm just watching," Thom said.

"Not a problem," Lake said. "I'll have them play with each other, maybe suck or fuck while you watch. Would that bother you? I know you're straight."

Thom laughed, "Hey, you know I'm not offended by what gay guys do—it's just not for me. I spent a weekend in the dorm on campus when I came down here to look the school over, and I promise you it won't be anything I didn't see in the shower there."

"Fine," Lake said. "I'll tell them to act like you aren't there while they do it."

"You said 'a few' tests. What else?"

"I want you to find out how you're going to feel being naked in front of a group. I'll announce that you're tentatively cast as Absalom, and in the first rehearsal I'll explain that I have to be sure you can be comfortable about being naked, and won't get a hard-on in front of an audience, so I'm going to have you walk around without any clothes while we read through the play the first time or two. Everybody in the cast is male, and so are all the techies, so they'll be sympathetic. And I suspect most of 'em will enjoy watching you. Will that embarrass you, being the only naked one — with fifteen or twenty guys looking at you like they want to eat you up? Most of them *would* like to, you know."

"Sure I'll be embarrassed," Thom laughed, "but I'm kinda used to getting cruised by now. It doesn't bother me. Besides, if I get the part, I'm gonna be the only one naked in my death scene anyway, right? Might as well get used to it."

"Well, remember that after Absalom dies, all the guys in the Greek Chorus come out and strip before the final curtain."

"Oh yeah," Tom said. "How about them — are they gonna get a 'no boner' test, too?"

"No, that's not really necessary," Lake replied. "I'll give them alternate blocking to use in case they get hard-ons. But Absalom has to lie there in David's lap, completely exposed — and you're supposed to be dead, so you can't very well move a leg to hide an erection. So...what do you think?"

"Sure, let's go for it," Thom said. "When's the first test?"

The first test was that night. Lake asked the two warriors who couldn't keep their hands off each other when they auditioned to help out, but only one was able to be on hand for the test; he asked Tobey to stand in for the other. Tobey was more than happy to oblige; he thought Thom was extremely hot, and was actually hoping Thom would fail the test and opt for sex with him—but in any case, he would get to play with the other 'warrior,' who was a walking wet dream. Tobey and the other warrior showed up that night, and Sean accompanied Tobey. No one objected to the diminutive boy's presence.

Mercifully for Thom's aspirations, he passed the test with flying colors, although Sean and both warriors were disappointed to see that his limp—but still very impressive—prick failed to grow when they did their best to make it do so. Sean had not planned to actually participate, but he got so excited a few minutes after the test began, that when he saw Tobey kneeling over the other warrior while they sucked each other's pricks in sixty-nine, he pulled off his clothes and knelt behind Tobey to fuck his ass. At Lake's suggestion, Sean pulled his prick out of Tobey's ass just before he blew his load, and shot it all over Tobey's back. Tobey abandoned the cock he was sucking, and knelt behind Sean to fuck him. The warrior Tobey had been sucking bent over him to lick Sean's come from his back and shoulders, then ate Tobey's ass while he was fucking Sean. Tobey blew his load inside Sean's ass, the other warrior took over and fucked Sean's cum-filled ass.

Thom admitted he had been forced to work hard to avoid getting an erection while he watched. "You guys are all fuckin' hot, there's no question about that—and if I was gonna fuck a guy, I sure would want him to have a body like you two," he said, indicating Tobey and the other warrior. To Sean he said, "And I guess I'd want him to have a cock like yours. Christ, Sean, I heard you were hung, but that's a real *monster!* And what a fuckin' *load!* "

"You shoulda felt the one Tobey blew in my butt,"
Sean laughed.

Tom laughed also. "I don't think that's gonna happen, somehow."

"And that is one helluva fuckin' shame," Tobey
added.

Clearly, Thom had passed the first test, and although
he felt strange doing it, he passed the other equally well. It
was much simpler, actually. He stayed naked throughout
the first two rehearsals, although everyone else in the
theatre was fully clothed. During that time, Thom's cock
remained flaccid—but very few others did, although they
were not on display. Of the twenty-five actors and
technicians present at those rehearsals, all but a few were
gay, and except for those who already felt that way before
the rehearsals began, by the time the 'test' rehearsals
ended every one of them was about halfway in love with
Thom Nelson, extremely hot for his body, and hoping
somehow for a chance to make love with him.

Within a week after beginning rehearsals for *Absalom*, all of Thom's potential suitors knew he was neither
gay nor interested in even so much as a blowjob from
them. No one pined away in despair, however: there were
so many boys in the cast who were interested in gay sex—
including all but one of the deliriously well-built studs
who made up the Greek chorus of warriors.

Long before the first rehearsal, Jason had been cast as
King David, father of Absalom. Sean had been the one to
suggest to Jason that he audition for the role of David, and
when Jason called Lake to say he was interested, Lake cast
him immediately, without audition, wondering why he
himself had not thought to ask him to take the role.

Jason's and Thom's roles were the leads, equally
important and equally demanding. Jason had seen Thom
on stage in several productions, and was well aware of
what a fine actor he was. He was also well aware of how
sexy Thom was both on-stage and at a couple of cast

parties he had attended where he had met the younger man. On those occasions Jason had learned, both from information relayed by Lake and other cast members whom he had gone to bed with, that Thom was straight. Even with that information, Jason had propositioned Thom, and had done so very candidly — learning at first hand that the information he had been given was correct. Thus, when Thom and Jason began working on *Absalom* together, the latter knew that Thom was straight, and the former knew that Jason was gay. Given that mutual understanding, each respected the other's orientation, and they got along well together; considerations of sex did not intrude on the mutual friendship they developed almost immediately.

Both Thom and Jason had an extremely large number of lines to speak in *Absalom* — in the parlance of the theatre, each had a heavy 'line load.' An actor normally likes to have a substantial line load in any play, since that means his role is an important one. However, the downside is that such a role brings about more pressure, and the memorization is more difficult and time-consuming. The two decided they would memorize lines together, each helping the other by feeding him other actors' lines when they were doing scenes not involving their own jointly shared dialogue.

Jason's house was more conducive to working on lines than Thom's apartment, so he and Thom met whenever they could, at scattered times during the day — or at night if they had no rehearsal. If they had the energy following a rehearsal they might also work for an hour or so then.

About the third time they met for line work, they wound up in the hot tub behind Jason's house. Thom was hesitant about working there when Jason suggested it, fearing that the atmosphere might encourage him to make sexual overtures.

Jason had said, "I'm not gonna tell you I don't want to make a pass at you, Thom. I assume you know I'd love to have sex with you. But unless you tell me you want to do it, I won't touch you, okay? No sweat—it's strictly up to you."

"But it isn't gonna happen, Jason," Tom answered. "I like you a lot, and if I were gay, you'd be the first guy I'd…" He laughed, "I guess if I'm gonna be completely honest with you, I'd have to say Tobey would be the first guy I'd want to sign my dance card. Jesus, he's so fucking handsome, and I don't think I've ever seen a guy with a more fantastic body. I gotta admit that while I watched Sean fucking Tobey's ass, I thought a lot about how my dick would feel in there—and that was when I had to concentrate hardest to keep from getting a hard-on. I've never looked at a guy's ass before, and thought 'goddamn, that's *beautiful*!' Of course his chest is… Look, Jason, don't repeat this, especially to Tobey, but his tits are so big and juicy, so fucking sexy, I think I could spend hours playing with them and sucking them!"

"Why don't you tell that to Tobey," Jason asked. "He'd love for you to play with his tits. You wouldn't believe how much time I've spent doing it—and Tobey enjoys it almost as much as I do."

'No way," Thom said. "We both know that would take us somewhere I don't wanna go."

"Well, I know he'd love to suck you off. If you got that turned on by his tits, you could let him blow you— that would be fun, wouldn't it?"

"I haven't let a guy blow me since my best friend did it a couple times in grade school," Thom said, "and even then I didn't *let* him, he did it while I was sleeping." Then he laughed, "I promise you, the *next* guy who gives me a blow job—if there is one—is gonna be you, okay? You do want to suck me off, don't you?"

"You bet your sweet ass I do," Jason replied.

"Ah, so you think my ass is sweet, huh?" He grinned at Jason, then happened to look down. "Christ, Jason, look at you. You got a hard-on from me talking about this, didn't you?" Jason nodded, sheepishly. "Stand up." Jason did as he was told, and his prick jutted straight out in front of him, throbbing and bobbing in full erection. Thom whistled, "Wow, nice dick, man!" He shook his head, "Okay, that's it. Sit down, we're changing the subject."

For two weeks Thom and Jason memorized lines together, mostly in the hot tub, and mostly uninterrupted. On one occasion, Tobey joined them, and Jason was amused to watch Thom almost drooling as he studied Tobey's magnificent chest, trying to hide his fascination. While the three of them talked, Tobey and Jason played with each other under the water, Soon, Tobey moved to sit in Jason's lap, and settled down over his cock. Jason had never told Tobey about Thom's admiration for his chest, but it almost appeared that he had, since after bobbing up and down on Jason's prick for a few minutes, Tobey began to moan while he squeezed and massaged his own tits, licking his lips and staring seductively into Thom's eyes while he reveled in the pleasure of Jason's fuck.

Tobey smiled crookedly at Thom. "You don't mind us doing this, do you?"

"No, go ahead," Thom said in a very shaky voice.

"Jesus, it feels so good," Tobey groaned as he squeezed his eyes shut and moaned in pleasure. Both he and Jason panted and groaned for several minutes before Jason cried out loudly, and blew his load inside Tobey. Tobey opened his eyes, glazed over with intense fuck-lust, and tried to focus them on Thom's. "Jesus, Thom, you don't know what you're missing."

Thom shook his head nervously, smiling weakly. Then Tobey stood up, turned around, and drove his prick into Jason's mouth. Jason sucked profoundly, and reached behind Tobey to fondle and squeeze his muscular buttocks. Remembering how Thom had also been fascinated by Tobey's ass, he ran his hands over it seductively, often pulling the asscheeks apart to reveal the still distended hole he had just fucked, which dripped with his own cum when he massaged the muscle stud's ass.

Since Tobey faced away from Thom, and his body blocked Jason's view of Thom, neither could see how he was reacting to the sight of their lovemaking. In fact, Thom had a fierce hard-on, which had developed while he watched Tobey play with his own tits, and which he was now stroking fiercely under water as he fought against the temptation to stand and to drive it inside Tobey's asshole, and to reach around the boy to squeeze his glorious tits while he fucked him.

Long before Tobey discharged in Jason's mouth, Thom raised his body up enough that his cock was free of the water, and he blew his own load into the palm of his hand. He flicked some of it off his hand and wiped almost all the rest off on the side of the tub. Then he sat back down in the water and washed his hands clean. When Jason finished blowing Tobey, the two sat back down, facing Thom, who was by then composed.

After a few minutes, Tobey left, grinning at Thom, "You really oughta try it, you know." Again, Thom demurred.

Watching Thom study Tobey as he was leaving, Jason asked, very quietly, "I think you may be ready to get that next blowjob now."

Thom turned to him and smiled. "Not yet, Jason." He was silent for a minute, thoughtful, and he gazed back toward where Tobey had just entered the house as he said, as much to himself as to Jason, "He's pretty fucking amazing, isn't he?" Then he turned to face Jason. And added, laughing nervously, "Jesus, did you see his balls?"

Jason laughed, "Thom, I've spent hours playing with those balls. I'd recognize them anywhere—biggest ones

I've ever seen, I think. You can't imagine how many hours I've spent draining them!"

"It's probably a good thing I don't have to lie in *his* lap naked for ten minutes at the end of the show. I might not make it."

Another time Sean joined them, and when he stripped to step into the tub, it was clear that Thom was still amazed at seeing such an enormous prick on such a small man. He had thought of Sean as a boy, since he was so diminutive, and since he was playing a child in the show, but it was clear he was no boy when he stripped. Sean flirted with Thom the whole time he sat in the tub with him and Jason, and when he stood to get out, his prick was fully hard — nine full inches of fat meat swaying in front of his little body — and he was clearly offering it to Thom if he wanted it. If Thom did want it, he did not indicate that he did.

Sean stopped by the hot tub another night when Thom and Jason were in it, working on their lines. Tony Lowe was with him, in uniform — a white one, as tight and revealing as ever. They asked if they could use Jason's bedroom for a while. Jason gave them permission, of course, and since he and Thom were almost through for the night, he said he'd join them there in a little while if they wanted some three-way action. They enthusiastically declared a threesome would be fun, and went off to begin it as a duo. Sean added, as he left with Tony, that it would be a lot more fun if Thom joined them.

Thom had almost goggled at the sight of Tony's dick outlined in his uniform pants. When Tony and Sean had gone into the house, he asked Jason, "Christamighty, how big is his cock?"

"It's ten inches, Thom — biggest one I've ever had, or even seen in person."

"Can you… " he began, and faltered.

"Can I take it up the butt?" Jason laughed. "Oh yeah. It's a challenge, but well worth the effort."

"How about Sean? Small as he is, surely he's not going to…"

Jason interrupted, "Believe me, before the night is over, Sean will have his butt pressing against Tony's belly and his asshole buried in Tony's pubic hair—just like I will. He enjoys getting fucked by Tony as much as I do—and that means he has a helluva good time with Tony!"

Shaking his head in wonder, but without implying any criticism, Thom said, "You guys are unbelievable!"

The last night Jason and Thom studied lines together in the hot tub—the night they decided they finally had them down cold—they shared a bottle of champagne to celebrate. Rehearsals for *Absalom* had been going well, and both were sanguine about the prospects for its success.

By then, Thom assumed that almost everyone in the cast, or even working on the show in other capacities, was gay. Jason explained that while he thought about half of them might be gay, the rest were better described as either bisexual, or situationally gay—meaning they enjoyed sex where they could find it, and at Paulik University, and even in Hus Bay generally, that meant gay sex.

"I imagine it's a lot more complicated being gay than being straight," Thom said, and Jason agreed it probably was. "So I can't imagine anyone really *wanting* to be queer if he wasn't, but I kinda wish I was, Jason, so I could really show you how much I like you, and appreciate your friendship." He had been sitting opposite Jason in the hot tub, and he stood and waded over to him. He cupped Jason's chin in his hand, leaned over, and just before he pressed his lips to Jason's he whispered, "Don't misunderstand, or make anything out of this that I don't mean when I say it, okay?" Jason nodded. "I love you, Jason."

Their lips met and they shared a long, romantic, chaste kiss while each held the other's head gently. Their lips opened, but, taking his cue from Thom, Jason did not press his tongue into his mouth.

The tender moment passed, and Thom rose up. Standing in the middle of the hot tub, he commented, "Water's a little hotter than usual; the air feels good." He closed his eyes and stood there, enjoying the cooling effect of the air for a few minutes. When he opened his eyes, he saw that Jason was sitting there, looking up at him and smiling. Neither said a word as they spent a long moment looking into each other's eyes. Then Jason's gaze drifted downward, admiringly, over Thom's shoulders, chest, and stomach; when it reached his cock, it remained fixed there. It was very fat prick, and quite generous, even though it was flaccid.

Their silence continued. The only sound was the hot tub pump. Thom studied Jason's face, and although he occasionally glanced up to share a brief glance with Thom, Jason continued to study the maddeningly limp dick hanging no more than a foot from his face.

Finally, Jason's obvious hunger and admiration were rewarded; Thom's prick began to lengthen and erect very, very slowly — almost imperceptibly. Jason continued to watch, holding his breath, afraid to utter a sound, as in the tiniest of increments, the limp, but promising cock in front of him grew, and grew, *and grew*, until it was standing upwards at an angle of ten or fifteen degrees above the horizontal, trembling and throbbing, and even longer than the stunning nine-inch prick that Thom had admired on Sean. Given its abnormal girth, it was extremely formidable, *enormous* — and completely desirable.

Jason held his breath, afraid to say a word that might break the spell. Finally, he looked back up into Thom's face again.

The stud gazed downward at his admirer, apparently as rapt as he by the charged atmosphere of the moment. Finally, he smiled, and put one hand on the nape of Jason's neck and began to draw his head in toward his cock. As Jason's mouth opened wide — *very* wide, to accommodate Thom's monstrous girth—Thom's other hand helped press Jason's lips down along his shaft.

Once he had Jason's lips buried in his pubic hair, with his balls resting on Jason's chin, Thom whispered only one word as he began to undulate his hips and hump into the moist heat of the vacuum Jason provided for his prick: *"Now!"*

While his hands held Jason's head firmly, Thom began a vigorous, serious mouth-fuck, and while his hands fondled Thom's wildly thrashing ass eagerly and lovingly, Jason sucked profoundly, and drove his tightly compressed lips all the way up and down the challenging shaft he had hungered for so long a time.

Jason occasionally moaned his thrill around the mouthful of cock that was inspiring it, and Thom's murmurs of satisfaction grew in excitement and intensity, until he was gasping and crying out in ecstasy, finally shouting "Take it!" loudly as he wrapped Jason's head in both arms and pulled it as tightly into his stomach as he could, holding it there as he filled Jason's ravenous mouth with hot cum. It was the kind of load that only a young man who had not had an orgasm for several days could produce—and Jason was the fortunate beneficiary of the uncharacteristic short period of celibacy Thom had endured.

Jason gagged at the force of Thom's orgasm, as well as on the volume, and was forced to allow a small portion escape his mouth, but he quickly recovered, and savored the large mouthful of thick semen, lapping Thom's cock as he did so, bathing it in its own discharge. Finally, Jason swallowed, and exhaled his satisfaction in loud panting.

"Jesus, that felt great," Thom gasped, still pressing Jason's head against his stomach. One of Jason's hands stopped playing with Thom's ass, and went underwater to stroke his own cock—which was painfully in need of release. "Yeah, beat off," Thom whispered.

In a moment, Jason rose to his feet quickly, pulling his head from Thom's grasp. He was masturbating wildly, and almost immediately aimed his prick at Thom's still hard one, crying out loudly as he covered it and Thom's belly with his own impressive load. Jason threw his arms around Thom's waist and rested his head against Thom's chest as he recovered from the intensity of his orgasm, and Thom returned the embrace, patting Jason's back gently, whispering, "That was good, Jason."

Finally, Jason broke the embrace and stepped back slightly, holding Thom's ribcage in his hands as he smiled at him, without saying anything. Thom grinned at him and stepped back, looking down at his cum-covered cock and stomach. "Aren't you gonna clean up after yourself?" Then he put both hands on top of Jason's head, and pushed him to his knees.

Jason licked his cum from Thom's stomach, and sucked it off his prick—which was finally beginning to lose its rigidity and enormity. When he finished, he stood, and once again put his arms around Thom's strong body. Thom smiled at him and returned the embrace as his lips again sought Jason's. One of Jason's hands caressed Thom's ample, unbelievably firm, muscular ass, and the other fondled his now almost completely flaccid, but still impressive prick. In return, Thom played with Jason's ass and stroked his still-hard prick. Just before they kissed, Thom snickered, "Shit, you've still got a hard-on." This time their kiss was a passionate, all-stops-out affair, with their tongues dancing inside each other's mouths and entwining hungrily while their busy hands continued to explore each other's bodies.

Finally, Thom broke their kiss and whispered in Jason's ear, "That's the first time I ever touched another guy's cock, and I've never kissed a guy before, either—except for my dad and my uncles when I was little. I don't know whose cum I tasted in your mouth, mine or yours, but I really enjoyed kissing you, Jason, and you gave me the best blow job I've ever had, by far—and I mean *really* by far! I could tell you were enjoying it as much as I was—and that made it special; I don't usually get that feeling when a girl is blowing me."

"I'm glad, Thom, " Jason whispered. "I wish we could…" He was cut off by Thom's hand covering his mouth.

"Jason, don't wish any more. This isn't gonna happen again. I enjoyed it, and I have to admit I really wanted it, too. And it was great. It was fantastic! But I'm straight, Jason. I want to keep being a close friend, but that's all. Can we do that?"

Jason knew Thom had already given him more than he could have expected, and even though he wished the situation could be different, he accepted it. "Of course we can. After all, I'll still always be able to remember the night I sucked Thom Nelson off."

"And there isn't gonna be a night Thom Nelson sucked you off, or fucked you, or got fucked by you. You sure you're okay with that?"

"I'm sure," Jason said, "but it's still the night I sucked Thom Nelson off, so how about giving me one more kiss before it ends, and then we'll finish off the champagne?"

Their last kiss was very long, and while their tongues were busy, it was a sweet kiss of friendship, not the kind Jason really wanted, but still a very memorable and treasured sign of their new relationship.

During the time they spent drinking the rest of the champagne and talking before he went home, Thom exacted a promise from Jason that he would tell *no one*—not even Tobey or Sean or Tony—what had passed between them. "All three of 'em are really hot guys," Thom said. "With Sean or Tony's cock, I might be tempted, and I'm sure Tobey's body and his tits would be a big temptation—and I really don't want to be tempted, Jason.

If they knew about what we did tonight...well, you know. Just promise you won't say anything."

Jason swore he would never tell anyone about 'the night I sucked Thom Nelson off.'

As he was leaving, Thom threw an arm around Jason's neck, saying, "You' re a good guy, Jason, and I mean it as a compliment when I say you're a great cocksucker!"

"I got to suck a great guy's cock tonight, Thom. Thanks — I'll never forget it."

"You know what, Jason? Neither will I."

9.

LIFE UPON THE WICKED STAGE — ACT TWO

The play *Absalom* depicts the conflict between the biblical King David, and his rebellious third son, Absalom, loosely adapting the legend set out in the Second Book of Samuel in the Bible. It ends with the death of the boy. Absalom's greatest act of rebellion has been to woo and seduce Jonathan, his father's 'great friend,' David's lover since Jonathan was fifteen years old.

At the beginning of the first act, Absalom — then an eleven-year-old boy — watches from concealment while his father and Jonathan bid each other a passionate goodbye as David goes off to battle following a night with his young lover. When Jonathan exits a moment later, the boy Absalom emerges and curses him, "Jonathan, my father gives you the love he owes me, and you take what, as my father, he must not give me."

In the second scene of Act Two, the now fifteen-year-old Absalom's wooing of Jonathan — then twenty years of age, but still David's lover — culminates in his seduction of the older man. Following a long kiss, Absalom's words to Jonathan echo the ones he used in cursing him in the opening scene: "The love you gave my father for so long, will from this day be mine to claim; the sustenance my father has given you since I was a child, I will now provide for you." As he begins to remove his tunic, he continues, "And I swear I will give that sustenance to you with greater frequency and in greater quantity than the King has ever provided." They kiss again, and Jonathan falls to his knees in front of Absalom as the younger man drops his tunic to the floor and stands naked before his father's lover. To the disappointment of most audiences, Jonathan's head blocks the audience's view of Absalom's genitals. Absalom looks down, placing one hand on Jonathan's head, and whispers, "Let the feast begin." *Quick* blackout.

Ironically, the actor playing Jonathan was straight, like Thom, who played Absalom—straighter, perhaps, when the play began its run, since at that point he had experienced nothing like what Thom had shared with Jason. The onstage kisses he shared with Thom were awkward for both of them at first, but by the time the show ended its run, they were driving their tongues into each other's mouths lustfully, fondling each other feverishly as they did so; by then, Thom's experience at kissing a man had grown exponentially, while at the same time his partner had yielded to the blandishments of the diminutive Sean Gayle, who had in that short time provided a comprehensive course in gay lovemaking, focusing on the lab work—and which his pupil passed with flying colors!

Prior to the final scene, Absalom is captured by David's men, sent to quell his rebellion, and even though his father had ordered that no harm should come to the boy, one of his men stabs him and strips off his clothing. The naked body of the dying Absalom is brought to David, who is seated in his throne on a raised platform far upstage. The king leaves his throne to kneel on the platform and receive the body of his son. The play ends with a long, touching reunion between father and son, with the son stretched out on his back, his head cradled in the arms of his father.

When Absalom dies, David calls out to the eight ultra-manly warriors, who have throughout the play commented on the action in the manner of the standard chorus of Greek tragedy, to come forward, crying "Warriors, clothe my beloved son in military finery; bury him with solemn ceremony." Individually, one by one, each warrior comes forward and removes the laurel crown from his head to lay it on Absalom's chest—symbolically clothing his corpse in military finery—then denudes himself by stripping off the simple band of cloth wrapped around his loins; except for the laurel wreath and his lace-up sandals, it is all he wears. He lays his rudimentary costume over the body of the dead boy, symbolically burying it with solemn ceremony. He then turns to face the audience, nude except for his sandals, and walks very slowly, mournfully, all the way downstage to turn around and kneel, facing away from the audience, toward Absalom and David. After all eight are arrayed with their bare backsides facing the audience, they prostrate themselves on an invisible signal, and lie face-down on the stage as David intones the words from the Bible, "Oh my son, Absalom! Would God I had died for thee, Oh Absalom, my son, my son." Blackout.

Since the play is a tragedy, there were no curtain calls; the lights came back up—however many times the audience demanded—to reveal a frozen tableau. During the blackout at the end of the play all characters return to the stage to get in position for the tableau, and all the naked warriors turn around to face the audience, sitting on their heels.

For the warriors in the last scene and in the curtain-call tableau, there were special instructions in the event any of them had a hard-on. For the last scene, those with erections were to back away from the body of Absalom, backing ceremoniously all the way to his downstage position, rather than turning around so that the audience could see his erection as he got in position for the final blackout. During the curtain call, they were instructed to mask any erections by placing their hands strategically in their laps. Once the play opened, however, the special instructions were ignored.

247

John Butler
THIS GAY UTOPIA

From where he sat on stage, Jason was amused to watch almost every warrior, during almost every performance, use his hand to 'fluff up' his prick before turning to walk toward the audience, so that it would appear especially large. Not one of them ever elected to back away from Absalom's body, and during the run of the show there were quite a number of erections swaying in front of warriors as they walked downstage for the ending — ranging from semi-hard ones, arcing out over a set of balls, to throbbing, rigid ones standing straight out or even pointing upward! Most of the warriors stroked their pricks during the blackout, so that when the lights came up again, revealing them facing the audience in tableau, their pricks looked big — many actually erect, but because of their kneeling position, they didn't necessarily appear to be so.

Neither members of the University Administration, nor anyone else were bothered by the imputation of homosexuality in Biblical characters — after all, David and Jonathan were clearly chummy to a suspiciously high degree — nor did they complain about the nudity, or (surprisingly) the erections. The stately parade of the naked warriors, whatever condition their cocks might be in — to say nothing about the sight of their eight naked, majestic asses for a few minutes before the blackout and the sight of them kneeling there with big cocks showing for the final tableau — was a very stimulating way to end a relatively intellectual and dramatically restrained tragedy.

Absalom was a hit, and the original planned run was extended twice, probably because of the number of people who came to see it repeatedly — principally to see the breathtaking muscle boys parade their cocks and asses, but also to view Thom's naked body, and (hopefully) to see a large number of erections!

Thom, as Absalom, however, could not show even a suggestion of an erection in the final scene. He was supposed to be dying — not a condition that causes a hard-

248

on—and for the last several minutes of the show, he is supposed to be dead (at which time, all bets are off for the likelihood of a hard-on).

During most of the rehearsals, visible hard-ons were not a consideration, since the actors were working in street clothes, fully dressed. Normally actors don actual costumes for only the last three or four rehearsals, but because of potential problems, Lake had everyone in costume for ten days before opening; for Thom—and, to a lesser extent, for the warriors—that sometimes meant wearing no costume at all.

Everything went fine during rehearsals. Thom never got a hard-on, and the warriors were mostly able to conceal theirs, although Lake bawled them out for working up erections during the blackout before the final curtain-call tableau. Secretly, Lake loved the plethora of erections to be seen once the show opened, and never got too shirty about it. ('Shirty' is a Briticism for 'angry,' which an English boy in the *Absalom* cast used once during a rehearsal, and all the actors gleefully adopted it as an 'in' expression.)

During the final dress rehearsal, the night before opening, the theatre was about half filled with an audience of almost two hundred people: everyone connected with the show in any way who was not actually working during the performance, invited friends of the director and the actors, and several members of the University administration. Administration representatives were there because Lake had asked them to come and certify that the nude scenes would not embarrass the University. Their approval was something of a formality, since the playwright had specified the nudity—and the playwright's stature in the dramatic and literary community was such that censoring his work would be potentially more embarrassing to the University than allowing it to proceed.

Nudity and other potentially controversial factors in Paulik Players productions had never been forbidden or changed as a result of administrative or public pressure in the past, nor did the Administration representatives fail to approve *Absalom*. A few of them were almost shocked by some of the warriors' cocks at the end—not by the cocks, but by the *condition* of them—but they said nothing. Virtually all of them decided they would try to see the show frequently, so they could, again and again, enjoy the spectacle of so many extremely muscular students showing their hard dicks; because of the 'hands off the students' policy of the University, it was as close as they were likely to get to those tantalizing studs in the nude.

Things also went smoothly during the final dress rehearsal, until the last scene. Thom, as Absalom, was carried in, in the nude, and stretched out on the platform at the feet of Jason, playing David. With a cry, Jason fell to his knees and hugged Thom's body to him, holding his shoulders and burying his face in Thom's neck as he sobbed. The two warriors who had borne Thom's body retired upstage to join the other six warriors, arrayed in a semi-circle around the upstage platform, three on each side of the throne.

Jason sat back, cradling Thom's naked body in his arms, with the boy's chest in his lap, his legs splayed out in front of him, and his head resting against Jason's chest.

Jason began to deliver David's lengthy monologue of a father's grief, but had only spoken the first few lines when he heard Thom hissing very quietly, so that only he could hear it. He looked down into Thom's face and realized his eyes were slitted open the least bit, enough that Jason could tell, but not the audience. It seemed obvious Thom wanted to communicate something to him, so Jason took a dramatic pause in the monologue while he hugged Thom's head so that the boy's mouth was near his ear.

Thom whispered, "I'm getting a hard-on. Move my leg to hide it. Hurry!"

250

Jason glanced down at Thom's cock, which was no longer lying limply against his inner thigh, as it had been when he, as Absalom, died. It now dipped down between his splayed legs, but instead of hanging there, it was standing out independently just a little, its growth and changed angle probably not noticeable to the audience. Yet.

Jason reached over Thom, and grasping his downstage thigh, he pulled Thom's body up and in to his own so that the boy now lay on his side, his backside facing the audience and his groin completely hidden. Jason sobbed into Thom's neck again, then continued with the monologue. He continued to cuddle Thom that way as the warriors came up to strip themselves and cover his body.

The first warrior to kneel and lay his wreath and sash on Thom's body looked over it, and saw that Thom's impressive prick was standing straight out between his and Jason's bodies. He took a few seconds longer than he normally would have before he turned and retreated downstage to clear the way for the next warrior. During those few seconds he grinned at Jason, mouthed the word "Wow!" and winked at him. In rehearsals the first warrior had always played with his own prick for a few seconds at that moment, to be sure it looked impressive when he turned to face the audience, but as he turned to walk downstage that night, he had no need to do so; the sight of the huge erection on Thom, whom he — like so many in the cast of the show — really *wanted*, caused his prick to arc out significantly over his balls. Since the sash he had lain on the body covered Thom's erection, none of the other warriors was able to see it.

In the blackout, while all the cast was assembling on stage for the final tableau, Jason reached down and grasped Thom's cock; it was completely hard, and enormous — just as big as he remembered from the one time Thom had given it to him. "Jesus, Thom!" He whispered, as he stroked the throbbing flesh lovingly.

Just before the lights came up, he heard Thom snicker, "Thanks for the help, Jason, but, that's enough." Jason was sorry he had not heard Thom say that his help had been enough *for now!*

There were several enthusiastic repetitions of the final-tableau 'curtain call.' Finally, at the end of the fourth one, the cast heard Lake call out from the wings, "That's it, clear the stage."

Lake collared Jason as soon as he entered the wings. "What happened?"

"Thom got a hard-on, and I had to hide it," Jason answered, knowing full well what Lake was referring to.

"Good thinking, Lake said. "I wonder why he got a hard-on? It hasn't happened before. I won't say anything to him about it right now. Be ready to cover again if you have to, and if it keeps happening, I'll talk to Thom; we can change the blocking a little bit if we have to. I don't want to, unless it's necessary, though; I like way Thom's body looks so vulnerable with his legs stretched out the way we have it blocked now."

Jason laughed, "Shit, I like the way Thom's body looks *any* time!"

"Amen," Lake said. "What a shame a *hunk* like that is straight. Such a terrible waste." He turned and went backstage to offer his congratulations to the cast.

Jason found Thom sitting in the small dressing room they shared — the only 'star' dressing room, designed for use by three or four actors at the most. Everyone else used the two huge dressing rooms designed for men and women, both of which were usually used for men. If just a few women were involved in the cast of a show — as was usually the case, at most — they shared the 'star' room. For *Absalom*, it made sense for Thom to share the small room with Jason — they were clearly the principal actors, and they had obviously become close friends. Besides, Lake thought the presence of an actor like Thom, who seemed so aggressively straight, might put a damper on the gay banter and horseplay that invariably took place in the large men's dressing rooms.

"What happened?" Jason asked as he entered his and Thom's dressing room.

"Beats the shit out of me," Tom said, shrugging his shoulders. "Suddenly, layin' there naked with all those people I couldn't even see, lookin' at my dick...I dunno, it got me excited. Thank God you helped me out."

"It was fun," Jason grinned. "Felt like I was greeting an old friend when I played with your dick during the blackout."

"I didn't mind. Hell, especially not after you saved me like that." He smiled, "Anyway, it really felt good. I wish we'da had enough time for you to finish me off."

"Hey," Jason said, "it's never too late."

"Nah, it's gone away now — and besides, I got a date later on."

"I still don't see why knowing a lot of people were looking at your cock gave you a hard-on, Jason said. "Were you especially horny, or something?"

"I shouldn't have been," Thom said. "I spent the night with Cassie last night, and I fucked her — but just once. I probably would have fucked her this morning, but her mother came in, so I fucked her instead."

"I'm surprised you didn't fuck both of 'em together," Jason laughed.

"Well, I don't really feel comfortable fucking either of them while the other one is there. Besides, I ain't that much of a stud, I guess. I've done it a few times, though. Cassie's mom is really a better fuck than she is, and I think Cassie gets jealous when I pay too much attention to her mother." He leered, "But none of 'em can suck cock like Jason Boone! I like a threesome, though, and...I mean a threesome with two girls and me, Jason; don't start to get any ideas."

"Understood," Jason laughed. "But I think you *are* that much of a stud. I know you got another great big hard-on not long after you let me suck you off that night in the hot tub; I'll bet you could have given me another load, if you just would have."

"Yeah, and I almost did. Hell, it was still 'the night I sucked Thom Nelson off,' like you called it. I shoulda let you."

"Like I said, never too late," Jason said.

"C'mon, Jason, I told you that night.... "

"I know, I know," Jason said, "just wishful thinking. So, do you think you're gonna get a hard-on again in that scene?"

"Christ, how do I know? I'll plan on thinking of something to keep my mind off it," Thom said. "Maybe, just to be sure, I can raise my leg before I die, so it'll hide my dick."

"I know Lake wants your dick showing, if possible, but..." Jason began, but Thom interrupted him, laughing.

"I think Lake would like to have everybody's dick showin' — all the time."

"I imagine that's about right. But anyway, he asked me a couple of minutes ago what happened, and I told him. He said he could change the blocking in case it might happen again, but he doesn't want to, if he can avoid it. Says he likes how vulnerable you look with your legs stretched out in front of you."

"Tell you what we'll do," Thom said. "If it happens again, if my dick starts getting hard again, you can reach down and play with it until it's a full boner — and then you can suck me off until it gets soft again. And then I can die. Whaddya think? I'll bet it would be a sensational way to end the play. You'd probably have to swallow my cum, though — it would look funny if you spit it out. Would you mind?"

"Nah, that would be cool. But I could gargle your cum for a while, then spit it out into my hand and say, 'Absalom my son, would to God I had done that while you were still alive.' Then I could hold my hand out to the warriors and say, 'C'mon boys, suppertime!' "

Thom laughed uproariously, and said: "I think maybe it would be better if I just think of a way to keep from getting a hard-on!"

"Okay," Jason said, "but I really liked your last suggestion."

"Tell you what, Jason. Keep a lookout, and if you see my dick getting hard again, or if I let you know it is, just do what you did tonight, and when we get back here to the dressing room you can suck me off then. And I mean that seriously. How's that grab you?"

"That's a deal. Seriously," Jason said. "You know I'm gonna be pulling for you to pop a boner every night, don't you?"

"But how about matinees?"

"Matinees, too," Jason said. "I think a mouthful of your cum would taste great around tea time."

"Don't hold your breath until it happens—but that *is* a promise, okay?" He kissed Jason lightly on the lips, and turned to begin removing his make-up.

The next night, as Thom and Jason met in the dressing room to prepare for the official opening night performance, Jason showed Thom a hard-rubber wedge he had brought, the kind designed to prop doors open.

"What's that for?" Thom asked.

"In case you get another hard-on tonight, this it to jam under the door to keep anyone from coming in here after the show, while *you're* coming!"

"I don't think that's gonna be needed," Thom smiled.

Unfortunately for Jason—fortunately, for Lake's blocking—Thom's prick remained flaccid during the closing scene that night. Jason asked him in the dressing room afterwards, "I guess the audience didn't bother you tonight—damn it!"

"I had an idea how to avoid that," Thom said. "About fifteen minutes before my entrance for the last scene I went into the bathroom and jacked off. Worked great—I would have had to *work* at getting a hard-on out there tonight."

"Shit! And I wasn't here to help you," Jason said. "You just *wasted* your load like that?

Tom laughed. "Fuckin' shame, huh?"

"No shit, Sherlock. And I'll bet you were thinking of fucking one of your women while you beat off and came."

"Yeah, most of the time," Thom said, "but I might as well tell you—and don't get any ideas, this doesn't mean anything—just when I started to blow, I thought about how great it felt when you were sucking the cum out of my dick."

Jason grinned, "So, maybe there's hope, after all."

"C'mon, Jason, I told you."

"I know, I know. But it still seems like a damned waste!"

The night after that, Thom's strategy worked again. The next night, during intermission, Jason asked him, "So you're gonna jack off again as soon as I go out on stage, right?"

Thom was silent for a minute, thinking; then he spoke hesitatingly, "Look, Jason...you were so great, helping me learn lines when we worked together, and I got to thinking, what the hell, why not let you keep helping me do the show, since you obviously want to do it? It sure as shit wouldn't hurt me; in fact...oh hell, in fact I'll admit it: I'll enjoy it a lot."

"I guess I should ask you to get to the point," Jason said, "but I know what you're saying. Instead of jacking off tonight, you want me to blow you, right?"

"Well, during every performance...if you want."

Jason grinned, "Before, during, after—whenever you'll let me."

Thom returned the grin as he slipped out of the tunic he wore in the second act until his final entrance in the nude. His prick was already semi-hard, and he stroked it as he leaned forward and kissed Jason before pressing him down to his knees, panting, "C'mon, Jason, suck the cum out of it!"

Jason's lips closed around Thom's fat prick, and sought its base as he sucked deeply, bringing it to full erection instantaneously. Thom moaned, "Oh shit, that feels so fuckin' good." He fucked Jason's mouth eagerly while Jason moved his tightly compressed lips all the way up and down the shaft, countering each forward thrust. At the same time, Jason fondled the cheeks of Thom's ass, which were busily undulating and humping as the boy drove his rapacious cock, until, after a delirious six or eight minutes, it unloaded explosively and copiously in Jason's throat. "Jesus, baby, eat my cum," Thom groaned, and kept fucking until Jason had sucked out every spurt and every last drop of his load.

Finally, Thom said, "Whew!" and backed up a step, pulling his cock from Jason's hungry mouth. "Did you swallow it?" he asked. Jason hadn't, but he did so just then, and nodded to Thom. "Christ, Jason, that was fantastic!" Thom said, embracing Jason as he pressed his lips to Jason's, and they kissed passionately for several minutes.

While he was kissing Jason, Thom could feel the other's hard cock pressing into his stomach. He stopped kissing and smiled, "You need to get off, too. I wish I could..."

Jason interrupted him, as he opened his own tunic and produced his erection. "It's okay, Thom — I know the rules," he said as he began to beat off.

"I'm sorry, Jason. If I was gonna do any guy, it would be you, I promise." He moved to stand behind Jason. Lifting up the back of Jason's tunic, he put his still-hard prick in between the older man's legs, just below his ass. Jason automatically spread his legs for a moment, so that Thom's prick could slide in between them, and the cock-head rose to rest against the back of his ball sac before he closed them tightly around the invading shaft. Reaching around Jason and taking over for him, Thom began to stroke his prick at the same time he began to fuck his legs. "I guess I can at least give you a handjob," he said into Jason's ear.

Jason gasped in pleasure, throwing his head back and squeezing his eyes shut as he reveled in the feel of Thom's fat prick thrusting in and out of his legs, Thom's mouth biting his shoulder and nibbling his ear, the excitement of Thom's rough hand stroking his throbbing prick, with the taste of Thom's cum still strong in his mouth. He reached behind to pull Thom's ass tightly against his own—grinding and humping as it had when Jason had been sucking the boy's cock.

With a loud cry, Jason's prick erupted, splattering cum all over the dressing table as Thom continued to pump it until he turned Jason's body around. He grinned ruefully, "I should have got you off while you were doing me—I've still got a hard-on." The side of his hand was coated with cum, where his fist had circled Jason's cock. He scraped it along the shaft of his own prick, then used his fingers to coat it before he poked the head under Jason's balls and whispered, "Open your legs for a second, and let me in."

With his arms around Jason, fondling his ass, and with Jason holding his head while they shared hungry, feverish kisses, Thom fucked for another five minutes. Jason's hands squeezed Thom's frantically pumping ass-cheeks while he panted into his mouth, "Fuck me, Thom!"

One of Thom's hands went between Jason's buttocks, and he penetrated his asshole slightly with one finger, wriggling it about as Jason moaned his pleasure. "That's where you should be fucking me."

"Jesus, Jason, you are so fuckin' hot!" Thom gasped, not commenting on the invitation Jason had just implied.

With a few extraordinarily deep and powerful thrusts, he cried "Aaaaaahhh!" and his cum began to spurt, coating the inside of Jason's legs. He held Jason's body painfully tight as his orgasm subsided, then he pushed him down on his back over the dressing table. He leaned over and spread Jason's legs, then—much to Jason's surprise— licked his own cum off them.

Thom surprised himself almost as much as he did Jason. He looked up from between Jason's legs, grinning at him, his lips and his chin covered with cum. "I never tasted my own cum, and I suddenly had the urge to do it."

Jason stood up and embraced Thom. "Tastes pretty damned good, doesn't it?"

"Yeah, it does. No wonder you like it," Thom said as he kissed him.

"But don't forget, Thom, you covered your dick with my cum before you started fucking me, so you were tasting it, too."

"I didn't think of that," Thom replied, looking slightly troubled. Then a smile dawned on his face as he looked into Jason's eyes, "I guess it didn't hurt me, did it? And I still think it tasted good."

"Christ!" Jason said as there was knock on the dressing room door, and a call for 'Places for Act Two,' "I've gotta get out there." He began putting on his tunic, hastily.

"Tomorrow we'd better get you off before you do me, or *while* you are, at least," Thom said. "I enjoyed giving you two loads, but it takes too much time. So—just one load tomorrow." He winked at Jason and added, "But I won't jack off in the morning, so I'll have an extra big one for you."

Jason took a moment, before he went out to start Act Two, to kneel and lick a drop of come from the end of Thom' prick—still, amazingly, almost fully erect—and to squeeze it and kiss it briefly. He was almost out the door when Thom said, "Jason."

Jason turned and asked, "What?"

"I enjoyed it—and I'm already looking forward to intermission tomorrow. But I better not think about it for a while, or you're gonna have to hide my hard-on again in the last scene."

The hard-rubber wedge had served its purposes that night, as it was to do until the end of the show's run.

The first week of the *Absalom* run ended with a Sunday matinee. By that time, Thom and Jason were making efficient use of their intermission break, and there had been no recurrence of Thom's hard-on problem during the final scene. Lake took Jason aside toward the end of the week and said, "I don't know what Thom is doing to avoid getting a hard-on again, but for your sake, I hope it's what I think he's doing." He winked.

Sean and Tobey—Jason's only close friends in the cast, other than Thom—both suspected what Thom and Jason were doing in the dressing room, although only Sean guessed they were doing it during intermission, rather than before the First Act, and both guessed wrong about exactly what they were doing. Individually both had suggested to Jason that they knew Thom was fucking him.

"I wish," Jason had countered. "There's nothing going on. Thom is just jacking off in the bathroom after Act Two begins." He didn't like lying to his friends, but he had promised Thom he would not tell anyone else what they did together—and when he extracted that promise, Thom had even specified that it extended to Tobey and Sean as well.

When the Sunday matinee performance ended, Thom lamented to Jason, as they were removing their makeup, "I guess I'm not gonna get another Jason Boone blowjob tomorrow. You know, I've really come to look forward to intermission more than anything else about this play. How'm I gonna hold off until Tuesday to fuck that hot mouth again?'

Jason stood and shed the robe he had thrown on to clean up before getting dressed. He completely hid his cock and balls by pressing them back as far as he could, and holding them between his tightly clenched legs. Only his bush of pubic hair showed at the "V" of his groin, and it looked like a woman's crotch. As he had often done during his Navy days when he was trying to get straight sailors to fuck him, he asked Thom, "You wanna fuck my pussy?"

The sight of Jason's fake 'pussy' and the invitation to fuck it, had often been enough for straight sailors to pretend they weren't about to fuck a shipmate; furthermore, the offer *seemed to be* presented humorously, so they felt like they were just 'going along' with a joke when they started playing around. Once a cock was inside the 'pussy,' held tight by Jason's legs, the fuck – perhaps started as a joke – almost always turned serious. Once the straight sailors were sufficiently caught up in serious lovemaking, they almost always got – and frequently gave – blowjobs, and often raised Jason's legs or rolled him over to fuck him properly. On a surprising number of those occasions, they returned the favor, offering their own asses for Jason to fill with dick.

Thom had obviously not been exposed to this fake-pussy ploy before, although it is quite common, even used by supposedly straight boys who are genuinely just playing around – or who think they are, anyway. He laughed and stood up. He was already naked, and the towel that had been in his lap fell to the floor. He reached out and stroked Jason's lower belly and pubic hair; he put his arms around him and said, "Yeah, I could stand some pussy," as he kissed him lightly. "I haven't fucked anything in..." He ran a finger over Jason's lips, "...oh, more than an hour."

Jason reached down and began to stroke Thom's cock, which immediately grew hard. Still acting as if it were a joke, he said, "C'mon and get it, big boy!"

Thom positioned the head of his prick at the base of the "V" and began trying to press it in between Jason's legs, having to push quite hard because Jason's legs were held together so tightly, in order to keep his cock and balls hidden. Having little success penetrating Jason's 'pussy,' Thom said, "Guess I need some Vaseline for a pussy as tight as this one."

Jason turned only the upper part of his body, reaching into his make-up kit for a tube of K-Y Jelly. He had been hoping for an occasion when it would be necessary ever since he had been assigned to the dressing room with Thom. He squeezed some on the palm of his hand and reached down to smear it over Thom's cock. "Now try," he grinned.

Thom pushed again, and his prick slipped in between Jason's legs. He snickered, "My God, this is what I call a tight pussy!" He began to fuck, the top of his cock sliding against the top of Jason's between Jason's legs. All pretense of 'kidding around' vanished almost at once, as Thom began to fuck in earnest and fondle Jason's ass feverishly. He whispered into his mouth and began to drive the tip of a finger in and out of his ass before he kissed him, "Jesus Christ, Jason, you're so fuckin' hot!"

He fucked for a few minutes before he pulled his prick out and said, "Put the door-stopper under the door while I get some towels." Jason quickly complied, his achingly hard prick popping out from between his legs as he did so. Thom spread a few towels on the floor and said, "Lay down here."

Lying down on his back on the towels, Jason tried to hide his prick and balls by pushing them back in between his legs again. He was having difficulty, since his freed prick had grown so unremittingly hard, it would not bend far enough back to return to its prison.

"Shit, I can't get it back in," he said.

"Never mind," Thom said, kneeling between his legs and applying more lubricant to his cock. "I'm gonna like it more this way. I don't want to pretend you're a girl Jason. I like you just the way your are." He took Jason's prick in hand and stroked it a minute before he said, "Close your legs tight again." Jason did so, and as Thom slipped his prick between his legs, under his balls, he said, as he lowered his body and began to fuck Jason's groin, "Why should I screw a fake pussy when I've got Jason Boone to fuck?"

Jason played his hands eagerly over Thom's writhing ass while he fucked him, and with a fingertip, teased Thom's asshole. When his finger actually penetrated Thom, and he began to push it in and out, the boy stopped fucking for a moment, and reached behind to pull it out. He simply said, "No, Jason," and resumed fucking.

"Then why don't you lift up my legs and fuck me right? Jason asked. "I want you inside me, Thom."

"Not here. This is fine for right now," Thom panted. "But I want to. I never thought I'd wanna fuck butt, but I know I want yours. I'll fuckin' *fill* your pretty little ass full of hard dick and hot cum. How's that sound?"

"Oh Jesus, Thom, I can hardly wait."

Nothing more was said, although both lovers panted and moaned in joy while Thom fucked savagely and they kissed ravenously. Jason had sucked an unusually large load out of Thom's cock during intermission, so it took a fairly long time before Thom shot another. As he did so, he cried out loudly and buried his face in Jason's neck, whimpering "Oh, baby! Jesus, I love it, Jason," while the passion of his orgasm faded somewhat.

Rising to his knees, Thom pushed Jason's legs apart so he could kneel between them. His cum coated the back of Jason's balls and his inner ass-cheeks; Jason's legs had been squeezed together so tightly, all Thom's load had been trapped in the pocket of hot flesh he had fucked. He reached in and spread cum over Jason's asshole, and used it as a lubricant to insert a finger. Driving his finger all the way in and out, he whispered, "Next time, I put my cum in your ass, and it's gonna shoot outa my dick, as far inside it as I can get it." Jason said nothing as he writhed in pleasure, whipping his head back and forth while he groaned appreciatively.

Abandoning the finger-fuck, Thom used his full hand to scoop up all the cum he could, which he then used to coat Jason's cock and jack it off — slowly and sensuously at first, but gaining in speed and intensity of stroke until his efforts were rewarded with Jason's orgasm exploding, sending jets of cum all the way up to his chin, crossing his chest and belly with ropes of it.

Jason was panting in exhaustion and ecstasy. Thom leaned over him and kissed him tenderly for a moment before he raised his head and smiled, saying nothing for a very long moment as he gazed happily down into Jason's eyes. Then he moved his head down and began to lick the cum from Jason's chin. Jason's hands held his head loosely and lovingly as Thom licked his way farther down, lapping up every drop of cum from Jason's neck, chest and stomach. He lightly kissed the head of Jason's still-formidable prick, licking off the drop of cum that still clung to it. From Jason's mid-section he smiled upward at him and said, "Another first. And the next time you blow me, it won't be one-sided, okay?" He rose to kiss him with cum-covered lips, "I can't believe I'd ever say this, but...I want to suck your dick, Jason! No...I'm *going* to suck your dick, and I'm gonna fuck your ass!"

"Oh Jesus, Thom! When? I can't wait."

"Well, you'll have to wait for a while. I'm all fucked out!" Thom grinned.

They lay there and cuddled for a few minutes, but the floor was hard and cold, so they were getting uncomfortable. Thom had no sooner said, "Let's get dressed" than there was a sharp rap on the door, and a voice called out, "Jason? You wanna go out and get a burger?" Thom and Jason held their breath. Then someone pushed against the door, but the rubber wedge kept it from opening. They heard the voice say, with a snicker, "Guess he's busy again. You still want to go, Tobey?" Tobey — presumably — grunted a muffled "Yeah," and their footsteps retreated down the hall.

"Who was that," Thom whispered.

"I'm pretty sure it was Sean. Obviously, Tobey was with him," Jason said.

"Christ! Do you suppose they knew both of us were in here?" Thom asked.

"I'd be willing to bet they did," Jason said. "Sean has made a few remarks lately about you and me being together a lot, and then the other night I was in bed with Tony — you remember, the sailor with the tight pants and the big cock? We had fucked each other, and were taking a break, watching TV, when Sean and Tobey came down from upstairs. They'd been screwing each other, and they needed a break, too; they knew Tony had come over to see me, so they came down to visit. We were talking, and Sean said he thought you and I must be getting to be *really* good friends."

"What did you say?"

"I reminded him that you were straight and I told him we were just good friends, that's all. Sean laughed and he said, 'Oh sure. Right! Hey, I'd like to get friendly like that with Thom — *real* friendly.' And then Tony said, "You know, he may be straight, but he sure checked out my box the night I came by with Sean.' And Tobey said, 'When he was watching me fuck Jason in the hot tub one night, I got the feeling he wanted me almost as much as I wanted him.' "

"Well, hell," Thom said. "What if they do know what we're doing? I don't suppose it makes any difference. Are any of you guys...*serious* about each other, though? You know what I mean?"

Jason laughed, "God, no. In fact, right after Tobey said he thought you wanted him, Tony said, something like, 'You're a god, Tobey, I can't resist you!" and shoved his cock up Tobey's ass and started to fuck him in Sean's cum. Then Sean fucked me in Tony's cum, and the four of us messed around with each for a couple of hours."

"I wonder how Tobey figured out I was hot for him that night," Thom said. "I thought I was being careful not to let him catch me staring at his body and his tits — then, and while we've been doing the show, too. And I might as well admit it; Sean kind of fascinates me, too. He's so small, and he's got that huge fuckin' dick and that cute little ass. But anyway, he and I are never on stage together in the show, so I don't see too much of him"

"I *thought* you had the hots for Tobey," Jason said. "Why don't you let him know? Obviously he wants you, too. He's damned good in bed, Thom. But so is Sean, if you're interested — and don't forget Tony. He's got the biggest dick I ever saw, and he uses it like a fuckin' artist, but I'll bet he'd love to take yours up his ass; he said he thought you were hot as hell."

"Nah, I've got you now," Thom said, joking — almost.

The next day was Monday, and there was no performance of *Absalom* scheduled. Thom called The Book Cellar about the time Jason was getting ready to close, and Tobey answered the phone. Thom asked to speak with Jason, and identified himself when Tobey asked if he could tell Jason who was calling. Tobey turned the phone over to Jason, holding it up to his chest so Thom could not hear as he said, "It's your straight lover boy. Oops, I mean your *good friend*."

Jason began to glare at Tobey, but then laughed and winked. His heart was beating heavily as he spoke, hoping that Thom had decided he couldn't wait until tomorrow to get together — and that tonight might be the night he was going to both suck and fuck him. "Hi, Thom. What's up?"

Tobey giggled, and whispered, very quietly, pointing at the phone, "His dick!"

Thom had not called to say he was coming over. Quite the contrary, he had a date that night with a woman he had been fucking with for quite a while. But he did say he wanted to call and tell Jason he was sorry they wouldn't be able to get together until the next day. Jason was touched – and encouraged by his thoughtfulness – and by the fact that Thom was going to miss their lovemaking.

"Are you gonna think of me at all when you fuck her?" Jason asked, aware that Tobey was still listening, but deciding it didn't make any difference now.

"I wouldn't be able to *not* think of you," Thom said. "I hope I can pay attention to her, and not slip up and call her 'Jason.' I'll probably be thinking about how I'm gonna fuck you while I'm fucking her. In fact, I'm thinking about it right now."

"How big is your dick right now?" Jason asked. Tobey tittered quietly.

Thom panted, "It's about as big as it's ever been, thinking about you, and what we do together, and how much I'm gonna miss it tonight – and I'm stroking it right now, listening to your voice. I'd better hang up, 'cause if I don't, I won't be able to stop jacking off until I come – and that would really piss off my date."

"I wish you were here right now, so I could do that for you. But I understand – get ready for your date. It was really sweet of you to call; I can hardly wait until I see you tomorrow."

"I can't either. Jesus, Jason, what's going on? Are you turning me queer, or what?"

Jason thought a second before he answered, "I'm not doing anything to force you to express yourself sexually with me, Thom. Are you doing anything with me you don't really *want* to?"

"No, not at all. I love what we do. Hell, I love..." He stopped abruptly.

"If you were going to say you that love me, you can say it, Thom. It's not a trap. I love you, too, but that doesn't mean either one of is probably *in love* with the other. I love a lotta guys, Thom, and not just because I fuck with them. I love Tony and Sean, too." He looked at Tobey, who looked like he was going to have his feelings hurt because Jason hadn't included him. Then Jason said, "And especially Tobey. I'm as eager to make love with him as I am with you, or as eager as *you* are to get him in bed." He winked at Tobey, who grinned back.

"I've gotta hang up, or I'm gonna start thinking about Tobey too," Thom said. "I love you, Jason. See you tomorrow."

"For sure," Jason said. "Enjoy your date."

Jason looked at Tobey after he hung up. "Just keep quiet about it, okay?"

"Sure," Tobey said. Then, after a pause, he grinned, "So he wants to get me in bed, huh?"

"I don't think even *he* realizes how impressed he is with you. He's dying to play with your tits and your ass. But just keep that to yourself for a while. You want him, don't you?"

"Shit yes, I do!" Tobey said.

"Well, I'll work on it, and set it up for you when he's ready. He's never sucked cock or fucked butt yet, much less taken a dick up his own."

"But I'll bet he's close, with you. Right?"

"Yeah, I think so. Anyway, when he's ready for the 'Tobey Barksdale Experience,' you'll be the first to know — probably even before he knows."

"Yeah, but is he ready for the total 'Jason Boone Experience'?

"We're almost there," Jason smiled. "How about you? You ready to swap the *Tobey Barksdale Experience* for the *Jason Boone* until then?"

"Hell yes," Tobey said. "Let's lock up the store and go upstairs so we can *express ourselves sexually!*"

*

During intermission the next evening, Thom spread towels on the dressing-room floor again, but instead of fucking Jason's legs, he kissed him, then kissed and licked his way down his body until he reached his cock. He opened his mouth wide, and administered his first blow-job. He didn't do a very good job of sucking Jason off, but he enjoyed it, and managed to contain every spurt of Jason's unduly large load inside his mouth. He swallowed the cum eagerly, licking his lips and savoring it long after he had done so.

While it was true Thom had proven fairly ineffective as a cocksucker in his maiden effort, it should be pointed out, in his defense, that at over eight inches, Jason's cock presented a serious challenge. But he rose to the challenge gladly: before *Absalom* ended its run, he was burying his lips deep in Jason's pubic hair, with his co-star's balls pressing against his chin every time he blew him — and he had done so at least a dozen times by then.

"I can't believe I'd ever be saying this," Thom whispered as he lay on top of Jason following the first blowjob he had ever given, "but I loved sucking you off, and even swallowing your cum. It was really exciting, especially when you blew your load. I wish I could take your dick all down my throat, the way you take mine."

"You'll be taking it down to the root in a week, if you want to keep doing it," Jason said.

"If I *want* to? Jesus, Jason, yes I do. Try to *keep* me from doing it! Hell, I'd suck you off again right now if I could."

"Turn around and kneel over me," Jason smiled. "We can sixty-nine, and I may not come again before you shoot your load, but I promise you it won't be long after."

Thom eagerly reversed his body, and returned to sucking Jason's cock as Jason sucked his. He was already able to take more of Jason's cock in his mouth. His cum did erupt and fill Jason's mouth before he sucked out Jason's cum again, but as he continued to working on his second blowjob, Jason released Thom's cock and turned his attention to his asshole.

Raising his head, Jason began to kiss the cheeks of Thom's ass, and lick his asshole. Thom started to groan and pant his pleasure around Jason's prick. When Jason drove his tongue as far inside Thom as he could, he forcefully squirted the mouthful of Thom's cum he had retained into the boy's own asshole. Thom raised his head and howled with excitement for a moment before returning to his work. As Jason's cock exploded in another orgasm, filling Thom's mouth almost as fully as before, Jason's tongue was driving and wriggling deep inside the boy.

Thom rose to his knees, and sat down over Jason's face, begging him to keep eating his ass while he rhapodized about how much he enjoyed *everything* he did with him. Then he turned over and lay atop Jason again while they hugged and kissed tenderly in the afterglow of their sexual sharing.

"You want me to fuck you after the show?" Thom whispered into Jason's mouth.

"Yes, Thom. Oh Jesus, *yes!* But it'd be a lot better if we didn't have to worry about someone interrupting us. Can you come over to my house and fuck me in my bed, so we can take our time and really enjoy it?"

By that time, Thom had a finger deep inside Jason's ass. "I'm going to enjoy it wherever we do it," he said, "but I really would like to make love with you in your bed."

"Make *love*?" Jason asked.

Thom kissed him very sweetly, "Yes. *Make love* to each other — not just blow each other or fuck each other."

"Fuck *each other*? Jason asked, "Does that mean you want me to…"

"Jason, I…don't know if I'll ever be ready to take you up the ass. I want to fuck you so bad I can't stand it, but I don't know if I can take it myself. I'm not even sure I *want* to, no matter how much I lo..." He froze for a moment, then smiled as he relaxed, "I almost said I, didn't I? What the hell, it's true. I'm not even sure I want to get fucked no matter how much I *love* you. I do love you, Jason."

"I love you, Thom."

"I promise you," Thom said, if I ever do take a dick up my ass — or try to, anyway — it'll be yours."

That was a promise Thom fully intended to keep, but Fate was going to step in and keep him from doing so.

As they embraced and kissed lovingly, Jason realized that for the first time he might actually be falling *in love*. He loved Tobey and Tony and Sean, and had loved quite a few others in the past; while it had been more than just beautiful boys and great bodies, big dicks and hot sex, he had never actually fallen *in love*. Of course when he was younger, he had mistaken adolescent crushes for love when he had sex with especially hot guys, especially the first ones he had sucked and fucked with.

Without any bitterness, Jason realized that he seemed to be, ironically, falling in love with an apparently straight boy — admittedly a straight boy who had just sucked him off. He had gone to bed with many, many straight partners in the past, straight boys who liked fucking or getting blown by a gay boy — and to Jason's amusement, quite a few of those liked sucking that gay boy's prick or taking it up the butt, and still claimed to be straight. He had to ask himself: *Why couldn't I fall in love with a gay boy? Or, at least, one who admitted he was gay?* But he was mature enough to realize he had little choice in the matter, and had to accept the role of Destiny in his life. Destiny had, apparently, brought Thom Nelson into his life.

10.

JASON TAKES A TRIPP

Following the performance that evening, Thom went home with Jason, and while he knelt on his bed in front of Thom, Jason introduced him to the wonderful world of buttfucking. If he hadn't been immediately an accomplished cocksucker, Thom took to fucking butt as if he had been doing it for years — and doing so with great skill! Also, his cocksucking ability was clearly going to grow exponentially; he almost deep-throated Jason both times he sucked him off that evening.

Several evenings that week, Thom came to Jason's bedroom to make love after the show, and by the end of the next week he was usually spending the entire night when he did. Tobey had once come down to Jason's bedroom to see if he wanted to fuck, and had overhead him having sex with Thom, so he went back upstairs and left the two to their lovemaking.

By the time the show ended its run, Thom and Jason were making love so often that the supposedly straight boy had not had sex with a woman in two weeks — nor had Jason had sex with anyone else since the first night Thom had fucked him. They spoke of their love often, but neither had yet professed that he was *in love* with the other. Neither was yet sure he *was* in love with the other.

Thom was worried that he might, indeed, be turning completely gay. It was something that, because of his upbringing and natural prejudices, he did not welcome, no matter how much he enjoyed sex with Jason — even though he admitted he must be bisexual, at least as far as Jason was concerned. He renewed his sexual contact with his female playmates aggressively, but didn't stop his love-making with Jason. He explained to Jason what he was doing, and Jason never tried to talk him out of it. In fact, Jason told Thom that he himself was ready to start having sex with other guys again, but he also wanted to continue their sexual relationship. Each was slightly hurt by the other's declaration, but their love and friendship survived the minor jealousy it naturally aroused.

Tobey, Tony, and Sean welcomed Jason back into their sex lives after the brief respite, and Jason made a few new casual conquests as well. Tobey and Sean were well aware that Thom and Jason had been making love regularly, and even Tony had learned. All three thought Thom was extremely hot, and each wanted to have sex with him; they asked Jason if that would bother him. Jason said it was strictly up to Thom; he even promised to sound Thom out about his sexual interest in any of them.

Jason approached Thom to see if he was interested in sex with Tobey or Sean or Tony. It would have been futile for Thom to deny his interest in Tobey; he had often expressed to Jason his special attraction to Tobey's glorious chest and his enormous balls. As for the others, he admitted that Tony, the incomparably sexy and mon-strously hung sailor, fascinated him as well. He was also in awe of Sean's prodigious cock, and curious about how it would feel to make love with a mature person whose body was so small. In short, while Thom's appetite for gay love-making was principally centered on Jason, he was clearly interested in branching out with Jason's friends.

In fact, Thom sheepishly confessed, one afternoon on campus the week after *Absalom* closed, he had encountered Matt and Cliff, two of the ultra-studly boys who played warriors in the play; they had made it clear they were on their way to have sex together, and would be particularly happy if Thom would go with them to make it a three-some. Thom succumbed to temptation, and joined in. He had sucked and played with their tits at great length, sucked Cliff's cock for a while, and then sucked Matt off. Thom spit Matt's load on Cliff's ass to lubricate it before he fucked him.

While Thom was fucking Cliff, Matt was sucking Cliff's cock, taking his load in his mouth about the time Thom's load exploded inside Cliff's ass. Matt kissed Thom, and squirted into his mouth the load of cum he had sucked out of Cliff, quickly urging him not to swallow it, but to spit it out on his own ass and fuck it also. It took Thom a long time to blow another load, in Matt's ass, but he managed.

Cliff begged Thom to let him fuck his ass, but Thom refused, although he did let the boy finger-fuck him while he screwed Matt. Cliff's disappointment was mollified when Thom sucked him off at the same time Cliff was eating Matt's ass, sucking Thom's cum from it.

Jason was somewhat stung by Thom's confession, but at the same time he was so excited by it that in the back of his mind he made plans to seek out Cliff and Matt so he might share in a threesome with them.

The three-way encounter with Cliff and Matt had been so gratifying, Thom said, that he hoped Jason would join in with him and Tobey, as well as with him and Tony, or with him and Sean, if those encounters materialized. It sounded hot as hell to Jason, and he quickly agreed.

Shortly after that, Thom finally got to have sex with Tobey, in a threesome with Jason. It was clear he adored it—so much so, that Jason often spent much of the time watching the other two making love to each other. Thom played with Tobey's tits almost constantly while he fucked him and sucked him—and even while Tobey was fucking Jason. When Tobey and Thom were sucking each other in sixty-nine, Thom suddenly stopped sucking and buried his face in Tobey's ass—eating it out as eagerly as Jason had eaten his. Although Jason had eaten Thom's ass countless times by then, Thom had never done the same for him— but the sight was so exciting, Jason didn't feel hurt.

Several nights after his three-way with Tobey and Jason, Thom broke a promise to Jason, when Sean joined him and Jason in bed.

Thom seemed as fascinated by Sean's diminutive body as he had been by Tobey's massive one. Jason was interested to note that Thom was able to deep-throat Sean's massive prick the first time he took it in his mouth. Perhaps Thom had been practicing on some other extremely well-hung stud? Or did either Matt or Cliff have a monster cock of similar dimensions as Sean's? Thom had said nothing about that, but it seemed logical to Jason that he would have said something if either Cliff or Matt had been hung with something like Sean's 9 ½ inches. Jason didn't ask, and never learned where Thom's improved skill in sucking cock had come from.

Thom had just blown a load in the tiny Sean's ass, and was kneeling, bent over Jason, sucking his prick. Jason was sitting up, leaning against the headboard, with Thom's head buried in his lap and his ass sticking up in the air.

Sean got behind Thom and began playing with his asshole. First he ate Thom out for a long time — to Thom's great enjoyment — and then he dipped into the lubricant freely, and greased Thom up. He inserted first one finger, then another, and although Thom grunted a little, he neither complained nor stopped sucking Jason's prick. Even when Sean gradually added a third finger, Thom only stopped sucking long enough to say, "No, Sean."

In spite of Thom's objection, Sean continued fucking him with three fingers, then pulled them out, greased up his cock, and positioned the head of it for entry. As he began to push forward, Thom rose up and said, "No, Sean, I don't do that."

Sean ignored the objection and continued to press his cock, pushing Thom's head back down into Jason's lap, saying: "Don't be a pussy, Thom. Take it like a man! You'll love it."

Thom objected a few times, but soon Sean had his prick completely buried inside his ass, and he whispered "Relax and enjoy it" as he began to fuck Thom slowly, with shallow strokes. Within a few minutes, Sean's stroke had greatly increased in rapidity and depth of penetration. He was soon fucking 'all stops out,' and Thom began backing his ass up to meet each plunge of the massive prick. "How is it?" Sean asked.

"My God, it feels fuckin' *great!*" Thom panted.

"Of course it does," Sean said as he threw his head back and pounded ass as fiercely as he knew how. "You're getting' every bit of it now, baby!"

Jason was astonished. He had figured Thom was going to take him up the ass fairly soon, and he planned to take this final step with his lover in a gentle, loving way, but here was Sean, driving a colossal cock into Thom without any holding back—a meeting of virgin ass and a cock that was *extremely* far removed from 'training size.' It seemed unlikely that such a combination could yield the utter *joy* Thom was obviously experiencing.

Thom gasped and groaned his pleasure, often panting words of encouragement to Sean, and often grunting incoherent words of ecstasy. His comments of appreciation, "God, that feels so fuckin' good!," "I love it!," "What a big fuckin' dick!," and the like, appeared to be directed to Jason, since Thom was staring into his eyes all the time, brows knitted, jaw slack, head shaking from side to side. But Thom's eyes were unfocused, too glazed over with mindless lust for Jason to believe he was addressing his comments to anyone in particular.

As Sean shoved his cock as deep inside Tom as it would go, and froze there while it erupted, he cried out, "Take it all, baby!" and Thom all but screamed his excited "Give it to me!" While Sean resumed pumping his cock, although more slowly and gently, Thom began to wriggle his ass around it while he resumed backing up on it in sync with Sean's thrusts. His eyes were still fixed on

Jason's but they came into focus as he said, "Jesus, Jason. That's the greatest feeling I ever had."

Jason gently took Thom's head in both hands and kissed him sweetly, whispering, "I know."

"But I promised you'd be the first guy to fuck me if I ever took it up the ass. I'm sorry, Jason, I didn't mean to break my promise."

Sean, still gently probing Thom's ass, laughed, "It's not like I gave you much choice, Thom." He leaned over, pressing his chest against Thom's back, and kissed him, then whispered into his ear. "And you really took it like a man. You are a helluva fine piece of ass, you know. Did you shoot your load while I was fucking you?"

"No," Thom said, "but I've got to, soon."

"Just get up there in Jason's lap and sit down on his cock," Sean said. "He can still fuck you the first time you got fucked — it's just that he can't start it out. You up for it, Jason?"

"What do *you* think?" Jason said.

"Go ahead," Sean said, pulling his cock out of Thom. "After you come, you're probably gonna hurt for a while, but if you take Jason up the butt right now, it's just gonna be more of your first fuck. Go on, do it!"

Jason slid his body down on the bed as Sean backed away, and whispered up at Thom, "Sit on it, baby. I've wanted to fuck your ass for such a long time!"

Positioning his asshole over the tip of Jason's prick, Thom sat down hard, impaling himself on a cock slightly smaller than Sean's, but still an extremely challenging one. Immediately, he began to bounce up and down on it, while Jason fucked upward into him, with Sean's volu- minous load of cum leaking out of Thom's ass and coating Jason's cock and pubes. The glaze of lust again descended over Thom's eyes as he rode, once more muttering and panting his enjoyment.

Fortunately for the recuperative period Thom's ass-hole was going to need following a maiden fuck by two cocks in excess of eight and nine inches, respectively, Jason was so excited that he was not able to prolong his fuck for a very long period. After only five minutes, he levered his ass high off the bed and blasted his cum deep inside Thom, who had been begun masturbating fran- tically when Jason went into high gear and announced the imminent arrival of his orgasm. Almost simultaneously with Jason's discharge, Thom's prick began spewing ropes and spatters of thick, white cum on his fist and all over Jason's head and upper body. Sean immediately seized Thom's hand and lapped the cum from it before he sucked the last drops out of his cock and began licking Jason's body clean.

In the afterglow of their exhausting sex, the three lay together and talked. Thom was amazed to find that he felt free to discuss what they had just shared, kidding about his getting fucked—something he had never thought he would do, much less feel happy and guiltless about. "God, Sean, your dick is so fuckin' *huge*," he said, "I don't know how I managed to take it.

Sean laughed, "Wait'll you get Tony's up your butt— it's even bigger. Biggest one I've ever had, in fact."

"Me too," added Jason.

"Who says I'm gonna let Tony fuck me?" Thom asked.

Jason and Sean laughed, both saying "I do." Jason went on, "Tony puts that big dick of his almost anywhere he wants. Not many guys want to say no to ten inches of fat cock."

True to form, Tony put his ten-inch cock where he wanted to when he went to bed with Thom and Jason, once again in Jason's bedroom. He put it all the way up Thom's ass, and fucked him twice in succession, without even withdrawing—although he did take a rest, in between and in place. Before Tony fucked Thom, he had encouraged Jason to fuck him first and prepare his ass for the onslaught. Jason was happy to oblige, of course, and left a nice load inside Thom to welcome Tony's enormous prick.

In the period between Sean taking his cherry, and Tony's fuck, Thom had been fucked by Jason quite a number of times, and once again by Sean. He was not too worried about being able to take Tony's monster—after all, it was only a half-inch longer than Sean's. As it happened, he found it was easier to take Tony's superior cock than it had been Sean's, since the sailor was gentle and cooed seductive words of encouragement while he slipped his gargantuan prick inside, not *shoving* it in the way Sean had.

Tony was an amazingly satisfying lover, Thom found, but so was Sean. Surprisingly, diminutive Sean was much more demanding and fierce than the tall, even better-hung Tony. But while Thom had adored sex with both of them, he knew that it was Jason he actually enjoyed more than either; he loved Jason—he just *wanted* Sean and Tony. He also wanted Tobey, but he knew that his degree of desire was much stronger for him than it was for Sean or Tony—close, in fact, to what he felt for Jason. He had only made love with Tobey once, and had yet to get fucked by the gloriously built stud. It was a simple matter to rectify that failing.

Thom called Tobey and asked him if he wanted to come over to his apartment to make love—just the two of them, without Jason present. Promising not to tell Jason, Tobey agreed.

Tobey was pleasantly surprised to hear that Thom had finally bottomed, and he wasted no time in starting to fuck him. After only a few minutes' foreplay, he had Thom lying on his back, with his legs spread wide. While he fucked Thom in missionary position, Thom played with his chest and his ass frantically. If Tobey wasn't as well-hung as either Sean or Tony—or Jason, for that matter—his cock was anything but small, and he fucked Thom slowly, deeply, lovingly. Before returning Tobey's first fuck that night—the first of two—Thom ate Tobey's ass at great length, licking and kissing everywhere, and tongue-fucking him as deeply as he could.

After their sex, Thom and Tobey lay together in each other's arms, kissing tenderly, their asses full of cum, and their tongues tasting of it. Tobey said, "You know, Thom, I used to think you were straight, even when I found out you and Jason were making it regularly, but after to-night..." He smiled, "I'm here to tell you—you *aren't* straight. I guess you still like pussy, though."

"Yeah," Thom said, after a meaningful pause. "But I have to admit, I find I like cock just as much. And I like fuckin' butt just as much as I do fuckin' pussy. But *getting* fucked is...I don't know, it's just..."

"The greatest?" Tobey asked. Thom nodded, shyly. "I know," Tobey said as he kissed him ad added, "So you're bisexual, so what?"

"I guess," Thom said as he started to fondle and kiss Tobey's chest. "But I know I've never seen a woman's tits that turned me on like these," and he began a new round of passionate body worship.

True to his word, Tobey said nothing to Jason about his meeting alone with Thom, but Thom himself admitted it to Jason. He also admitted he was so attracted to Tobey that he was beginning to think he might, in fact, be turning queer. "Tobey told me I was at least bisexual," he said.

"Does it bother you?" Jason asked.

"I thought it would, but...no, it doesn't. Does it...get in the way of...how you feel about me?" Thom asked.

"Not really, I guess. No, to be honest, it does. I've got to admit I've started falling in love with you, Thom; I've never really been in love with anyone before, and I thought you might be starting to feel the same way about me. Am I right?" Thom hesitated a moment before he nodded. " But I'm beginning to think you may be feeling that way about Tobey, too," Jason continued.

"I'm just confused, Jason," Thom admitted, clearly troubled. "I do love you, and making love with you means more to me than I can tell you. But I find Tobey so fucking attractive I don't think I can leave him alone if he wants to make love with me. The real problem is that I still like girls, and... I've never talked about this with you, but some day I'd like to have kids. What can I do, Jason?"

"I don't like to give advice to anyone, Thom. Usually I just tell someone who wants it, that all I can do is tell him what *I* would do if I were in his situation. But I'm stumped on this one — I can't even relate to being torn between sex with girls and guys. But I will say this, Thom. You have to admit you're at least halfway queer. I don't think you could really be happy if you had to give up sucking and fucking with guys permanently, but I have no idea how you would feel if you completely stopped having sex with women. I will give you this advice: If you can't give up either men or women *completely*, be sure you leave yourself a way to be honest to your own desires, but also to be honest with your male or female partner — or the two of them, if that's the way it works out. Having kids would probably make you feel more loyal to your wife, but if you still have to find a guy to have sex with, even if it's only now and then, don't jeopardize your relationship with your wife by being caught out in a seamy, secret life. Basically, I'm saying just be honest; it may create some problems, but it's the only way for a long-term relationship of any kind to work." Jason grinned, and kissed Thom lightly. "Long-winded speech, but it all boils down to the fact that you've got to decide for yourself — but then, I guess it always does."

Thom's problem was brought to a head shortly after that, when Lisa, one of the girls he had been fucking for a long time, announced that she was pregnant, and she said no one had fucked her but Thom. Thom offered to marry her if she wanted, or to pay for an abortion if that was her preference. She wanted the baby, but she didn't want to get married, and finally admitted to Thom that she had a female lover.

Lisa said she liked Thom and enjoyed sex with him, but her lesbian companion was the most important thing in her life. "Besides," she said, "I think you may want to be with Tobey more than you do me."

"What do you know about Tobey?" Thom asked, shocked.

"Only that you've been saying his name in your sleep for the last month or so. "You fuck me, then you lay there and sleep a while, and he's the one you're obviously dreaming about. Who is he?"

"He's just a friend, Lisa. For God's sake."

"Well, he's a friend who gives you a hard-on, obviously. And more than that, I'll bet. I've sucked your hard-on a few times when you were asleep and saying Tobey's name, and from what I can make out by what you say, you and Tobey have obviously been blowing each other." She laughed. "Figures. I thought you were the only straight guy in this miserable town, but I was wrong as usual. Do you fuck him, too?"

"Yes, Lisa, I fuck him! And he fucks me—and I love it. But I like getting fucked by Sean even better; he's only about five feet tall, but he's got the second-biggest prick I've ever seen. The biggest one is Tony's, but he's only fucked me with it once—*so far*. But I loved that, too."

"Christ, Thom—you big, fucking *fairy!*"

"Yeah?" Thom snarled. "Well, I know I never even touched another guy's dick until after I started screwing you. Maybe it was because you were a dyke, even though I didn't know it."

She slapped him—hard.

Thom's reaction was more of shock than pain, although Lisa packed a pretty good wallop. He seized her arm in a fierce grip, feeling a surge of anger that quickly gave way to his fundamental decency. "Okay, I deserved that. I apologize, Lisa." He released her arm and sat down in a chair on the other side of the room. "What do you want to do about this?"

Lisa was not as easily mollified as Thom. "Go to your fairy friends, Thom. I don't care. Shannon wants me to go to New York to live with her so we can both be mothers to the baby. I told her I had to stay here so the baby could knows its father, but you know what? I don't want to give you that much satisfaction. I'm off to New York, and you'll never see your kid—never know if it's a boy or a girl. But I promise you one thing, Thom: If it's a boy, I'm gonna have him playing with my make-up and jewelry and dresses as soon as I can, and I'm gonna make sure he's the biggest, nelliest *queen* in the city of New York. I know how much you hate that, Thom.

"Not as much as I hate you right at this minute." He turned and walked from the room, never to see Lisa again, or hear news of the son she bore in New York seven months later.

Thom went directly to The Book Cellar, and found Tobey working. He asked Jason if Tobey could be spared. He could.

In Tobey's apartment, Thom embraced him and unloaded on him. He admitted that for the last few months every time he had made love to a girl or a woman, he had been thinking of a guy—usually about him. He told him all about Lisa, and declared he was through with women as sex partners. He said that although the reali- zation had dawned relatively late in life, he knew he was basically queer. The most meaningful and enjoyable sex he had ever shared had been with him and Jason and Sean and Tony, and even with Matt and Cliff. Learning about Thom's tryst with Matt and Cliff surprised Tobey, but did not necessarily shock him, since he knew from experience how persuasive and satisfying the two muscular studs were.

284

"But if I could be with you all the time, I'd be glad to give all of them up, if that was what you wanted," Thom said. "I love you, Tobey. You're the most beautiful and exciting thing I've ever seen. If you want me, I'm yours for the asking." He kissed Tobey passionately, for a long time. Then he squeezed him and smiled. "You don't have to say anything right now—especially if you're gonna say 'no.' But think about it, okay?"

Tobey was astonished, but he thought about it as he stood there holding Thom in his arms. He had sensed that Thom was falling in love with him, or was at least fascinated by him. He also knew that Thom was extremely fond of Jason, who was close to falling in love with Thom. He asked Thom how he felt about that.

"I love Jason, Tobey. I could easily be in love with him—and I think he already feels that way about me. But, the important thing is that even though I don't want to stop making love with Jason—or Sean or Tony, or maybe someone else who might come along, for that matter—I want to be with you more than anything else. I want to be your partner, to be *married*, in a way. If that means giving up sex with anybody else, it's worth it. But I don't know if you feel like that about me."

"I want to say I want to be your partner, Thom, but..."

"Then *say* it," Thom interrupted.

Ignoring the interruption, Tobey continued, "but could we be partners—be *married*, like you say—and still have sex with other guys? I don't think I'm ready to settle down completely yet."

"We can *try*," Thom said. "It basically hinges on one thing: do you love me?"

Tobey enfolded Thom in his magnificent strong arms, and pressed his colossal chest to Thom's own impressive one. He said, very seriously, "Yeah, I do." Then he gave him a very long, tender kiss, and a grin dawned as he added, "Let's try!"

They tried. Thom moved in with Tobey, in the apartment over Jason's. Jason was hurt and disappointed that Thom had chosen Tobey over him, but he was not surprised — Tobey was one of the most glorious physical specimens he had ever seen, and was a good and likeable person as well. But in a way he was relieved, also. He had been close to asking Thom to be his partner, himself, but he realized he was even less ready to settle down than Tobey. The fact that both Tobey and Thom made it clear that they could all continue making love with each other alleviated the hurt and disappointment.

For the next year, Tobey and Thom came downstairs to drop in on Jason at all hours of the day and night, sometimes singly, sometimes together, sometimes looking for sex with Jason and sometimes not. When either or both of them was looking for sex with Jason, and found him already making love with someone else, they sometimes left him alone and sometimes joined in, depending on what they thought might be desirable, based on what could be overheard. If the door was closed, they knew Jason did not want to be disturbed — but he seldom closed it, since a threesome or a four-way with one or both of them was usually welcome. If Tony or Sean (or both) came to fuck with Jason, they frequently called up the stairs after a while to invite Thom or Tobey (or both) down to join them.

Tobey and Thom graduated together the following year, and they moved to Columbia, where Tobey could be near — but not *too* near — his family in Lugoff, and where Thom could be far enough away — but not *too* far away — from his parents in Greenville. They went to work for a high-powered real estate developer, and learned enough from him that ten years later they began their own development company.

They both worked out in a gym near the University of South Carolina campus, where they attracted enough attention that a string of especially toothsome USC boys visited their bed regularly—sometimes making love with just one or the other, often with both at the same time.

Within a few years the specter of AIDS had become sufficiently threatening that they insisted on condom usage with all their sex partners, and, because there were so many of those, even with each other.

Paulik University had reacted to the AIDS situation by conducting one of the earliest, and most thorough safe-sex education programs in the country—no doubt because the 'powers that be' at Paulik were well aware of the special importance of safe sex at their all-male, gay-friendly school. Paulik students soon generally refused to have sex with anyone without a condom, and as a result, the sailors, the Marines, and the townspeople who fucked with them—men like Jason—all adopted condom usage as well.

About that time, Tony Lowe was mustered out of the Navy and headed to California, accompanied by Sean Gayle.

Sean had graduated from Paulik before Tony's separation from service, but at that point had no idea what he wanted to do with his life. He moved into the apartment Tobey had vacated, and he and Jason frequently welcomed each other with open arms and open legs, but he also lured a regular parade of sailors and Paulik students into his bed, and not infrequently brought one down to share with Jason. Few Marines ever picked Sean up unless they got a look at his monster cock first. He also needed to earn money, and he built up a select clientele of older, generous men who appreciated his charms—and who were willing to pay generously for sharing them.

Tony visited both Jason and Sean separately at their respective apartments, and the three frequently fucked as a trio.

A boyhood friend of Spike Jefferson had cruised Tony one night a few months before he went to California, and was thrilled when the tall sailor wearing skin-tight uniform pants that revealed something very special agreed to come home with him and spend a few hours of 'quality time' for a hundred dollars. The man was so overwhelmed by Tony's looks and by his astonishing prick that he asked if Tony might be interested in appearing in fuck movies.

Tony had planned on going to college when he be-came a civilian again, using the money Max had left him, supplemented by a Navy program that would help pay the cost of his education. He reasoned that if he spent a few years doing lucrative porn work, which would help pay for his schooling, his higher education could wait a few years if it had to. He let the man take a few Polaroid snapshots of him, both in uniform and naked — his face, his body, and his enormous prick. The man mailed them to Spike.

Spike Jefferson was excited by the pictures of Tony, and called him, offering to send him a round-trip ticket to come to California for a screen test and interview. Tony flew out to L.A. He liked Spike Jefferson, and Spike adored Tony. Moreover, Tony was not only gorgeous, extremely sexy, and hung like a horse, he also proved to be extremely photogenic. Perfect!

Spike painted a tempting picture for Tony of the glamorous life of a porn star, but was honest enough to tell him that the real money lay in 'escorting,' and that the length of his 'stardom' would be relatively short-lived. Could he 'escort,' he asked? Could he get it up and keep it up long enough to please a john, even if he was an older man — very likely a considerably older man — one quite probably not attractive to him? Tony had done so on occasion, and thought he could so on a regular basis. He went out on a couple of well-paid 'dates' with wealthy older men, arranged for by Spike. He performed well, and his 'clients' raved about his personality, his cooperation, and especially about his ten-inch cock! Spike promised to turn him over to an 'agent' who would manage the prostitution part of his career.

Tony agreed to come out and start shooting a video for Spike as soon as he was released from the Navy. When Spike asked if he had any friends or boyfriends who might be interested in the same kind of work, Tony described Sean, and suggested that he might be very marketable, both as porn star and escort, since he was an adult who could pass for a twelve-year-old boy, but one with a cock almost as big as his own. Spike was more than interested. "Send me pictures, and talk him into coming out here with you to interview," he said.

Tony posed with Sean for the pictures they sent Spike, so that he could compare Sean's size—his stature on one end of the scale, his cock on the other. Spike telephoned Sean directly, wildly enthusiastic about putting him in porn. "I want to use you! You don't even need to audition, just get out here as soon as you can so we can start. You are every *chicken queen*'s wet dream. Even if you just lie there, every one of 'em will be whacking off over you, and every 'size queen' too! And if you're as hot in bed as Tony tells me you are, you're gonna make a lot of money!" He went on to caution Sean about the need to 'escort' if he wanted make a really good living, but Sean assured him he was already doing that.

Sean moved to Los Angeles, and Tony followed him out there a few months later. Tony was officially a civilian by then, but he brought all his uniforms with him, since Spike told him he was going to have him playing a sailor whenever he could. "Nobody has ever looked sexier in a uniform than you do—well, not since I got out of the Navy!"

Tony moved to L.A., into a house with Sean. The porn videos that Tony began making, and which Sean had already been filming, were enormously successful, and both were soon porn stars of the first magnitude. They were both utilized mostly as tops, but when either one was paired with an unusually well-hung actor, or a major porn star who never bottomed on camera, he also bottomed. Every time they appeared in a video together—as they often did—each fucked the other one, and almost always double-fucked another actor at some point in the film. Uncharacteristically, they did not adopt aliases, electing instead to use no last names at all. Like 'Cher' or 'Madonna,' they were mononymic—known to the porn world simply as 'Tony' and 'Sean.'

In the trade it was generally understood that Sean and Tony were lovers, and they were, insofar as their porn and escorting careers would allow. They made love with each other whenever they could, but both were so busy with video work—which usually involved at least two orgasms during a day's filming—and with johns who paid them extremely well for their privately delivered orgasms, that their lovemaking was often limited to cuddling and kissing and—if neither of them had an 'overnight' trick with a john—sleeping in each other's arms. They also brought other major porn stars—some of the hottest, most desirable men in the world—home with them for sex. Their agent was a wonder in screening out relatively undesirable clients for their prostitution, and finding extremely generous ones. He also was quite successful in finding wealthy men who wanted the two of them to perform together for their private pleasure.

Shortly after they began their own development company, Tobey and Thom began work on a pet project at Hus Bay, a new housing development called "Paulik Shores." It was to be a complex of small houses, condominiums, service buildings and amenities built on a large bayshore tract of land. Tobey and Thom had convinced a number of wealthy Paulik graduates to finance the project.

All preferred that Paulik Shores be adjacent to the University campus, but since they insisted that it front on the waters of the Bay—allowing for swimming and boating—it was not possible to actually link campus and development. The campus is the only thing separating the City from City Park, so bayfront property on both sides is public land. Tobey and Tom were able to acquire a sufficiently large waterfront parcel on the edge of the city opposite the University, near the western limits of the Naval Station, and construction began there in 1990.

Purchase of houses and condominiums at Paulik Shores was limited to University alumni. By terms of the sale, an owner could not sell his unit or even rent it to anyone but another Paulik alumnus. For an independently determined value, he could sell it back to the corporation from which it was purchased, however. It was an "adults only" facility; minor children were not allowed, although pets were permitted, under fairly restricted conditions.

The houses and condominiums were elegantly designed and appointed, with amenities commensurate with their very high price range. The beach at bayside was improved, and a private golf course was built. Meeting rooms, a well-equipped gymnasium and sauna, a marina, and an Olympic-sized swimming pool—with diving tank and lap pool—were built. The gym and sauna were connected to a large Men's Club that had a bar, lounges, television rooms, and a dozen private rooms allegedly designed for private, one-on-one meetings on a rental basis.

A staff of trainers was on hand at the gymnasium that could be engaged privately by the members on an hourly basis. Most of them were porn stars who, (with one or two exceptions), had left the porn business and were pursuing careers as physical trainers. All of them were still active as escorts, although their work in that area was now almost exclusively conducted on the Men's Club premises. The porn stars—active and retired—normally carried a few of their own porn videos in their bags, to watch with their clients while they re-enacted some of the video scenes together.

The private rooms at the Men's Club rented by the hour, although half-day and overnight rates were offered as well. Each included a full bathroom, a television set and VCR, easy chairs, a mini-bar, and a daybed. Videocassettes were available for use, and could be checked out when engaging a room. Condoms and lubricant were as much a part of the furnishings as soap and towels.

As part of the Men's Club, the private rooms were available only to men, and only residents of the complex could rent one. A renter was allowed to invite one, or even a small number of male guests to accompany him to the room. The videocassettes available were of one kind only; not surprisingly, they were all-male pornographic tapes, and the selection was large and up-to-date. By all odds, the most popular videos were those that starred the Czech porn star Johan Paulik; his last name (even though it was probably an assumed one) attracted Paulik University alumni who liked to watch young men making love, but Johan was both amazingly cute and astonishingly sexy as well! Tapes were also available for rental to Paulik Shore residents in their homes or condominiums.

Videotapes featuring Sean and Tobey were even more popular—at Paulik Shores as well as on the Paulik campus and in town—since everyone seemed to know of the stars' Hus Bay roots. Jason ordered each of their videos by the hundreds for sale at The Book Cellar. Tobey and Thom had tried to convince the two porn stars to return to Hus Bay, to head up the gym/training business at the Paulik Shores Men's Club, and oversee and participate in the escorting phase of that business. Both were too busy in California with the video work—which by then involved directing and producing as well—and servicing a regular base of loyal clients for their escort work.

Homes and condominiums at Paulik Shores were all relatively spacious, but each had only one modest-sized bedroom. While wives and live-in girlfriends were welcome, the units were obviously designed for one person—

and since residents had to be Paulik University alumni, they were, *de facto*, designed for occupancy by single men. If a man and wife, or man and mistress, wished to share a single bedroom, they were free to do so, of course. In fact, all but a few of the units were occupied by lone men — mainly bachelors, divorcees and widowers, but quite a few were owned by men who wanted to have a place away from their principal residences, where they could enjoy gay trysts.

Given the specifications of the housing units and the Men's Club, it seemed Paulik Shores had been developed to encourage occupancy by gay men, and to provide them with facilities to allow for sexual dalliance away from home, if that were desirable. That was definitely *not* coincidental; to a man, everyone involved in planning and financing the development was either homosexual or at least bisexual — and the former far outnumbered the latter. All, without exception, were Paulik alumni with fond memories of a permissive gay lifestyle during their student years in Hus Bay.

In the early 1990's several large, single-occupancy apartment buildings had been built in the city, near the Paulik campus, which were designed for students who wanted to avoid the intense sexual atmosphere of the University dormitory — or for anyone who wanted a small apartment, of course; there was no 'males only' policy. Many of the apartments were rented by Naval officers (and a very small number of Marine officers) who wanted a place to live off-base, where they could pursue a private life in off-duty hours — which often meant having a place to conduct sexual rendezvous with Paulik students or fellow Navy and Marine officers (very few had sex with enlisted men — far too risky for their careers). Until Paulik Shores opened, quite a few well-to-do University alumni rented apartments for the same reason the military officers did, but they welcomed enlisted sailors and Marines into their clutches as eagerly as they did students.

293

Quite a few enterprising University students who earned a substantial income through 'escorting' rented apartments to entertain their clients, mostly older men who, for whatever reason, could not entertain an 'escort' at home.

By the time the apartments were built, most Paulik students had computers, which proved to be extremely useful for those who were looking to make contact with other guys for sex—both for fun and for pay. By the time Paulik Shores opened, every student was required to have a computer of some kind. Most of the sailors and Marines who wanted to, were able to access computers in some way, for the same purpose. For all who were willing to sell their sexual services for money, and who could perform satisfactorily with older men—often *much* older men—the computer was a godsend beyond compare.

Many young men selling themselves who might not be able to 'get it up' with an older man under normal circumstances, found that money was a remarkable aphrodisiac—and most of their Paulik-alumnus clients were quite well-to-do, and willing to pay generously for their young bodies.

High school boys in Hus Bay, and other nearby communities, often advertised the availability of their sexual services on the computer as well, and a surprising proportion of the sexual trysts arranged in 'Cyberia' involved them. They all claimed to be Seniors, of course, and of legal age. All their clients *completely* accepted the truth of those claims to adulthood, of course—surely no one would misrepresent himself in that respect!

The ease with which Paulik students had found sex in the dormitory or (along with the sailors and Marines) in City Park was extended electronically to both the older and younger horny citizens of Hus Bay. Except for the necessity of adopting safe-sex practices twenty years earlier, this gay Utopia had grown even more Utopian by the onset of the twenty-first century.

As the Paulik Shores project was under development and construction, Thom and Tobey had to be in Hus Bay frequently, and often for a fairly long time. The apartment on the top story of Jason's house, where Tobey had lived for several years, was unoccupied, and they offered to rent it for their use during that time, but Jason insisted they stay there as his guests.

Jason had seen both Thom and Tobey regularly, if not frequently, over the years. They were both still enormously attractive, and the chemistry between all three of them was still strong—as evidenced by the passionate and deeply satisfying sex they continued to share when they got together. Jason was still in love with Thom, but he had long ago conceded that he had lost him to Tobey, and regretted that he had not acted more quickly to win him. Jason envied Tobey, but any time he saw Tobey's body he envied Thom almost as much. However, his friendship and affection for both men overrode any latent jealousy.

By then Jason had found that sales of books in his business had shrunk considerably, largely because of the availability of cheaper, more varied stock for sale on the Internet, but also because the popularity of reading for pleasure on the part of college-age boys had shrunk so alarmingly. As book sales had tapered off, he had gradually added more stock in videocassettes and DVDs, for sale or for rental. Since the State of South Carolina no longer allowed, as they once had, the open sale or rental of hardcore pornography, Jason developed a private video club for the hundreds upon hundreds of his clients who clamored for gay adult videos—'fuck movies,' as they less elegantly termed them. As members of the club, they were able to buy and rent the hot videocassettes and DVDs they wanted to see.

The private video section was a separate part of the store, created by expanding the area at the basement level of the house that was dedicated to the business. It was run by a young man named Tripp Robinson, who lived on the main floor, and shared Jason's bed and Jason's life.

It had been a stage play that brought Jason together with Tripp, as it had been a play that united him and Thom many years earlier. When Lake McCoy asked Jason to play the part of Sir Thomas More in a late Fall production by the Hus Bay Community Theatre of *A Man for All Seasons*, he had to be convinced to do so. He had not been on stage since *Absalom*, some fifteen years earlier, and dreaded the thought of the lengthy rehearsal period, to say nothing of the enormous line load and the dramatic ability that is required of the actor who plays Sir Thomas More in that show. This time there would be no nudity or a group of nearly naked warriors to provide eye candy to compensate for the work involved.

He reflected wryly that it was much easier now to play an older man than it had been when he had played David to Thom's Absalom; he had recently passed his fortieth birthday. But Lake McCoy was nothing if not convincing, and although Jason had laughed off Lake's suggestion that he might meet another Thom Nelson in this play, he probably held out some subliminal hope that the magic might actually strike again. As a forty-year-old whose taste in sex partners generally ran to men much younger than himself, he realized that it was highly unlikely. Still, he accepted the part and began rehearsals.

Most of the actors in the show were adults, but there were a few reasonably attractive young men playing lesser roles. Jason had already been to bed with one of those, and another proved susceptible to his seduction within a few weeks of rehearsals. Since the last of his 'regular' sex partners had left when Tony and Sean moved to California, Jason had made do with sailors or Marines and University students he either picked up or met when they visited his store. As always, there was a plentiful supply, and a sufficient number of those were eager to go to bed with a more mature man that he had kept his sexual needs more than adequately supplied. In spite of his age, he was still an extremely satisfying sex partner, and quite a few of his tricks returned to his bed frequently. If he hadn't discovered another dick like Tony's, or a body like Tobey's, he came close surprisingly often. With one—a nineteen-year-old sailor—he came close to finding Tony's dick *and* Tobey's body wrapped up in one magnificent specimen, and they had a half-dozen stupendously satisfying encounters before a Chief Petty Officer about Jason's age came in The Book Cellar one day and introduced himself as the boy's lover, and then offered to beat the living shit out of Jason—as he put it—if Jason didn't keep his hands off his boy. The Chief was very large and very convincing, and Jason ruefully stepped aside.

Jason was getting all the sex he needed, but the idea of a life partner—someone to take the place of Thom, who might have been that partner—seemed more appealing all the time. It didn't appear that he was sharing the stage with another Thom as rehearsals for *A Man for All Seasons* progressed.

There was one boy in the show whom Jason almost overlooked. He was twenty-two years old, short (although not as much so as Sean), with a slight build that fairly baggy clothes tended to conceal. He wore large, almost owlish glasses, and was very shy and self-effacing. Had it not been for a mop of glorious golden-blond, curly hair, Jason might have ignored him altogether. He appeared to be much younger than he actually was, and Jason had first assumed he was about fifteen, until the woman who was playing the part of Alice More, his wife in the show, told him the boy's age—which she knew only too well, since she had given birth to him twenty-two years earlier! The boy—and Jason still thought of him as such—was named Tripp Robinson.

Tripp's part in the play was so minor that he had only one spoken line, although he was on stage fairly often, playing the part of a page—and even then, his single line of dialogue had been added to the script by Lake McCoy to cover a bit of stage business he had introduced. Jason had not realized how very *cute* Tripp was until he saw him without his glasses one evening. He had large green eyes and long eyelashes; when he laughed, the laugh-lines crinkling his eyes were almost as deep as the adorable dimples that appeared in his cheeks at the same time.

The idea of seducing Tripp began to grow in Jason's mind, but after the first rehearsal where the cast wore their costumes, the idea became an urgent desire. With the stage lights highlighting his glorious blond hair, and with his face no longer hidden behind his glasses, Tripp looked adorable. He appeared bare-chested, wearing a ruff—a starched, pleated collar—around his neck, and dressed below the waist only in light-colored, blue-gray tights, with minimal shoes. When he first walked out onto the stage in his tights, Jason was impressed with the boy's fine body—slight, but lightly muscled, with unblemished skin that looked almost like golden velvet. His rounded breasts were capped with dark-brown nipples, subtly skewed to the outside, which somehow, Jason thought, looked especially sexy. The crotch of his tights bulged roundly, but as round and sexy and inviting as the bulge looked, it didn't excite Jason especially, since he knew it was caused by a codpiece, worn to conceal Tripp's genitals so they would not be individually outlined by the clinging tights. His well-shaped legs were so closely contained in the tights that it almost appeared that he wasn't wearing anything over them, but that he had light blue-gray skin from the waist down. The tights were low-slung, revealing Tripp's minuscule waist, his 'outie' navel, and his flat belly.

When Tripp turned away to cross the stage, walking away from him, Jason virtually gasped, and 'went up' in his lines (forgot them, in theatrical parlance)—something he rarely did. The boy's ass was breathtakingly beautiful—

literally so! The cloth was stretched so tightly over it that it gave Jason the same impression he had when he looked at Tripp's legs, that it was like a smooth, blue-gray skin. The cloth was pulled so tightly and deeply between the buttocks, that it even clearly outlined the inside of the crevice between them, and gave definition to the well-rounded hemispheres it concealed. The effect was that instead of seeming to conceal Tripp's perfect little 'bubble butt' ass, the tights actually emphasized its perfection. Jason realized that Tripp's ass was probably more desirable encased in the tights than it would have been if it were completely naked—and he was eager to check out that theory! It was perfectly obvious Tripp was wearing nothing but the codpiece under his tights.

Jason could not immediately remember having seen an ass that was more perfectly formed and sublimely desirable. He managed to catch himself, and focus on his lines after a long moment, but only after Lake had called out, "Jason? Do we have a problem?"

After the rehearsal was over, Jason asked Tripp if he would like to go out for coffee before going home. Jason knew the boy lived at home, with his mother, and normally went there with her following rehearsals, but he seemed flattered that Jason had asked him, and he readily accepted, telling his mother where he was going.

As they talked in the all-night diner where they sat drinking coffee, Jason learned that Tripp was the only child of parents who had both been raised in Hus Bay. His father had been a groundskeeper at Paulik University who had begun dating the girl who was to become his wife when they were in high school. They had married quite young and were, in fact, only two years older than Jason. They had divorced when Tripp was fairly young, and he hardly knew his father, although he got Christmas and birthday cards from him annually until he was ten years old, when the older Robinson died of some ailment his mother never fully explained to her son.

299

There was no money for Tripp to attend an expensive school like Paulik, but by means of a scholarship and a student work program, he had attended the University of South Carolina for two years; he realized he didn't yet know what he wanted to do with his life, so he returned home to live with his mother and work for a few years until he decided. That had been two years earlier, and he still wasn't sure. He knew the job he held as clerk in a stationery store in Hus Bay was not going to become his life's work.

Tripp only gradually revealed the basic facts about his life to Jason, and he was very shy in doing so. Jason had to do most of the talking. It even took a half-hour before he convinced the boy he should call him by his first name, instead of "Mr. Boone." Tripp asked as many questions about Jason and his life as he answered about his own.

Tripp had never been on stage before the play they were working on, but his mother had convinced him to accept it. "She's worried that I don't have enough friends," he explained.

"Is that true?" Jason asked.

"I guess maybe it is. But I have friends she doesn't know about." He blushed as he said that, and Jason suspected the 'friends' might be boys or men he was having sex with. Several indicators suggested Tripp might be gay: he was living with his mother at age twenty-two; he apparently wasn't dating; he was clearly sensitive; he was carefully groomed, obviously interested in keeping his great natural beauty looking its best. Still, he was not remotely effeminate, and had said nothing to suggest a gay sex life—or *any* sex life, come to think of it—until he mentioned his secret 'friends.'

"Would I know any of the friends your mother doesn't know about?"

Tripp's blush deepened as he said, quietly, "Yes, probably." Then he seemed to pull himself together, and he looked Jason directly in the eye. "Will you answer me honestly if I ask you an odd question?"

"Sure, Tripp."

"Why did you ask me to go out with you tonight?" the boy asked.

"Well, we're working on the play together, and I thought we should…"

Tripp interrupted him. "I'm hardly in this play, and I don't see you going out with the other guys. Getting to know the other cast members isn't why we're here; I haven't seen you taking my mom out for coffee, for instance, and you and her work together all the time in the show. I thought you said you'd answer honestly."

"I'm sorry, Tripp. Yes, you're right; that wasn't an honest answer. But to be fair, your mother and I have gotten to know each other pretty well because, like you said, we've worked together a great deal in rehearsals and talked a lot when we weren't actually rehearsing. The same thing is true for several other people in the cast."

"So what's the honest answer?" Tripp asked.

Jason thought for a moment before he said, "I saw you wearing tights tonight for the first time—and I've never seen anyone that looked as good as you do in tights."

"And that's it?"

"Do you realize how attractive you are, Tripp?" Jason asked. "You must. I thought you were cute when we started working on the play, and then when you stopped wearing your glasses in rehearsals, and I could really see your face and your eyes, I realized you're actually…I'm sorry to put it this way, but, you're actually beautiful." Tripp blushed again, but said nothing. "And seeing you tonight without a shirt, and wearing those tights, I realized your body is just as beautiful as your face. As perfect as your chest and your arms look naked, the way those tights stretch over your legs, they make them look even more… attractive than if they were naked, too."

After Jason said nothing for a few seconds, Tripp smiled slyly, and said, "You're not gonna mention my ass?"

Again looking directly into Tripp's eyes, Jason said, evenly, "After seeing your ass in those tights, I don't believe I have words to describe it. 'Perfection' is so weak a word to describe anything as breathtaking as your ass."

Still smiling, but wryly, Tripp said, "So I guess I know why you wanted to get to know me."

Jason quickly replied, "But that's not the only reason, Tripp. Please believe me. You really do seem like a nice kid, and I'd like to know you better in any case, but seeing you in those tights just made me want to know you a lot better, and a lot sooner. Does that shock you? Am I out of line here?"

"No, you certainly don't shock me, Jason," Tripp said. "I may look young, but I'm not a kid. And besides, while you may have been finding me attractive, and seeing me almost naked sent you over the top, I've felt the same way about you since the first rehearsal, but I've never had a chance to see you almost naked."

"But I'm in my forties, Tripp, and you're..."

"Old enough to know what I like," Tripp interrupted. "And if you're interested, I'd like to go somewhere where you can check me out when I'm not just *nearly* naked, and I can check you out the same way."

They did not linger over their coffee!

Back at his home over The Book Cellar, Jason gradually removed Tripp's clothing, kissing and licking each part of his body as it was revealed. His prick was raging hard when it popped out as Jason pulled his shorts below it. It was not large—average, perhaps, at something a bit under six inches. But that did not bother Jason in the least; it was as beautiful as the boy himself was, and it fit very nicely in his throat.

Tripp smiled as he stepped out of his shorts and slowly turned around to reveal his naked ass to Jason's gaze, arching his body so that his perfect, round buttocks projected outward, actually *presenting* them for Jason's approval: golden, hairless, unblemished, with a deep, tight chasm protecting the entrance to the beautiful boy's body. Jason had encountered thousands of bare asses in his sexual adventures; he honestly believed he had never seen one more beautiful or tempting.

Although he had been caressing and fondling the firm, cool flesh of the boy's ass while he had been sucking his cock, the sight of it took the older man's breath away. Tripp reached behind himself and spread his cheeks, almost revealing the pink pucker hidden so deeply between them. Jason gasped in appreciation as his hands reached up from behind to fondle Tripp's chest as he buried his face in the boy's hot ass, and began to lick and tongue-fuck him. Tripp groaned with joy, and released his buttocks to allow them to trap Jason's face inside while he reached farther back to pull the older man's head as deeply between them as he could.

Turning around, Tripp disengaged Jason's tongue from his ass, and he raised the older man to his feet. They embraced, and their kiss was long and sweet, gradually growing intensely passionate until Tripp broke away and panted, "Get naked. Strip for me."

Jason quickly complied, and it was clear that Tripp was almost as eager to make love as Jason was. Tripp's shyness and reservation completely disappeared when he was making love. The joy he had registered when Jason ate his ass turned into fierce, vocal ecstasy when he was getting fucked.

Jason's unusual ability to produce multiple orgasms still persisted, but it was tested that night. Before dawn broke, he had fucked Tripp four times, and Tripp had sucked him off once. Tripp, on the other hand, had not fucked Jason at all, much to Jason's dismay, although the boy had three orgasms: one when he and Jason sucked each other off in sixty-nine, one when he was riding Jason's cock, and another when Jason was fucking him in missionary position. Tripp confessed that as much as he loved to get fucked, he simply was not a top, that when he tried to fuck someone, his prick—fiercely hard any time he was being fucked—refused to cooperate by staying erect. He was, fortunately, able to stay hard and come while he was getting blown.

They snuggled and kiss for long stretches between bouts of fucking, and Tripp's sweet, shy nature reasserted itself during those times.

Jason wooed the younger man assiduously, and even encountered outside encouragement to do so, from an unexpected source: Adele Robinson, Tripp's mother! Her son had raved about Jason so much on the day following the first night he had gone to bed with the older man that she knew what had happened. She had known Tripp was gay almost from the onset of his puberty; she recognized the signs probably even before he did—she had learned what they meant when she had been married to Tripp's father, before he left her and his son for an older man. Adele still loved the boy's father, although now only in memory. During his lifetime she had no trouble forgiving him the pursuit of his true nature; she had her beautiful boy to console the hurt she felt over his having deceived her by marrying her. His death in New York in the 1980's had been AIDS-related.

By the time *A Man for All Seasons* ended its run, Tripp was spending almost every night in Jason's bed, and within a few weeks after that had moved in with him. For the first time, Jason was completely in love, but his much younger lover had been in love several times before, always with a man considerably older than he, but never with a man who was completely honest with him—and the dishonesty had ranged from infidelity to secret wives, and has always been the cause of Tripp's breaking off relations. With Jason, Tripp fell in love all over again, but insisted that he could only be Jason's lover if they could be completely honest with each other.

Jason confessed that as much as he enjoyed sex with Tripp, and he enjoyed it to an unparalleled degree, he still wanted — no, to be honest, he *needed* — to bottom once in a while. Tripp used dildos on him regularly, but they both knew that no artificial substitute for a hard cock could fully scratch the itch that can only be fully satisfied when a hot man or boy drives a real prick deep inside one's ass.

The compromise Jason and Tripp reached was that when Jason needed to bottom, he could do so, with the clear understanding that Tripp was fully aware he was doing so, and that he never got emotionally involved with another sex partner. He was even free to top the man or boy for whom he bottomed, so long as Tripp was on hand to bottom for the third party as well. Tripp was especially happy with that arrangement; he was a very hungry bottom, and never quite seemed to get fucked as often as he wanted. Furthermore, while Jason's big prick was extremely satisfying, the occasional bigger prick a stranger could bring to their lovemaking was even more exciting.

A sailor named Jackson (he always wanted to be known by his last name alone) with a full eleven inches of cock was a frequent visitor to their bed, even though he would not suck dick or take one up his ass; both Tripp and Jason were happy to content themselves with blowing each other while Jackson plowed both of them repeatedly.

As it worked out, Tripp was very often on hand when Jason went to bed with third parties, since so many recognized what a luscious ass the boy could bring to their lovemaking with Jason. Between Tripp's ass and Jason's cock, they presented a very satisfactory package. In fact, almost half of the sexual threesomes they engaged in came about through Tripp agreeing to let someone fuck him if they also fucked Jason, although he was careful to ask them to proposition Jason to set things up.

Tripp left the stationery store where he worked, and became Jason's partner in The Book Cellar as he was in Jason's bed. Six months after they became lovers, Tripp's mother asked when they were going to get married. She was actually joking, but the more Jason thought about it, the more he wanted to show his young lover how serious he was about their union. Consequently, he asked Tripp if he would marry him formally, although the union would not, of course, be a legal wedding. Tripp readily accepted.

The wedding, presided over by a liberal Episcopalian minister, took place in the largest meeting room at the Paulik Shores Men's Club, where the wedding reception was also held. Adele Robinson, the only female in attendance—and one of the few females who had ever been inside the Men's Club—'gave' her son away. Thom and Tobey took care of the arrangements, and also secretly had Sean and Tony flown in from California for the occasion.

In lieu of the formal honeymoon they planned for later in the year, Jason and Tripp—with Tony and Sean, Thom and Tobey on hand to participate—celebrated a three-day orgy at their house. Every one of them carried 'the bride' (Tripp) over the threshold at some point, and then fucked him! Although Tony and Sean, as porn stars and professional escorts, were accustomed to extended periods of intense sex play, the other four were fairly exhausted by the time the 'honeymoon' was over. Tripp had been fucked so many times he lost count, and at one point the sight of Tobey's magnificent body lying before him, and the two enormous pricks Sean and Tony were poking in his face, so inspired him that he stayed hard when he attempted to fuck Tobey. And he succeeded admirably in his attempt while his new 'husband' and Thom were taking turns fucking him.

Another 'first' occurred when Jackson was invited to join the group the second afternoon. Jason and Tripp had talked about him, and the others wanted to see for themselves. The sailor was happy to join the fun that day, and showed up in a uniform as tight as Tony's had ever been, causing a sensation when he unreeled all eleven inches of the monster prick Jason and Tripp had raved about. Jackson fucked every one at some point, although he didn't blow a load each time he fucked. He was so excited by the sight of the diminutive Sean making love with Tony, and with the pair's enormous pricks—almost as long as his own—that he sucked them both off while he was fucking Tobey and Tripp was eating his ass. The sailor declared it was the first time he had ever sucked dick, but after he left, Sean and Tony agreed he had done so well at almost deep-throating their cocks and eating their loads, that he was either lying or was the most instinctively talented cocksucker in the world.

Every time after that, Jackson freely sucked dick when he was with Tripp and Jason, and eventually even took Jason up the ass—and with the same kind of suspiciously 'instinctive talent' he had displayed when he sucked off Sean and Tony!

Jackson's rampaging eleven inches of cock hammering his exquisite ass one afternoon inspired Tripp to top again, and this time his 'husband' was the lucky recipient. From that point on, Tripp's new-found ability to top returned occasionally, usually on visits by the spectacularly-hung sailor, but on other, widely-spaced occasions he would turn the tables and plow Jason or a third party to their lovemaking—including Jackson, the sailor who inspired his ability to do so. The only constant that was present on all those latter occasions, as far as Tripp or Jason could determine, was that the matchlessly beautiful Czech porn star Lukas Ridgeston was on-screen when they were watching one of his videos while they fucked. Tripp's contention that Lukas was the most beautiful, sexy and exciting man alive met with no argument from Jason.

CODA: THE PERSISTENCE OF UTOPIA

T ime will tell if Jason and Tripp's 'marriage' will last, but as this account is written they have celebrated the eighth anniversary of their union, and are as much in love as they ever were.

There has been — and continues to be — a steady parade of new faces from the Paulik student body and from the Naval Station and Parris Island in their bed. Jason is nearing fifty, although he is still in fine physical shape, and looking more dignified as he matures. Tripp could still pass for twenty, and is as fresh-looking and beautiful as ever; when he can, he wears clothing that shows off his trim young body and breathtakingly sexy ass to best advantage. Together, the two attract a wide variety of admirers eager to make love with them, but they have managed to separate the recreational aspect of lovemaking with those other men and boys from the genuine love-making they share only with each other.

Things have changed, of course.

At Thom and Tobey's urging, Sean and Tony moved to Hus Bay as managers of the health club at Paulik Shores, which entails managing the prostitution services the trainers provide as well. They are themselves still very popular with patrons for their 'personal services,' and even though they have retired from porn, they are still called on to provide those same services all over the country for fans of their video work. They still live together, but they consider themselves as fuckbuddies, rather than lovers; both might welcome a real partner into their lives, but neither has found one whom he thinks might actually be *Mr. Right*. They are very good friends, and the sex they share with each other is still as exciting as what they share with others to whom they are attracted, or who pay for their services, and who do not arouse jealousy in their relationship; that may be the best formula for a continuing relationship, after all. They often—singly, or as a pair—visit with Jason and Tripp, who usually welcome one or both of them to bed as a pair, but who are willing to swap partners and use two beds on occasion.

Thom and Tobey have relocated their development projects office to San Antonio, but manage to return to Hus Bay occasionally, and always stay with Jason and Tripp when they do. Their partnership had never been formally solemnized as a marriage, but that's what it actually is. Like Jason and Tripp's, theirs is an open relationship that seems to work for them—never better than when they are with their old friends and former fuckbuddies in Hus Bay.

Given the increasing acknowledgment of homosexulity by young people generally, Paulik University has become even more accepting of it, although that would almost seem impossible.

In spite of the military witch-hunts that the Navy and Marine Corps occasionally conduct—more properly called 'warlock hunts,' perhaps—the hunger for cock is as much a facet of military life as ever. Swabbies and jarheads continue to prowl the streets of Hus Bay and the Paulik campus looking to get laid, and meeting with as many ready men and boys with the same objective as ever.

While only the oldest residents of Paulik Shores recall the orgy that took place in City Park following the announcement of the Japanese surrender, virtually all the other residents have fond memories of gay sex there while they were students, and most find ways to re-create the joy of those days.

310

For current Paulik students and servicemen, the clearing in the park is still a favorite place to find fun, or to take a fun-seeking partner.

Whether this unique city along the waters of the South Carolina coast will suffer the same fate as that other ideal settlement, Camelot, remains to be seen, but to date it remains a relative paradise, especially for Jason, who finally met his life partner in this gay Utopia; oddly enough, he did so when he was performing in *A Man for All Seasons* as Sir Thomas More, the man who provided that synonym for paradise in his book of the same name.

The above photograph was taken in 1996.
The reader is left to imagine
what the portrait in the attic looks like!

ABOUT THE AUTHOR

John Butler retired after a thirty-six year career in teaching and administration, ranging from elementary and secondary school music, to Dean of Arts and Sciences at a major American University, where he also served as Professor and Department Head for twenty-seven years.

Although he has published widely in his primary career field, his first literary achievement in the field of interest that has occupied his mind since he started fooling around with the little boy next door at the age of nine, however, was realized with the publication of his erotic novel *model/escort* for STARbooks Press in 1998. Subsequent novels include *WanderLUST: Ships that Pass in the Night, Boys Hard at Work (and Playing with Fire); The Boy*

Next Door, The Year the Pigs Were Aloft, and now, *This Gay Utopia.* Besides his novels, Mr. Butler's shorter fiction has appeared in various STARbooks anthologies.

Following the death of STARbooks Press founder John Patrick, John Butler completed the editing of Mr. Patrick's posthumously-released anthologies, *Seduced 2* and *Wild and Willing,* and is the editor of *Living Vicariously,* a collection of John Patrick's best writing—all still available from STARbooks Press.

vearing any underwear. "Excuse me," I said, having a hard time l

blinded by that bulge in his crotch. "but don't I know you?" "May

kind of t

with Ra

at loser?

said. "Lik

nice body

fully, he l

ou up to t

nistaking

Uh, I coul

blood rac

cing with

t we go o

will see u

red?" he

privacy.

—hard. I

ack, traci

ezed it, ha

it with my

obbing, I

The sound of unzipping filled the small space. I don't know who'

st, but before I knew it, I had his rod in my hand, and mine was in

ant to do?" he asked, his tone challenging. I knew exactly, and sa

www.ingramcontent.com/pod-product-compliance
Lightning Source LLC
Chambersburg PA
CBHW072058020726

47501CB00003B/624